An Orphan's Wish

Elizabeth Gill was born in Newcastle upon Tyne and as a child lived in Tow Law in County Durham where her family owned a steelworks. She has spent all her life in Durham but recently moved to North West Wales to be near her family. She can see the sea from her windows and spends a lot of time eating seafood, drinking orange wine and walking the family Labrador, Izzie, on the beautiful beaches.

Also by Elizabeth Gill

Miss Appleby's Academy
The Fall and Rise of Lucy Charlton
Far from My Father's House
Doctor of the High Fells
Nobody's Child
Snow Angels
The Guardian Angel
The Quarryman's Wife
The Foundling School for Girls
A Widow's Hope
The Runaway Children
The Pit Girl
The Miller's Daughter
The Lost Child
A Miner's Daughter
A Daughter's Wish

. . . and many more!

An Orphan's Wish

Elizabeth Gill

QUERCUS

First published in Great Britain in 2022
This paperback edition published in 2023 by

QUERCUS

Quercus Editions Ltd
Carmelite House
50 Victoria Embankment
London EC4Y 0DZ

An Hachette UK company

A CIP catalogue record for this book is available
from the British Library

PB ISBN 978 1 52942 107 1
EB ISBN 978 1 52942 108 8

10 9 8 7 6 5 4 3 2 1

Typeset by CC Book Production
Printed and bound in Great Britain by Clays Ltd, Elcograf S.p.A.

Papers used by Quercus are from well-managed forests and other responsible sources.

For my wonderful son-in-law, Allan Betty, who buys me Maltesers

Author's Note

I named this series, Blessed St Hilda's Orphanage, after Hilda of Whitby, abbess of the monastery, who led one of the most important religious centres in the Saxon world.

My other favourite Hilda is Hildegard of Bingen, also a very influential woman. She was a Benedictine abbess, writer, composer and philosopher.

From what I can gather the Seamen's Mission was in South Shields in 1900. I have moved it into Newcastle because it suited my story.

One

The point of Christmas, Flo Butler had always thought, was to lighten the darkness with festivities, that was what was taught in the churches and chapels in Weardale. You spent all the rest of the year toiling and working but Christmas would light up that special day just after what some folk called the Winter Solstice. So on December 21st that year she was ready to bring in holly and sing carols in her head. She had been baking and cooking, her Christmas puddings and her Christmas cake had long since been made and one of the local farmers would bring their chicken for Christmas dinner all dressed and ready for the table. She was determined it would be good that year. They had had so many bad times.

In older days she had done such things herself but the little shop and keeping the house going took up all of her time and she therefore didn't choose to wring a chicken's neck, cut off its head and feet and go through all the palaver of putting it into boiling water, plucking it, taking out its insides and so on. What with the shop and the big garden behind it – even though Joshua had not worked at the quarry for a long time now and she was glad of it – there was enough to do. Neither of us is getting any younger, she told herself but with some satisfaction.

Sometimes in the streets of the little town she would look longingly at the big families, people who had children and grand-children. She and Joshua were not as lucky as that. They had had but one son and he had disgraced himself, running off to strange lands with a lass who was already fat with her first. She had pulled the wool over their Michael's eyes and they had run off together.

That was almost twenty years ago. After he went Flo and Joshua had to live out the shame. The one thing they had to do was choose where they worshipped. Their families had been good chapel-goers but after Michael left they went to the parish church. Neither of them could bear the sympathy nor the looks that their fellow chapel-goers bestowed on them and Flo needed her prayers and the strength that God could give her. She found peace by being in a church. She thought at the time that if one more friend sympathized and asked where she thought they had gone wrong she would scream.

It always had to be somebody's fault and since they were his parents something they had done had turned him into this person they didn't recognize. She tried telling herself that this was not true, that people were born in a certain way and their upbringing did not determine everything about them.

Even after all this time she could not think any better of him. It had been on this day when he had left. There had been letters in the early days but Joshua threw them on the fire and much as she wanted to protest because she was desperate to find out how Michael did he ignored her. Since she knew he was just as hurt as she was but showed it in anger, she had learned to say nothing, what else could she have done?

However could they have borne it? If he was having a bad time they would worry, if he was having a good time they would resent that he had left.

After a long while the letters stopped and they did not talk about him, just went on with their day-to-day lives as best they could. Flo staggered about, heartbroken day in and day out, and Joshua dug in the garden and they ate and slept, at least sometimes. It was strange how good weather made it worse. You would think that bad weather, cold nights and staying indoors would make your grief more real but it was the summer days when the children played outside long into the evenings and she could hear their mothers and grandmothers calling their names that hurt most of all.

The summer made her restless and she felt as though she should be joyful because everything was at its brightest and best but somehow the flowers looked too gaudy, the leaves on the trees were so green that they scorched her eyes and she spent many a long afternoon wishing she could have the relief of rain. She slept better to the sound of it. The sun was somehow harsh and relentless, it showed up the dusty corners of her memories, cobwebs of the time she had lost without her son over the years. Each day, each hour, each minute, every single second.

Strange then that that very morning she received a letter. Letters were usually something to be read, reread and cherished but this one she could tell, right from the beginning, was trouble, with what Joshua called a capital T.

She almost dropped it as though it had burned her but she knew it was something unusual. It was written in an educated hand on expensive thick cream paper with fine sloping handwriting, the characters almost curled around they were so distinct.

She and Joshua never got letters like that and she did not want this one now, did not want to know what terrible news it must contain.

She thought she might put it on the kitchen fire before Joshua had time to see it and complain and get rid of it but she couldn't do that. She just pretended it hadn't got there, she tucked it into her pinny pocket but she was so aware of it like a hot coal that she took it back out again. She put it in the dresser drawer and then removed it, thinking Joshua might find it when he was looking at the bills for the shop and such, and so she ran upstairs and placed it in her dressing table drawer under her knickers. He would not go looking in there. She then went downstairs and pretended that nothing had happened.

Joshua came in for his dinner and she had thought it was going well when he suddenly looked at her over his mince, carrots and taties and said,

'All right then, Flo, what is it?'

She tried to look innocent and failed. They had been married for forty years, she could hide nothing from him but still she made the attempt. She looked down at the dinner she couldn't eat, and usually she loved mince and dumplings, and then she said in a wobbly voice,

'There was a letter this morning.'

'What sort of letter?'

'An important one, I think.'

He sat there, knife and fork down on his plate, and she did the same thing, while their dinners got cold and the day seemed to turn darker. The shortest day of the year, the longest night and now this. She could tell that it had been as big a shock for him as it was for her and half wished she had burned it without saying anything, yet how could she when it might be very important?

Joshua scraped back his chair and went outside into the garden even though at this hour it was only in his mind that he could see much beyond the walls. What little light there was had disappeared into evening already. Their house was on the edge of the village where the road wound away towards Crook and Bishop Auckland, up on to the hills where the little pit towns lay, but here at the dale's beginning it was a landscape quite different.

The farms here were a thousand years old and most of them had been fortified in the days of the twelfth century when the border reivers stole land, cattle and any valuable goods they could lay their hands and weapons on.

Now it was a poor place, the lead mines were played out, what prosperity, little as it was, had gone and the old squires did their best with their land but it was mostly hill country as you went up through the dale towards Cumbria and Northumberland. It became a bare and almost arid landscape, fit for nothing but the hardy sheep that lived there and constituted most of the money the farmers could make and many of them had nothing much more than a smallholding.

This place where the Butler family had lived, for how many generations back they did not know, was falling to pieces. Joshua had always been proud to live there but he was proud no more. It had been in a bad way when his father died and there was no money to do anything to make the house more than barely habitable. When he had an accident at the quarry and could work no more, he and Flo had turned their only decent room into a shop. A fall had crushed his foot so he now walked with a limp and dragging that leg around tired him so much he could not go back.

It must have been a fine house once, now it was just a ruin

within a few minutes' walk for the villagers who came to Flo's shop to buy the things she made and the foodstuffs she sold.

They had nothing outside other than chickens, it was eggs and goods made with eggs, the few things she could not make herself and ordered from Hexham, and then she turned her attention to garments she could knit, or sew. Joshua did the outside work and grew as many vegetables as he could. It was their main source of income. He looked out across the fields, it was the view he had seen all his life, his mind gave him the light the day did not at that hour, early afternoon, and he thought now for perhaps the thousandth time that it had not been surprising Michael had longed to get away. There was nothing left here beyond the acres behind the building.

He wished now that he had been able to get away but they had been too poor to go anywhere. Joshua had been proud that he could provide but he rued the day that Michael had ever spoken of his ambition to leave this country and go off to convert people in that far-off eastern land to Christianity. If Michael had stayed Joshua did not know what would have happened. In his dreams Michael had remained and had his own parish. He'd married a lovely girl who gave them lots of grandchildren and gave his parents time and love. Sometimes when he awoke in the early morning he thought that he had dreamed this so hard that he would find the house repaired and warm, Michael would have employed the best workmen and, most importantly of all, there would have been grandsons to carry on the house where the family had lived for so long.

They had nothing but four rooms altogether, two bedrooms and a back kitchen where they spent their lives. The rest of the buildings had fallen down, there was nothing but rubble outside and a garden shed until you reached the river where his land ended.

It was a cold wet day and although it had started out bright when the sunrise finally made its appearance at nearly nine o'clock the light was gone and the rain suddenly began to bucket down. He stood there with the door open until wind blew the rain all the way down the street from the marketplace, around the end building and into the pantry. Flo came downstairs and gave the letter into his hands.

He tried to take it, she knew he did, but his fingers shook. They always shook these days whenever anything went wrong and things always did, no matter how hard you tried to deflect them. So it ended up on the tablecloth and they sat there looking at it like it was a rat their Nell had found in the henhouse and brought in by the back door.

Nell had been Michael's sheepdog. After he left Nell didn't know what was going on and wouldn't be comforted. In the end they did what they had said they would never do and took the dog to bed with them. It brought all three of them comfort when she lay between them like a warm bolster, snoring softly in the only peace that she had found, the release of sleep.

Flo listened to the rain on her windows and thought about the vegetables. Much more of this and the Brussels sprouts would rot and the last few red roses would lie like blood in the wet soil, irretrievable as their petals turned brown. Nell had lived for ten years after Michael went and then she died by the fire one Sunday morning while they were at church. She had been the only thing they had after Michael had gone off and left them.

Joshua bravely picked up the letter, looked at it, turned it over, stared at the handwriting – he wouldn't wear his glasses – and then he turned it over a couple more times, got up, went to the mantelshelf and got down the knife which cut open any letter they did get and then he unfurled it.

Flo couldn't move. She didn't think she would ever move again. He went on reading until she wanted to cry out, or grab it from him or both, and then he lowered the letter and his face was so pale it was like snow. Just yesterday they had talked to one another about the possibility of snow. Joshua said he could smell it like the sheep who huddled together by the stone walls, taking what shelter they could from the relentless wind which sent the big square flakes blowing horizontally across the whitening fells.

Flo liked snow at Christmas though it didn't often actually happen until the festive season was over. It was even more welcome by January because the days were dark and at least it made a change, it lightened her mood and the hills and the village roofs and even the roads and pavements. After that she began to feel better because they were heading into spring and although it came late in the north the seasons were a fixed thing and she took comfort from that.

Finally she saw the look on his face. It was disbelief. Neither of them spoke for a long time and then she could wait no longer. She got up and threw coal onto the back of the fire and began to pull some of it forward into the blaze and then she went and sat down again. She wanted to clear the table, she usually did that straight away, but somehow it would have made too much noise, too much movement, like when people coughed and sneezed and blew their noses at funerals it would change and cheapen the mood.

He pushed the letter over to her but didn't give her time to read it.

'Our Michael's dead,' he said.

Dear Mr and Mrs Butler,

I have taken some time to find you and only through vigorous efforts have I managed. I understand from various contacts in Japan that your son Michael Butler, whom I understand you have not heard of for some time, has died of typhoid fever while undertaking a perilous journey into unknown places. You may not be surprised to know that this was some time ago and we have been trying to contact you ever since.

His wife Rosa died just three weeks later. The circumstances are uncertain. There are children. The authorities decided that they should be sent back to England as two of them are quite young and there has been no provision made for them here nor anyone to take care of them.

The two elder children are seventeen-year-old twins but although Dominic helped his father in most of his work this time he was thankfully as it happens left at home. Constance was her mother's helper and joy. They had no place here, they are foreign both to the local people and to anyone of our church, or indeed to any Christians as their father and mother were, I hate to add, bereft of God and therefore but for the work he did in various villages, and that was only to offer medical aid, the family they have left has no place here. Nobody wants them.

They seem to have no family but you. Although Michael did not belong to our church we have raised the money to get them home to you. We hope that you as their closest relatives will be able to pay back what it has cost us as it is a great deal of money. We would have liked to ask you for the money before the children set sail but they had nowhere to go and we had no option but to put them onto a ship and we did the best that we could in extremely difficult circumstances.

Therefore they left here some weeks since and will dock in Liverpool any day now from what I understand. I will write to you again and let you know exactly when this will be so that you can go and assist them as they come here to nobody but you and have nothing and no place to go. Although we are aware that Michael did not succeed in his vain attempt to become a missionary we understand that he managed to do some good and therefore it seems only fair to let you know that his children are in need of support and a home with their family.

You have of course my heartfelt sympathy and best wishes,

Dr Hartley Davies
Methodist Overseas Department
Westminster Methodist Hall
115 Westminster Avenue
London

As Joshua flung down the letter upon the kitchen table Flo eyed it. They had not spoken Michael's name in twenty years but he had been their only child and she had adored him. Everybody in the dale knew he had broken his parents' hearts by running after a traveller's daughter and then she was expecting a child and the scandal had been enormous. He had come back from London after three years training to be a Methodist minister and was planning to work overseas. They had been hoping to talk him out of it since ministers went there alone for the first three years and they wanted him close since he had been studying for so long, and then everything had gone wrong.

He had been such a good son and they had been proud of him and then he had gone to a fair in Hexham and it was the darkest day of all. For there he met a merry black-haired girl who sang bawdy songs in the marketplace and she had enticed him with her laughter and her charms. He fell in love with her and after that his parents had no more influence with him.

Flo had gone over this in her mind thousands of times. His father had told him he could not marry such a woman even when he said that she was expecting his child, so the couple had run off and that was the last anybody had seen of them.

He would have been unable to take up the post he was meant to in Japan. He had in effect lost everything for the sake of a loose woman with no background or family. Flo had let herself be ruled by Joshua on this matter for all these years though often she longed to know what had happened but his grief was too much. Michael was dead to the dale and to his parents. He had ruined the future and now – what on earth was to be done?

She read the letter and then she read it again while Joshua stood in front of the kitchen fire, which he did when cold or upset or both, and after a long time he broke the silence.

'They cannot come here.'

Flo still hadn't taken in the idea that she had grandchildren. Her first instinct had been joy even though Michael was dead. He had left somebody to come after him. She said nothing. Perhaps when Joshua grew used to the idea he would soften. It was just that he was hurting once again and he could not stomach it or the idea that their lives would change yet again. They had had enough of that. It was all they could do to take day by day the time which was still allotted to them and be grateful for each other.

'Four children,' Flo said. She thought of it, Michael's twins and two later. It would be a joy if they came back here, it would be real family and a way forward other than a dire old age, at last.

'We must write and tell him that we cannot have them here,' Joshua said.

'But where are they to go?'

'Who cares?' he threw back at her and he went out into the sodden garden in the by now thick darkness and slammed the back door.

Flo was angry with him now and yet she knew him and understood him so well. He had been her only love and she was aware how he longed to have her agree with him because of the respect that she owed to her husband but she was frustrated.

After Michael had gone she had never forgotten what the weather was like. That Christmas had done itself out for beauty. The sunrises were pink and grey and the light came twinkling across the fields while the grass was diamonded with heavy dew and later white frost. It had snowed on Christmas Day such as Michael had always wanted it to as a little boy. When he was seven his father had gone outside into the back garden and helped him to build a snowman and she had provided coal for his eyes and buttons and a carrot for his nose, a twig for his mouth and an old scarf for his neck.

Since he had left they had been alone, just the two of them on Christmas Day. The local Methodist minister had gone to see them that first Christmas but Joshua would not allow him inside and since that day few people had been into the house unless they were buying something at the shop.

Michael had gone to the seminary in Richmond near London

to train before he and Rosa ran away. Joshua was still working hard to help put Michael through. His parents had toiled so that he would be successful and have enough money to help him win an overseas post such as he had wished for more than anything.

Michael and Rosa had gone. Then there had been Joshua's accident and they opened the shop to make ends meet. Flo blamed her son, it seemed fitting that Michael had caused it and what a good bitterness to feel when the supposed culprit was absent and could not state his case.

Flo still made cakes and puddings but she never uttered the word 'Christmas'. They ate them like they ate any winter stodge because the weather was so bad that you had to fill up your stomach against weeks of snow, sleet, icy rain and wind which screamed down from the hilltops and froze the streets in silver. They had only the one fire and it was in the kitchen so had they not gone to bed on full stomachs they would not have slept but he had to tend the garden and she had to tend the shop and yet even when they had eaten their fill they always lost weight over the winter so that they dreaded the long cold season.

Flo loved the few snowdrops that grew in the back garden. They were the first signs that things would get better and that spring would finally arrive, though often it was late up here in the dale and on a bad year even April and May could be bitterly cold. They had once had snow in July.

After Christmas that first year everything had frozen hard for weeks. Joshua had been ill, begun to cough and then developed bronchitis, so the doctor said. It was not bronchitis, she thought, it was heartbreak

They didn't need the money to help Michael any more. They had saved so that he could go to Japan as a missionary. He would go alone, that was the way of these things, for the first three years and only when he had proved to his betters that he could manage such a difficult life he might send for the woman of his dreams. Instead of that Michael took with him the traveller's daughter, there was no wedding as far as they were aware, only that he took every penny they had.

After that they made do with what the shop profited them but there was nothing left over for luxuries and the house was theirs so they could apply to no landlord to fill in the walls or mend the roof and howling draughts blew cold breaths through the cracked windows. Joshua had taken to stuffing the holes with old clothes until old clothes were all they had on their backs and Flo sold everything she could think of in the shop. Sometimes they had not enough food for themselves, they had to live so cheaply.

The next day Flo set about her household tasks and she opened up the shop. Several people came in quite early, they were stocking up for Christmas. One of her best sellers was lucky bags. She didn't call them Christmas lucky bags but slyly, she thought, wrapped them in special paper. She was proud that she bought cheap paper and then drew pictures on it, snowflakes and holly with red berries and mistletoe, green and white. She and Joshua did not discuss any of this, they regarded it as sale items. Also she made fudge and tied ribbons around it. The sweets she bought in big jars from Hexham and was sent refills. It was quite a lucrative sale because children loved such things, spending a farthing or two that their parents gave them.

She sold cabbages, carrots, leeks, parsnips, potatoes and Brussels sprouts, anything which would keep upstairs in the room that had been Michael's. Sometimes she would go in there just to take in the smell, which was predominantly of apples – they had three apple trees in their back garden and she had become grateful for the huge bounty these trees gave them. And strings of onions were held from the ceiling when Joshua had dug them free of the earth.

Joshua's father had farmed the land behind the house and like Joshua he had worked in the lead mines. Joshua had inherited his father's ability to make the best of what land he owned.

Flo had made a big pan of broth two days ago because she knew she would have little time to cook in these few last days before Christmas. There would be pease pudding and ham sandwiches which they would have for tea.

That day, however, and the following day, one or both of them struggled to eat or think of anything to say and she was only glad to have to serve on in the shop and show a cheerful face. Joshua began to cough and sat over the fire so long that she wanted to object but she knew there was no point. He could not help his feelings and neither could she.

They would be closed on Christmas Day. It was the tradition but always a bad day for them. This Christmas morning she went downstairs and usually the first thing she had seen of late was the letter standing on the mantelpiece propped up against the clock. It had gone.

Nobody spoke. She raked and rekindled the fire and then she put on the kettle for water to boil and she set about the breakfast porridge as she always did. When it was ready she put it aside to keep warm and then she went out and fed the hens.

It was a frosty morning and usually that made her feel better. Today it didn't. The hens had virtually given over laying. It was far too cold for such activity. She fed them every scrap of food she could spare since they were vital to her existence. She liked the henhut. Michael had made it when he had been half grown and would boast that it was the Hen Hotel. It was large and wooden and ornate. He had been such a clever child and they had been so proud of him. It still held together well and she liked how the hens went up and down their little ramp to get in or out.

She always locked them up at night and they were good about coming back from the part of the garden where they were allowed. It was set aside from the rest as hens could make a mess of anything. In the summer they loved having dust baths in the flower beds so Joshua kept them strictly to where there were no flowers and no vegetables.

Both of them were fond of the hens, they were in a daft way all that was left. The early days when they had kept a few sheep, a pig and several cows, and further down where the pond had housed ducks, were long since gone. Sometimes Flo talked to the hens. She called herself stupid but she had to tell her woes to somebody.

At one time they had kept bees and she remembered how you had to tell the bees when somebody died. Bees knew a lot about death. There were certain drones who could find a dead fellow within a few minutes and dispose of him. Flo had told them so much and now the hens put up with her secrets.

She loved how fluffy they were in spring and now in winter she made sure they were well fed and that if they did not want to come outside, if it was too dark and cold and wet, at least they were safe in the house that Michael had made carefully for them so very long ago.

It was big and square and held the warmth so that on a bad day she would go in there for the very comfort of the straw which to her held summer in its odour, and somehow in that there was hope. The land at the back of the house was theirs. Joshua made hay every year and there were fields of wheat and the straw was taken for the henhouse. Nothing was wasted.

They ate their porridge and it was only then that she could not stop herself from saying,

'Where did the letter go?'

'I put it on the fire last night. It was the best thing to do. It will be as if it never was. We won't talk about it again.' Nor did they.

Two

Amos Adams, the local Methodist minister in Wolsingham, had been born there but had left at an early age. He well remembered the Butlers, Flo and Joshua, indeed his father had been Joshua's brother. Apparently they had quarrelled and he and his wife Lena had left, taking their son with them and never gone back.

Amos could not accept that he and his father had been turned off from the place he regarded not just as his home but as the most important place on earth. He did not remember his father and his uncle quarrelling, he remembered such happy times when his mother and father and himself had a place there. The family had pulled together in those days and it seemed to him that they would always be like that.

He had no idea what prosperity or poverty was, just that he was cared for and loved, that he had enough food to eat, the riverside and the fields to play in and that he had loved his aunt Flo and his uncle Joshua. So it was a shock when his father woke him in the night when he was seven and took him away.

Perhaps there had been some quarrel between the brothers, he didn't know just that he had been flung from his paradise and nothing had ever been the same.

His father took his family to Newcastle and then walked out on them so Amos was known by his mother's name and that was all. They were poor and he remembered the streets when he was a little boy and the winter where she coughed until she died and then he had nobody but the dreams of the house by the river in the beautiful valley where he had been happy for those few short years before everything went wrong.

It was not all bad, however. He had found different kinds of work, he managed scraps of education and then he met a boy of about his age when they were playing football on the streets. He was called James Leslie, and his father was a Methodist minister in Newcastle. James took Amos home and the kindly family helped him and when James went to Leeds to the seminary Amos was able to go with him. The Methodist church thought that he had sufficient talent as a minister and they encouraged him so that was what he became.

It did occur to him that he wanted to do something else but all he thought about was the house by the river and that over time he might be able to fulfill his dearest dreams and go back there as the minister.

He discovered from local gossip that Michael Butler, the only child of Flo and Joshua, had run away with his chosen woman and never returned. Amos remembered him vaguely and had disliked him, perhaps they were jealous of one another, perhaps Michael had been unpleasant. He wished his memory would give him more than feelings and half pictures but it did not. Had he wiped out whatever unpleasantness there was? Amos waited and waited to see whether Michael would come back, hoping against hope that he never would and in time his hopes were realized. There was a rumour that Michael Butler had died. Amos prayed that it was so.

He had been a happy child but leaving the house by the riverside, which had been his home, took all that from him and he was cast out into the wilderness. He had nobody and nothing but his own wits and hard days, hot or icy, an empty belly and no friends. He knew that somebody was responsible, someone was to blame, but Michael did not come back and Joshua and Flo held on to that house with all their might when they should have kept him there. Did they not know his parents had died? Did they not care what happened to him? He was family. They should have cared. There was a great big hole in his heart where nobody cared and nothing could fill it.

Amos began to think that he had been sent back to Weardale with a purpose. He had managed to get this far. His other luck had not held. He had been obliged to marry the woman he got with child since she had come from a respectable Scarborough family and was staying in the area. Now they had two children. Having lost several before, he had imagined these scrawny two would make him thankful but the truth was that they did not. They never stopped crying, all they did was suck up his meagre income. His wife was not much better. She was thin and ugly with her whining voice, greasy hair and sunken cheeks. She did nothing but complain.

He knew the day would come when he would present himself as the heir to the two old people so that he would inherit Holy Well Hall and live there like a lord and not as a Methodist minister. It had at one time been a much bigger building but a large part of it had fallen down and it was difficult to see that it had once been a pele tower. The farm to the side was all that was left, other than the crenellated ruin beside it.

He had come to loathe the manse. That first winter and ever after it the weather was foul and the trees in the garden which his study looked out on were black, the dead leaves disintegrating upon the bare soil, and the wind howled around the little town.

It was not the way he had thought it would be. He could not go to his aunt and uncle and present himself to them as heir to the property. There was always the chance that Michael would come back. He hoped against hope that it was not true. It was the only positive thought he could hang on to. They went to the parish church to worship so he saw nothing of them.

These were country people. A lot of them lived barely. They did turn up to chapel on Sundays but their clothes were shabby and they were for the most part thin because all they had were small businesses or tiny farms which were little more than a large back garden. Many had numerous children which dragged them further down. At least that was one cross he did not have to bear yet. He dreaded his wife having more children, poverty awaited them.

The days before Christmas the year that Flo and Joshua had the letter about their grandchildren were barely light and the manse was shrouded in gloom. He could hardly afford to heat the place and small fires made no impression on the cold walls and bare floors. It was an old house. It had no water in it, all had to be drawn from the pipe in the street and Sally, their small maid, spent many hours trekking back and forth for this precious commodity. The girl was known as Sarah Charles but his wife had thought it too good a name for such a pathetic creature and renamed her.

There was no plumbing and it was a case of going down the garden for your body's waste and sitting there with ripped-up newspaper, sleet drumming on the tin roof. At night it was pots under the bed, which made him shudder, he had lived better than this. He had belonged to the land. Now he belonged nowhere but this dry existence where everything seemed almost impossible.

He hated it. He had lived in a decent house in Newcastle with the Leslie family. Sometimes he thought it was the best things had ever been. Now it was gone so he clung to his ideas that things would get better when the old people knew who he was. He would tell them and he would go to Samuel East, the local solicitor, and see where his prospects lay.

He pressed to him these thoughts as the weather grew worse. Winters were very long here. They started in November and often went on into early June.

Sometimes if Amos was restless and the night was clear he would put on his clothes and walk to Holy Well Hall and look over his inheritance and think positively about the future and how sweet it would be when he took the land for his. He would ask for no more, he told God. It would be all he would ever need.

And yet he could not go to them and tell them who he was. He did not think they would believe him, and since from gossip he gleaned that they had cast off their son why should they take to their nephew? He preferred to live in his head where they took him to them with glad cries and he could be that child again who'd had so many good times through each season.

He'd even had a pony and a dog and there were cats in the stables and pigs and sheep and cows in the fields, and it seemed to him to be always summer. Or if it was not, he was warm in bed where his mother had tucked him up and kissed him goodnight and it had seemed to him that life would go on indefinitely in that wonderful way. He could never accept that it had been over when he was a small and helpless child.

One day in December he got a letter in a stiff white envelope and that was when everything changed.

The week after Christmas Flo made the best of things and it was a cold snowy day when she trod carefully, in case there was ice along the main street, to the haberdashery which was kept by an old lady called Miss Hutton. It was Flo's favourite shop. As a shopkeeper herself you might think that shopping was not her favourite pastime but she tried to put happiness into everything she did, she now had so little in her life.

She missed going to chapel but understood how much it hurt her husband, and although she was civil to everyone scandal died hard here and Michael had caused the biggest scandal ever to hit Wolsingham.

Miss Hutton was always more than polite and Flo thought they might have been friends had circumstances been different. She kept wool and silks and cottons and tablecloths and tray cloths to be embroidered and knitting patterns and various-coloured wools. She also made clothes for the women of the area and had several different materials and patterns and colours for these.

The choosing was one of the few things that Flo enjoyed. She told herself that it was shop business and not an indulgence. In the long winter evenings Flo knitted and sewed. She made quilts from various-coloured squares of old material. These she sold in the shop and she knitted baby clothes, bootees, caps and mittens in blue and pink and white and yellow.

She made sure not to compete with Miss Hutton who made more intricate things such as clothes for children and adults, socks and shirts, and her brother ran the tailoring business next door.

There was a separate cobbler's just beyond and then the sweet shop which Flo would have loved to have gone to on many occasions but stayed out of because the village gossip was rife there and having suffered from this for years she kept away and made her fudge at home. Also the confectioner, Mrs Pringle, who made all her own sweets rather than buying them in, did not appreciate Flo selling fudge or sweets in her lucky bags so that was another reason they were rather cool to one another if they did happen to meet and then there was nothing beyond a nod while keeping their eyes averted. Flo's argument was that she would not have sold fudge and sweets had she not needed the money.

That morning she had stepped into the road to avoid the doctor's horse. The doctor was called Thomas Neville, a good Durham name, and he was a popular man, partly because he was young, had not been there long and had not yet taken a wife. She did not therefore see the minister, Amos Adams, until she bumped into him and raising her eyes from beneath her hat her heart sank.

Mr Adams was not one of her favourite people and he was not well liked. A few years ago he had taken over from the old minister who had been there for seventeen years. He would never have retired, he died and Mr Adams had come to replace him but he had completely different ideas and old ideas lasted in such places as Weardale. Nobody appreciated a new broom. Flo kept the idea that a new broom swept clean but an old broom knew where the dirt was and he did not endear himself to people of the dale because, unlike the lovely old minister, he had a nasty habit of telling folk what to do and how to do it.

She felt ashamed but the trouble was that Mr Adams was physically unattractive with a large nose and tiny mouth and small dark eyes which missed nothing. His voice was thin and reedy, almost whining even, or especially so folk said when he gave a sermon and his sermons were very long.

Worst of all he was not particular in his dress and while the farmers often gave off a healthy smell of cow muck and would ask your pardon for stepping inside the shop Mr Adams gave off the reek of unwashed linen, sweat and urine. Flo wondered why his wife did not tell him that he needed to wash occasionally but then she could not imagine Mr Adams' meek wife saying anything to him. The poor woman was completely cowed. If you met her in the street she never looked at you. She had no friends and since nobody was invited to the manse other than for religious purposes no one went there.

The rumour was that Mr Adams knocked his wife about though nobody could ever see any evidence of this on her. It was just that she was skinny and miserable, his children were snotty and crying, their clothes always too small and they were not allowed out to play with other children.

They did not, Flo surmised, have a good time of it at the manse. Also there was that poor girl Sarah Charles who had been taken in by the minister and his wife and though nobody said he hurt her or even disliked her she also fell beneath the dark cloak that seemed to surround the manse and the chapel and had such a dour look on her face that nobody spoke to her.

Mr Adams tried to insist on people going to his chapel. Those who didn't attend out of either duty or faith he would go and see. If they did not attend twice on Sundays he thought it was a falling from grace. Also he preferred that people did not keep alcohol in their houses. It was quite usual for tots of whisky or brandy to be administered as an aid in some homes and there were housewives who thought Mr Adams was getting in their way by telling them what to do and how to live.

Mr Adams did not include himself in these ideas. He was their minister and was there to guide and govern them. He did not need guidance and was in charge of such matters. He told himself since he was above them in intelligence and education he always knew what he was doing and he had had a harder life than anyone he had ever met so he did not think that alcohol hurt him. He thought to himself sometimes that it was spirit to guard the spirit. He liked the notion.

'Mrs Butler, how are you?' he said now.

Mr Adams did not approve of the Butlers. The old minister had known very well why they didn't go to his chapel. He was the man who had helped Michael to get to college and when Michael had run off with Rosa he had been very sympathetic and also seemed to understand that they found it too hard to appear at chapel each week as though nothing had happened and as though their son had never preached within its walls.

Flo had the idea that Mr Adams was not overly impressed with women and, though he did not object to them cleaning and looking after the place and raising money, he did not ask for their opinions. She had the idea that he thought women well beneath men and having but little brain. He was not alone in that, she knew.

She could not help thinking that he was about the same age as Michael would have been had he lived. It was rumoured that he had once been a street child in Newcastle and been taken in by kind people but he showed no signs of gratitude or joy in his demeanour and neither he nor his wife ever looked well. Also she doubted Methodist ministers were decently paid and he was a slight skinny man who spent his winters coughing and sitting over his fire when he did not have to go out and visit his parishioners.

He was a good man, she admonished herself, who had taken on a hard task in this remote area and although he put on a front Flo was convinced he did his duty and nothing else because he had been sent here by his church.

He had not been there when Michael and that awful lass had run away, presumably he was still then learning to become a minister of the Methodist faith, but she did not doubt that his ears had been filled with talk when he first got there and he must be aware that she and Joshua had not set foot in the chapel since.

When she merely bobbed in excuse and acknowledgement and tried to walk round him he glanced about to make sure there was no one near and then he said, with a modicum of disapproval in his voice,

'When do you go to Liverpool?'

If Flo's heart had not already been in her boots it certainly would have been there now.

'What?'

'It has nothing to do with me, of course, I just wanted to wish you well and hope that things may get better for your family.'

He said this in so starchy a voice that far from being any comfort to Flo it produced the opposite effect and made her panic.

'You knew?'

'I was informed of the matter as I am the minister in this area though I have to say I was surprised that the Methodist church paid for the return of your grandchildren, two of whom as far as I can make out ought long since have been paying their own way and not leaning all over their parents, and I feel sure that you will be obliged to pay back what the church has expended. We are after all, unlike the parish church in Weardale, very poor.'

The Church of England was very rich here, all to do with bishops and silver and lead and landowning. It was one of the reasons why Flo and Joshua had disliked it but since Michael had left they had gone to the parish church and been welcomed there very civilly and accepted openly. The vicar was like the old Methodist minister. He had been there a long time, it had been his first appointment and he was well liked by almost everyone.

She didn't want to blurt out anything to a man she barely knew but she thought her heart would burst in her chest if she didn't confide in someone and so she said very softly,

'We cannot go.'

She would have run away at that point but her legs shook and so did her lips and all she wanted was to cry, her throat throbbed so badly and took up all the space she used for breathing until she panted.

'But they . . . but I . . . I thought they had docked several days ago,' he said.

'You heard that too?' Once again she was forced to look into his stormy dark eyes which she thought were very cold.

'I had two letters,' he said, 'the second saying that the ship would be there any day and I assumed that you were in Liverpool and—'

'A second letter?'

'Did you not get one? 'He realized he had blundered and badly, she could see by the look on his face, and though he could not have felt such a thing she thought she discerned a look of triumph as though he was pleased to know and surprise her with it. He was enjoying her discomfort.

She understood that he was not the only one who had blundered and without saying another word she scattered along the icy pavement like somebody half her age and ran into the vegetable garden where the Brussels sprouts stood out like tall green bullets against the snow. There her husband was standing doing nothing.

'We got a second letter?'

She thought at first he would deny it and then she saw more

closely that the tears began to run down his face as she did not remember them ever having done before. He nodded and began to sob.

'You burned it?' She could not believe he had done such a thing and without telling her, without giving her any options or chance to do what she knew was the right thing. She wanted to see her grandchildren, she wanted to hold in her arms all there was left of Michael. Why did Joshua not understand that, why had he taken from her the chance of a better future?

'I did.'

'Then you must go to the minister and ask for directions. Whatever will happen to those children?'

'I will do no such thing. That man is unpleasant. He can take them in,' Joshua said bitterly and Flo could see the tears which he did not normally allow to fall from his eyes and they cascaded down his face in a sorrow that had built up for years and could no longer be contained. He could bear nothing more from Michael and she could bear nothing less than the children Michael had left. What else was she to do with the rest of her old age, was there to be no joy at all in her life?

'But the church didn't send anybody,' she said, hurt and cross and wanting to lash out. 'We were meant to go. We were meant to be there.' She began to batter his chest with her small fists and he didn't stop her. She wished he would, she wished he would push her away or shout at her or perhaps even strike her, something he had never done and even now she knew would never do, and yet it would have given her cause to hate what he had done and a place for her anger and despair to go.

Three

Thomas Neville had been looking forward to Christmas. He was to spend it with his parents in Durham. Becoming the doctor here in Wolsingham was his first ever post, he had finished training, come back from London excited and proud and had his parents look on him with pride and joy. He was their only child and he knew how much he was adored, how they gloried in his success and were glad that he had managed to find his first post so near to them.

The dale was only a few miles from the city. He knew they had suspected he would stay in London or in the south where things were easier and while they had never said that they wished he would come back he had and was full of enthusiasm and looking forward to whatever the dale might bring him – farmers who had broken a limb calving a cow, slipped in manure and bruised their bodies, children going down with various fevers he could work his magic upon.

Midwifery had been his speciality and he wanted to prove to every woman in the dale that he would be there for her and would make sure she had all the care she needed. He knew how to set children's bones, he had learned a great deal about the problems of ageing and he was convinced he could make a difference here.

There were two doctors further up the dale but he was to take care of Wolsingham, Stanhope, Eastgate, Westgate, Daddry Shields and St John's Chapel. Even the sound of the names enthralled him. There were a lot of outlying farms too up on the tops and down by the river and he would be responsible for all these people. He had loved the whole idea.

He had fallen in love with Weardale as a small child when plodging in the river, staying in an old farmhouse where his father's friends lived and getting to know the animals in the fields and barns and stables. He loved the little farms, the grey streams, the rich green grass in the square fields and he had known that he would come here and would make it a better place for people to live.

He had gone to look at the house and the surgery when he came home from London that autumn and had been delighted with the prospect. He went back to London for the last time to see his friends and colleagues before returning to Durham.

Then he got a message from their local doctor, Crawcrook, saying that his father had died suddenly and his mother needed him.

So he left without delay. Was this not to work out as he had hoped? He had loved London and would have liked to settle down there in some ways but he was aware of being an only child. Though they were too kind to say so he also knew it was their dearest wish he should come back to the north-east – they missed him and he missed them so really there was no contest and so he had settled nearby.

They had been the best parents anybody ever had. They sent him to Scorton Grammar school though he knew they would selfishly have preferred to keep him at home. The public school in Durham was one of the oldest in the country but he would have been a day boy and have missed out on so many things, his father said. His father had loved his school in Yorkshire and wanted nothing less for his son. In the holidays as he got older they took him all over Europe and encouraged him to take a friend so that he should not be lonely.

He went to Oxford and medical school and practised in London at a hospital until he was judged competent enough not to kill too many patients when he should be sent among the general public.

His parents had never mentioned wanting more children. They had always given him the impression that he was enough and everything to them but he knew his mother felt the lack. His lovely mother would have adored them no matter how many children were given to her but it was not to be.

So he took the train back to Durham and wished things otherwise. His mother was pretending that nothing had happened and greeted him so merrily that his heart ached. He had forgotten how small she was, almost dainty, and how large was the hall of his home and how dark and gloomy on that afternoon. When the door closed the place echoed. She was so white-faced he was afraid she would faint but she never did such things. Neither did she cry.

He was appalled when he saw the state of her. Her white hair was loose and down past her shoulders, her dress was shabby and everything about her spoke of shock and lack of care. She directed him to see the doctor who had gone there especially to greet him.

Dr Crawcrook, alone with Thomas in the vast drawing room, was not so reticent.

'He killed himself, Thomas.' Dr Crawcrook watched the floor as though something fascinated him.

Thomas stared at the top of the man's head. Stupidly, Dr Crawcrook had always seemed much larger to him. His wonderful, funny, kind and brilliant father had killed himself?

'I don't believe it. Somebody made a medical mistake. Were you treating him for something awful? Was he given the wrong medicine?'

Dr Crawcrook was trying not to be insulted, Thomas could see, and he understood how upset the young man was and how much easier for him if it had been an error of judgement or simply that his father's heart had stopped. He could have accepted that but this?

'He shot himself,' Dr Crawcrook said, giving the floor a last lingering look as the awful truth was spoken.

Thomas didn't move. It was too hard to accept.

His father had loved the odd day's shooting up on the Durham moors with his dogs and his gun. He hated driven pheasant shoots and called them slaughter. Thomas wanted to be told that it was an accident, that his father had tripped and fallen over his shotgun though it could never have happened because his father was the most careful of men and always broke the gun over his arm and that was so that he would not injure a dog or another person.

The doctors pretended it had been an accident but few people were fooled, Thomas thought when he had been there for a couple of days. He wanted to ask his mother for details but he could not hurt her any further so he tried to believe what he had been told.

His father's cousin, Iain, who lived in the Scottish lowlands, came down and took the dogs away to his small estate. Thomas knew he would never forget the worst moment of his life, early on the morning of his father's funeral, when the middle dog, a Labrador, Juniper, tried to climb into the hearse with his master.

Iain said gruffly that he was afraid he could not stay for the funeral, he had to get back. Thomas watched the dogs as they were driven away on the morning of the funeral, Juniper regarding him dolefully from sad dark eyes.

Thomas had always loved his home. Now it seemed to him the loneliest place on earth. It had never been so big that it echoed. It was as though the very house itself mourned its master's passing.

Everything went wrong, perhaps trying to distract Thomas and his mother. The roof, which had never leaked before, poured water into the attics which came through into the bedrooms so the bedroom ceilings cracked in turn and broke and plaster fell to the floor and in two rooms the water ran down the walls and dripped into the reception rooms below.

Howling gales threw sleet over the small grey city and the windows rattled so that Thomas did not sleep. He blamed it on the trees which toppled over in the garden and the wind blew down the chimneys so hard that the fires went out and the rooms were filled with reeking soot and smoke. It was as if the elements knew his father had died and were venting their bitterness. Thomas lay in bed, eyes open, and wondered why such an awful thing had happened to them. He would have liked to call it unfair but having dealt with so many illnesses and deaths by then he knew there was no such thing as fair.

The stupidest thing about it was that he found his mother, who had not cried once, in tears the week after his father died. Her cat, Meadow, had run away the day that her husband died and not come back.

'Even the damned cat,' she said bitterly, revealing her pit village background as she spoke. 'Even Meadow has bailed out on me.'

And later,

'How could your father do this to me?' It was the first time she had spoken of her beloved husband.

'He didn't mean to.' The words were out of Thomas's mouth before he could stop them but, after all, what else could he say?

'Oh, of course,' his mother said, glaring at him. 'He put a loaded shotgun to his head by mistake.'

'Dr Crawcrook said he had not intended to,' Thomas said, adding worse to bad.

His mother 'Dr Damned Crawcrooked' the man so that Thomas cursed himself for having spoken.

'I wish I hadn't had to go to my stupid husband's bloody funeral,' she said and clashed herself out of the drawing room. Thomas watched the door shudder and was almost grateful. It had been appalling and he could not put from his mind the way that his father's funeral ought to have been and the way that it had been. He thought it would linger with him for years, the images of his mother's bitterness, grief and sorrow.

The advice had been that the funeral should take place at the cathedral. His parents had met there and so it was his father's favourite church though God knew they had hardly ventured there since, his father disliked all houses of God, thinking privately that so far God had made a bit of a hash of things.

His mother had been a teacher and her parents were proud of her. Even prouder when she met the city's most brilliant barrister one Sunday morning when the dean had invited people to his house for coffee after the morning service.

Thomas suggested that the funeral should be there. His mother flatly refused.

'Can you imagine the cathedral, you, me, our closest friends and some reluctant clergyman who has been talked into giving the service?'

'People loved him. They will want to pay their respects.'

'Everybody knows he killed himself, no matter what the doctors say. They won't come and they'll blame me. The wife is always to blame. They won't want to be associated with us ever again. We'll ask for St Margaret's, at least it's so small that it won't matter.'

He hated how his mother was right. St Margaret's church contained his father's coffin, his mother, himself and five good friends. He half wished he could have been like Iain and left. He envied everyone who had found an excuse to stay away.

He had tried to talk his mother into putting up her hair, wearing black and presenting herself as best she might but all she did was to shrug into her winter coat and pull a large hat down so that few people would be able to see her eyes.

In the end they went to Wolsingham for Christmas. Things could hardly be any worse, he thought.

It was obvious from the start that his mother would hate the house. She had told him to leave her in Durham, which she said she would prefer, but it would have taken a more stony-hearted man than he to let her be lonely as well as heartbroken so he talked her into going with him.

'Just for a visit,' he said.

'I want to stay here.'

For once Thomas insisted. In fact he thought it was the first time he had insisted on anything with regard to his mother and it seemed to him that she needed to get away from the city where things had gone so wrong so he steeled himself.

'The house isn't fit to keep anybody and the last thing you need is more to cope with. Why don't you come to Wolsingham and stay with me? It's not much of a place but there are good fires and hot meals and the servants are kind, well-meaning people.'

He had approached the subject with trepidation and could not put from his mind how difficult it had been, most of all because he wanted to be there all on his own. His mother's presence would be an intrusion but what else could he do?

She had stubbed out her cigarette into an overflowing ashtray and lifted the silver cigarette box which his father had bought for her with her name etched on it so that she could take another.

'What, to the country?' she had said scathingly.

'People do live in the country, you know, Mother.'

'What on earth for?' she said and went back to the Pallisers. Anthony Trollope was her favourite writer. She read his books again and again for comfort and she had never needed that refuge more than she did now, Thomas knew.

'I can't leave you here alone.'

She stopped reading once more and gazed at him over her spectacles with the blue-green eyes his father had so adored, in a way in which he was certain was meant to wither him. It did that.

'Do not think,' she said severely, 'that I have not seen you look down your father's beautiful nose at me disapprovingly because I smoke and drink. I am not going where you can lecture me on my faults.'

'Smoking and drinking will shorten your life,' he said and that was when she laughed and that was when she decided she would give him a dog's life in Wolsingham so she would go, he knew.

She let herself be persuaded but Thomas had no idea how long she would stay with him. The awful thing about it was that he didn't want her there. He was ready to revel in the only freedom he felt he had.

The surgery was small and the house was shabby. Ada and

Fiona looked after the house and Oswald, the stable lad, took care of the horses and gardens and Thomas was ready to sit over his fire and smoke a pipe and enjoy the fact that he was the doctor and happy to be here among the people of Weardale.

His mother had never been a large woman. Now she seemed to him to be shrinking. She had refused to go into mourning – not that he asked her but she went around wearing totally unsuitable clothes, including several evening dresses, fit for the weather but velvet, mid-blue, claret-coloured and bottle green. Perhaps they made her think of how happy she had been at the various dinner dances she'd gone to with her husband year after year.

She had several fur coats, gorgeous shoes and lots of gems which he had bought for his beloved wife as anniversary gifts, birthday presents or just because he had seen a bracelet or a brooch in the local jeweller's window as he went by on his way to the courts and thought she might like it. His mother's life then had been full of velvet jewellery boxes and she had loved each one.

She wore the same diamonds every day as though they could bring her solace and also kept her hair down as if imagining that she was young again and so it would bring back Harry, the love of her life. It made her look like a witch. Thomas was just glad that she did not add her only tiara. It would have convinced him she had lost her mind.

She had started smoking more. She always had three or four cigarettes in the evening and owned several different-coloured holders but she began to smoke from early in the day until late at night. She spent most of her time sitting by the library fire, coughing over fumes from the chimney and her lungs, drinking sherry and reading.

A short visit, he reminded himself when he realized what he

had done. What on earth people in Wolsingham would think he could not imagine. He thought that in small insular communities like that people would talk about the strangeness of the doctor's mother. He wished that she would dress appropriately but there was no point in saying anything and so she came to Wolsingham with her hair all over the place.

It had turned white – whether it had been a gradual process, he had no idea – but suddenly she had aged ten years and when he handed her down from the trap as they reached their destination she stumbled and he had to catch her. She had not spoken from the moment she left her home until now, she had ignored everyone on the train, and when Oswald turned up at the station she ignored him too. Oswald looked hard at the doctor's mother but of course he said little.

Wolsingham in December was very different from Wolsingham on a bright day in mid-October. It had been a perfect autumn day then but the weather seemed to know that he was taking his mother to the dale with him and the rain fell sideways all the way from Durham, cold sleet drenched everything and turned the housetops to silver, the pavements to dark grey and the houses to square black splodges.

His mother stared out at the gloom and was silent and he could almost hear her thinking,

'So this is what the country looks like. How dreadful.'

The little town, when they finally got down the banks into the valley, was sodden. He helped his mother inside and wished she had not brought half the house with her though he hadn't dared say so.

Most of her many trunks of luggage, which he was convinced were books, cigarettes and bottles of sherry, were directed upstairs to the biggest bedroom where she told Oswald where to place each box, where to put them down. She even changed her mind a couple of times and complained how small the room was.

Then she summoned Ada, a lovely woman who was a good cook and a fine housekeeper. She and Fiona made certain the fires were stoked and the rooms were cleaned and Thomas felt sure they would be as good to him as he had heard they had been to the doctor who had retired and gone to Northumberland to live by the sea.

'This fire must be kept on all day until I go to bed,' his mother said.

'Yes, 'm,' Ada said, obviously terrified.

'You will call me Mrs Neville.'

'Yes, Mrs Neville,' Ada agreed hastily.

She bobbed herself out of the room and almost ran down the stairs.

Four

It was bitterly cold, was Connie Butler's first thought when they disembarked. She was so glad she was wearing most of her clothes, layer upon layer of padded robes finished with her big warm jacket. It was a strange kind of cold, nipping at your cheeks and biting your neck, the kind she had known during the first winters of her childhood in Japan when they lived in the south and when it snowed it shut people into their homes and villages and nobody could go any place for months.

Thatched wooden houses in the snow country. She could remember as a small child having to stay inside, when her mother taught them to read and write and to speak various languages. She made up poetry and songs for them and played her guitar so that they could dance and they drew many pictures which she would prop against the walls, she was so proud of everything her children accomplished.

After they had moved to Tokyo Connie had never seen it like that again and was not sure she cared much for it now. Other winters she could remember were different, so many times when the rain fell and the fields flooded, but this was different again and it was because it was a place she had never been to and knew nothing of and perhaps it was tinged with fear of the future and a land where foreign devils lived. She tried to lighten her mood in this way but it smelled gritty, as though the air had been breathed in and out a great many times, and there was nothing new here, it was all old and tired and poor, used up and sad.

The buildings seemed to her to close ranks and huddle nearer and shut her out. Her feet felt strange, they had for so long been used to the ships' movement, especially the third one which had carried them so far. She felt a kind of longing for it, the only certainty in their lives. It was gone.

Dom said nothing. They were twins and usually she waited to see what he said, what he thought, but he had run out of ideas and she was not surprised. It had been a long and uncomfortable journey and their parents were buried in a far-off land as it was now and they had had no choice but to come back to England. That far-off land was home and she wished herself back there and with them and even without them. This place was strange and alien to her.

Her parents had never spoken of it, there were apparently no ties, no family, nobody left here, but she and Dom had gone to Phadeus Small, the head of the local missionaries, and asked him for advice. She didn't want to go, their parents had never had anything to do with the authorities. The missionaries lived in a compound. Their father had despised such people.

Their mother was unacceptable because of her origins and her nomadic past and their father would never have done anything to hurt her, she was his first concern. His second concern had been the people who lived so often in squalor and these were the folk he tried to help, it was the main work of his life and Rosa and the children were dear to him.

It had therefore become a necessity that Dom should take advice. Tria, their servant, would see to the two children and so Connie accompanied Dom to talk to the minister. Dom would have gone on his own but she knew he would feel better if she went with him.

She had never been into the compound until then and hadn't liked what she'd seen of the big houses with their long wide windows, the air of prosperity. Once inside Mr Small's house she saw stout furniture, many books such as she had longed for, the smell of good food. It was not pretty but it was luxurious. Mr Small had gone through two wives while he had been here, that was what their father had said. Often people here died of diseases they were unused to. Her father claimed that Europeans had brought many of the diseases with them, their diseases and their stupid ideas was what he called them.

Her father had liked none of these men. He had laughed at their narrow minds and belittled their attempts to convert millions of people to a religion which they cared nothing for, it was despicable, he thought, it was disrespectful and worst of all it did nothing for the people except frustrate and anger them.

Connie was surprised to be taken into Mr Small's study and how the man got up, smiling. She suspected that smile and she could see Dom's fingers clench as he made them into fists but they stayed by his sides, he must try to see this through as she must. 'That dreadful little man' as her father called Mr Small privately. He was Small by name and small by nature. She could hear her father's acerbic voice, the man had small ideas and small eyes quite close together. It was said that he had reported another missionary to the authorities for dancing.

'I am so sorry for your losses,' he had said, he meant their father and mother, their father having died of typhoid miles away, where his medical skills were needed and their mother had died of a broken heart. It was not called that of course but she had given up when she heard of his death. It had been suggested to her that she should take her four children and go back to England and she had laughed bitterly at the suggestion.

There was nobody to take them back to and she had nothing. After Mickey died she had told them of his parents – this was the first Connie had ever heard of them and her lovely mother's voice was so bitter when she spoke of them – how they had hated her and of how she and Mickey had come here for a better life and now it was all over.

Everything she did have had been given to other people. There was nothing left to sell that would bring money. Mickey had looked after them, he was a warrior, a clever thinker and a gatherer, he provided everything that they needed. Now he was gone. After Mickey had died she had struggled for three weeks and then she had killed herself.

The English people here thought it was a sin, but to the Asian mind it was a reputable and understandable way out. You were in charge of your life and your death. Connie could not forgive her mother, was too English to think in the same way. Her mother's two children were now almost adult, the others had been adopted by Rosa and Mickey after the children lost their parents, Leo was ten and Pearl was four, without prospects of any kind.

Mr Small was not much bigger when he got up but it was not his shortness that she disliked, Connie thought now, it was the smallness of his mind, her father had been right. It was how men thought that mattered, not their stature.

He greeted them politely enough but did not ask them to sit down. He must show them that they were not respected, that they were not good enough to sit with civilized people, that they had no place here, could play no part. They both understood it well but Dom said what they had rehearsed he would.

'Thank you, Mr Small, it was very good of you to see us.'

At home inside their own doors they were as rude as they liked, outside they were the very opposite and here in the compound they behaved as English people did, though she was aware of the huge differences. It occurred to her that she and Dom belonged nowhere, not here and not to the people outside, they had no home and nobody but themselves.

'We thought that you might be the person to put us in touch with anyone who could help us contact any family that we might have left in England.'

They had sat up for many hours discussing what they could possibly do and this had seemed an option. They were not old enough to do anything else. Their mother had taught them all they knew. English children were sent 'home' for their education as soon as they were seven but her parents would never have done such a thing. Their father had always impressed upon them that this was their home in a way which had made it harder and harder to imagine anywhere else where they would feel the same sense of belonging.

'We are a family,' her father had said. 'Why would we send you away? We can teach you the things you need to know.'

Mr Small coughed and looked down and Connie had to bite her lips because her first thought was, Mr Small is not so tall, not tall at all, and such is his fall for no matter his height, had he been a mountain he will be forever small.

'I did have another prospect in mind for you. Perhaps you would like to sit down?'

They did and the chairs were so comfortable Connie thought she might never rise again.

'I thought that perhaps you would like to move in here.'

At first Connie didn't understand. They were not liked there, at least her parents had not been. Was all forgiven now they were dead? On what terms could they – and there her mind went in quite a different direction. It was said that she was the spit of her mother and her mother had been so beautiful that men stopped in their tracks to watch her walk down the road.

Her children took after her but then their father had been dark-haired with brown eyes and a skin which grew dark under sunshine. He told her he had Scottish ancestry from somewhere and that in the Highlands people looked like him, so it was as though their children's hair and eye colour were inherited from both sides.

She had understood that it was not quite seen as respectable. The English people in the compound were fair-skinned and a lot of the girls had pale golden hair and blue eyes and looked fragile, not something which could have ever been applied to her mother or herself.

Leo and Pearl's parents had been Japanese but had died of typhus in a village where they too had been trying to help poorer people than themselves. The children had been left behind with Rosa and that was where they stayed. Leo had been a small child then and Pearl just a few months old. The younger children therefore knew no other home than the huge bustling city of Tokyo.

'I wondered whether you, Miss Butler, might do me the honour of marrying me,' the man said.

Connie thought Dom was going to hit him, indeed she grabbed his sleeve and then his arm in case he moved. Dom was fast as a warrior and he was skilled in martial arts. It was yet another thing his father had learned there and taught him. In a country where there was danger from people of different kinds and all sorts of problems like diseases and floods you had to learn to take care of yourself in every possible way.

Also he had a terrible temper when he was not in command

of himself and she knew how protective of her he was. He would laugh when his mother reproached him for his temper and now he was flashing murder from his eyes that this man would insult his sister. Beneath her grasp he was shaking but she had known for several seconds what was happening and was able to reply very calmly that although it was indeed kind of him she could not presume.

She understood at least a little, even though in some countries she thought she would be considered young at seventeen to become a wife. Here sons were preferred and often daughters were put into orphanages if their parents could not afford to feed them. They were taken in and brought up and then if they were beautiful they became concubines, if they were useful they were married off to poor men who would buy them.

Women were expected to work as hard as men, bear lots of sons and do as they were told. Sometimes when men prospered they took on other wives. The first wives were turned off or neglected and became servants once again. Better-off people divorced and began once more. She should have been honoured by the prospect of marrying an Englishman. He could have tried to get her without marriage and still she would have had to think herself lucky. Some girls might have agreed to the proposal through fear but Connie was her mother's daughter. She tried to put a little sanity into the mix here.

'We think we ought to go home,' she said levelly. It had long since dawned on her that they had no future here. Their education came from their parents and while they had lived here all their lives they were still seen as foreign. Dom had learned skills from his father but nonetheless he was out of place here, belonging neither to the Japanese people nor to the missionaries, who were hated and feared.

'You do not know where your home is,' Mr Small said, as though he didn't want her to have options and why should he when he could buy himself a wife?

'I understand that my father went to college in London, that is what he said, and I feel certain there will be an address from when he was there because surely he would have gone home from time to time. We would like to go back there should it be possible.'

Mr Small said nothing. She knew if he did not help her because he had designs on her body she could apply to someone else in the compound. Although they did not like her family some of them were sufficiently honourable to give aid at this time, thinking in some dreadful superior way that as Christians they were above the rest of humanity. She might not want to play their tiny game but if it was for herself and Dom and the children she would do it.

'I wish that you would consider my offer more carefully,' Mr Small said. 'I do not suppose that you will get a better one. Your father – forgive me for speaking so freely of him – but he had unorthodox views about so many things and I'm afraid in these circumstances it works against you. If you have no money and no influence you cannot go anywhere and even if you did who could be left back there? Surely you would have heard from them long before now had someone wanted you in England?'

Connie was well aware of it. None of these people had said a kind word after her parents had died. They had disliked her father and despised her mother. To them Connie and her siblings were only a little better than the poor among the Japanese. It was even said that they had common ancestry.

Connie thought nothing could have been further from the truth, though she considered it her loss, while her father cared little either way, but it made him smile as their looks were European, their father Scottish and their mother's family had come from Spain and perhaps even further back from Egypt, as far as she knew. Did it matter? It did here. In this small compound status was everything. Was it like that in England? She had begun to think ruefully that it was probably like that everywhere and so she and Dom and the children were in for a bad time.

Not one single woman had come out of the compound and crossed the street to their house where they lived among the ordinary people. Her father would never have forgiven himself for doing anything less. He thought it was cowardly that they clustered together, like hovering gnats.

She knew also that the Japanese despised these so-called ministers, named them foreign devils, stole from them, cheated them when they could and only accepted what Mr Small would call the word of Christ if they were paid for it or given something they thought valuable. They had their own customs, their own ideas, so that the English despised the Japanese and the Japanese hated the English.

Somewhere between the two were she and Dom and Pearl and Leo. All alone, left, unwanted and unneeded here now. The people who cared had no money to help anybody. Connie had become scared and then horrified at the prospects but she had kept her voice steady and level. She didn't want to have to come into this wretched compound where they still insisted on eating things the Japanese considered savage and in huge amounts so that their teeth were bad and their bodies fat. Too much dairy, she shuddered, too much sitting around, too much sugar and flour, too much leisure, too much meat and no work, too much food wastage. Mr Small went on trying to tell her that it was best for her and for her family to come and live with him within the compound when he had been told they would leave.

Connie said that she didn't think it would work out.

'And whatever would happen to the two children who live with you?' he said. 'They have nowhere to go.'

'We would take them with us of course.'

'Really?' He looked genuinely taken aback and she could tell by his nasty sour face that he was thinking, surely any family you have left in England would not want orphans such as these who speak little English and have been brought up as savages.

He was rude, yes, the children could be difficult but they had endured many hardships in their short lives before her parents had taken them in and after that as far as she and Dom were concerned they were family and would go wherever she and her brother went.

In the end when Mr Small could see that she was implacable he looked disappointed and surprised. Had he really thought she would marry a smelly old man of forty, who was balding and getting stout, whose breath smelled of sour milk and thick red meat? After several pauses he agreed he would write to the head of his church in England and ask if he could help.

They waited until the gates of the compound were closed and then Dom swore in Japanese, what he would like to do to Mr Small, how he would cut off his penis and shove it in his mouth, how he would make soup of his bollocks.

Nobody took any notice and it was just as well for his voice was not soft. The people in the compound did not speak Japanese thankfully, for Connie thought Mr Small would have been mightily offended.

Late that night when the children were asleep they talked it all over. Dom did not want to leave, Connie could see, but she knew they could not belong here without their parents, they were too different. On the other hand they could not leave without the children so she must somehow contrive to make sure at least that they all left together. If she abandoned them they would die. Dom tried to make an argument for staying here but her instincts told her it was not the thing to do.

In the end she and Dom went back to Mr Small and he did say that he would ensure they could go back to England and make some kind of life for themselves. He did not voice the main problem, that there was a good chance they would not be accepted in a place they had never been to. English was their second language and sometimes Pearl could not think of the correct words to say. Leo in a bad mood would not speak and Connie feared greatly for their future. Dom wanted to wait and she could see that he was hoping they would not be able to leave.

It soon became obvious they could not stay. Yes, they had friends around them but the situation was different now and when they slept people came in and stole everything they had. It felt like the last straw. All they had left were clothes and most of those had gone. Mr Small arranged for them to leave and Connie, afraid Dom would find out who had stolen from them and retaliate, wanted to get him away in fear that he should be killed, that perhaps there was such hatred of foreign people that they might be murdered in their beds.

It seemed that the Methodist church had helped them to go back to England and though she could not imagine why they should be so generous she did not question it. She wanted to leave here so badly and the good news was that her father had parents in northern England. His parents were still alive. Connie was elated. To think that they could go to a new country and belong to somebody. It was exciting.

Five

Flo could not be at ease. She felt as if she and Joshua ought to have done the right thing. Her mother used to say, 'Two wrongs don't make a right.' Just because Michael had made a mess of his life, it wasn't to say that she and Joshua should not try to help their grandchildren. If they did not who would?

Joshua was still against it and his will was implacable so she did not discuss it with him any more. He knew he was doing wrong but he wouldn't alter it. He blamed his son for what had happened.

Flo didn't go far. The shop was to see to and the weather was vile. It was always at its worst in January and February so that nobody went outside unless they had to. The very next day after they found the children were in England she said that she was going out and went.

She did this from time to time, otherwise everything would be shut when she needed supplies from Miss Hutton or the hardware store. Joshua would suspect nothing. He was in the garden digging over the beds and turning up new soil because the ground was not hard at the moment. The weather had momentarily turned soft and since it would not last he was out there as often as he could be because when the frost returned it would help to break up the soil. Flo was glad of some breathing space. They were barely speaking.

She put on heavy coat and boots and ventured down the street towards the centre of the village. The market square was in the middle with shops and houses mixed on either side so everybody knew what everybody was doing, therefore somebody was bound to see her whatever she did. She had taken this into consideration, been obliged to admit it and still go forward.

The chapel was halfway down on the left-hand side, a pretty building but not a patch on the parish church, she always thought, honestly.

It was likely that Mr Adams would be in the chapel. She didn't want to go in but she made herself. She could no longer just sit at home and do nothing.

When she opened the heavy door and stepped inside her footsteps echoed just slightly but he had acute hearing. He looked up from where he had been writing at a table just to the side of the aisle and he got up.

It was only then that she admitted to herself she had long since missed this place of worship. The parish church here was old and lovely and much more pleasing and ornate but this had been home and she had been happy here before everything had gone wrong and Michael had run away.

There were a thousand pictures in her mind of him here and that was one of the reasons she and Joshua had had to leave. Neither of them could bear to remember the sight of him in this place which she had loved so very much.

She said his name over and over under her breath since nobody ever spoke of him. She wished she could have kept his image better in her mind, it had long since faded. She could only picture him as young and how fine-looking he had been and they had been so proud of him when he turned out to be clever. So much for intelligence, she thought now, many a lad of his age who had not half his brains had married and kept his wife and bairns on his wits. She had longed for grandchildren. It was a case of 'be careful what you wish for', she thought now with a pang of sorrow. She had never wished for any of that for years, she thought to chide God and then rebuked herself. She was in God's house.

It was so plain and she liked the plainness of it, it was somehow neat and clean and yet spacious to her eyes, and she remembered the pew where they had sat and she remembered also how Michael had got up and preached there. It had been the best moment of her life.

He said that he had lost his faith after he met Rosa and it seemed to her that now he was dead – she could not accept that, he would never be dead to her, but he was and she must try to understand how badly things had gone for them – and yet from beyond the grave in some far-off strange place he had made another huge mess which she and Joshua, despite what they thought, must try to deal with somehow.

Mr Adams ushered her somewhat unwillingly into a little back room which was very cold, there being no fire. Her heart had been beating wildly as though she had no business being here, not telling Joshua where she was going.

'What can I do for you, Mrs Butler?' he said, not sitting down himself nor offering her a seat.

There was no point in hesitating because this man did not like her and resented that she and Joshua did not come to his church.

'I think you probably know,' she said. 'It's about my son's children. What will happen to them?'

'I understand that they have your name and address and sufficient money to get here by themselves.'

Flo felt as though she was being swept away.

'They are coming then?'

'They have no other place to go and since you did not meet them at the docks I'm sure they will be here very soon.'

'But – but they can't,' was all Flo managed. 'Joshua will never allow it.'

'I fear it is out of Mr Butler's hands,' Mr Adams said.

'But we have no room, we cannot house more people. We cannot afford to keep them, we cannot—' She ran out of breath and comprehension at that point and the tears began to brim over and slide down her cheeks.

'Your son forfeited his right to practise within our church a very long time ago and after the church had provided money to help take him to Japan. He never offered to repay a penny of it but we cannot turn our backs on his children. It is our Christian duty. The older ones could doubtless be found some kind of work. As for the young children I do not know what to advise, if you will not help. The only orphanage nearby is up on the tops and is in ruins.'

She went home now nervous as well as downhearted. The situation seemed to her to be getting worse and worse.

Six

Laura Neville already hated the country. She had lived in Durham City after she married. Her childhood was spent just outside the city in a pit town. Weardale was strange to her. There was not enough space somehow. The valley was narrow and the fields were full of sheep, the stupidest animals on earth. The villages, what she had seen of them, looked all alike, the people were sour-faced and poor by their dress, they spoke in a different accent than hers and seemed to have little knowledge of anything beyond sheep and home.

Some of the farmers stank of manure, at least she imagined that was what it was, when they came to see the doctor so that Fiona was always washing floors. They made a great deal of work, Laura thought, but she didn't think she could do anything about it so she said nothing and kept to her part of the house where nobody ventured but herself, Thomas and the maids.

In her heart she was still in Durham with Harry. Their beautiful house also was right by the river and she remembered how very happy she had been as though the city wrapped its arms around her and her husband and her house and indeed her whole life.

She tried not to think of how she had been able to have only one child. When her bleeding dried up so early and she felt strange with warmth in her face and strange sensations in her body, she went to Dr Crawcrook who sympathetically told her she would not have any more children, middle age had crept upon her when she was young and what a hard thing it was.

She had gone home tearful, only for Harry to tell her there was no need for any more, they had got it right the first time. No wonder, she thought, that she had so adored the only child she had.

To be fair they had done their best for him and he had been worthy of it right from the start, a happy bright little boy who walked and talked very early and always brought joy to them. He was what they called 'not a scrap of bother' in Durham. He was tall and handsome for he looked just like Harry, she said, though her husband disagreed and said that the child looked like her.

Thomas was always ahead of the class in school, not that his school was in Durham. When he was seven they sent him to Scorton Grammar school. Laura had worried in case Thomas should dislike boarding school but Thomas loved his school, the little independence he got and his friends there. He loved cricket and rugby and Greek and Latin. There was little the boy could not do. He was merry and bright and to them could not have done any better, they were so very proud of him. When he decided to become a doctor Laura's heart almost burst with pride. She thought that Harry might have been disappointed for the law was seen to be the senior profession but he was happy to let his son be who he was.

Thomas went to Oxford where he made friends but always he found time to come home to Durham and his loving parents.

It was over, the happiness was finished, Laura reminded herself. Harry was gone and yet here she was in Wolsingham and she heard her lovely boy's voice a dozen times a day. She would learn to be thankful for that.

From her window which looked out over the garden she glimpsed, just beyond, a young woman and a tall figure almost in shade not far from the garden gate. They were laughing and talking. How could she envy a young woman a lover when she had been so lucky to have married the man of her dreams? And yet she did. She felt so unwanted, so unneeded, so unnecessary now. She had no place here. She had no place anywhere.

Seven

Pearl cried to go home and Leo stood around scowling. He mimicked everything Dom did, quite unwittingly, and took up his moods. Connie had begged of Dom to speak English and not to swear but he didn't seem to want to do anything much and did not talk to her until he had to as he did now.

'What in the name of God do we do?' he said, when the other people who had been on board disappeared into various vehicles and up a number of streets and alleyways.

Connie had never felt less at home than she did here. There were people of all kinds and dress, tall, short, fat, thin, they seemed to be speaking different languages, she caught an English word here and there but that was all. Dom was frowning and fidgeting and he also was lost and scared, she knew, even though he was trying hard to act like the man he thought he was.

They had been told there would be members of their family to meet them, apparently they had their father's parents still alive and they were meant to be here, but nobody turned up and they soon became tired and hungry and Pearl sobbed hard against Connie's shoulder. Connie knew the little girl could barely stand for tiredness and she lifted the child into her arms.

Somebody needed to make a decision.

'Do you think we should try to find where we get on a train

or should we seek out some place to stay?' she said to Dom but he only shrugged.

The area around the docks was filled with huge buildings which threatened to overwhelm her but she had an idea. The last of the crew were coming off the ship. She thought they might find her somewhere to stay but as she took the first steps Dom stopped her. She stared at him as he shook his head.

'What?' she asked.

'I don't think we should trust them.'

'We have to trust somebody.'

'Why don't we move away and see if we can find a place for ourselves?'

'What, with all this stuff?'

'If they get hold of you there's no saying what they might do. Women like you aren't to be found everywhere and very young. You know what I mean.'

'That's stupid, Dom.'

'Well it might be but I'm not bloody fighting sailors over your maidenhood. Please yourself.'

She wanted to laugh but it was true that she had spent a lot of time down below on the ship even though the place reeked of stale salt water and damp sweat and rotting timbers because when she went on deck the sailors stood about, staring at her, whistling after her and offering to do various disgusting things to her in odd manners, most of which she understood even though they spoke in other languages. Some of their stances and actions were lewd. Dom might not be right but she could not afford to take any chances.

In the end Dom shouldered the two big bundles they had brought, Leo insisted on taking another though he staggered under the weight of it and she held on to Pearl and also carried one bag in her free hand and another on her shoulder. She was aware of the darkness between the streets and alleys, they could be robbed and beaten or worse, she knew, but they must have somewhere to stay in safety and some comfort if it could possibly be managed.

Finally away from the vicinity of the ships there were several streets and to her they looked respectable. There were a number of small hotels with unlikely names, The Ship Inn, The Sailors Hotel, the Overseas Mission, whatever that was, but in the end she went to the nearest decent-looking place and banged on the door.

A woman in a grubby patterned frock was not long in opening it.

'Can't you read?' she said and then Connie saw the placard in the window, 'No Chinese, no Irish, no Black people.'

'But we aren't—' Connie, nonplussed, couldn't help voicing denial.

The woman slammed the door in her face. Connie stared at the notice. She now saw similar notices everywhere they went and understood. Their faces made them look like foreigners even if people didn't know where they had come from or belonged and people were somehow naturally afraid of everything that they did not know or understand. Mickey had always said half in jest that the lads of Rookhope would fight with the lads from Stanhope even though it was but a few miles away.

In the end Connie stopped a woman who was clean and neat and asked politely how to get to the station. The woman stood back gazing at them but the two lads did not come near and Pearl had fallen asleep so Connie looked pleadingly at her and the woman explained that it was but a twenty-minute walk to Lime Street Station and gave them directions.

This cheered Connie and, memorizing the directions because Dom would pretend he hadn't heard or wouldn't or couldn't remember, she knew what she must do. She set off and the lads followed her. It was very cold and in fact took rather longer than that but eventually they found the station and it was enormous.

It was scary, that was her first thought, and busy. She felt as though she had been on her feet forever but it was only the middle of the day.

A mingling crowd of people stood before her and there was a great deal of noise, huge steam engines graced the tall building and there were whistles and the sound of steam hissing and people had suitcases with them. Some people were very well-dressed, fashion obviously mattered here. She had thought people would mostly be poor but they were not. Women wore gorgeous hats with feathers in them and long skirts and neat boots and the men wore what she could tell were tailored suits which fitted them and they all had on tall hats and they were talking in a very polite fashion.

Further over were less well-off people but nobody was badly dressed. Presumably if you had no money you didn't take a train. She handed the sleeping Pearl to Dom and then she went into the ticket office where people were queuing. She was panicked now. She didn't understand a lot of what was said so when she got to the person behind the counter she thrust the address at him and asked if he could help her.

He spoke so quickly and with a thick accent which sounded like some kind of song to her that she had to ask him to repeat it all. He asked for what she thought was a great deal of money but there was nothing she could do about it and so she paid him. By the end of the journey she knew they would have very little left. He told her which platform the train was leaving from and how long to wait and that it went to Manchester and then on up to Leeds. They would have to change trains at Leeds and go to Darlington. Then they would change trains again so that they could get to Durham. After that it was what he called 'a small branch line' so he was not quite sure how much further it was from there but they could get a train to Wolsingham from Durham. She was only relieved that they could travel all the way. She had imagined a lot of walking and between Pearl and all the baggage it would have been very hard.

Eight

Flo could not put the children from her mind. She went over and over what had happened and it beggared belief. What if they had not arrived? What if something had happened on the voyage? What if they did not know how to find their way here? What if they had lost the address? What if they decided to go some other way? She didn't sleep and couldn't eat and Joshua was the same but they did not talk about it. She tried to go on with her work as usual but it was hard and yet she was glad of it, that people came to the shop, that she had to appear as though nothing was the matter.

Nobody but Mr Adams knew anything about it. Further than that she could not think but as two days turned into three her anxiety grew worse. Just as the shop was about to close several people came in. Why she did not notice them or look up from where she was counting her money she never knew.

Darkness and cold had fallen and she was not expecting anybody except that there were one or two old people in the village who almost deliberately waited until two minutes before half past five and then kept her talking.

She knew those living alone got fed up of their own company and were aware they got more attention if her shop was empty but for them. She finished her sums and then she looked up and got such a shock that she felt faint.

She had never fainted in her life but before her stood Michael when he was seventeen, clever, handsome, tall with those glinting eyes surrounded by thick lashes. The only difference was that he was dressed in expensive black clothes such as Michael had never been. She was convinced that his clothes had been tailored to him, they were some material she knew nothing about and made him look even better than he had ever appeared to her in her mind. How silly, how unlikely and yet there he stood and she had never been as glad to see him and could not convince herself immediately that it was not her beloved and long-despaired-of only son.

His name was instantly on her lips and the tears which had filled her eyes for so many years came back like an unwanted old friend. Her vision blurred and she shook her head and sniffed and dashed away the water and then she saw the four of them, the elder girl – the two oldest children were near in age, she guessed – and she was exactly like Rosa. Flo had hated Rosa so much, had blamed her for everything she had done, for having wrecked all their lives, so that even now she could feel the hot temper rise up in her.

The girl had a child in her arms and by her side there was a boy of about ten. Nobody spoke for what felt like a long time and then the girl very politely and in a strangely accented though clear voice said,

'Are you Mrs Butler? We are your grandchildren.'

Flo's hands began to shake. She had not imagined them like this but with white skin and brown hair and brown eyes but then Michael had been very dark and Rosa as a traveller even more so and these children were as foreign as they could be in their strange expensive black clothes.

How could these be her grandchildren? There was such a

huge gap in age between the two older ones and the two small children so that her mind filled with strange ideas, that Michael had married again, that Rosa had died much earlier, that he had had another woman, a mistress, that was what the upper classes called it. Was Michael worse than she had thought, and what on earth would Joshua say and think if that were so? She could not stop looking at them, they were so beautiful, tall and slender and of a completely different world. She was stunned into silence.

They were pale and looked tired. Indeed the little girl with the sleek black hair was asleep in the older girl's arms.

At that moment Joshua came into the shop. He would be wondering what they were having for tea. He stopped short and stared. Flo was beginning to think that nobody would ever break the silence. The children didn't move. It was as though the single moment of shock went on and on like a pebble thrown into a pond.

'These people are not like us,' he said hoarsely when he found his voice and he stared at them in disdain. It was shock, Flo thought, he was not used to such things. Who would be? Presumably he had not thought that any grandchild of his could look so utterly foreign, so out of place, like strange beings from an alien planet. 'Do they speak English?'

And that was when the older boy said clearly,

'Yes, we speak English. We also speak Japanese, Spanish and Egyptian, a form of Arabic. You can talk directly to me. I am Dominic, this is my sister, Constance, the boy is Leo and the little one is Pearl. We have travelled halfway across the world to meet you.'

His voice was so assured, so cultured, so intelligent. Flo was amazed. He was nothing like Michael, she could see the differ-ence now, and despite his looks the boy was a stranger. Michael had had a northern accent, a soft beautiful lilting dales voice. This young man spoke to her not quite like a southerner or a foreigner but as though he was not quite sure of his language – it was his second tongue, she could tell, and it was slow and careful and clipped and very precise – and he had a straight look such as Michael would never have had.

It was, she thought, less respectful as though he stood his ground because it was his right and that was never the way here, especially when you spoke to older members of your family. Accuracy was his first concern and then his second was to make sure that he was accepted. He assumed that he would be. There was a certain arrogance about him which she did not appreciate.

Then the girl spoke and she was the same. Very certain of who she was. Was this really Rosa's daughter? The traveller's offspring?

'May we sit down? Pearl has become very heavy. I have carried her for hours.'

'You cannot stay here,' Joshua said. 'We have no room for anyone. Go and make your way up to the ruined orphanage, that's good enough for the likes of you,' and he went into the back room and closed the door.

Flo didn't know what to do. She dithered, that was the name for it. She had always thought that since Joshua was the man in the family and her husband and the only person left for whom she felt any love that she must let him have the last word but she wanted to tell the children that they could stay, even though it was impractical, even though two of them were as big as adults, the little girl was small and the boy looked weary. Her heart hurt so much she thought she would die.

They stood there looking inquiringly at her and she wanted to greet them with joy, but she couldn't do it, not after what

Joshua had said. He was implacable, he would not give in and he was right, they were not like anybody here, they were incredibly odd-looking with jet black hair and the older boy and girl were confident such as she had not seen before.

They were nothing like her or Joshua and not like she remembered their Michael. He had been modest and self-effacing, one of the reasons he would have made such a good preacher, at least until he met that awful woman. Flo stared at the older children, yes, they looked like Rosa. She had always had that horrible bright stare about her as though ready to take on the world. She had ruined their lives and now Michael was dead and these ghastly offspring assumed they could come here and be accepted. She would be ashamed that the village should see them, that the whole world would talk. She and Joshua would be a laughing stock as though their lives were not difficult enough and yet the mother in her yearned for them.

She was relieved and sorry when they turned and left and yet as they did so she could not contain herself and stood there weeping in the empty shop, gazing down the street after them as though there was something to see, as though anything could be done. They disappeared into the darkness and she could not help thinking that there was no way they could ever have stayed here, they would not fit, they were so out of place, they would never be accepted.

Then she locked the shop door and went into the back. There was but one candle as though Joshua could not have lit another, the low mood he was in.

'They are not like us,' he said again. It was not an accusatory tone, it was closer to despair, his voice very low and almost broken, as though things had turned out even worse than he had thought and it was more than he could endure 'They'll have to go, to the workhouse if necessary. Things are bad enough. Michael shamed us and now his vile offspring have come here to haunt us and shame us all over again. I thought things would get better. I never imagined this.'

His voice snapped and tears sped fat and round down his weathered cheeks. Flo could think of nothing to say. She tried to imagine that she was back just a couple of weeks with Christmas approaching. She had thought things were bad then but they were nothing compared to this. She felt as though she wanted to go out and lie down and freeze so that she got colder and colder and went to sleep and died. What a relief and release, she thought, it would be.

Nine

Turned out, the little family walked the short distance into the market square, one long street, a bridge and then the road veered to the right. There they stopped again. Connie couldn't think of anything to say. It had not occurred to her that their grandparents would not want them, would not take them in.

Dom stopped. She had been afraid he would do so. She knew he blamed her that they had come here. They had tried not to shout at one another in front of the younger ones but she understood how exasperated he felt.

'I wish we'd never left home,' he said.

'It was a joint decision.'

'It was nothing of the sort. You pushed me into it like you always push everybody into everything,' her brother said.

'You know very well what would have happened,' she said. 'You would have got us all killed, taking it out on other people, and don't let me think you threw that knife away. I know you carry it on you. Things like that don't help.'

'And where in the name of hell do you think we can go now?'

She couldn't think but she needed to.

'The church,' she said, 'we'll go and talk to the minister.'

'I'm not going anywhere near anybody to do with churches,' Dom said.

'Have you got a better idea?'

He didn't answer. It was cold and dark and she was so weary. They trudged on just a little way and then she saw a church with the inscription '1865' over the door. It was plain and small and on the pavement of the street so unlikely to be the parish church. Just to the side and set back was a house, not like the vicarages she had been told of which were enormous apparently, it was a very modest house and not quite in darkness because the sky was clear with a big moon and stars. Encouraged and unable to think of what more to do she began to walk towards it and Dom, who by now had put an arm around Leo, followed her without a word.

Neither of her parents had explained much of the past, so that they were going forward as though it had nothing to do with them. She could not believe that woman was her grandmother, that little wizened-up tiny bird without dignity, without decent clothing, wearing what at home would have been considered little more than rags for the poorest.

She could not believe that her father's parents had so little, that they were this poor in their tumbling-down house and shoddy little shop. Shopkeepers of all things. She had not known all those years that she had family anywhere and now that she had come thousands of miles they didn't want her, or Dom or the younger ones.

What cowards these people were. How closed-minded and insular and rude. Ignorant peasants in tiny dirty houses with grubby cold streets and the hills here beyond the town seemed to dominate everything in the narrow valley. She could not believe her parents had ever lived anywhere so awful. No wonder they had left.

Dom knocked on the door and a woman came to answer it.

Middle-aged, badly dressed and shabby, plain-faced with her hair drawn back from her sharply pointed cheeks, she stared into the darkness from the comparative light of the hall where an oil lamp burned. Snow had fallen and the night was bitter.

'Could you direct us to an inn? We don't mean to impose but we have just arrived. We are the Butler family.' Dom spoke in such a friendly manner, Connie thought, and the woman fell for his confidence straight away. Connie had seen women do that a hundred times. He was mesmerizing. It was like a spell he cast over them. Was he aware of his effect? She was sure he understood. He did it on purpose so that he would get what he wanted and this time she wasn't sorry. They needed to use what wiles they possessed.

Women would do anything for him, he was beautiful, intriguing, softly spoken. They had not seen him like an animal, snarling and growling and using his body to defend those he cared for, and yet she knew also that that was attractive if a woman should need protection and care. He looked unselfconscious and that was part of the pull, he had a touch of arrogance about him which spoke of his upbringing and self-belief.

He had several times defended his father when his father went to a village to help aid the sick and he had had rocks thrown at him but his father just ran. Dom had told Connie about it and the idea of their father running like that made them smile.

She didn't think Mickey had been like that or Rosa, it was just Dom and to some extent herself too. They had been brought up in a proud place and taught that they were the very best they could be and had had it reinforced by the people they lived amongst.

Connie just wished now that her father had not given away every penny he possessed, everything of value, to help others.

It was the reason they had nothing now but their pride and Connie was beginning to think it ill-bought, though she sighed in apology to her father's memory. He had brought them up to do the same. They had good clothes which their mother made and good food and their education but that was all.

'Nobody can take your education from you,' her father said and she knew he had given away everything in the knowledge they would save themselves.

It was the first time Connie had thought she and Dom really did come from another land, they had not been born into a place like this where they were regarded as nobody and nothing. She and Dom had always been very proud of who they were, they had been brought up to it but also it was part of the culture. When you were educated, when you were clever, then you had status and her father and mother had been greatly regarded, respected and admired as much for who they were as what they had done. They had been loved by the people they served, they really had. She had thought to find an affection here, had hoped for it, but she had been wrong. She wished there had been any-where to go but this miserable little backwater in the middle of nowhere in this sparse and inhospitable land.

'Yes, yes of course,' the woman almost stuttered as she gazed at the glorious young man in front of her in the street which was glittering with ice on snow and above it stars in the clear sky with a huge blue moon.

Dom was tall, he was getting taller, Connie thought, he was six feet two at least. She was tall too but she didn't think she was as imposing. She was like the other side of him, the lighter side, a light in the darkness, wasn't that what her father had called it? Oh hell, she thought, I miss you so much, Mickey. They had never referred to their parents as Mother and Father. Rosa thought it was beneath them and wanted all her family to be on an equal and adult footing. Michael went with her on this issue no matter whether he liked it or not but since all their children spoke so lovingly there was no crime in it.

It had not occurred to Connie that houses could be other than the one her father and mother had made for them in Tokyo, the city she loved. Her mother had built a special garden there and Connie missed the libraries and the parks, the shops and the smells, the street markets and the sounds of people selling their wares, and she missed the music and poetry and the food, most especially the food.

Were there cities here or was it all like this, with houses crowded together as though there was no space? They had come through bigger towns but in her confusion she had not noticed them except that everywhere seemed equally unfriendly, beginning with Liverpool which she admitted to herself now had scared her. Nobody had spoken to her on the trains and when she had been confused in the stations she had been ignored, despite asking for aid. People had glanced away from her and her little family, as though they were low animals, to be avoided, to be shunned. The children and Dom had slept as they moved but she could not and now felt utter weariness creep over her.

Inside she thought that the house smelled damp and she recognized poverty because she had seen it so often when she and her mother went to poor houses within the city to help. Yet this was quite a big house. The hall echoed with the sound of her feet, on the thin carpet which was so bare that it muffled little noise. She wanted to turn and run but Dom was ahead of her, leading the way.

Depending on the situation one of them always took over and instinctively they knew when to hold back and when to go forwards, she wasn't sure whether sisters and brothers usually felt like that or was it just twins? She loved their relationship and felt sorry for people who were not twins. She knew what he would say, sometimes how he would think, and often when they were away from one another she could feel his presence close and safe.

She had led when they had left the ship and found their way to the railway station, now it was his turn. Dom had picked up Leo because the boy was scared and tired and although he was far too big for such things Connie thought Dom had timed it right. The poor boy was past himself, as Rosa would say. He hid his face in against Dom's shoulder and enfolded his arms around Dom's neck to get as close as he could. Usually he was a courageous boy but too much had happened and she could tell he could not stand any more.

Pearl was almost asleep in her arms but the little girl's face was raw and red as she had cried so very much that day and rubbed her cheeks against Connie's jacket. She was exhausted. Connie's arms ached. She would have given a great deal to put the child down but she knew Pearl would cry away from the comfort of her arms so she clung on, knowing she needed the comfort too of having the little girl so very close.

The woman led the way into the nearest room where a short skinny man in worn clothes stood up from some kind of desk. A small fire burned in the grate but when he spoke Connie could see his breath. He looked astonished and well he might, Connie thought. He stared. He stared for a lot longer than would have been considered polite in Tokyo, you looked somebody in the eyes for a brief time only. It was considered rude to do more except that Dom was doing the same thing now, as a form of dominance even if he was unaware of it. He owned the room in seconds.

'I am Dominic Butler, this is my sister Constance and the two younger ones are Leo and Pearl. We understand that you might help us to find an inn for the night.'

The man stared for such a long time that Connie was embarrassed for him. She could feel the heat on her face. She felt she ought to have been grateful even for that, it was the only warmth she had. The man remembered his manners then and told them that he was Amos Adams , the local Methodist minister.

'Did you not locate your grandparents?' Mr Adams said in a strange flat accent like a poor man who had no home. He did not greet them and to ask a question so immediately was unusual and considered rude.

'We could not stay there. I think their house is a ruin.'

Mr Adams looked confused and tried several times to be constructive. Perhaps he was unpractised at such matters, Connie thought, perhaps good relations between people when they first met had somehow been lost in this dark poor vile little country.

'I imagine they were shocked to see you.'

'We had been told that we were expected,' Connie said.

Mr Adams said nothing. After a while Dom said,

'Is there some kind of an inn we could go to until we have slept and eaten?'

'You could not go to such a place,' Mr Adams said.

'There is no inn here?'

For a few moments Connie smiled. They had kept Christmas, her father cared very little for religious ceremonies, traditions and beliefs but Christmas was his weakness and when she had been a very little girl he told her of Mary and Joseph and the baby Jesus and how there was no room at the inn. It had for a long time been her favourite story. She had liked to hear it before she fell asleep. Even here in this strange land they must have inns with stables like the one where Jesus had been born. She had always felt sorry for him being born into a poor land. She knew very well that he had been born in the east so probably nothing like this weird place. She sincerely trusted not.

'Then what are we to do?'

'You had better stay here for tonight.' Mr Adams spoke grudgingly, he was doing what he had always been told was his duty, Connie thought. You did your duty but usually you could manage more than that. Their form of hospitality was the worst she had ever come across.

'Thank you,' Dom said, giving him a little bow. 'You are most kind. May we sit down? I fear my sisters are weary.' Which was irony but Mr Adams didn't even hear it, Connie could see.

Tired as she was she didn't want to sit down in such a dingy place. She was certain that it wasn't very clean and that all kinds of pests lived here and would bite her and crawl on her body and into her hair. Her mother, having lived in a caravan for most of her young life, had taught them that they must be tidy or there would be a mess and as they had many servants the house was spotless. Nobody wore shoes inside, nobody could abide dirty dishes or dishevelled clothes or food which was not prepared with love and care. Such things were part of the culture as she understood it. Her father employed as many servants as he could afford because it gave people a place, a home and an income. Also they got food three times a day. If they had children her mother would teach them light things like singing but also to read and write in their own language.

Everything about their home was good. She had not forgotten how the servants wept after her father died. It was not entirely altruistic, they would lose everything too. Connie felt guilty about it, she wanted to bring all their friends and servants to this country but she could see now that it was just as well she could do no such thing. Tokyo was a palace compared to this. And she reminded herself that they could no longer belong there. This was the future. How truly awful.

There was little furniture and she thought she could smell mouse wee. The curtains looked as though they were mouldy. In fact the whole place could have done with what her mother used to call 'a spring clean'. However, she had little choice. Pearl huddled closer and shut her eyes against this new development.

Connie wished she too could shut out the world but most of all she longed to eat. As soon as she sat down in a most uncomfortable armchair, it bristled with something that seemed to stick into her and she wanted to cry. She remembered her mother talking of horse hair. How revolting. Their chairs had been better than this, she knew for she had made the padded cushions for each one. She felt like she was sitting on spikes.

She hadn't cried up till now, she could not start crying about the lack of a decent chair when she had not cried as they had brought back the news of her father's death, nor when she had had to say goodbye to her mother and taken care of her body, nor when they had lost their home.

She and Dom had laughed over disgusting Mr Small. She tried to remember that day and how they had gone home pretending to be amused by his assumption that she would ever contemplate marriage to a man like that, and yet in the end they had been grateful to him because he had helped them to get here so she didn't feel as though they ought to laugh at the man even if they didn't like him. It was childish and she was attempting to put such things behind her. Then she remembered that her father had always made fun of Mr Small and that felt even worse. Now she couldn't bring anything positive to mind. Her head ached and her feet ached and her arms ached and the water in her eyes stung. Whatever were they to do?

She blinked away the tears. If Pearl saw them she would cry as well and they would be letting their family down in front of people they did not know.

'Would you be able to allow us tea and perhaps rice?' Dom said.

He looked at Mrs Adams.

She returned the look blankly. 'We could give you bread and butter.'

'That would be very kind,' Connie said.

'A couple of pounds would help,' Mr Adams said.

Connie was appalled but she kept the look from her face and watched Dom give into Mr Adams' eager fingers most of the money they still had. She wanted to turn and walk out but she was too tired and she thought the man knew and took advantage of it.

A servant came in, a small girl with a scared look carrying a plate of thinly sliced bread, barely spread with butter, and four cups of water. They did not have much food to spare, Connie surmised. She tried to eat slowly because they had not been able to spare much money for food and she was very hungry. Sitting there, however, she felt so ill that she could hardly keep down the little she was given. She felt she would choke on sobs if she had much more to endure this day.

They were seen upstairs into a large room and left with a candle.

'Aren't you beginning to wish we had stayed where we were now?' Dom said and as often happened he was echoing her thoughts. Would they have been so much worse off in a place they knew, where they understood the customs and culture and could probably have done better than this? The trouble was, she knew that they had hoped for family, somebody to care for them, somebody to be sorry for what had happened to them. Somebody to welcome them as if they were going home. They had no home now.

'Don't go on about it,' she said. 'You would have ended up like those boys who looted our house, who would kill their grand-mothers for money, who care for nobody.'

'That's not fair,' he said.

'Dom, this was the only sensible thing to do. We have to find a place to live our lives.'

'Huh,' Dom said and she didn't think that was very mature.

The bedcovers – there was one big bed – were icy to the touch but the children went to sleep immediately when Connie pulled back the covers for them to climb in. They had had something to eat and their lives were shattered. Connie wished she could sleep like that. She went over to the window. There was no fire in the tiny grate and the curtains at the window were thin but she did not want to shut out the night. The moon lit the sky. She could not believe it was the same moon as she had seen in Tokyo, the same moon her mother and father had loved so much.

From here the streets held no light. The houses were black-windowed as if there was nobody in them or as though people went early to bed because they could not escape from the cold and hunger until they lost consciousness. She tried not to think about food or dwell on the kind of reception she had hoped she might get. How silly it seemed now. At her lowest, after her mother died, when she was told she had grandparents she'd been so relieved that she would belong to someone, that she could go there and be welcomed.

She tried to think what they were like. She had known that her mother had no family, had never known her own mother and her father had died when she was fifteen and she had danced and sung for money and had no home, but she knew now that her father had had a home.

She had dreamed of what it would be like. Was it a castle such as her mother had told her about, which lined the border there, or a big country house where people had fires in every room and glass houses which held every fruit she could imagine? They might have big ponds so that fish could be caught and eaten every day and they would have wonderful gardens full of cherry blossom.

What a stupid idea it had been. How different this was. What was it like to feel unloved by your son and abandoned by him and the woman you thought of as a whore and therefore want nothing to do with their children?

She hated the idea of people closing out the darkness as though they were afraid of it. There were so many more things to fear than night time. Her parents had both loved the night. They liked the glitter of the stars and if they were near a river the sounds at night, how the water ran, how the birds quietened, how the country slept, the flapping wings of the night birds, and in summer how the stars were so much lower and glittered like diamonds, so her mother said. Her mother had had no diamonds, only her children.

When Connie had been a little girl they would all lie outside under the stars. Her mother had a saying that went something like 'How could I be afraid of the night when I have seen the stars' and her father would tell them stories, fairy tales he called them, and bible stories. Dom liked Daniel and the lion best and her mother would sing Spanish songs and sometimes she would dance as she had as a young girl dancing for pennies in the marketplace of the towns she went to with her father.

They had had a horse and a caravan and her mother would explain that caravan was the eastern word for travelling wagon, her father moved from place to place, mending pans and other hardware. Connie could remember her mother telling of this and how he would get up and dance with her and they would all laugh with joy.

Dom knew she was about to cry, he always did. He came and stood by the window with her. They were demonstrative people, it was her Spanish mother that had done it, it was not usual for people to touch as much as they did but Dom came over.

'It will be all right, we will manage,' he said. She didn't think he believed it for a second and now neither did she.

In the end they huddled together for warmth under the eiderdown at either side of the bed, she behind Pearl and he behind Leo so the children were saved from any danger or draught and she was so tired that she fell thankfully out of consciousness.

She came to and there was candlelight. As her eyes focused she saw that Dom was out of bed and had lit the candle and was at the big dressing table.

'What are you doing?' she whispered and he came over to the bed with a big jug in one hand and something white in the other. The two children awoke and then he gave each of them a long swallow from the big jug and then he gave huge chunks of bread into their hands.

They ate and drank greedily.

'You stole?' Connie said, but unable to care as she bit into the bread and enjoyed the milk when it was her turn.

'Do you want us to starve?' he whispered back. 'The last time we had a decent meal was before we left Japan. We will have no energy to go on if we don't eat something soon.'

There was also a huge piece of fruit cake which he divided into four and when there was not a crumb left he set the jug down by the bed. Connie could not worry about it, she was too tired, and her stomach was too full for her not to fall asleep.

When she woke up Dom and the jug and the candle had gone but he came back soon afterwards and they dressed and went downstairs.

She was not looking forward to what would probably be bread and butter again for breakfast. There might even be tea. She hadn't tasted tea in so long that she watched the door eagerly. They were ushered into the kitchen by the little servant girl.

It was a dark room which overlooked the back garden, poorly furnished with wooden forms at either side of the table so it was obvious that Mr Adams and his wife didn't breakfast there. Also Connie could smell something like eggs and toasted bread and her mouth watered. They sat down at the table to eat – she was not quite sure what the white globs of stuff were in the small cracked bowls which the servant girl put in front of them. Dirt hid in cracks, she knew. How disgusting. A big spoon each was given to them. Connie was used to ceremony with meals but there was nothing of the ceremony about this, it was as basic as it could be.

'What is it?' Leo asked, staring and solemn. Pearl took up her spoon eagerly for she was hungry and put the first spoonful into her mouth, paused and then her face changed into a grimace and she spat it back out into the bowl and started to howl.

The servant stared at them, more scared than she had been the night before, and Connie wondered whether she was afraid of them. She was not very clean and she wore some disgusting dress which looked as though she had never had it off her back. It was stiff with dirt.

'Is it some kind of milk pudding?' Connie asked in horror at the whole idea. She had heard of such things. Her mother had a distaste for dairy and never gave them anything as weird. They did eat congee, rice porridge, but it was nothing like this.

'I think it's oatmeal,' Dom said, voice full of wonder as he stared down at the strange concoction in his bowl. Connie looked down at the porridge once more. Oatmeal was something they ate a lot of in noodles, pancakes, rolls and dumplings but never like this.

'Do you have any rice?' Dom asked the servant and she stared at him.

'Rice pudding for breakfast?'

Dom and Connie looked at each other. The servant fled, no doubt she would be blamed for this somehow, Connie thought, unsure of whether the girl was more scared of the strange visitors or the people who employed her and perhaps would blame her for the wasted food. Who could have eaten such a thing, Connie could not imagine. Hungry as she was it would not do.

Mr Adams asked them into the room they had sat in the previous evening. Connie would have stood had it been mannerly because the chair she sat in was so awful but after a night in a freezing room with little sleep and nothing for breakfast but cold water she was not keen to put herself through any more so in the end she chose a different chair. To her dismay it was no better and the smell of mice was somehow worse this morning, that horrible rancid smell of urine.

Connie was a bit worried that Leo wasn't speaking any English.

He was whispering to Dom, asking if he could have something more to eat. He could speak English very well and Pearl too was talking what the Adams' would think was gibberish, a mixture of several languages all at once. Since Rosa had died Pearl had begun sucking her thumb. She hid against Connie's shoulder and Connie took comfort in the fact that the little girl probably didn't remember anything except what had happened recently and therefore she wouldn't react.

There was a tiny fire burning but Connie could see her breath and her instincts screamed at her to get out of there because no good could come of it. She pushed away the idea and tried to concentrate on what was happening but the whole atmosphere was negative somehow, not just unfriendly but almost evil. It was frightening and yet she could see nothing that might have given her such thoughts. These people were poor and could not afford to take in other folk, because they had so little themselves. She could not get up and run away but it took everything she could summon for her to sit there as though nothing was happening.

Mrs Adams smiled just a little like she felt obliged but wished to be rid of her odd visitors and Mr Adams coughed and said that the situation must be resolved.

'The thing is that we understand your grandparents are very poor and cannot help you. The only thing I can suggest is that you should both try to find work at a farm nearby, the more prosperous ones have servants. I doubt any of them would take young children such as these. After that there is nothing but the workhouse.'

The silence that followed this was a new low. Connie and Dom were skilled people, he had learned martial arts, his father had taught him that and how to talk to people when they were upset or worried, how to catch fish without any rod. He also read a good deal and kept his father's paperwork in order, something Mickey had been notoriously bad at.

Connie was good at needlework, her mother had taught her how to sew, how to make garments, but they knew nothing of the kind of work servants did. This was the very lowest of the most humble of people. They were not this and never had been and never could be. It was a matter of pride but right now she was ready to consign her pride to the gutter if it should have to go there. Dom, however, had a different idea.

'My grandfather—' he paused there and Connie understood. He had never used these words before and she could see the effort it took. 'He talked of an orphanage. Is it the sort of place which might help us?'

'It was a school many years ago for children who had nothing and nobody. After the man who built the town died there was an effort to make it into an orphanage but it failed and there is nothing up there now. I believe that the Catholic church still owns it but it is private so I don't think you could go there. Other than that the town is no more since the work dried up twenty years ago, so I understand. I would suggest that you try various farms and ask if they have any work. Whether they will take you on at this time of the year is doubtful and I think also that they would not want the children.'

Dom looked hard at him.

'I do not understand what you mean.'

'You are foreigners, people here are not used to those who are incomers or so different. You come from very far away, they will not have you there because they fear the unknown and that you might have odd habits and customs and that perhaps you do not understand what it is to live decently.'

Dom said nothing. Connie held her breath. She was outraged.

Two pounds for this. If Dom started yelling and then kicked this man in the face God only knew what would happen but her brother had evidently learned a lot since his parents had died. He merely stayed silent for several long moments and then he said,

'And your workhouse?'

'It takes in those who have nothing. I am not sure whether they would have you. It is in Stanhope which is a village six miles further up the dale. You could walk it easily but they are unused to strangers.'

'I see.' Dom glanced at Connie and she read him and got to her feet. He bowed.

'We thank you so much for your hospitality, Mr and Mrs Adams, but we will trouble you no more.'

She was proud of Dom and even to a certain extent herself. He was implacable when he was like this, just like Mickey had been and Mickey had always done the right thing. She followed him out of the room and up the stairs where they gathered their bundles once again and then they took the children and walked out.

The day got no better. Dom went into the shops they passed to see if he could find work either for himself or Connie but he came back out again quickly.

'We can stop at the farms we go past, perhaps they will take us in. We are both very strong and capable,' he said.

He stopped again when they reached a shop which had groceries in the window.

'I would go in but I think they will take it better from you,' and he handed her a fistful of money. Connie stared at him.

'I thought we had nothing left. You gave the two pounds to Mr Adams.'

'Let's just say I redeemed it,' he said with a certain amount of pride.

'But Dom, that's stealing.'

'He stole from us. He shouldn't have done it. He was as unpleasant as Mr Small. In fact if he had had the same name they could have been brothers, disgusting man. Besides, we are not going to starve because these people are so vulgar and rude and inhospitable.'

Connie was unhappy but couldn't think what else to do so she went into the shop and the others stood outside and waited. She loved shops, you never knew what you were going to find when you went into one you had not been to before. The big windows at the front threw a little light to the inside and Connie looked eagerly at all the goods before her. There were lots of tins and packets but also there was the smell of fresh bread and best of all she could see a big packet of rice. She didn't think it was the kind of rice they usually ate but it would do if she ever came across a fire and pan and water. That seemed like a big ask at this point and she reprimanded herself silently for being impractical but she bought the rice, a bag of flour, two loaves of bread and a pitcher of milk, they could drink from that in the street and hand it back, she knew.

The woman behind the counter was not local, Connie could see, and she did not know where the woman came from. She greeted Connie in English but in an accent that Connie didn't understand and yet it sounded to her vaguely like Spanish. It was therefore a western European language, Latin-based. And then it dawned because of the produce on the shelves, hams and long stems of sausages and there was cheese and potatoes and cabbage. She was Italian.

How wonderful to see such good food and to find a woman who was polite and smiling.

'Bring your family in,' she said. 'I would like to meet them,' so Connie did and Mrs Rizzi told them that they were all very handsome and she was glad to know them but when Dom talked of work she shook her head.

'I found it very hard when I first got here. These people are very suspicious of those they do not know and that's not just those from other lands like we are.'

Mrs Rizzi gave them bread and milk and a sweet cake which Connie loved and she talked to them about the orphanage up the hill.

'The nuns used to be there and I feel certain they would leave it habitable for others. Go and see what you can do with it. There were always big gardens and also if you are a huntsman,' she nodded at Dom, 'if you can supply me with rabbits and you say you fish, I would be glad of those too and I could give you sugar and flour and yeast and I could make wonderful meals for you to take up there. It will not be so bad, I promise.'

Connie was pleased to have met somebody kind and felt cheered and eager now.

They walked out of the town and up the hills, calling at every house and farmhouse for work but always they were chased away by dogs or shouted at in language they could not understand and when they reached the top of the second hill she thought she could see buildings in the distance.

It was about three miles, the road went down and then up and then they reached the hilltop village.

Connie was surprised and disappointed to find that it was not the same as Wolsingham. Here things were even worse. It was more bleak because there was nothing to stop the cold winter, but it was worse than that. The village straggled into the valley and a lot of the houses were empty, some of them were tumbling down. The children walked up the first hill they came to and here was snow and a biting wind. Some of the houses had doors which had blown back and snow was piled up inside. Broken glass littered the pavements which themselves were cracked and broken.

The whole place was one main street after you got up to the hill. It wound down through the village itself where the houses petered out into country at the far side.

The orphanage was at the top end of the village before the streets turned into fell. There was some kind of church nearby but no sign of habitation. A broken sign declared the building to be 'Blessed St Hilda's Orphanage'.

Dom tried the door. It was unlocked. Inside everything was dark and gloomy. The floor crunched under Connie's feet as she followed Dom slowly into the building. Leo was beside him and Pearl was in her arms.

It was big. First of all the entrance led to a long hall with rooms on either side. It was achingly cold in there but the rooms had big fireplaces.

Neither asked the other what they would do. Now would have to be enough. Their parents had taught them to live in the present because it was all you had so they had learned to smile over the good times and not to speak of how awful it had been when their father had died and how they had somehow known that their mother would not be able to go on without him. She had adored him, that was the word for it. Connie had seen how other people behaved, shouting and kicking against one another's ideas, but her parents were like one person, devoted, and so she and Dom had known that their mother could not live without their father.

Indeed Dom had seen her and spoken to her and told her that she was not to worry about anything because he and Connie would see the four of them forward into whatever would happen next and so she had gone to her death believing him.

Connie and Dom looked around, she carrying Pearl, Leo tight beside Dom's left knee. It was a very big building but it had been left in a bad way. Somebody had been living there at one time but not recently. Next door the church or chapel or whatever it was was also in a bad state. The windows had been smashed and the door kicked in or perhaps had just fallen in.

'Do you think people did this on purpose?' she ventured.

'I think it's just poverty, bad weather and neglect, like most things,' Dom said comfortingly. He was probably right, why would anyone come here where there was nothing and nobody and make things worse unless they resented the place so much that they could no longer contain themselves? It seemed unlikely.

From the outside Connie viewed the building and then suddenly she understood and her heart soared like a bird for the first time since her father had died.

'It's the shape of a butterfly,' she said.

'What?' Dom wasn't into imagination.

'The house, it's like a butterfly,' she said.

They stood back and stared and she was right. At either side it ballooned and in the middle came together at the front door. For some reason it gave Connie hope. They walked around the back and the building looked as though some strange genius had designed it like that on purpose, perhaps to give people something to be happy about. It made her want to smile. She even laughed just for a moment and so did Dom, awed to find beauty among chaos.

They explored further. The steep hill up to this point was where they had walked but there was also a long straggling main street, if you could call it that. There was little to see. Empty shops and snowed-up back lanes led into yards and houses. Gates were broken and on the ground and windows gaped where glass had filled them. It was as well there was snow, Connie could not imagine how much less attractive it would look when the snow melted and the ground was black and the day was grey and the nights were bitter with a howling wind.

It was the very opposite of what she thought of as the divine wind, the warriors of her country knew such a thing, when they battled against enormous odds where they would sacrifice themselves for the greater good.

There was nothing divine about this wind, it was harsh and came from the north and north of here was the coldest place on earth. She knew about Iceland and Greenland and the North Pole and that they were inhospitable. She did not think they could be any more inhospitable than this place. But now they had the butterfly house and the roof, windows and doors were sound and its walls were thick. It was not the ruin she had been told of. Her heart began to soar.

Dom went into one or two of the shops in search of anything he could find and she was glad that Leo was keen to go with him and even laughed and found some crockery amid the dust and rubbish. She followed to the door of one shop and Pearl turned around in her arms and asked to be let down and so they all went inside.

It had been a hardware shop once. Connie found two pans which had fallen on the floor, slightly dented but no worse for that. Also there was cutlery which they would need. No chopsticks here but there were bowls which she could make good use of and further over Dom cried out with glee, he had discovered matches and candles. He struck a match. Nothing happened but the third match lit. Knowing how important it was, Connie watched the flame with a feeling that was almost glee and she was cheered.

Leaving the hardware store and main street they moved further until they found some disused gardens. Fruit trees grew, which of course were empty at this time of year, though she did find a few rotten apples in the long grass. The people here had grown vegetables and there were quite a lot left but most had rotted too so she and Dom took what they could carry and noted where the best ones were. Connie swore to herself she would treat her meagre supplies with care. The trouble was that they all had keen appetites and had gone without good food for a long time, it could not be healthy for them.

There were outhouses beyond the back of the orphanage and best of all coal and wood and various papers. Everything was damp but she struggled on, determined to have warmth, and she did eventually manage to strike a flame so that it licked around the paper. When the sticks began to spit and crackle Connie felt so much better and wanted to cry with relief that she had managed though it was several hours before the fire gave out any heat into the enormous kitchen.

Dom took pans down to the bottom of the hill and filled them with water from the millstream, as it had once been, and then walked all the way back – though he said that they must find a better method of transporting water.

It was a triumph when she was able to put in front of her family rice and vegetables. It was amazing how cheered you felt when you had eaten.

'There will be fish in that stream,' Dom said. She smiled at him. It was progress.

That night they dragged two old chairs into the room and placed them as close to the fire as they could get for warmth without the danger of getting too close and there they wound themselves into the coverlets they had brought with them and for the first time since her father had died Connie felt good and she slept as soundly as though she was at home and her parents were just next door and the world had nothing more to offer.

The following morning Dom went down the bank to the stream, taking the pans with him. He would not come back without fish, he never had done and did not now. It was a real art form which she thought Mickey had shown him, so perhaps it was something that came from this strange place of narrow valleys and shallow streams. All he had to do was spot a fish and seeing it startled and hiding under the bank, get down to it and very gently hold it in his hands.

He caught two trout big enough for a meal for all four of them and filled up the pans with water and with a bag over his shoulder for the fish and with the pans he went back up the hill.

He was smiling when he reached the orphanage. Now Connie felt rich. This was the first good food they had had since they had left their home and it was almost enough to make her happy. They slept well that night once again and in the morning Dom announced that he knew there were coal pits, his father could remember them on the surface above the dale, and he set off with a big sack over the fell.

He was gone a long time and Connie had just begun to worry and the little ones to fret when he came back with all the coal he could manage and he had discovered a rusted though working little trolley on wheels to carry it and it made a pile in the old building at the back of the house. He went back again and again over the next few days.

Connie's skills included never letting a fire go out, being able to leave the embers and bring them back to life in the morning, and with such wealth they could leave the fire on all night.

Lack of cultivation in the garden at the back of the orphanage perhaps meant that the vegetables were seeding themselves year by year. There were cabbages, leeks and even some carrots and potatoes, and though they were small once she had cleaned the dirt from them they were edible. Food was her main concern and they still did not really have enough to eat but her mother had taught her to make much of little and rice went a long way to feeding hungry children.

Connie managed to make dumplings in boiling water and pancakes in the flatter of the two pans. She eked out the rice and flour and Dom caught fish every day though water was precious because he could only carry so much.

They needed to make money somehow because they would soon run out of it but in such a place as the dale few skills would sell so she didn't know quite what to do.

Dom discovered a well at the very back of the property, in its own little house, and it made their lives much easier. He primed it from a big trough which once must have been a field for cattle and held rain water. They now had water whenever they wanted. Connie was so pleased.

The following night she awoke and it was because she sensed Dom was awake though what he was doing or why he was stirring at that hour she had no idea.

'There's an animal in the room,' he said, very softly. Dom had good eyesight. So did she but she wasn't sure she wanted to see any animal in the room so she didn't really look.

'A rat?'

He looked at her, she could see him turn by the firelight.

'I don't think so. It moves differently.'

'So what is it then?'

'From what Mickey said I think it's a polecat.'

'That makes it a whole lot clearer.'

'He used to keep them when he was a boy. You know, ferrets, they fish and go down rabbit holes.'

She stared and didn't have to look far. The small animal had come inside, presumably because it was frozen and half-starved, and it was quite beautiful from what she could see by the obliging moon. Long and sleek, it was almost elegant.

'It looks hungry,' Dom said and he got up and put down a plate and onto it a piece of raw fish which she had covered up. She would have protested but that the polecat took one look at the offering, demolished it more delicately than she would have thought possible in a hungry weasel, cleaned its whiskers or whatever they were with its paws and then lay down and went to sleep by the fire.

'Do they bite?' she said nervously.

'If you feed and don't scare it nothing bites,' Dom said.

Having been brought up where snakes were sacred she went back to sleep. That was her father all over, he was afraid of nothing. She could remember him crouching down to dogs that were considered savage. He would get on one knee and beckon them in his sweet lilting voice, holding out his arms, and they always ended up coming to him and letting their ears be fondled. Also, although Rosa protested, he would feed every animal he found so that their house was always full of other people, unwanted babies and every form of animal from off the streets. Connie had never been afraid, her father was always there. Now she would look to Dom. He would always be there.

Her mother had so often said that they would have been

able to live a lot more lavishly if her father had not brought back every hurt or sick animal he had ever encountered. He did the same with people. He could never go past anything or anybody who needed him. Their mother didn't mean it, Connie was aware even then, she was proud of Mickey and his ideas and his ways, and that he had been born to help other people she never doubted. Dom was rather like his father but had not his empathy. She thought he helped people because he believed it was the right thing to do, but he lacked his father's skills and could not put people at their ease with a laugh and a joke and a kind warm hand.

It seemed strange to her now that her father had come from this cold unsympathetic land and yet he was like that. It didn't look as if his parents had been, and Dom had been brought up in another country and though he was in some ways like his father he was not like him in so many others. Connie tried not to think that he would be a lesser man.

In the morning Leo got up and stroked the polecat and named it Sid. They had once known a snake named Sid and that was all the connection she could think of.

That day Dom went up onto the moors with Sid and came back with two dead rabbits. With his knife he skinned the rabbits and then they had meat to go with their vegetables. Sid also became adept at catching fish and Dom was pleased because it was easier on his frozen fingers and thumbs.

Sid became the children's constant companion and it made things easier, Connie thought. They had been brought up to fear nothing and to value everything, and since Sid was kept well fed and watered he took to sleeping with the children and he was a bigger comfort than Connie could ever have thought a small wild animal might be.

Sid was fearless but he liked to be the hunter. Connie told Dom that he and Sid could have been brothers. Dom carried Sid in the top of his jacket for warmth when they went on their expeditions. Sid was white when snow fell. The rest of the time he was cream and brown and tremendously handsome with bright dark eyes and glossy coat.

Ten

As soon as the children had left Mrs Adams went to her husband who was sitting in front of the study fire wondering how much whisky he could buy with the two extra pounds he now had. He tried not to drink, he hated the smell and even the taste, but he had not been able to bear his life at one low point and had taken a drink. He had remembered the old adage 'The man takes a drink, the drink takes a drink and the drink takes the man.'

He hated who he was becoming and yet he could not help it. It was against everything he had been taught but he needed something so that he could go on in his daily life and now he had an arrangement with a man who lived just outside the village that Amos would buy the whisky from him and nobody would know.

Amos had never asked where it came from, he just knew that it was his secret, his delight, his comfort blanket. Every time he bought a bottle he told himself that it would be the last, that he could manage without it, but as he'd looked at the money he forgot all that he had promised himself and longed for the taste and the smell he had so much hated and now could not do without.

Usually his wife was reluctant to go into the study and he didn't want her there. She knew he liked to be left alone but even when he glared at her as she burst into the room he realized something had gone wrong and it was bound to be something to do with those children.

'They stole,' she announced with some excitement in her voice. 'They took bread and cake and a big pail of milk. I wonder what else they took?'

Amos got up quickly and went to the bureau where he kept his money. It had gone, not just the two pounds he had put there last night but all the rest of it as well. There had been nigh on five pounds which he had gathered so carefully over the last months. He did not care that it meant there was not enough to feed them so his wife would moan. He needed the whisky more than the food, in fact he was eating very little now and the children were small and he did not care about her. He could have hated her had he given his mind more to it.

'Sally probably ate the food,' he said, 'she's a greedy little witch,' but he went off to see Mr Whitty who was all the policeman they had in the village.

Part of Amos was astounded. He had thought he was doing well taking two pounds from that haughty lad, it was sickening to think that such a boy had taken advantage of his hospitality, eaten him out of house and home and then stolen every penny he possessed.

His wife had wept when he had blamed her but it was not just the money, it was the fact she was inept at everything she did. She didn't keep her children quiet, she couldn't keep the house clean, the food was awful, she was a bad cook, she was inadequate all round and Sally was no better. She could reduce a pan of potatoes and cabbage into some kind of slop he wouldn't have fed to pigs.

To think that he had taken in and fed those children and put them up for the night and they had treated his hospitality in such a way.

Amos didn't like Mr Whitty because Mr Whitty seemed prosperous without actually doing anything. Most of the crime in the dale was petty pilfering and arguments among the farmers or the disgusting way that the local men got drunk and fought on Saturday nights. Amos would never have gone inside a public house and preferred his drinking to be his own.

Mr Whitty always seemed to be at home with his wife in his lovely house in Meadhope Street. It was the big house on the end, Amos envied him this. He seemed to avoid telling people not to do things or solving any problem which did arise. Perhaps Mrs Whitty had come to him with money, Amos didn't know, just that Mr Whitty was idle and much better off than he was for doing nothing.

Mrs Whitty had a library. That was what she called it. Amos didn't approve of such things. Women ought to have better things to do than read. If they were looking after their homes, husbands and families, doing their sewing, knitting and repairing garments when they had time, it was unlikely they could fit in book reading. Amos thought that novels were a nearer thing to the devil than anything else in the world.

The local squire, John Reginald, had donated the books because there was a big sitting room in Mr Whitty's house and there women gathered in the afternoons, gossiping and eating cake. Amos deplored it.

There were also evenings for the men to go to when Mr Whitty presided over coffee in his sitting room. A great many of these people either did not go to chapel or went to the parish church instead, and though they could have gone to chapel activities which would have been much better for them, they went to Mr Whitty's instead and forgot their prayers and their bibles.

Mr Whitty had a sort of office in his house. It was just off the kitchen with no luxury such as Amos presumed he had. It was a stark little room with nothing but a table and two chairs. There was not even any paperwork and Mr Whitty did not offer him anything but a seat.

Amos poured out the story of the children.

'I know nothing about them,' Mr Whitty said. So much for the local policeman knowing everything, Amos thought.

Therefore Amos was obliged to tell him about where they came from, how they had got here, their grandfather turning them out and how he, Amos, had been good enough to offer them food and shelter and now they had stolen money and food from his house and he had no idea where they had gone.

'I don't think they ought to have been allowed back here,' Amos said.

'Who paid for their passage?' Mr Whitty asked.

'My church,' Amos said regretfully. 'I don't know why, they had no reason to. Their father was an unbeliever and their mother was a traveller's daughter. He had belonged to the church at one time and of course they have grandparents here though old Joshua is a hard man and wouldn't give them house room.'

Mr Whitty ignored the chance to put down his neighbour. He would do anything for a quiet life, Amos thought.

'Where do you think they have gone?'

'I told them about the workhouse,' Amos said. 'But I doubt they take in anyone who is not of this parish and these children are not even English. They could have gone to the ruined orphanage up on the tops but they couldn't hope to live in such a place where there is nothing to eat and no shelter.'

Mr Whitty told his wife about this. He told her everything.

'I can't believe their grandmother wouldn't have them,' she said.

'Old Joshua rules the roost there and hasn't spoken about his son that I ever heard of.'

'But his poor wife,' Mrs Whitty said. She looked carefully at her husband over the tea table. 'Do you think they stole the money?'

'It depends how desperate they were and whether anybody knows where they are,' Mr Whitty said.

He did think about going to look for the children but he realized then how much he disliked Mr Adams. He had long since suspected him of mistreating his wife and perhaps even the girl who lived with them. It was not something he could interfere with but neither did he think there was any reason he should believe Mr Adams when he said that the foreigners had stolen from him. He was the kind of man who would get people he disliked or had a grudge against into trouble just for the sake of it.

Eleven

Thomas Neville admitted to himself almost from the beginning how hard his life was now. He missed his father. He missed the woman he had thought his mother was. Almost sick with grief here they were, living in the same house somehow attempting to go forward and getting nowhere.

He remembered the visions of what his life would be like here in this beautiful place. He had been ready to fall in love with the dale, with the people, with those he had asked to look after him and his practice – Ada who was local, Fiona who was from the far north of Scotland, Jimmy who was good in the pharmacy but spoke almost indecipherable pitmatic, being from Tow Law originally, and Oswald, the lad who looked after the two horses and stables and whatever needed to be done outside.

How this worked Thomas did not understand but he didn't care as long as everything was managed so that he could aid the people of the lower dale. It had long since been his passion but he had not thought his mother would be there with him. He had escaped the parental home a while ago but now he felt as though in some ways he had gone backwards and she was watching him as a parent did, though to be fair she had not been that kind of parent and neither had his father. Even thinking of what life had been like when his father was alive hurt him.

He had thought this house was just right. Compared to his parents' house in Durham it was small, inconvenient, on the main street with nothing but the pavement to save it, a neat garden at the back, a couple of old though sound stables and just enough acreage behind the house to feed a couple of horses. This and the trap that he hoped would enable him to reach most of his patients except those in outlying areas was all there was to the place.

Both the maids lived in and shared a room which was perfectly respectable and even more so now that his mother lived there. Had there been only one maid living in it would never have worked so he was grateful for the two women and how they kept his house so clean and made his favourite meals and most of all from the beginning they were kind to his mother.

The two lads were similarly placed, Oswald lived with his mother in the cottage beside the yard and Jimmy had a room there too. Thomas was so glad that after he and his mother had pretended to eat in the evenings they were left alone.

He had had no idea how awful it would be in those rooms which had never seemed small before now, his mother filling the space with cigarette smoke and sherry fumes and the fire dying because nobody saw to it after Ada had retreated to the kitchen for the evening.

In desperation a couple of weeks after he got there he had staggered into the Bay Horse, the pub at the bottom of the hill, before the road wound its way up two steep hills to the deserted village which housed St Hilda's Orphanage.

He regretted it the moment he walked into the bar. Silence fell. He wanted to run away but knew if he did he would never be able to go in there again and so he stepped up to the bar and boldly ordered a pint of beer. Whereupon, after a short pause, a young man whom he did not know came to him from where he had been sitting by the window at a small table with his friends, and he said,

'Do you play dominoes?'

Thomas could have wept with joy. He was careful not to sound enthusiastic. He wasn't sure it would have gone down very well in a place where people knew he was the doctor who had recently moved there. He knew he had no place here other than that which they chose to give him. Nor did he offer to buy a drink.

'Sometimes,' he said and the young man nodded at his cronies and they let him join them.

Laura Neville, left alone over the sitting room fire, could not believe that she was widowed. Somehow it had not pierced her mind. She had known that she could not be but now that idea was fraying at the edges and had settled itself like a nest of vipers inside her conscious head.

She was no older than fifty. Yet she had become more and more aware that she had nowhere to go, no place to be. She was stranded here in this godforsaken hole but she knew that had she stayed in Durham she would have put herself in the Wear.

She had tried not to agree to coming here but how could she get by in the house by the river which held so many good memories and yet they were over? Nobody had come to see her. A few friends – all women – had written stilted letters but she had become an outsider, a leper. Her husband had taken his life and they thought she had caused it. Somebody had to take the blame and who better than she?

She lay awake and thought back to what she had done and not done and the memories appalled her. She had thought she was a good person. Dr Crawcrook had told her over and over again that her husband had worked too hard but she could not be convinced. Why leave someone you loved who loved you?

Day after day she picked up the same book. It was called *Can You Forgive Her.* How apt, she thought, and there she sat, smoking and drinking and having sandwiches brought to her which she never ate. Bread stuck in her throat and often she had to run out to find somewhere to be sick and then her empty stomach ached and in the mornings she wished she hadn't drunk so much without eating and her throat hurt with cigarette fumes and despair.

She went nowhere. Thomas had suggested she might like to go to the parish church of a Sunday whereupon she had turned to him and said,

'After what God's done to me?'

Her son looked hard at her and then took no more notice. She didn't want to go anywhere. She read her Trollope novels and stayed where she was. Unfortunately she had been reading his novels for years and although he had been prolific she yearned for new material and so when she was told there was a small library in the village she made herself go there one Thursday afternoon.

Most of the local women who had time would gather there and in the evenings when Mr Whitty was in charge a lot of the local men went there and drank coffee and smoked and talked and sometimes even took a book home with them.

Laura, hesitating, forced herself to go from sheer boredom but she made sure she was wearing a long musquash coat and her best hat so that she could sweep into the room easily. It was the first time she had put up her hair or worn a decent dress since Harry's funeral and she was surprised how much better it made her feel. Talk ceased. Nobody moved.

It was a very big room and Laura loved the way that every wall was covered in books. Doubtless the squire had also donated the bookcases and this house had been chosen less because of the local policeman and his wife and more because it was exactly the right building.

About two dozen women were standing about the room with teacups. Laura had no doubt that they were aware of who she was. She didn't quite know what to do. She had no idea what Mrs Whitty looked like but a woman with dark hair came over with a warm smile on her face and greeted her.

'Mrs Neville. I am Norah Whitty. How good of you to join us. Can I give you tea?'

Mrs Neville politely refused.

'Coffee?'

'A glass of dry sherry would be more acceptable if you have such a thing.'

Mrs Whitty didn't even blink.

'But of course,' she said and sailed out of the room.

Laura occupied herself with browsing the shelves and talk started up again but nobody came to her and she didn't know how to go to them, she was so new at this.

Mrs Whitty duly returned with such a large glass that even Laura had to appreciate it. She was thanking her hostess when a tall lean figure appeared behind Mrs Whitty, an elegant old man with silver grey hair.

'Ah, madam,' he boomed, 'I see you appreciate the finer things of life.'

It was the squire and he was beaming at her. He also had a large glass of dry sherry in his thin hand.

Mrs Whitty introduced them and he said to her,

'I knew your husband long since. He was a very good man.'

Laura couldn't have been better pleased. She could have cried, she was so grateful.

'How did you meet?'

'Up on the moors. He was a fine shot.'

Nobody else had said something so insensitive but the squire was not the man to care about having put his foot in it and she discovered that she preferred his way of doing things.

'I was very sorry to hear of his death,' the man went on and she breathed out more easily than she had done in weeks. 'As younger men we spent many days up on the moors where the old orphanage is now. I used to come back, having shot one pheasant all day, with aching limbs, dogs with scratched eyes because of the gorse and too tired even to swallow their dinner. My wife was a fine cook – she didn't like anyone else in her kitchen on special days – and so we had pheasant on Saturday nights and a bottle of claret.'

This made Laura think of the dogs and how they had gone to live with Iain. It was all for the best she knew but she missed Juniper almost as much as she missed Harry. They were one and the same to her.

'You must miss Harry as much as I miss my beloved Phoebe.'

Laura gulped at her sherry.

'That woman was Phoebe's favourite writer,' the squire went on. 'Those were her books. Do you like the Brontës?'

She said that she did. She stood there with *Jane Eyre* in her hands. It was a fine leather-bound copy and she wondered how long it was since Phoebe had sat over a fire and read.

The squire had visited Haworth and talked of the steep hill and how Branwell climbed out of the pub window as his father tried to take him home, how desolate the moors and how Reginald and his wife, Phoebe, had gone there to stay with friends and walk over the moors with their Labradors in soft falling snow.

When the squire left Laura made her way slowly back to the little street house and then she went upstairs to her bedroom and sat over the fire for a while, recalling Harry and the dogs with so much sorrow and affection that she smiled among her tears.

Twelve

Amos Adams had never given a thought to whether Michael Butler had children. It seemed stupid to him now. Had he been pretending? Had he been hoping so hard that it seemed impossible? His life had changed and not for the better when the Butler children turned up at his front door. He thought he had died and gone to hell. How cruel, how impossible that this should happen to him after all he had gone through already in his life.

To his joy the children were arrogant and nobody would ever want such like anywhere near them. He hoped they had a really bad time, he thought of them having nowhere to go. They knew nothing of weather like this and times like these. The orphanage was very run down as far as he could remember and they had no chance of the workhouse, looking as strange as they did.

The few times he had dared to look at the possibility of the idea he had reasoned that any children Michael Butler had had would not come back halfway across the world. They would have no reason to and no means and now ironically he felt that the Methodist church had done more than its bit and enabled them to land here and disrupt his plans and spoil his life. He could no longer live in the dream which allowed him to go forward in this place and with these people whom he could not like nor feel anything good towards.

Everything was over. He could not steal out when he needed to see the land and the house which had seemed rightfully his and was no more. Hope was gone. The future was over. Life had been cruel to him once again.

Finding the children turning up at the manse seemed like a trick. He thought back again and again, sure that they would get nowhere here. Two of them were obviously Asian. The older two would never be accepted, either, with their golden brown skins such as local people only had during long hot summers here. They were too strange, too alien. They spoke with weird accents and wore odd clothing.

The only thing that had mollified him about having them in his house was that he felt the hatred, the resentment. If they could go to the workhouse he would be glad or, better still, he hoped nobody would help and they would go away and he would hear nothing more about them.

In the meanwhile they had no idea how much two pounds was worth. He lay awake as he had lain awake every night since the letter had arrived and he had understood that they were coming back. They could not survive long here, he assured himself. They had been taken from their place of safety.

He wished he had been there when old Joshua had turned them out. The workhouse would not be glad of them and they would not last long in alien conditions such as these where they were not welcome. What on earth would they do then, without food or shelter, friends or family?

When he heard that the foreign children had gone up onto the tops and inhabited the old buildings which had not been lived in for years he was disappointed, especially since they had taken his money. They could not survive there without help though, he felt sure. In a short time they would have to admit defeat and go to the workhouse.

Like the rest of the village he waited to see what would happen and the talk was all of the Butler family and these newcomers.

Thirteen

It was March when Connie and Dom had a visitor. Somebody banged on the outside door. Dom went to answer it. He kept his knife on him which made Connie feel better though she had long since wished he had left it behind him. Now she felt need of the protection he could give her. So far he had not used it but Connie knew he could and would if the circumstances depended on it.

She did not go to the door, she stood back inside with the children, but she would help him if he called for her. He did not. She heard some kind of quiet conversation and when she ventured into the hall she saw the old man she had managed not to hate standing outside.

She had striven to understand that he was old and set in his ways and had had a terrible shock having found out his only son was dead and that he had left four offspring to the world. She and Dom must strive to be kind to the two old people, she knew it would benefit them in the end. He was smaller and more bent over than she remembered and he was no warrior, which was why Dom was leaning towards him, inviting him in. She was so pleased that her heart warmed toward them both.

The old man hesitated, afraid perhaps, but his other problems overcame his fear and within a minute or two he was by the kitchen fire and the children had given him the sofa and she had sat him down and now she kneeled to him so that he should understand they would help him. He said nothing for so long that she wanted to fuss but she had learned not to. She just sat and Dom stood and the children made no noise.

Eventually she held out her hand and touched his fingers.

'Grandfather?' she said and then he gradually looked at her and in his eyes there was a kind of anguish that she had seen before. It was there for those who had lost their loved ones. It was there for those who were grieving and for those who were in despair and he shook his head and because he did not know how to cry before her he just gazed at her.

'How is Grandmother?' Connie said.

He hesitated for such a long time that she was beginning to worry when he said suddenly,

'She has a fever, Dr Neville says, and may not live much longer. She wants our Michael.'

Connie and Dom exchanged looks and understood. The woman wanted back the son she had lost, the boy who had run away. They thought that their father and mother must have had reason to do such a thing and to Connie that good reason was this dreadful insular place where people were uneducated and stupid and living from hand to mouth. But then again Connie knew millions of people all over the world had no better and that she and Dom had been lucky to have parents who understood so much more and to have been raised in a culture where most people could read and write and the arts like poetry, painting and all kinds of special skills and crafts were valued. The people there were proud and the men were warriors.

'You must go with him,' she said to Dom.

'I'm not leaving you here alone.'

'With Sid and your knife I will be safe.'

She talked him into it because nothing beyond duty and a love for his parents would have got him to walk the three miles back down to Wolsingham. He could not love this old man, he was almost a man himself, she reminded herself, men did not give in to their feelings as easily as women, and Dom had lost both his beloved parents and just now was blaming the old people, he needed somebody to blame. Too much had gone on, dislike and bad feeling had entered into the souls of these people, and even now the old man thought only of his old woman and not of his grandchildren but Dom would go anyway because he was honourable and understood that it was the right thing to do. He would not turn the old man away no matter what privately he thought of him.

'I will be back tonight,' he said and she was comforted.

She tried to talk him into staying over there but he would not leave them for a single night. She wanted to say to him, what if Grandmother doesn't remember her son, or doesn't understand or doesn't want you there, but he only said, understanding,

'Then I will be back sooner,' and he left and the old man went without a word of thanks.

Flo couldn't rest after the children went away. She couldn't sleep and she couldn't eat. She felt sick. She wanted things to go back to how they had been before the letter. That letter had ruined their lives and then she thought, no, their lives had been ruined twenty years ago when Michael walked away and took joy and any chance of future happiness with him.

Until now they had been trying to live with it. That was swept away, the thin layer which had been their daily comfort was all gone and reality was once more upon them. The children's coming had been like the explosive which was used in the nearby limestone quarries. It had blown up in their faces and everything was over.

She was angry with Joshua. She knew there was no point in being angry, it achieved nothing and upset her. This was not his fault, he was reacting in the only way he knew how, pretending that he could shut his eyes and the horror would retreat. It was not his fault and it was not hers and though they had blamed themselves for what Michael had done they had brought up their child as well as they could and done everything possible for him and a lot more besides, they had broken their backs for his education and he had broken their hearts with his actions.

Worst of all she lay awake in the night and knew something which she had been aware of for several days but had not allowed herself to acknowledge. That boy was not as old as nineteen or twenty and that meant Michael's nasty woman had lost at least one child before she had him. For some reason that Flo couldn't work out, this bothered her. Had it happened sooner would he still have married her? Had she miscarried within the first few weeks would he have considered it a lucky break? Did he marry her because he felt obliged? Did he feel trapped or was it just that he was so infatuated it wouldn't have mattered, or would he have been heartbroken because she had lost his child?

Flo had lost three children in miscarriage. There had been very little fuss. It was so common that nobody took any notice. All the doctor said was that it would be better next time but Michael was an only child. She tried to think of how different her life would have been could she have had three or four children like so many other women, like Michael's dreadful woman. Or was the truth different, considering that the two younger children looked nothing like him?

Worst of all somehow was that Flo understood how hard it would have been when Michael's woman miscarried. Perhaps they were at sea. Maybe it had been painless and a non-event and then Flo's true self told her that these things always mattered.

With her there had never been any point in saying anything to Joshua, men didn't understand, they thought you could just go on and have another and the world would still turn, but Flo had in her own mind named each child she lost, it was as though she had built a memorial to them in her head and heart because she was never allowed to speak as if any of them had been real.

It had been the biggest grief of her life, just as Michael had been the biggest joy, her sheer delight at her only child. She had failed over and over again to bring a child to full birth and it seemed cruel beyond words that their one child had deserted them for a life in which they were not allowed to take part.

Now his children had come back and seemed to mock her.

In the darkness she fell on the ice on the path in their back garden. If she had lived alone she would probably have frozen to death because it was almost dark and nobody would have seen or heard her calling out for help, nobody would have come to help her. She slipped and fell and hurt herself.

At first, winded, she couldn't get her breath or make any noise and then she realized she had hurt herself as never before and could not get up, she was in such a lot of pain. She didn't know how long she lay there but it could have been only a few minutes before Joshua noticed she was outside. She had left the back door open because she was just going out for a few vegetables and could see by the light from the back door that was her aid.

She told herself she ought to have gone out before darkness, that was what she usually did, but her worries and griefs had so distracted her that she had forgotten all about food and Joshua would be wanting his tea. So the kitchen light spilled out to where she lay and she watched the still and silent garden around her until Joshua came.

He carried her back into the warmth, complaining and asking what on earth she was doing out there in the gloom at this time of the day. It had been dark for hours, in fact it had barely been light that day. As a little girl Flo had loved the winter, snowmen, slides and watching the big flakes fall while she was safe on her mother's knee with the snow beyond the window, now she dreaded it and never more so than having acknowledged she was old enough to fall and hurt herself.

By the time he got her onto the kitchen settle she was in a lot of pain. She cried for sheer helplessness, for being so old that she hurt. She had never hurt herself falling over before, she had always bounced. Now she was old and skinny and her bones wouldn't stand up to such things.

When they had first met Joshua had called her his sparrow because she had been so tiny. She was glad of that now. If she had been as hefty as some women she would have had to lie there until he could fetch help and that would have been even more humiliating.

He wrapped her in a blanket and made tea.

Watching him as he bent over the kettle and the big brown teapot she thought of what he had been like when they had met, how proud she had been of his Scottish looks, his dark brown eyes and black hair. His hair was white now and his eyes were pale with age and had big red bags under them from the suffering he had gone through over the years but somewhere the lad she had fallen in love with was still there beneath the hurts and the failures.

The boy, the tall grandson, looked exactly as Joshua had looked when they had just met. It was the first time she had acknowledged to herself that the boy was not the spit of his mother. It would have been so easy to go on hating him as his mother's and nothing to do with them.

'Don't cry, Flo,' Joshua said to her, having stopped telling her off for going outside. He was hopeless at making tea, he rarely did it. He didn't put enough tea into the pot to make a decent brew and he had not let the water boil. There was too much milk in it and it was very weak. In fact it was disgusting. He had sugared it liberally but she drank it down, thinking that it was good for the shock.

By the time they went to bed she was in a lot of pain and when she tried to turn over in bed it hurt so much that it made her cry out. Joshua insisted on getting the doctor. Doctors cost money and they never had him out, neither of them had ever been ill before now.

He was lovely was young Dr Neville. It seemed to her he was little more than a boy himself for all his pretended confidence. He was nervous, she could see, and trying not to show it and probably at the same time proud of himself for having taken all before him as he must have done to become a doctor in his early twenties.

He was the sort of man Flo wanted to tell all her troubles to. A good many lasses in Wolsingham and beyond were hoping he would marry one of them, he was a bit of a catch, being young and handsome. There was, however, one drawback to the doctor's life. He lived with his mother, or she lived with him. His father had been a wealthy man, it was rumoured, and they owned a big detached house on the river in Durham City but his mother had insisted on coming to live with him and nobody liked her.

She seemed to think she was a cut above everybody else and showed herself off in furs and black gloves but everybody knew she had been a pitman's daughter from Esh Winning so she had nothing to be proud about other than that at one time she had been bonny enough to catch a lawyer with money. It was rumoured also that she had behaved so badly to him that he had done himself in. Flo knew it was a sin to kill yourself. The whole thing was shocking. She drank like a fish and smoked like a man and was trying to catch the squire now all because he had bothered to speak to her at one of Mrs Whitty's book afternoons. As though the squire would have anything to do with a barrister's widow never mind the daughter of a pitman.

When the doctor sat down beside her and touched her ribs Flo nearly fell off the settle with pain.

'You've cracked your ribs, Mrs Butler, or broken at least one.'

'What can you do about it?'

'I can give you a bottle to kill the pain. You will feel a lot better in three or four weeks.'

'Four weeks?' Flo stared into the doctor's kind face. 'I can't sit here for four weeks.'

'I don't think you have much option. You can get up and down as you must but it will take time.'

When he had gone, saying he would send a lad from the surgery with a bottle, Flo couldn't think.

She didn't get better. Sometimes she did ail but this was different, this was to do with those strange children showing up at the door and being turned away, as Joshua thought. It had to do with Michael and that dreadful woman and how Joshua had reacted to the children and how they had gone away. She had strange dreams where Michael and that woman came back and back and then left again and again so that she could see them just beyond the horizon.

She was so hot, she was so cold, she was so guilty, she was so bereft and most of all she yearned for her child. He came to her in dreams, not as himself but as a different boy, as a different animal, as a man she barely recognized and from somewhere she could hear Rosa's laughter and see her singing and dancing and stealing Michael away.

The bed was too small, the room was too big, the ceiling went round and round and she called out for water but when it came she found that it made her stomach bad and so she threw it up again and again, calling on her husband to be there, calling on her child not to go off like this and leave her.

She felt the wet cloths on her forehead and was grateful but the dreams took over so that everything she saw was unreal. She knew it was so and nothing like the everyday stuff that she had been used to. She struggled to get out of bed but it was like climbing a huge mountain, she could not do it for the pain and fell back, weeping because she had lost Michael and Joshua was not there.

Fourteen

It was strange going down the hills into Wolsingham with the old man. He didn't speak so Dom said nothing either, even when they walked through the village and took the road out to the house beyond the terraces, on the edge of the settlement. Dom was astonished at how big the land was which his grandfather owned. He had seen nothing but the shop on the front street but it had so obviously been there a long time, judging by the way that half of it was in ruins but it had been a house of some importance he could see right from the beginning and there was a small part of him, which he instantly denied, that thought his father had come from people of substance even though it had fallen into disrepair. Nobody had done any maintenance here in a very long time. Here Dom paused and his grandfather stopped when he noticed and came back to him.

'This is Holy Well Hall. My ancestors have lived on this site for upwards of a thousand years.'

Various sheds in the big back garden had fallen down and now it was at its worst with nothing to show but last year's plants dead or dying. The old man led him in by the back door. Dom almost reeled at the smell and stared at the chaos in the house.

The old woman must have been ill almost from when they had left to go up to the orphanage. It was dirty, his boots sounded and felt gritty on the floor, there were piles of unwashed dishes and the fire was out. Everything was so dark. The shop was shut and the shelves were empty.

The old man didn't pause. He led the way upstairs, very steep they were, and Dom became more and more aware of what a bad state of repair the house was in. It was like they had no money or that it did not matter, perhaps both. The windows were badly fitted and draughts howled through everywhere and daylight came in through the holes in the roof.

At last the old man led him into a dingy bedroom. They obviously thought it too cold to open a window, the air had been breathed in and out so often that it stank, and there the wizened-up old woman lay with her eyes closed. Her cheeks looked as thin as paper and had sunk until there was very little flesh on her face. Her forehead was wrinkled and her hair lay in a grey tatty mess on an even greyer pillow. Her breathing was low and ragged.

'Have you had a doctor?'

'He says she is very ill.'

Dom sat down. She didn't move.

'She wants her son,' the old man said.

'Her son is dead.'

'She doesn't remember that.'

Dom saw then for the first time that the old man was not stupid, he had brought Dom here hoping to deceive his wife into thinking their son had returned and she might be a little better or at least die with a positive thought in her mind.

Dom tried to think of what Mickey would have done but the answer as usual was obvious. She needed care and warmth and decent food and companionship.

She must have felt him sit down on the bed because she

opened her eyes. They were old and pale and watery and did not focus too well. The odd tear trickled down her lined and shrunken cheek like it came from an almost dried-up well.

Dom turned slightly as his grandfather sat down on the only and rickety chair in the room. It was then he saw that both his grandparents had a look of his father. Yes, they were old but there was definitely a resemblance. He was not sure how he felt about that.

He couldn't think of anything to say and the old woman closed her eyes again.

'Her mind wanders,' the old man said. 'She has forgotten who she is and I believe it is your coming back here which has caused it. We thought that was all over and now—'

The old man stopped. Dom said fiercely,

'Do you think we wanted to come here? We had no choice. We could not stay. Our parents were dead and we were left.'

'Your mother was a whore,' the old man said.

Dom was about to swear at him, that he would fill his mouth with pus, that his head would shrivel on his shoulders, that he would piss in his grandfather's gob.

There he stopped even in his head because the old man looked scared and Dom had forgotten how loud his voice was because since his parents had died the villagers were the only people he spoke to in English.

The idea shocked and dismayed him. If he started to think in English everything would feel as if it was over. He was trembling with anger but at least he had not disgraced himself, he had not shouted, he had kept his temper in check and his emotions as evenly balanced as he thought he had ever managed.

And then Dom saw that his grandfather could not stand that he should feel any affection for this boy-man who looked like him and like his own son who had abandoned him in this ghastly hole of a land. The old man was so badly hurt that all he could do was to hit out and ache and wish that the past had been different and most of all that his son had not died. What parent ever wanted his child to die before him? The hate was easier.

The old woman was sleeping. Even with such tension in the room he could hear her laboured breathing, short and harsh, and her chest moved as though each breath hurt her. This was a dark place where little seemed to prosper. There was no colour here, no culture, no decorations, no paintings, none of the joys which he had been used to and somehow no pride. Here in this godforsaken land there was no way to get out and the people had to endure it. He felt sorry for them.

Apart from her breathing he and the old man sat there in silence. Then the old man said her name so softly and sadly.

Dom didn't hear his grandfather's words. He heard, 'An old pond, frog jumps, sound of water.'

His grandfather's voice was almost like a haiku, it was poetry. Dom was amazed. Basho would have been pleased with his grandfather now as his voice settled on the sleeping woman, urging her so very gently to awaken and come back to him.

She opened her eyes. At first it was clear to Dom that she saw nothing and then her gaze altered in recognition of her husband and her husband said,

'Michael has come,' and that was when Dom saw how very ill she was and he was glad that he had gone there, for all his misgivings, for all that he was such a good hater and so angry. He was there whatever the outcome would be and it was the right thing to have done.

This was Mickey's father and this was Mickey's mother and Mickey had been such a fine father, such a good man, and Dom had loved him as no son had ever loved his father before and his loss was great. He must therefore now pay homage to these people because they were bereft and lost and grieving still for the son who had gone from them so very long ago.

She saw him and that was when she said his father's name. His mother had always called his father Mickey and so had they because she spoke of him as such and they had never understood the word father, it seemed to have little to do with this light in their life.

'Michael,' she said.

His father was always laughing. His father would carry Leo around on his shoulders and play-fight with them and most of all his father had been so very proud of his warrior son and had teased him and caressed him and tousled his hair and thumped his shoulder and told him that he was the most precious son a man had ever had but since he told Leo exactly the same thing Dom put it to one side and allowed it to flow over him.

She put up her thin fingers and they were cold where they reached his cheek and he could see how she was hurt and grateful and that all the years she had not seen her son rose up in her now like a huge wave and when it washed over her the tears leaked from her eyes in regret and guilt and loss.

Dom was good at being still, he had long since learned to govern his body, so he just sat there, watching the old woman find her son after twenty years. The three of them went on sitting as the day got darker and darker and sleet fell beyond the windows. Dom had very good hearing or was it just that he thought he could hear the sleet as it met the ground and even though it was a soft sound it was music to his ears and he loved it. He was so glad suddenly that he could find anything to love here.

When the woman slept the old man made a nudge with his head indicating that they should go downstairs so Dom got silently to his feet and followed him down the creaking steps and into the back room which was all their living quarters.

'What did your father do?'

Dom saw now that the old man had been restraining his curiosity and was eager for knowledge of what his son had been like.

'Do?'

The old man actually looked at him, possibly for the first time, and there was a yearning in his gaze, that he could not fill all those years gone by, that it was over and he had lost so much other people took for granted. Hunger filled his face.

The old man cleared his throat. 'He was trained as a minister here, you must have known that.'

'He helped people.'

'Helped them?' The old man frowned but it was well intentioned and he was staring at Dom with all his face. 'What, to pray?'

The old man suddenly looked hopeful and Dom was inclined to say that yes, he had urged his stupid religion onto them, but it wasn't true and he wasn't inclined to lessen the old man's pain with lies. He felt it would be disrespectful to the memories of his father and they were always good ones.

'My father didn't believe in religion, he thought it was stupid and divisive and that people should be educated and take responsibility for their own lives instead of unloading it onto the closest deity,' Dom said flatly.

His grandfather's eyes widened in dismay and disbelief.

'Didn't you have religion in this – this strange country you come from?'

Dom resented the term but ignored the insult.

'Lots of people do and my father respected the various beliefs but he did not care for religion personally. It is not considered polite to force one's view onto other people there.'

The old man so obviously had no idea what Dom was talking about, it was too far from his comprehension or experience. He was like so many people, clinging to a raft that was sinking.

Dom's father had told them bible stories and Dom knew all about Noah but he had been inclined to ask whatever happened to all the animals who were left behind. Did they drown?

And what about the unicorns who got the day wrong and turned up when the ark had already set sail and so missed their chance to survive? This had been one of his father's jokes but for a long while, and even now sometimes, Dom really believed in unicorns, it was such a beautiful idea. And also that despite the ark sailing without them they still lived somewhere in the universe, safe and well, and so did all the other animals who had not been rescued.

Dom could remember how his father had laughed and liked Dom's ideas and jokes and always nodded his head as though he had said something sage, no matter how often he had heard it before. And then his father said that had Noah been of a practical bent he would have come up with a much better idea or at least a bigger ark, one which would have encompassed all living creatures so that he could have saved the earth.

Dom was so taken with these memories that he said,

'Mickey loved people.'

He had not intended saying anything as intimate and as the words got past his lips he regretted them and his face burned for his indelicacy.

'Mickey?' the old man said, looking shocked.

'My father.'

'That was what you called him?'

'My mother was Rosa. She was very beautiful. Connie looks just like her. She taught us to speak other languages and she would sing and dance and play the guitar. She taught Connie to make wonderful meals and how to sew delicate seams and to choose the best cloth. My father taught people how to look after themselves, to make the best of their lives, to live as long as they could. He didn't believe in any kind of heaven, he thought you had to make the most of things now. He wouldn't say that to them of course, but he acted to keep them here on earth for as long as he could. He knew quite a lot about various fevers and different problems and ailments they had and that was how he died. They had typhoid in the village and he went.'

'Could she not have stopped him?' His grandfather, Dom could see, was in such pain that he could not pronounce Rosa's name.

He wished that his grandfather would not refer to his mother so disrespectfully but he replied coolly,

'Rosa would never have asked him to do such a thing. She would not have kept him from doing what he thought was right.'

Dom looked around him at the dead fire and the dirty dishes piled in the sink and was about to ask whether they had any help when his grandfather said,

'I don't understand how anybody would go to a place where there was such a disease. He must have known that it would kill him and he had a wife and children. He was still young.'

Dom shrugged.

'Many people die before they grow old. A flood, a famine, bad times and they are gone. He had taken such risks many times before.'

'Were there other missionaries to help him?'

Dom shook his head.

'My father despised missionaries. They lived together behind a big wall in rich houses and squabbled amongst themselves. They were ungenerous people.'

His grandfather was staring.

'Your father had a gift from God.'

Dom said nothing about that. He was trying not to argue, to keep on telling himself that this man was his family, these two old people were all that was left.

'And what did your mother do? How did she die?'

'She did the honourable thing, at least she considered it to be.'

'And what was that?'

'She took opium.'

His grandfather stared and then recoiled.

'He should never have married her. She was a harlot.'

Dom had to keep still and not shout and not react and in the end he said, with scorn,

'He never did marry her. Nor did she want him to,' and then he walked out before he should be tempted to hit the old man. He would not have forgiven himself.

Connie was glad that Dom had assured her he would be back. She felt so lonely with the two young children. It was very quiet up there. She could not think there was anyone in the whole village besides the four of them. When light turned to dusk she was afraid. She heard an owl hooting. It made her feel even more isolated.

The children were restless and Leo was so aware Dom had gone that despite how cold it was he kept wanting to go outside and see whether Dom was coming back. Pearl had to be kept entertained. Connie sang to her and told her stories but as the light fled she became anxious and thought she had never been as glad to see anybody as she was when the outside door opened. Leo flung himself into his brother's arms and Pearl left Connie and ran forward.

Dom didn't say anything about the visit to Wolsingham until both children were asleep and then he told Connie how ill their grandmother was and how dirty and neglected was the house and the two old folk.

'Don't people here help one another?' Connie said.

'I think he's the kind of old man who wouldn't let anybody help. I don't think they have eaten for days and Grandmother stank. She'll die and then he'll be left by himself. Serve the old bugger right,' Dom said.

She knew he didn't mean it and was just letting go of his worst feelings.

'We could have them here if we had more food and a bed for them to sleep in.'

'He will never leave that place,' Dom said. 'Besides, we have only sufficient for ourselves. It isn't practical to take anybody else in. We can only keep one fire going and we're running out of money. The coal is getting more difficult to find and the wood is so damp.'

He was right, they would have to sacrifice themselves for an old woman they had never known of until recently, and yet Connie could not let it go.

'Then we must persuade him,' she said, 'and we must manage somehow.'

Dom stared at her and he thought Connie might look like her mother but she had her father's sense of right, she always wanted to aid others as he had done. It had cost him his life but Dom would never have suggested to his sister that their father should not have gone. He would not have done such a thing.

'Their house is falling to pieces,' he said and then he told her that it had been some kind of manor house, a hall where the family had lived for many years and she smiled and was pleased.

In the end they decided he would stay with the children and she would set off at first light the next day and go and see whether anything could be done for the old people and if possible she would stay for at least one night or maybe two.

Connie was glad to get out by herself. She loved the two little ones but she was tired of being there with them. She strode away in her stout boots and thick padded layers of clothing and enjoyed the way the sun shone because it was eight o'clock and just light and the morning had been pink and grey clouds and now it promised fair as blue took over the sky.

Going to Wolsingham was the easy part, it was mostly downhill, but she thought it was strange that although you always thought going downhill was better it wasn't really because your feet went forward and banged into the front of your boots, whereas going uphill, although the climb was hard, at least your feet absorbed it without faltering and also you admired the view as you stopped for breath along the way.

She went straight to her grandparents' house and in by the back door which was unlocked. She stared into her grandfather's eyes while he said to her,

'You have no right to come here. Go away.'

'I will do nothing of the sort,' Connie said, briskly. She had decided that she would stand no nonsense from the old man. 'Dom told me what this was like and I will not let my grandmother die because you are too stubborn to let anybody help you.'

'I don't want you and your like in my house.'

'You don't want anybody in your house, though how far you think it will get you I am not sure. Now come out of the way while I sort the fire.'

She thought he was going to go on shouting, she thought he might even force her from the house, but she could hear a frail voice from upstairs so she went there and her grandmother needed water.

Dom had been right, the whole place reeked of old dirty people and it would not do. She took her grandmother some water and then she began to rake out the ashes and she laid paper, sticks and coal and soon the kitchen fire took hold.

She poured water into the boiler so that when it was warm she could do washing and make tea and then she went into the shop at the front of the house. It was dark and cold and the curtains were pulled across the front of the window. She pushed back the curtains and saw that there were vegetables which had survived. In the kitchen cupboards there was plenty of flour and sugar. She put the kettle on to boil. Her grandfather sat there like somebody stuffed but he was too much of a man to hurt a girl, she had been right in her estimation, whereas she was not sure he would have put up with Dom doing such things. Dom wasn't terribly domesticated anyway, he was clumsy in the kitchen like nowhere else and did not understand obvious things about pots and pans.

When the kettle boiled she made tea. There was no milk. She stirred sugar into it and put a cup and saucer beside where her grandfather sat at the table, unmoving, and then she went upstairs and took tea for her grandmother. The old woman cried.

Connie sat down beside her, lifted her into a sitting position, plumped up the pillows and then helped her grandma to swallow the tea. After that she took the chamber pot from under the bed, carried it downstairs and deposited it in the outside lavatory. She washed it and returned it under the bed without a word.

When the fire burned up she took a small flat pan and made pancakes with flour and water and the single egg she discovered in a bowl, she sprinkled them with sugar and rolled them up and then she gave four of these to her grandfather. The rest she took upstairs to her grandmother, cut them into small pieces and fed them to the starving woman.

When she went back downstairs her grandfather, looking shamefaced, had eaten his pancakes. When the water had heated she took a basin and cloths to wash and dry her grandmother's face and hands and she did this gently so that the old woman went to sleep.

She told the old man to wash his face and hands. She thought he would refuse but he didn't. These were not people who were used to dirty conditions, it was just that things were too difficult for them at their age. So she gave him soap and a towel and while he washed she chopped up onions, potatoes, carrots and parsnips and she put them into water with pearl barley and split peas and salt and pepper, all of which she found in the cupboard.

She told the old man to watch it didn't boil over and showed him what to do and then she said,

'I am going out to get some things you need. You must give me some money and if you lock the door when I am gone I swear I will smash the window.'

Thus bullied he gave her money and she went back to the Italian food shop where Mrs Rizzi knew her brother well by now because he traded fish and pigeons and rabbits for basics like flour and sugar.

The woman recognized her and Connie told her about her

grandparents and then she brought yeast and milk and butter and eggs. The woman would not accept her money, she said she owed Dom for what he had given her. Connie had a feeling he was taking rabbits to her almost daily and when she saw pâté advertised she knew that it was so.

She bought pâté and fresh bread and Mrs Rizzi, hearing that it was for her grandparents and aware that they would not let anybody inside, went into the back and came out with a big pan of pigeon stew. Connie said how grateful she was but Mrs Rizzi waved away her thanks.

'Your brother provided the pigeon – I have a horrible feeling he downed it with a stone – and the vegetables are from my garden. Take it and I hope it does them good.'

Connie kept the money her grandfather had given her, she would need it for her grandparents in the future. When she went into the house he left but he went only as far as the back garden and when he came back in he had a handful of snowdrops which he handed to her wordlessly. She put these into a glass filled with water and took them to the bedroom.

'He always gives these to me, at the end of the winter. They are the first signs of spring,' her grandmother said.

Connie fed them broth and bread and butter and pâté for lunch. She remembered that here it was known as meat paste so she called it that and they seemed happy with it.

She scrubbed the floors. Her grandfather stayed outside. The weather was getting better and she could see him digging, turning over the earth and perhaps even planting seeds. She wished her mother was here. She had not listened attentively to her knowledge of such things. She had not thought she would need it.

She did not like to tell her grandfather that she wanted them to come and live up at the orphanage because she felt certain he would refuse. It was the only practical solution but she would suggest nothing until her grandmother felt better and before then she would require more help, a bed, blankets, pillows and sheets, towels and even clothes that might fit the old people and she would need to be able to provide more food. She didn't know how she would do that but she determined that she would make it happen.

She understood why they loved this place so much even though it was of no use to them now. As far as she could see nobody had repaired anything for a hundred years, but at one time it must have been a place for rich people. There was some kind of fortification though it was in ruins and the land outside was presumably all that was left of a much bigger concern. It was beyond redemption now unless somebody had a fortune to repair it. Compared to the orphanage it was hopeless. She thought of the nuns who had lived there and even though it was in a bad way she thought they had dedicated time and effort which was why it was still standing and looking sturdy, though there could be lots done to make it sound and up to date. One day, she told herself, she would make such things happen.

She went outside to take a look round and that was when her grandfather spoke civilly to her for the first time. She wished she had thought of the topic sooner but now she said to him,

'How old is this place?' She knew he had told Dom but she wanted to make a connection with the old man and she knew how proud he was of it.

He turned from his digging and she could see the way that the light came into his eyes.

'Butlers have lived here for as long as people can remember. We were a rich family once. There was a series of underground passages. The place was several-storeyed and could be held against marauders and there was a big hall where the family gathered to eat. They had feast days. They had horses and cattle because the land was fertile by the river and also there were big ponds full of fish. There were shooting and hunting days. The Bishops of Durham used to hunt in the dale, Eastgate and Westgate contained the hunting park and they used to stay here. The whole area was well off.' He stopped there, coming back into the present and sighing as though he couldn't bear it.

'It's all gone,' he said, 'there's nothing left beyond these four rooms and they aren't sound to keep out the snow and the rain,' and he walked back to the house. Connie went with him and she felt a sudden thrill. It was the first time she had felt as though she belonged anywhere in this godforsaken country. How terrible and sad and somehow ironically amusing that it should be somewhere as barren and poor as this.

The pigeon stew was even better than she had thought it would be. Mrs Rizzi was a wonderful cook. Her grandparents ate it greedily. A few more decent meals and they would be ready to move if they could be persuaded, but coming into her mind again and again was how they would all survive together on so little.

When her grandfather went to bed she lay down on the settle by the fire and was pleased with what she had achieved and considering she was lying in a big chair with a pillow and blanket over her she slept quite well. Dom would cope somehow though she could not leave him for much longer with the children, he soon became impatient and bored. He would not go out and leave them but she worried that Pearl might fall upon the fire or that Leo would go outside and get lost because Dom had not noticed him missing.

The following day she got the old lady into the tin bath by the kitchen fire and left her husband to soap and clean her with towels nearby and she changed the sheets on the bed. When the water was hot enough she scrubbed them.

Then she persuaded her grandfather to change and bathe. She stayed upstairs until he had done this. So far he had not thanked her for anything she had done but that afternoon he went outside and she could see that he was moving big covers from the garden and he came back with a whole host of vegetables, many of which she did not recognize. He didn't say so but many of them were obviously to feed her family.

'Grandfather, I must go back to the others soon. Dom has had the two little ones to deal with on his own for long enough but I will come back.'

'You must not,' he said but he sounded feeble and as though although he didn't want her there she had become necessary to his wife's health and possibly even his own.

'You don't want Grandmother to die and you don't want to die so we need to help you. I'm sorry you don't like us but we cannot have you starving to death, the whole thing is silly. It probably wouldn't have come to this had you let people in.'

'I don't like having anybody here.'

'I shall be back very soon. In the meanwhile try to keep the fire going, heat the broth and watch it carefully so that you do not burn it and use a tea towel so that you don't burn your fingers and I have left plenty of meat paste and butter and even sliced the bread. There is enough pigeon stew for two more days. You just need to put it over the fire in a pan on the arm that goes over the fire and take care that you don't burn it or yourself. Look after Grandmother and don't go outside again.' She showed him how to keep the fire going so that the oven and the water were hot, the boiler being to one side of the fire and the oven to the other, but he was so inept that she no longer wondered from where Dom had inherited his lack of domesticity. His father had been deft and delicate but Dom, like Joshua, was neither of these things, at least in the house.

'We can't have you to live here,' her grandfather said.

'We don't want to live here. We know that it is impractical. This house is too small and cold, it is no friend to you and Grandmother, so you must let us help you until you can manage without us.'

'I want to die here,' the old man said.

'Hopefully not yet if I can prevent it,' Connie said, bossily, because he needed to hear it and then she went off up the hill to Dom and the children.

She and Dom could not make up their minds as to how they could get the old people up to the tops without upsetting and humiliating their grandfather. He was proud and why should he not be? He had educated his only child, he had looked after and loved his wife. They must not make him despise himself now. Nor must he despise them. That would be much harder to tackle, she thought.

If their grandparents would agree to move themselves and their furniture, and their grandfather would show them how to grow vegetables all year round, Connie and Dom felt that this would work, but how to get them there when they did not want to come? How could their grandfather give up his home now?

They decided they would find out how their grandparents and furniture and other goods could be conveyed up to the village but only when they had solved the problem of getting their grandparents up there after however many generations of

Butlers had lived in that tiny wretched house. Memories, be they real or imagined, kept you in such places, made you cleave to things you should long since have discarded. The mind was a cruel thing, pretending it had all been better than it was, that it had been dearer, that it was something you wanted back to the exclusion of now and the future and it would have been dearly bought. However, Connie could not say such things to her grandparents, it would have been rude and unforgivable.

She was starting to feel warm towards the old people. It wasn't a pure feeling, she had disliked if not hated them after what she thought they had done to Mickey and Rosa, but it was to do with blood. Her grandfather turned towards her and from her with the same movement as her father had done and she could see him in his mother.

She only wished that her mother had had family but she didn't remember, only that her father had been content to have her dance for pennies in the streets of northern towns. Connie tried to think positively about him. He too must have had his troubles, heartbreaks and heartaches. Had he loved Rosa's mother? If she had looked anything like her mother looked then he must have. Who could see such beauty and move beyond it without feeling bereft and scared?

She had already seen what her gift, if you thought of it in such a way, did to men but she saw how if her mother had not fallen into the safe hands of her father she could have had a life of hell. He had saved her. Perhaps they had saved one another. She had to be careful. Men like Mr Small had already and she had the feeling would go on lusting after her but that was not what she wanted. She had the example of the love between her parents. Nothing less than that would do for her.

Connie went to her grandparents' house when two more days had elapsed. She didn't think she could leave them by themselves for any longer, she worried so, and as she had thought the fire was out, the food was gone and her grandfather sat over the empty grate in the kitchen. He didn't speak or even look up.

She went straight upstairs to see how her grandmother was. She looked slightly better, Connie thought, but she was parched and hungry so she did what she had done before, making sure they were warm and full before she spoke to her grandfather of moving up to the village.

That was when he looked at her and she saw that he had known she was going to say this and that he would not now and possibly ever agree to it. She could see by the straight line that his mouth went into, it was all determination.

'We cannot leave this place.'

'You must leave it. I cannot do this all the time and you won't let anybody help you.'

'I want to die here.'

'You will die here if you don't try to do something about it and more to the point so will Grandmother. I'm going to hire a horse and cart to carry your belongings and your furniture but you and Grandmother must go first.'

He refused and she did not know what to do. In the end she went back up to the orphanage and almost cried over Dom in frustration.

'If they won't come we can't make them,' he said.

'What if they die?'

'Everybody dies and they are old.'

'They are all we have.'

'We have one another and the little ones.'

From somewhere it frustrated Connie that the future was all

you had. Was it all anybody had, were children everything? Was not the present and even the past just as important? Could it be that the selfishness of continuity was the worst thing anybody could want?

It was a sad business, Dom thought, living in a place when everybody had left. There was no work here, no money, the pits were obviously played out though he continued to find enough coal for them to get by on by going a little further every few days, and the lead mining had long since gone. What else did anybody do? It was a barren land, nothing happening, and as he had seen before when people left nature moved in.

No wonder Sid had found them, the place was full of birds and small animals and grass grew up everywhere. If nobody came it would be a dull strange place to continue living in but at the moment he couldn't think of anything else.

Connie worried. Was there some way that she and Dom could move into Wolsingham? Up here there was no school for the children, there were no shops and the vegetables that had lasted until early spring were now exhausted and since nobody had looked after them in so long the new vegetables grew very slowly.

These people too, she thought, like her grandparents, had made the best of what little they had and it was little, she could see now. They were poor, they were uneducated, there had been no books in the house, no pictures, no poetry, she doubted they could read and write very well. It was an existence such as only happened to very poor people indeed that she had ever known.

She could remember how rich her life had been in Japan. Her

mother had spent a lot of time helping people to start gardens wherever they could in the city so that they could have blue and pink and purple, white, orange, yellow and green. Where had her mother's knowledge come from?

Rosa could produce so much from so little, she could bring on what she called 'seedlings to weedlings'. She always laughed when she spoke these silly words. Connie's heart smote her for how much she missed her mother.

Rosa had been modest about her abilities, she could produce a flower as if by magic so that it would grow in the middle of a cracked road and be trampled underfoot even after a day but still she went on. Her mother too had been trampled underfoot because the man she adored was dead and she could do no more.

Her mother had specialized in poppies, red like blood, orange like flames in the fire's depth on a cold dark night. They would grow anywhere, she said, they grew lavender coloured in the broken pavements, they embedded themselves in people's hearts with their persistence and their fragile flowers.

They came from Egypt, she said. And relieved pain, people there would eat the seeds to banish heartaches. Sad then that she had needed poppies to relieve her of a life she could no longer bear. Connie thought she had understood that her mother wanted to go because she had nothing more to offer and felt her time on earth was over and hoped she would not learn to resent her mother's decision but she missed her so much now.

It was no good. You could not live your mother's life. It had to be the life she chose and you got to choose your life. It wasn't sad. Hadn't her mother said that after love it was choice that mattered? That had been her mother's choice. It was not that she did not love her children, it was only that she had thought she could be of no further help to them.

Fifteen

Thomas Neville was only too aware of what people were saying about his mother and none of it was charitable. He went into a lot of houses, he heard a lot of gossip, he dealt with the local people day after day and they were unkind about her.

The women resented that she was rich and perhaps that she was elegant and good-looking still and that she did what she wanted. Few of these women would ever have the chance to do what they chose. He was upset for her and just hoped she didn't know what people were saying of her, that her husband had killed himself because she was running around with other men, because she was not his equal, that he had married badly and rued it, that she was unpleasant to him and nagged and scolded him.

Thomas hurt for his mother as she had been none of these things. Last of all she had gained the squire's attention. That was unforgivable apparently. Since the squire's wife had died three years ago all the local women single or widowed had put themselves about to gain his attention but she had walked into the library and captured his gaze straight away. For that she would not be forgiven.

He almost wished he had left her in Durham. It could not have been any more painful than this. She pretended she knew nothing but as the weeks went on he realized his mother was too clever to miss anything and he thought it was awful for her.

She did not go back to the library afternoons. One day in late spring at teatime when Thomas had just finished the evening surgery a horse and trap stopped outside the door and a box was deposited in the hall, Ada having declared that it was too much for her to carry.

Thomas therefore carried it into the kitchen where Ada said she would unpack it but his mother was curious and so to distract her he got her to open the box.

'The lad said it was heavy and it must be bottles, I can hear them chink,' Ada said, hovering.

Inside the box was a note and when his mother read the note and didn't say anything to him he saw that her cheeks went pink. They were six bottles of dry sherry. His mother stopped and stared at the bottle in her hand and then she put it down and walked out of the room.

Thomas put the box in the pantry and followed her. She was standing over the fire smoking a cigarette newly lit and he did not pretend that he was unaware she was hurt.

'I'm sure he meant it as a compliment,' Thomas said.

'People are talking about me.'

'Well, they say the only thing worse than people talking about you is people not talking about you,' Thomas said and she gave him such a look that he wished not for the first time that he had not opened his mouth.

'Silly old bugger,' his mother said, presumably of the squire.

'You told me he liked and knew my father. It was probably something to do with that.'

'He spoke almost lovingly of your father,' she said and her voice caught in her throat and Thomas did not think that it was the cigarette smoke. He did not know what to do to help her. There were so few opportunities in the dale for widows and she was exceptional in so many ways. He escaped to the Bay Horse a couple of times a week and left her sitting over the fire with her books. He took guilt there with him every time.

Despite how his mother had reacted he knew she was pleased the squire had paid her such a compliment and he thought he could discern in her eyes a slight gleam such as women who were admired sometimes did have, happy to think that a rich and influential man had shown a likeness for them, however harmless it was meant to be. It must soften the blow of folk saying hard things about her.

And then Thomas thought about the gesture and wondered whether there might be some kind of future here in the dale for his mother. In places like this surely it was most unusual for men like the squire to send presents to women unless they meant something.

Perhaps he missed female company and although Laura was twenty years younger than the squire, her son thought that perhaps that only made it better. She would not think of him as old, only as well respected, and so in turn he could pass on that self-respect to any woman he admired.

Thomas was glad that his mother had something more to her days than sorrow and grief, her loneliness and the bitterness that sometimes seemed to enshroud her. This possible friendship was some kind of hope for both of them, he thought.

Laura got fed up in the end, fed up of having no purpose, fed up of dreaming that she would see the squire again, so she decided to go to another of Mrs Whitty's book afternoons. At least it would break the monotony of her days. She had never felt old before. Now she looked into the mirror and saw lines and bags on her face, and worst of all somehow she saw grief, not the grief of old age but the resentful grief that younger widows had, and she cursed herself and then Harry and she went that very day to the book afternoon.

The room became quiet but she merely breezed up to Mrs Whitty and said that she had nothing to read and she hoped she had not presumed too much in coming here to join in something. She had been feeling lonely.

After that the room was silent for several seconds and then Mrs Whitty beamed at her and said she was most welcome and then she began to introduce Laura to other women. Laura could feel the atmosphere thaw and she was quite proud of herself for how brave she had been and then she thought it wasn't brave at all, you were acting like a coward. What was it Harry used to say? Taking a bull by the horns and that was what this was.

She met and immediately liked Miss Hutton, the woman who ran the dress shop. Mrs Whitty said how much she loved Laura's fur coat and they began to talk about fashion and clothes and materials and Laura began to think that perhaps she might make a friend here or more than one.

She also thought that as Miss Hutton was a single woman perhaps she too was lonely and Laura felt lucky that she had married such a lovely man and had such a gorgeous handsome boy and she felt sympathy for the woman who had had none of these things and yet Miss Hutton was not the kind of woman who would care for being pitied.

The women were also keen to tell her what a wonderful doctor her son was and Laura was proud and tried not to show it. He was wonderful but his mother must not be seen to think so.

Laura did not ask for sherry, she had enough to think about with regard to sherry. She even put from her the idea that the squire might have been there. She had two cups of tea and took two books home and it was only then that she knew she had enjoyed her afternoon.

She was therefore able to announce rather loftily to the surprised Ada that she did not need tea that afternoon, she had been out for tea.

She told Thomas later what she had done and could hardly bear the look of relief on his face. He was so young. His father had died and it seemed to him that his mother had given up. Well, she wasn't done yet, not for a long time.

Dom took Sid to meet Mrs Rizzi. A lot of people were scared of weasels but Mrs Rizzi was not that kind of person. She actually took hold of Sid and you had to do that carefully because even good-natured weasels sometimes bit unsuspecting folk. Dom didn't blame them, it must be difficult being approached clumsily by people you didn't know, but she held him by the back of his neck and Dom would have shown her had he thought she didn't know what she was doing. Mrs Rizzi purred over Sid like he was a lapdog. Dom was not convinced that Sid liked being treated as if he was a spaniel but Sid was too well-mannered to indicate that this was how he felt so he endured kisses and cuddles.

Nevertheless Dom was pleased to give Mrs Rizzi the fish he had caught and the rabbits Sid had caught and there was quite a big bag. Mrs Rizzi looked pleased and she gave him homemade rabbit pâté, fish pie, and the usual flour, sugar, yeast and milk. She also gave him eggs and butter so Dom was very pleased with his haul.

He missed his home. He missed the company of other boys his age. He had discovered that a boy called Jimmy who looked after the doctor's pharmacy was not that much older than him and he envied Jimmy's job. Dom knew he would never be accepted in such a place doing such a thing but he also remembered what his father had taught him of herbs and ways of aiding people, but there again he did not dare approach the doctor.

Also although he had enjoyed doing these things when he had been with his father the ideas palled now and, seeing Mr Adams leave the Methodist church, Dom ventured inside. He knew his father had preached here and hoped he might feel closer to him in such a place. He had been in various churches but he thought them strangely ornate and somehow they made him feel uncomfortable. If the church could spend such a lot of money in that way why were so many people here so poor?

The chapel was different and all he did was go inside and the idea of his father there made him instantly feel better. Also it was his kind of building. The windows were plain and there were no velvet hangings or rich gold statues such as he had seen before. The man who had built this place was a very good builder. Its plainness made it somehow and he was lucky in that the sunlight was pouring in through the clear windows and he could see the way that the hills went up beyond the little town and how the sheep were like white dots in the grass. Above it was a clear blue sky and there was something so magically majestic about it all that Dom stood still and when he did he understood why his father had wanted to be a minister in the first place. He was glad that meeting Mr Adams had not given him a prejudiced view of such things.

He heard the door and saw Mr Adams. He knew instantly that the man was his enemy.

'You stole from me,' the man accused him.

'You robbed me,' Dom said and he did not wait. He walked out of the chapel and in his ears he heard the man's voice.

'I will have the law on you!' he said.

Dom was shaken. Could such a thing happen, would he have enough face to deny it and would Connie despise that he would tell lies? What else could he do? He could never admit to it, he might be flung in gaol and then what would Connie and the others do without him?

He knew the law here was Mr Whitty. He wondered whether he should go and confess what he had done but he didn't think that would help. He didn't know Mr Whitty and although he knew Mrs Whitty gave library afternoons to the women of the area he didn't think he wanted to go there and risk becoming involved in something that sounded like an old ladies' tea party.

He promised himself another look inside the chapel, however, when the minister was not there. He had been very impressed with the place and its atmosphere and every time he thought of the building it made him feel happy.

Sixteen

It was April and wind bit the land. Connie and Dom struggled to keep themselves and the children warm and fed but every time they went out it was an effort and told on them. They became weary and she would lie there at night and think that perhaps spring never reached this life, that it was like some awful dwelling place on earth where there was but one season. She could not bear it. The passing of the seasons, the changing, was what made life worthwhile. If you were to get up to constant sun or constant rain it would be unendurable.

And then she woke up one morning and it was light. She hadn't noticed that the nights were drawing out. Was that what you called it? She had heard of drawing in but now she thought they were drawing out and she liked it. She was getting up in the daylight and at five o'clock it was not quite evening and the grass was beginning to grow and what trees there were up in the village were showing a distinct green tinge amongst their branches and she thought it was a brighter green than she had met before. On some days now the sunlight came straight into the rooms so that she could sit in a patch of warmth and enjoy it.

Her grandmother got better. Connie was so glad of it. Perhaps they were used to the ruin they called home but she got up and began to light the fire and cooked meals and she opened the shop. She also seemed to delight in seeing Connie and the first time that her husband was not there she took the girl into her arms and said roughly,

'I am so grateful you came home.'

Connie hugged the old woman to her and closed her eyes.

'Oh, Grandmother,' she said, 'I thought I would never meet you.'

Connie liked going there now that she felt less responsibility. She liked seeing her grandfather in the garden, going about his digging. She would not have said such a thing to anyone but she had begun to love the land there and to feel that it was blood of her blood or something like that, she liked the idea that her ancestors had lived there for hundreds of years.

Her grandmother would send her out with cups of tea for him and Connie would linger and she got the feeling that he liked her lingering, that he knew she also felt a love for that place. She knew her father had not felt such love and that her grandfather regretted it. She understood that people wanted to get away but she had the feeling that had her father lived to be older he would have felt the tug of his mother country and wanted to come home.

Would she feel like that about Japan when she was older? Would she want to bring back the youthful joy that had been her first feelings and to have the idea that her parents who had died there had somehow left something important behind them? She knew they had. They had cared for so many people, had given their lives for that country. It had become the best part of them.

It made her feel displaced and strange that she was torn in two between her grandfather's acres and his tumbledown house and the land where her parents were buried. Would she always feel like that?

She and Dom walked down to Wolsingham twice a week. Her grandparents felt little for the two children who were not bound to them in blood and the children sensed it and did not like being there. Pearl clung and cried and Leo was so difficult that it annoyed Connie and yet she understood. If her grandparents had been softer and kinder to the little ones she would have been satisfied and might even have urged Dom to give up the orphanage and move here, but her grandparents would not like it and neither would the children and so they stayed up there and endured the weather. They could not afford to have nowhere to go.

Her grandparents went on ignoring the younger children. Connie watched Leo and Dom through the window as Dom ventured out into the vegetable patch to speak to his grandfather but the old man went on hoeing the rows as though Dom and Leo were not there and the child knew he was unwanted and put both arms around Dom's leg, something he rarely did now.

She wished her grandmother would take to Pearl who was the most beautiful child and yet her grandmother did not even acknowledge the little girl. It grieved Connie so much and made her angry. She wished in some ways that she and Dom could be hard-hearted enough to stop going down there to help but they could not. Always there were things to see to. She would clean the house and put coal on the fire. She made meals for them and brought food from Mrs Rizzi and Dom would bring rabbits and pheasants all ready for the oven and yet he was not thanked.

Rabbits and fish were their main source of food and they got everything else from Mrs Rizzi. When Connie went to see her grandparents her grandfather had taken to giving her the first vegetables. He had more than enough of such things and she was grateful, though when she tried to thank him he just ignored her. He didn't even acknowledge that he was giving them to her, he just left them by the outside door.

She would make sure they had clean clothes and bedding and yet she thought it was taken for granted. Dom said nothing, but she knew he felt the same.

'I feel we are paying for Mickey's mistakes,' Dom said one night when they got back to the orphanage.

It was the first time they had acknowledged that their father was imperfect and in some ways it was a relief.

The hardest thing of all was to be here and not have her parents with her and yet her grandparents lived and she knew how much they hated Rosa and how much they missed their son. She wanted to make it better, to be a bandage on the wound and yet there was no bandage big enough and the little that she and Dom achieved was nowhere near enough to make up for what had been done before they were alive. How could you ever get that back?

There was also inside her a thought that people here, like many others, were undemonstrative and that it was considered a sign of weakness to show love. It must be implicit so perhaps that was how her grandfather and to a certain extent her grandmother looked at it but as children of Mickey and Rosa she and Dom expected so much more than their grandparents managed and therefore they failed them every day.

The local people worked out when she and Dom were in the village and much to her surprise they seemed to want to help. Mrs Rizzi knew Dom very well by then and Connie just a little but she encouraged Connie to take Pearl to see her.

Connie loved the shop. It smelled of warm biscuits baking and it was clean and tidy but full of all the ingredients she would love to take home with her.

Also Mrs Rizzi would speak directly to Pearl in English and the child responded in the same language, which really pleased Connie and lifted her spirits.

Mrs Rizzi, unlike many native Weardale folk, did not believe in hanging back when she liked people and she would come from behind the counter and hug them both.

'I would hug your brother too, but I feel he might take it amiss,' she said, laughing. 'And lovely Leo. You are such a good family.'

Mrs Whitty invited Connie to bring Pearl to her house and there she produced picture books and read to Pearl and got her to read back. Mrs Whitty also tried to get Connie to read but although Connie thought it was kind of her she did not treasure reading as Dom did and she would take the books and pass them on to him. He could not be made to go to Mrs Whitty's afternoons and Connie always felt that she had too much to do to enjoy sitting down with a book for any length of time.

Mr Smithers owned the local hardware store and also had a horse and cart to move people and belongings throughout the lower dale. Prompted by Dr Neville, who had taken to bringing supplies to them, he seemed to consider himself a kind of honorary parent and he would put Pearl up on his horse, something she loved.

Connie was glad of these kind deeds because she sometimes saw people looking at her across the street. She ignored them as they ignored her but to be surrounded by kindness made a lot of difference to all their lives.

It was late May when Connie heard a knocking on the door. She was afraid it might be her grandfather with news that her grandmother was unwell again but it was not the same kind of sound, it was no large man wanting to be in, indeed it was faint, and had she not been in the hall she might never have heard it.

When she opened the door the diminutive maid from the manse stood before her, dirty face tear-streaked and so white that Connie was aghast. The girl backed away but Connie managed a smile.

'Hello,' she said, 'are you all right?'

The dirty girl shook her head and didn't say anything. And then she blurted out,

'I ate your porridge.' It reminded Connie of Goldilocks and the Three Bears, except that this child did not have yellow hair, at least she didn't think so. Whether it had ever seen soap and water was another matter. Connie had gathered together ingredients from the chemist in Wolsingham – she was by now on good terms with Mrs Southern and her son, Frank – and had managed to make her own soap. Mrs Southern and Frank made up all the prescriptions which Thomas thought too complicated for Jimmy to get right. Mrs Southern also was used by the local people for coughs and colds and rashes and falls, anything which they thought too trivial to go to the doctor for. They trusted her and everybody in the village liked her.

Connie's mother had taught her so many things which were now coming in useful. In the long run soap was cheaper to make and it was something she enjoyed, Pearl liked helping with the safe parts and Connie was finding herbs in the garden which withstood the weather. And she had been thinking fun had long since been left behind.

The bartering system which Connie used was helping with everything but Dom did most of it and everybody was glad of fresh fish and rabbits.

Rosemary was the chief herb and now tiny shoots of peppermint. She could remember her mother's voice – 'Spearmint, eau de cologne mint, pineapple mint, apple mint and horse mint, ginger mint and pennyroyal' – and Connie kept smelling them as they were beginning to come through the soil, somehow reminding her of her mother.

She was understanding more of how this place had once been a haven for children and that there had been skilled hands at work in this garden. The lavender was starting to turn green with purple tips and the long hedge of chives which somebody had planted lovingly, she thought, would be so useful in a little while as the weather warmed and the sun came out.

Already they had had several bright days and she and Pearl had gone outside to investigate. Also there were a lot of yellow dandelions and pink and white daises, flowers which grew regardless of whether there was anybody to mind them.

There were diaries around the house, so old that they were smudged and some of it was hard to decipher, written by the nun who'd helped to run this place, Sister Madeline. There were a lot of entries about how the children had been taken in, given beds and food and been generally so well looked after that Connie began to wish she had been there all those years ago when this place had been well used and much loved.

She was now, she thought, being given such an opportunity. Perhaps she would become the Sister Madeline of her day and aid people and make her parents proud of her in heaven. They didn't believe in heaven, at least her father certainly didn't, but she felt sure they were there looking down and admiring that she and Dom were trying to instigate their ideas here once again.

The little girl's eyes were full of tears and she was older than Connie had first thought. She must be thirteen but she was small.

'It doesn't matter about the porridge,' Connie said, smiling.

The girl said nothing.

'What is your name?'

'Sarah.'

'It's a pretty name.'

'The missus called me Sally.'

'Mrs Adams?'

'I ran away. I ran off.'

Connie opened the door wider.

'Do come in,' she said. 'Why did she change your name?'

'She said Sarah was a bible name and I wasn't worth it. I couldn't stay there and I heard them talking about you and where you'd gone and I had nowhere else to go.'

Pearl had hidden behind Connie but now she sensed that the girl was harmless she peeped around Connie's skirts. Connie picked Pearl up and took Sarah into the kitchen. She sat Sarah down by the fire and gave her soup. Vegetables which had been planted long ago were now popping up here and there, having reseeded themselves. That, along with what Grandfather gave her, helped their everyday needs.

She passed the girl a big bowl and before Connie could give her a spoon she took the bowl to her lips and started to eat. It was almost like home where such things were acceptable, whereas here you were supposed to scoop the food a long way before it got to your mouth. It made Connie feel warm and pleased. She gave Sarah another bowlful and after that the girl smiled at her and thanked her.

'Mr and Mrs Adams, they don't have much,' Sarah said. 'They took me in because they thought it was their duty but they didn't like me and there was so often nothing to eat and I had to do all the housework and look after the children.'

Connie had not forgotten the bread and butter and she could only wonder at this poor girl eating that disgusting porridge with relish.

'But they have a big house,' Connie said and then she remembered Mrs Adams' shabby dress, pale face and thin hands.

'There's another bairn on the way,' Sarah said.

Connie hadn't noticed such things but then Mrs Adams was a small woman. 'She lost one last year and one the year before an' all,' Sarah said. 'There's two to be looked after but they are miserable little things, crying all the time and so messy. I had to cook and nobody taught me so I didn't know how to do it and Mrs Adams kept getting cross with me. I don't think Mr Adams makes much money but then he doesn't have a real job. He sometimes goes out to visit folk and he preaches of a Sunday but neither of them does much at all except complain about everything I did so I ran away. He wasn't always nice to me either.'

Sarah didn't elaborate but there were faint marks on her arms and neck where somebody had obviously taken out their frustration on the nearest thing they could hurt and Connie wondered whether it had been Mr Adams and if he treated his wife and children just the same way.

Connie made the best of the fact that Dom and Leo had taken Sid fishing and she persuaded Sarah, who didn't seem to understand very well, that she ought to take off her clothes and wash.

'All of me?'

'There's nobody here so you needn't be afraid and I can find you something better to wear.'

In the end Sarah liked the smell of the soap and she let Connie wash her hair and when she was clean and dry Connie gave her some of her own clothes. The girl laughed over how long the clothes were so that the skirts had to be turned over at the waist so they didn't trail on the floor. Connie helped her to roll up the sleeves so that they rested on her skinny wrists and she found a scarf for Sarah to tie around her waist to hold everything up.

Sarah was reluctant to accept it and sighed over it and said it was much too pretty for her. It had been Rosa's favourite and Connie could not bear to have left it but she was also glad that it could be used for this poor girl.

'What if I get it dirty?' she said nervously.

'It washes.'

'But it's so pretty and feels so good.' Sarah did a twirl and laughed and her whole face lit up.

Sarah had long hair. Connie combed it out for her and they sat over the fire while Sarah's hair dried.

'Do I have to go now?' she said timidly once this was accomplished. 'And will you want your clothes back?'

'You must stay.'

Sarah stared at her.

'Here?'

'Yes.'

'What about the lad, your brother? What about him? He won't want me here.'

'Dom wouldn't turn anybody away,' Connie said.

'Poor shaffling little soul,' was how Dom described Sarah.

This had been one of their mother's favourite expressions for people she pitied. He and Connie looked at one another in recognition and remembrance.

Sarah was scared of Dom but he was sensitive enough to understand that she had not been well treated by Mr and Mrs

Adams and that he frightened her so he spoke softly to her. They didn't question her about her family or where she had come from. Connie hoped that in time she might tell them. If not they didn't mind.

Having given a home to this girl made Connie feel worthy of her parents and that she might do useful things given the chance.

However, she was not prepared to find Mr Adams at her door three days later and he was not smiling.

'Is Sally here?' he said.

No greeting, no warmth, nothing. And he peered past her into the house.

'We have looked everywhere for her. We did our duty by taking her in and she ran away, at least I presume that she did. You had no right to take her in if that is what you did. In fact you have no right to be here. Who on earth do you think you are?'

Connie was beginning to regret that her brother was not there, especially when Mr Adams barged through into the kitchen and scanned the room, though happily Sarah was nowhere to be seen. Maybe she had feared his voice and slipped into another room or out of the back door.

Connie was unhappy, not scared but she didn't like being spoken to in that way and felt it was unmerited.

'Mr Adams, we were very grateful that you took us in but I don't think Sarah is some kind of indentured servant,' she said. 'Surely she was free to leave if she chose.'

'Is she here?' He glared at her. 'You are beginning to upset the local people with your doings,' he said. 'There is talk of stealing and I know you took a lot of things from my house. I put it before Mr Whitty but of course he has done nothing. I won't forget it.'

'Stealing?' Connie looked hard at him but the guilt rushed her.

'You are not meant to be in this place. It's private.'

Connie was starting to feel sick and miserable as she remembered the money Dom took and the bread and cake and milk.

'I shall have the local law on you and where is Sally?'

'I have no idea,' Connie said.

Mr Adams got hold of her by the wrist. Connie looked at the hold.

'Please don't touch me,' she said. 'Take your hand away.'

He tightened his grip.

'I won't tell you again,' she warned him and when he pressed his fingers into her flesh and smiled Connie kicked his kneecap hard enough so that her foot hurt a little even though she had used the side of it as she was meant to. The hand went and she heard a sharp cry of pain as he clutched at his leg and danced in a neat little circle.

'I would like you to leave now.'

'I shall do nothing of the kind,' he said but not with any conviction.

'Oh yes, you will because if you don't I shall kick you out and I mean it literally.'

He stared.

'You?' he scorned.

'Me,' Connie said.

He hesitated and then he danced away, still obviously in pain. Connie closed the door as. Sarah emerged from behind her.

'You hit him,' she said, eyes round.

'I could have broken his kneecap but it wasn't necessary.'

'I never saw a lass do such a thing. Do you think I could do it?'

'Certainly. It doesn't require strength, just dexterity and aim,' Connie said.

'Who taught you to do that?'

'My father,' Connie said.

Sarah, wide-eyed, followed her back into the kitchen. Mr Amos was another stupid narrow-minded man just like Mr Small, Connie thought. Was the world full of Mr Smalls? Sarah looked a lot better after this happened. She was protected and by another girl and she could learn to protect herself in the same way. She was much cheered, Connie could see.

When she told the story to Dom he laughed over the tale as she meant him to but also he said,

'I don't think Mr Adams likes women or that maybe he likes them too much in a nasty way.'

'He certainly enjoyed hanging on to my wrist.' There was a bruise where the man's fingers had closed.

'I wonder if that's why Mrs Adams is so miserable,' Dom said.

Connie stared at him.

'You think he treats her like that?'

'Just a guess.'

'And she's having another child. Sarah said she lost at least two. She is so skinny, I don't think they eat properly.'

'Or that he won't give out money for food.'

Dom didn't tell Connie that Mr Adams had threatened to go to the law about the money he had taken. He didn't see any point in worrying her until something actually happened.

Neither did she tell him that Mr Adams had threatened her in the same way.

Seventeen

Amos, after his ill-judged meeting with Connie, went to see Mr Whitty in Mr Whitty's capacity as the law-keeper.

Amos explained the problem once again and slightly embellished while Mr Whitty sat back in his chair and listened as though he had not heard it all before which made Amos furious.

'You do know about these strange people?' Amos said. 'Their father ran off with a woman from the backstreets and they have come here where their grandparents couldn't afford to have them and now they are creating a number of problems.'

Mr Whitty knew everything that went on in his area. He had heard nothing about stealing from anyone else so he was sceptical about Mr Adams' claim. He sat back and remembered how little he loved Mr Adams.

'I have heard something of them,' he said. 'Didn't they come from Asia? I hear young Miss Butler is a bonny piece.' Mr Whitty was something of a scholar and knew that orient meant rising of the sun, which he thought was as pretty a meaning as he had ever known. His wife was not the only member of the family who read.

'Her mother was a street walker from what I understand and when Michael Butler married it was the biggest disgrace the area had ever seen,' Amos said.

Mr Whitty privately thought that if an ill marriage was the worst thing that ever happened it would make life much easier for him.

Amos went on.

'Sally Charles, the girl we took in as our daughter, has gone up to that place where they are living after we took her in and clothed and fed her. Disgraceful way to behave after all we did for her. None of them has any right to be there. I believe the Catholic church owns it.'

Mr Whitty was a good church-going man but he had no love for Methodists or Catholics. In fact he thought they were well below his social level though he would never have said so. The best people in the area went to the parish church.

'The boy has taken to stealing, first from us and now I gather other people. He also hunts and shoots illegally and over other people's land. I'm surprised the squire hasn't had something done about him. The man is after all a magistrate,' Amos said.

'Really? Stealing what?'

'All kinds of things,' Amos said vaguely. 'Coal and food and they go fishing where they aren't meant to. And that boy shoots pheasants and partridges. The farmers think he is stealing their lambs, knocking them on the head and carrying them away. People like that – foreigners – well that's what they do. And they ought not to be in that building, I feel sure.'

'The village is not within my jurisdiction,' Mr Whitty said. 'Nobody has lived up there for as long as I can remember. I understand that after Mr Gilbraith died there was no money and I don't have the full story but it's very sad to think that such a good institution could not be kept going. There are many needy souls around. I don't see that these young people could be doing any harm living in what is virtually a ruin where nobody has lived for as long as I can remember.'

He saw by the minister's expression that policemen were not supposed to think there was any such thing, that bad people should be locked up.

'There is the workhouse,' Mr Adams said. 'Perhaps they could be taken in there.'

'I have no jurisdiction over that either,' Mr Whitty said, thankful though he didn't say so. He didn't very often say what he did mean, it kept him out of a lot of unnecessary trouble. It didn't do to stir things up and he had no intention of making life difficult for himself. He liked this place, it was pretty and law-abiding and his wife was happy in her library with her friends.

His wife was somebody who heard all the gossip so he asked her about the children who had moved into the orphanage.

'Rosa McCready's daughter,' his wife said and Mr Whitty was thankful that his wife took in detail that he didn't need to and had been born in Stanhope. 'She was apparently a lightskirt.'

'Oh.'

'The daughter is beautiful.'

Mr Whitty thought it would be tactless to acknowledge this.

'He's a hard man is old Joshua.'

'I think he may have met his match there. Mrs Southern' – this was the chemist, 'says the girl was in buying ingredients to make soap and she cleaned and fed the old people. Mrs Butler won't last long according to Dr Neville, Mrs Southern said she took another bad turn this morning and had to go back to bed.'

'Mr Adams says they have been stealing.'

Mrs Whitty raised her eyes to her sitting room ceiling and tutted in disbelief.

'You would have heard surely by now Walter, long before Mr Adams if anything like that had gone on.'

'He's a disagreeable man at best,' Mr Whitty said. 'And that lass the Adams took in has gone up there to live with them.'

'I'm not surprised. If that's the best the Adams can do keeping lasses thin and unkempt, then they don't deserve any child.'

Eighteen

The next person Connie had to visit her was a tall dark-haired man. He wore a very nice suit, she knew the cloth was good and well-cut, it had been made especially for him. He smiled at her. Connie had never met anybody she really liked before but all of a sudden she understood her parents' marriage, how happy they had been, how well-suited, how fine-looking, and she could not help but stare at the young man in front of her. They had met before and she had taken to him so fast that she could hardly breathe. He said,

'Miss Butler, Good morning. I've come to talk to you about your grandmother. May I come in for a few moments?'

The doctor had been kind helping to bring supplies from the village and urging Mr Smithers to lend them his cart. The doctor had assured Connie that he paid for nothing but he was becoming known as a very generous man and she liked him but suddenly Connie felt awkward. She had denied to herself that she had felt something before but there was no denying it now.

Really, she thought to herself, the house was getting like her memory of Lime Street Station, busy. She found she had to distract herself to avoid the blushes that began to heat her face and she was angry at herself for these feelings she had for somebody she didn't know well. The whole idea was silly. She had never thought her body would disobey her in such a case.

She ushered him in and introduced him to Sarah who was so shy that she went white and ran away. Connie sat him down. She didn't imagine he had come with good news and she was right.

'Your grandmother has taken another bad turn,' he said. 'I know you and your brother have tried to help but that house will finish her off. I know you want to bring them up here and that your grandfather isn't keen but might you be able to push the matter forward?'

Connie liked how the doctor got straight to the matter but she found it difficult to meet his gaze. He was well-spoken, at least she thought so, he was a gentleman, well-mannered and well-dressed, and she had never seen anybody like him before in her life. He could only have been English with his fair skin and bright eyes and he smiled at her so much that she couldn't help smiling back.

'Grandfather won't move,' Connie said, hoping to keep to the matter in hand, 'I have tried to persuade him and since they won't have us there and they won't come here there's very little I can do.'

'Would you like me to try talking to him?'

Connie shook her head and then she thought that the doctor had authority and learning and was older than she was so perhaps he could help. Why not? Most men in authority in her experience were not like this. She thought she would have known he was a doctor even if he did not say so. He had gorgeous brown eyes, lit like dark topaz.

'I will go and ask him and you and your brother could talk about the possibility of moving the old people. If it was agreeable to you I could ask Mr Smithers and his son, Arnold, to bring their belongings and Oswald and I would bring your grandparents here in my trap.'

Connie had tried not to take favours from him but Mrs Smithers had met Dom and Connie one day as they struggled with supplies in the main street and had a quiet word with her husband. Connie was both grateful and embarrassed at so much kindness and tried to repay it. She made a blue dress for Mrs Smithers. The woman was so flattered she could not speak.

'Good luck with Grandfather,' Connie said to the doctor now. She felt better knowing that the doctor was on her side. She had the feeling that he would make a good friend.

Thomas got onto his horse and made his way slowly back to Wolsingham. He was amazed at Connie Butler. He had imagined that eventually he would marry and he had had a few friends who were female. There had been one young woman in London and he was still of the impression that had he stayed they would have got married, but even she had not made an impression on him like Connie Butler.

He tried telling himself how silly he was and that she was just a pretty young girl from another country and couldn't possibly matter to him. As a medical man he had scoffed at the whole idea of love, thought it ridiculous, but it was ridiculous no more and made him feel uncomfortable.

She was not the kind of woman he could have anything to do with other than medically, he told himself that she was too young, that they could have nothing in common, that he had met a great many young women as beautiful as she was, but he knew the truth was he had never met anybody like her before and could not get her out of his mind.

Nobody had ever got in the way of his concentration before. He attempted to rein in his emotions but the more he tried the more he thought about her.

He went to the Butler house when he got back to the village and had stabled his horse. He went to talk to Joshua but the old man ignored him.

'Your wife will die if she is not better taken care of, Mr Butler,' he said.

'Go away and mind your own business,' the old man said, 'and don't come back. I've got no money to pay you,' and he slammed the door in the doctor's face.

Connie couldn't rest and when the doctor had come back with the news that her grandmother needed better looking after she went down to the village to see how bad she was. The doctor had been right. Her grandfather let her in but he didn't speak to her. Even though she was going there as much as she could it was not enough any more. As soon as she left the place became cold, dirty and her grandfather was incapable of keeping the fire going or feeding himself or his wife.

'If you won't come to us then at least let me take Grandmother,' she begged her grandfather after three weeks of this when she thought she could stand no more.

'If she's going to die then she's best off dying in her own home.'

Connie was angry at such stubbornness and rather glad that it ended her patience.

'She will live a lot longer if she can be properly looked after but since you won't have anybody in and I can't come every day she must come up to the Hilda House.' Dom had named it that. She liked it.

'I don't know why you bother coming here and telling me what to do,' he said.

'You are a wicked, selfish, old man,' she said finally losing her temper and then she set to on the house and tried to make it right and to get some food into her grandmother.

He went out to hide in his vegetable patch and didn't come in again until she had left, as she had known he would. She cried on the way home but managed to dry her tears before she reached the Hilda House. Dom and Leo had just got home and it seemed that Pearl had been happy with Sarah and that Sarah was learning to be good with the little girl.

That was the best thing about Connie's day but later when they sat around and talked she told Dom and Sarah about her grandmother and none of them could think what to say.

Dom's best idea was that he should go to Wolsingham and talk to the doctor and since Leo wouldn't be left they could go together. Dom, after they arrived, got confused. There was a sign which said, 'Surgery' beside the front door and so he ventured in by the gate to a side door and there he rang the bell only to find the young woman who opened it, stared and slammed the door shut, her face crimson at the good-looking boy in front of her. Dom knocked again but it was not answered so in the end he went to the front again and was confronted by a lad of about his own age. Though the boy was skinny and ill clothed, he got a less unfriendly though rather strange reception.

'We's thoo?' the lad said.

Dom's language skills were of no use here so he said in plain tones,

'I have come to see the doctor.'

'He's not here,' Jimmy said and he too slammed the door.

Dom wasn't sure what to do. He didn't think his grandfather

would want him at the house so he and Leo stood and waited and it was not long before Thomas Neville came walking briskly down the street. Dom accosted him with,

'Good morning. My sister sent me to see you. We think you are right and that we must act to move our grandmother as soon as possible and you said you will help.'

'Yes, of course,' Thomas said genially and he shook Dom's and then Leo's hand and Dom liked him straight away. 'Do come inside.'

Dom had longed to see inside the surgery and had also wondered what the pharmacy was like but his interest in such things had been overtaken by his private visit to the chapel and he wished that he could go there, but Mr Adams disliked him so much that he felt he could not be comfortable.

It was not just that he thought of his father there, it was as though he had picked up ideas of his father's when his father had been perhaps as young as he was now and had felt he could do good work within the church. Yes, his father had lost his faith but Dom was very taken with the idea of helping people. He had always hated missionaries, how strange he felt now that he could perhaps become one.

The lad of the half hour before was nowhere to be seen so they followed the doctor into the room which had a big desk. He ushered them into chairs and then he sat on the front of the desk which Dom thought was very tactful of him because it meant there was no barrier between them. Presumably he had to hit the middle ground between respecting his patients and getting them to talk easily to him and to accept his advice so he would sit behind the desk or at the front of it, judging as best he could what was the right thing to do.

'You were so kind as to care,' Dom said.

'It's my job,' the doctor said as though he was embarrassed.

For a few moments Dom thought of Mickey, this man was a bit like him, more concerned for the welfare of others than for himself. It was a rare quality.

'If he will not come then we cannot make him,' the doctor said, 'but your grandmother needs proper care and you and your sister cannot be in two places at once. If you think it best I will take Mr Smithers and we will abduct her. I can't think of anything else and I wouldn't like to have her demise on my conscience. Do you have a bed for her?'

Dom shook his head.

'Then I shall provide it.'

Dom thanked him and left. The doctor said he would do his best to get a bed and mattress and other necessities up to the Hilda House the day after tomorrow which was the earliest he thought he could manage it.

When Dom and Leo had gone Laura confronted her son in the hallway. She had been looking out of the window.

'Who were those strangers?' she asked.

'They are the grandchildren of Mr and Mrs Butler who run a shop on the outskirts of village. They were born in the east.'

'What a very handsome boy,' his mother observed.

'They need help to persuade their grandfather to let them take their grandmother up to the village where they can look after her.'

'What can I do?' his mother said.

It had never occurred to Thomas that his mother would be sympathetic but then his father had been a barrister and Thomas knew very well that he came home and told his wife everything and she had always been discreet. It made things easier for his father to be able to confide in the woman he loved, had married and relied upon.

Thomas led the way into his surgery and closed the door behind them. He told her all about the old people, mentioning Connie in passing so his mother would not think he cared about a girl who was so unusual. He was angry at himself for caring but there was little he could do to get rid of the feelings that Connie Butler had stirred in him.

'I could order things for you,' his mother said eagerly, 'beds, blankets and all that kind of thing. And I could see Mr Smithers if you like. He and Arnold are not ones to gossip and they are so kind.'

Thomas had not known that his mother was on speaking terms with Mr Smithers and his son or family from the big hardware store where you could buy furniture and bed linen. She seemed pleased to have something to do and went about it straight away. He could see the beginnings of joy in her face now that she was getting out more. She went to church every Sunday and he went with her and there she talked to the vicar and his wife and other people in the village who had become friends.

Thomas did not pretend to himself that it meant she was any happier, but his mother had always been one to make the best of things and she was even beginning to look better, not smoking all day and sitting over the fire. Also since the squire's donation of the sherry she had taken to being slightly offended that he should send her such a thing and, to Thomas's joy, was not drinking nearly as much. The squire may not have known what he was doing but he was making the right kind of impression on Laura.

It was a cold wet day despite the fact it was summer but Laura left her furs at home and wore a black coat, plain hat and gloves and smiled politely at everyone she met and it was not long before she reached the hardware store.

She had not been in before. She could remember as a small child loving such places and this one was enormous because it had a back room full of furniture. Mr Smithers looked very professional, she thought, he wore a dark grey overall which had obviously been ironed recently.

Mr Smithers knew everybody.

'Mrs Neville,' he said as though they had met many times before, 'what a cold morning for you to come out and what can I show you?'

She told him without explanation that she needed three big beds. Thomas hadn't asked her for three but by all accounts the orphanage was a huge place and if the adult children were moving their grandparents into it – and how brave of them – they would need such things. She also ordered mattresses, blankets, pillows, sheets and pillowslips and towels and blithely put them on Thomas's account.

Then she explained her mission and found that he would be available to help in three days' time and would pick everything up for her from the shop. She told him that her son would sort out the moving of the old people but if he and Arnold could help with that it would be a blessing. He agreed immediately. And here she incurred more expense by telling Mr Smithers that if he sent in his bill it would be dealt with straight away.

She felt better now than she had felt since Harry had died. She wished that there were more things she could do. Since the squire had sent her the six bottles of sherry she had been hoping she might see him again but so far nothing had happened and her frustration at this made her want something else to happen and so she was getting about and doing her best to stay cheerful. It was only in her bed at night that she cried into the pillow for the loneliness of Harry not being there.

The atmosphere at the surgery house was what she had made it, she thought with slight satisfaction as she walked back. After initially scaring the two maids she had been easier and more polite. She summoned Ada to her now. She often consulted both girls on what to do. Ada was a sensible woman who came from a large family in Rookhope. Fiona was Scottish.

'Thomas is attending the family and Miss Butler wants her grandparents to go and live with them,' Laura said.

'It would be a fine idea,' Ada said, for she had lived in Wolsingham all her working life. 'Everybody has always felt awful that the two old people were left and neither of them very well. We could help with jam and eggs and such if you think it is a good idea.'

Ada was a very good baker too and loved making cakes and bread and puddings and scones and was so enthusiastic that it helped a lot. So Laura and Ada made a list of all the things they could do to aid the old couple and also Connie Butler.

Thomas went every day to see Mrs Butler and only hoped she would live long enough so that he could get her to the Hilda House. Her husband had been very bitter about the doctor entering the house when he had insisted. In the end when Thomas Neville let his impatience show the old man stormed off into his back garden and so Thomas, although calling himself names for his reaction, also thought that the only way he would see Mrs Butler was to climb the stairs of the increasingly dirty and ill-kept house and find every day that his patient had had nothing to eat or drink.

After that he took Ada or Fiona with him, they brought soup and milk, and made time for clearing up and putting on the fire while they were there. When all was ready up at the orphanage, the beds in place and made-up, he was able to move the old lady. He didn't hesitate or ask questions because he knew if he gave old Joshua a chance the man would forbid it and rant and rave so he kidnapped Mrs Butler. He walked in with a huge blanket, lifted her out of her bed and settled her on cushions in his trap which Oswald drove and they took her out into the cold air but on to the tops where she would be looked after.

Joshua could feel the hot tears running down his face as he tended to his vegetable patch. He knew they had taken his wife away. He had gone on telling himself that she had always got better before and would do so now but in his heart he doubted it. He went on digging until it got dark and then he went back into the house and sat over the black grate. He crawled into bed and willed himself back to better times when his son was a small child and his wife was a young woman and a good wife and mother, and then he slept.

Connie felt awful. She was pleased to have her grandmother here but worried that her grandmother wanted to be with her grandfather and yet if she had been left there she would have died. She was so underweight and dehydrated that she was very weak and did nothing but sleep.

'I understand how you feel, Miss Butler,' the doctor had said, 'but there was no option.'

'I know,' she said, and he thought that she was the most beautiful creature he had ever seen and even though she came from a country he knew nothing about he could see how at home she looked here amongst this wilderness. He remembered what people said of her mother being of low morals and a traveller's daughter and yet he thought that Connie had some wonderful essential quality he had seen before only in the wind and the snow and the rain and the sea. She was of nature and yet in her eyes there was a depth of experience and intelligence such as he had never witnessed before. Perhaps she got those qualities from her mother.

He told her that he would go and see her grandfather and try to ensure that he had care, clean clothes, a warm hearth and good food. He didn't know how he would accomplish it but for Connie's sake and for the sake of his own high principles he could not let the old man be neglected and die in that place without his wife's presence or his granddaughter's help.

Ada and Fiona took to going there when they had a little free time but Thomas didn't want to take up all their own time, it wasn't good. He began to pay both Ada and Fiona more money and made sure they had a chance to do whatever they chose two or three times a week. It wasn't fair to try and solve the problem that way but he didn't know what more to do and it worried him when he couldn't solve difficulties.

Flo woke up to sunlight. At first she thought she was at home in bed with Joshua but she was too warm and comfortable for that. The bed felt soft and new and they had never had a new bed.

All their money had been spent on Michael. The curtains were always closed at home in a vain attempt to shut out the draughts which ran around the rooms like lost souls. She didn't think she had ever been so cosy in her life. She went back to sleep.

The second time she woke up somebody was just about to sit down on the bed and to her joy her granddaughter Connie was there, all smiles and with tea and buttered toast on a tray.

'Sit up, Grandmother, and have this.'

Flo then realized that she had been carried here the day before. She had not wanted to leave her husband alone and now she brought him to mind she said,

'Joshua?'

'He wouldn't come.'

'I can't leave him. We've been married for forty years.'

'When you are better you will be able to go back to him.'

Sarah surprised Connie by saying that she could go down and help the old man.

'If there's anything I do know it's housework and since you are to be looking after the old lady here it will be much easier and faster and even if he doesn't like it I could do a bit of shopping on the way there and leave it outside if he won't have me in the house.'

'But what if he is awful to you?'

Sarah smiled.

'It'll be water off a duck's back, knowing I can come back here afterwards. I could maybe take Pearl with me when he gets used to me. Who couldn't love such a bairn?'

Grandfather had so far managed to ignore the foreign children as though they were nothing more than pictures on a wall.

Connie thought life was getting easier because Pearl had taken to Sarah whereas before she would barely let Connie out of the room without her. Now she was feeling more secure.

Also it was strange that Pearl had taken to Sarah because since their parents had died Pearl had barely spoken a word of English unless she was with other people. Sarah seemed to comprehend perfectly and it made Connie's life easier. Connie didn't like to say anything because the communication between the two girls was a lot more basic than language, it was like sisters and yet more.

Pearl was happier than she had been since they had lost their parents. She was turning into a joyful little girl up here in the middle of nowhere, having Sarah to dance with her, and Sarah knew lots of nursery rhymes and childhood songs and hymns. Connie didn't like to be inquisitive and ask, she was content to let this new friendship grow and flourish.

Nineteen

Amos could not think when he had been more pleased than he had the day he found out that old Mrs Butler had been taken up to the orphanage on the top of the hill. He was well rid of her. Now it was only the old man to deal with and he didn't suppose a nasty interfering slut like Connie Butler would leave things alone and she would be doing what Amos wanted her to do, taking the old man up there and leaving Amos's childhood home empty and ready for him.

He lay awake at night thinking of how good it would be when the old man was gone and the house was his once again. He had not thought how glad he would feel when the strange children took their grandparents to live with them. He had been gleeful to think of how old the grandparents were, how frail Mrs Butler was now.

He had been able to watch the house before in the darkness though summer caused problems because the sun rarely went down before eleven and was back up again at four but he would leave the manse and creep down there and look upon the place of his dreams. They had stolen from him his rightful inheritance. The old woman was gone but the old man hung on until Amos became frustrated and wondered what he could do to get rid of him.

How keen of hearing was old Joshua and would he know if someone entered the house at night? The door was always locked, Amos had ascertained, having tried to get in quietly just to sit inside and remember all the things that he thought he could bring to mind: laughter and good food, the warmth of people who loved him, the peace of being in the right place. If he could just sit there in the darkness he knew he could bring it all back to him.

Amos blotted out the parts of his life which he did not like, the way his father and Joshua had quarrelled because they both thought they were entitled to own the house. Joshua was only fifteen months older and it was unfair when Amos's father had a son too. They should both have been given a share and yet it had not worked out that way. Amos's father in a rage had taken his little family away and that was how they had lost everything.

They had been so unhappy in Newcastle and in time his father had gone away and left his wife and child. It seemed he could not stomach being away from his beloved Weardale yet Amos had not been able to ascertain whether his father had ever returned and he dared not ask many questions in a place where everybody knew everybody and everything about them. He could not afford to upset anybody or get anyone involved. This was for him only. Amos understood that so completely. This was their home, his home, and he had come back to it and he would have it for his own, he would restore the happiness that they had had when he was a small child and everything was good.

After several frustrating nights he found that the windows did not lock and some were so badly rotted they would open to his touch and so he chose the biggest which was in the kitchen and at the back, easy to get to without being seen. He would stay here for the rest of the night, lying on the old couch, and he would sleep there sometimes and there he could block out all the horrors of his life. He could become the boy he had been and bring it all to him again and enfold it in his arms and sleep.

Twenty

Flo cried. She had thought she would soon be back home but she did not get well enough for that. She missed her husband, she missed her home and her surroundings, but Connie fed her good meals and kept her warm and when she became a little better Connie gave her just a little knitting and sewing to do from Miss Hutton's shop in Wolsingham.

When she had first arrived Connie had gone to the shop to see if she could buy sewing and knitting materials and had got talking to Miss Hutton. Miss Hutton was what they politely called a maiden lady. Connie liked her. She had a good fund of common sense and Connie could see that Miss Hutton liked her right from the beginning.

Miss Hutton was lonely in her own way. She went to church but few other places, though she did like to attend Mrs Whitty's book afternoons. It was not so much that she was a big reader, she confided to Connie, but she enjoyed the company and a lot of women in the village would go to her for advice on sewing and knitting. Miss Hutton joined a quilting class which went on in the back room of the chemist's shop and she told Connie that she thought Connie would be welcomed there though Connie said she knew nothing of quilting.

Miss Hutton smiled.

'But you have told me that you make all the clothes for your family. Quilting is much easier than that but you get something special out of it as well. Do come and I will introduce you to the others.'

Connie was shy. They were all older than she was and she was unsure about being accepted but these people had already been kind to her so she went. She would come down the hills with Connie and Pearl and spend part of the day with the quilting group and another part discussing clothes with Miss Hutton. Some women were good at plain sewing but could not do the more intricate things, like alterations, making clothes good again when they had been worn by several children and were shabby. Miss Hutton taught her to knit on four needles which had been a mystery to Connie but it turned out to be just another skill that she could acquire and be proud of.

Also Miss Hutton was the only person who ever discussed her mother sympathetically and she remembered Connie's mother as a young girl and was so kind when speaking of her that it made Connie glow with happiness.

The only fly in the ointment, Connie thought, feeling slightly guilty, was that when she and Pearl and Sarah went off to the village Dom and Leo and Sid were left to look after Grandmother and Dom did not pretend to like it.

Leo was restless and hated having to stay indoors because Grandmother only ventured outside to sit on a bench in the sunshine when Dom carried her and of course she could walk nowhere. Leo would complain both to Connie and to Dom that he wanted to go somewhere and do something and not have to listen to the old woman rambling on as she had to be watched all the time. Dom did not like to say anything sharp to him because Connie knew he felt the same way but it had to be done.

'You still have plenty of time for fishing and going on the fells but you must help by seeing to Grandmother while I'm gone. Miss Hutton is starting to put work my way. You go down there to see Mrs Whitty and Mrs Rizzi—'

'I don't have people my own age,' Dom complained, 'and neither does Leo. It gets boring up here without you.'

'You'll just have to get on with it,' Connie said firmly to her brother, and to Leo, 'You can't always have things your own way,' which was hard, she knew. They would have to learn there were other people in this world and they too were entitled to do things that gave them pleasure especially when it made money.

After Connie began to spend time with Miss Hutton as her grandmother got better she would come back with all the village gossip and encourage her grandmother to get dressed and sit up for a short while each day. Her bed and special chair were downstairs in a big sitting room and there the fire was kept going all day. Connie would sit with her in the afternoons, talking to her, and they would sew and knit and it gave Flo something which she had never had, another woman's companionship. She wondered sometimes had things been different would she and Rosa have spent time like this and then she felt guilty and bereft and sad and it filled her heart that Rosa's daughter had come back to her and was sitting here now as though it was a usual thing to do.

Also Connie was going to the market in Wolsingham each week. Pearl could be left with Sarah and then she would bring back second-hand clothing which they would wash and she would unpick and make up into garments for Miss Hutton's shop.

Miss Hutton told Connie that some of the better-off farmers' wives had started coming to the shop more often to see what she had and that one was going to a ball. Connie had bought new but discarded shiny blue material on the market. Somebody's house had been cleared and there was a bolt of this cloth which Connie proudly took to Miss Hutton because a rich farmer's wife wanted a ball gown designing.

Connie made a sketch of the dress and Mrs Castle approved it and Miss Hutton thought that half the women of the area would envy her this apparently simple dress with a white underskirt and bodice which Connie's nimble fingers fashioned with expertise and deftness. Mrs Castle was thirty, had a beautiful figure and a lovely face, she was creamy-skinned and yellow-haired and blue suited her perfectly. She was tall enough to carry it off and she was, best of all Connie thought, an enthusiast and told Miss Butler that she was a genius.

'The best place to show anything off is a ball,' Miss Hutton said, having never been to one herself but Connie understood what she meant. Miss Hutton paid for the material which Connie had bought, and then they went halves on the profits, Connie for making it and Miss Hutton for selling it. Mr and Mrs Castle would be staying over in Darlington with friends for two nights and no doubt everybody would find out where she had had the dress made. Connie was ecstatic.

Sarah was worried about going 'to do', as they called it, for old Mr Butler though she didn't say so. She didn't know him but she had heard stern things said of him and she didn't like to say to Connie that she was scared because it would have been daft but she was. Pearl went with her from the start and children made everything so much easier, Sarah thought. It moved the focus of your day.

She was happy enough to begin with and it was a lovely day, almost warm, but when they got into Wolsingham and near to the house, Pearl came close to Sarah's skirts as she had used to do with Connie, Sarah knew, and so Sarah picked her up and carried her, but just for a little while as she was now much too heavy to be carried for long.

It was not far into the morning when she got there but the old man was up and out in his vegetable patch at the back of the house. Sarah could see the door standing open and so she went to him and told him that she had come to clean the house and see to the fire. Would he like some tea when the kettle boiled?

He didn't speak but Sarah tried not to mind and remembered her upbringing. She had met plenty of opposition in her thirteen years, including a dad who yelled at her and a grandfather of her own who had taken to spitting at her so she didn't think overly much of it but she and Pearl went into the house.

Sarah put on the fire and heated water for tea. Then she poured water into the boiler at the side and when it got hot she wiped the floors and surfaces and she began to clean. Pearl was a good help.

Sarah gave her a scrubbing brush and later, when Sarah made something to eat in the middle of the day, Pearl took a sandwich out to the garden for her grandfather.

Sarah tried to think of positive memories about her childhood but she remembered the mint in the black earth, the flowers, the potatoes and the cabbages, how it had been lost and she had been lost and then she blotted it all out. She did try to think about it but her mind was too afraid. She felt instinctively that the old man would not hurt her, he was just grumpy.

Sarah hadn't known it was such a wonderful place here or so big. And there was a greenhouse. He had been busy in the greenhouse. She didn't know much about such things but she liked what she saw and in the end she couldn't help exclaiming,

'It's so bonny here,' and the old man looked out across his land.

Pearl ran around the garden like a butterfly let out of an almost closed window. Sarah had thought the old man might object even though Pearl kept strictly to the paths and in sheer joy of being a small child she raced around the garden, pausing here and there in a patch of sunlight, and he watched her and Sarah thought that inwardly he rejoiced.

Pearl was too absorbed in what she was doing to notice the old man or think that he did not like her and she was not very old and had been taught that the people around her loved her. She had been uprooted from the only soil she knew and brought here and she was no relation to this old man and yet he saw the youth in her and stood rooted as she swooped and dived like a swallow.

'What are you growing?' Sarah asked, nodding at the greenhouse.

'Tomatoes.'

It was the very continuity that kept him there, she knew it. The going on of things mattered so much. It was his way of life and no doubt had been the way of life of his ancestors for hundreds of years. She could understand even if Connie found it hard, why he would not leave this place. In so many ways it was all he had but she did not doubt that he missed his wife and wished that she could have been there or that he could have followed her to a new place but he did not know how to leave.

She went after him into the greenhouse. The tomato plants

were two feet high and smelled very strange and warm. The old man kept going and watering them. The fruit was large and dark red. He picked and handed her a tomato. It tasted better than anything she had ever eaten before.

Silently he went on with his work, the black soil colouring his hands, and there was something almost holy about it, Sarah thought, and she remembered how her own grandfather had turned weird and he had died when she had needed him so much and her eyes misted until she remembered that she must look to Pearl and she could see the little child running and running around and around as though she had never been let loose in such a good place before.

'Does she speak English?' he asked abruptly.

'Sometimes but she is shy and doesn't know you very well yet.'

He knew what Sarah meant, she thought, that he was frightening and very old to a little girl, even if he didn't speak to her, but he just went on with his gardening and said nothing.

As they talked Pearl came to an abrupt halt, finally out of breath, and she walked slowly across to the greenhouse and then she said, distinctly,

'Grandfather, I need you to come out here with me,' and so the old man, as if magically transformed, took the fingers that she extended to him and followed her into the part of the garden where she showed him her favourite flowers.

Sarah let herself remember her mother's father after that but it was not easy. He had been a lovely man, so she thought, and then something had gone wrong in his head and after that he was changed and wandered the streets at night, neglecting his house and garden and looking for something but nobody knew what. He had been all she had and after he died from the cold when he stayed out overnight, probably not knowing how to get home, she had nobody, her parents having been long since gone from her.

When Mr and Mrs Adams had taken her in she had thought that she was in luck. They were godly people apparently though she knew nothing about churches other than the outside of them. Her grandfather never went and so neither did she. There was nobody else so when he died she was glad to be taken to the big house in Wolsingham but the joy did not last long.

Mrs Adams told her what she must do and it started early in the morning when she had to get up and light the kitchen fire so that there was tea. She must prepare breakfast for the family though it was never anything more than porridge for the boys but they fought across the table and since they ate separately from their parents there was nobody to see to them. Mr and Mrs Adams had toast and tea except that now and then they had bacon and eggs and Sarah wished she had been offered even just a little of this. She had porridge if the boys left any.

Sarah must empty the chamber pots and clean the bedrooms. There was the washing to do and the ironing and there was dusting and she must peel potatoes and put various meals into the oven and since she knew very little of such things Mrs Adams complained that the meat was tough and the vegetables were soggy and that her rice pudding was grit hard.

She slept in the attic. That was the worst thing of all. They had six good bedrooms on the floor below but she slept in the attic which she shared with a small family of rats. She liked the rats. They had become her nearest companions and she shared the little food she had with them.

She kept all the crumbs, put them into the only handkerchief she owned and anything else she could at night so that Mr and Mrs Rat and their one offspring – why they only had the one

Sarah didn't like to enquire – could share out the goodies such as they were.

The attic was stifling in hot weather and freezing the rest of the time and the roof leaked so that sometimes it was rather damp though to be fair never in the bed since Sarah pushed it away from the wet spots, it being thin and light. When things got the better of her in the end her only regret was the rat family though she did sneak several pieces of bread and cheese into the attic room before she left.

Twenty-One

Sarah told Connie and Dom how the old man had behaved with Pearl and although they were pleased they didn't think it meant he would give in and come up here, he was too stubborn for that. Connie would have called in to see him more often but Sarah was still finding her place there and Connie didn't want to get in the way. Also she wasn't happy at leaving her grandmother. In the end she said to Dom, for about the fifth time because he was sulky and obviously resented it, that he must stay with their grandmother while Sarah was with their grandfather and she was in Miss Hutton's shop sorting out the new clothes which women had begun to order. This made the majority of their money.

He said nothing.

'Does that mean you will or you won't?' Connie said. 'Don't stand there twisting your face, you have to do something useful surely.'

'I don't think that looking after old people is really my job.'

'Then what do you suggest? You aren't pulling your weight around here. You and Sid spend all your time away from the house and I know it's very useful with the rabbits and pigeons but it doesn't take that much time. It means one of us has to stay here when we need to be somewhere else.'

'Grandmother calls me Michael,' he said.

Connie stared at him.

'She doesn't know who I am.' He looked away beyond her.

'I think she wants you to be him.'

'I'm nothing like him,' Dom said, in desperation, she knew. 'I don't look like him or think like him. I am a foreigner, a real foreigner, I'm not Michael the local boy come back. I'm not a failed clergyman turned doctor and I'm certainly no nurse.'

'You think you're warrior boy.'

'I think my natural ancestors were.'

'Dom, your natural ancestors came from here and were farmers and lead miners.'

'I wasn't brought up here, I don't belong. I don't want to belong. I want to go back home. I miss it. I miss the people and the ways and the food and everything about it, this place is little and narrow-minded and I am the warrior, it's what I was brought up to be and always will be.'

'There are lots of narrow-minded people in Japan.'

'Most of them are outsiders and do-gooders who think they know better. My God, what arrogance.'

'You're the one who's arrogant,' she said.

He stormed out. Dom was the opposite of the natural door slammer, Connie thought, he flung open the doors and left them so she had to go around closing them after him. She thought it might have been easier had there been boys his age around them but there was nobody and in any case he would stand out like a sore thumb. He was as unlike the country lads here as anybody possibly could be.

The odds of him making friends didn't exist. He was too much of everything, too clever, too learned, too beautiful, too canny, too well schooled. He had been playful when his father was alive but that had almost gone, she thought, and who could blame him? Even his clothes were different. To be fair lads here wore dark colours for practicality's sake but they did not wear them like a gentleman.

Mickey had been a gentleman in how he treated other people but Dom was deft and meticulous and graceful. He was a thousand years old in so many ways and would never have been like that had he been brought up here. And now he was stuck in a place he was beginning to hate and she didn't know what to do. She was not happy, she could not be happy without her parents, but she was learning to like the place, and she liked her grandmother and even the old man, disagreeable as he was, she was learning to love because he had acknowledged the little sister she loved so very much.

One of the most important things about what had happened here was that Pearl had started speaking English every day and it was so well pronounced, so well put together. Their mother had taught them all about sentence construction and how different languages had different tenses and strange origins.

Dom was only gone for an hour. He was not the person to sulk for long.

'All right,' he said when he came back. 'When one of you isn't here I will stay with the old woman but it means that you will have to take Leo as well as Pearl. I can't expect him to sit all day like that at his age.'

So by solving one problem, Connie thought with a sigh, they had created another. Leo would not be happy at Miss Hutton's shop, he was too much of a boy for that, so they decided that Sarah would take Leo to his grandfather's and she would take Pearl to the shop and they would see how that worked.

'And you will have to feed her,' Connie insisted to her brother.

Flo was a problem. She didn't like rice or fish. She was happier on the diet she had always had but it included a lot of things which Connie didn't approve of like cake and cream and sweet biscuits and what Flo called 'proper Sunday dinner' which was lamb or pork with various potatoes and vegetables. Connie had had to learn to make Yorkshire puddings and gravy and stuff like apple pie and custard which she loathed.

Sarah was the only one who wolfed down her Sunday dinner with relish and she liked her fish cooked and her rice with sugar and milk. It was a bit like running a third-class hotel, Connie thought.

It was strange, Dom thought, that he was the only person his grandmother didn't know or was it because she didn't want to? He had the feeling that all these years she had been waiting for her son to come home. It would never have mattered to her whether her son took his children or the woman she despised away, she just wanted him back and she had somehow made Dom into him. He thought Connie was much more like their father than he was.

He was like his mother, he moved well and fast, he was quick-silver. He and Mickey had taught Connie how to defend herself but it had taken quite a while for her to catch on. She was not nimble, she had to think about it before she moved, whereas a good warrior did not need to think and used stillness and movement with grace.

His sister was very beautiful but she was not graceful. It was like she was the dog and he was the cat. Also he had tried to teach her how to use weapons and she was clumsy. Unlike the person who could sew and cook, she was not a natural at such things. Her dancing was not as good as her mother's and she could not hold a tune or play a musical instrument.

He thought it was probably just as well that they had different skills and ideas. He made money with hunting and Connie with sewing.

The first day that Dom was left with his grandmother after this he determined to do better, he moved her bed into the sunshine so that she could see out of the windows. He gave her buttered toast and tea and cut up the bread into triangles. She hadn't seen that done before and smiled over it. Also he read to her. It was something he loved doing anyway and as Leo had gone down to the village with Connie and Sarah there was nobody getting under his feet, as his grandmother called it.

Dom now went to see Mrs Whitty occasionally because Connie didn't bring the right books for him and anyway he wanted to choose his own and so he was brave among the various women of the area and she had given him copies of *The Three Musketeers*, *Robinson Crusoe*, various works by Charles Dickens, Jane Austen which he thought clever but a bit soppy and several books by people who were called Brontë. There was also quite a lot of poetry and so he read his grandmother to sleep in the afternoons. He had a good memory and introduced her to all the haiku he could remember but also English poets. He thought it was the sound of his voice rather than the stories which she liked.

Sometimes when he thought she was asleep he would find her smiling at him and remembering his father, he knew. If it kept her happy then he could put up with it, even though she did not remember his name.

As the weather grew hot in August he became restless and would carry her outside, wrapped in a big rug, and take out one of the armchairs and sit her down while he worked on the garden. He was eighteen now and felt even more like a man than he had done before and wanted to go out and do bold things and here he was stuck with his grandmother, almost like an old person.

He didn't like gardening but it had to be done because they needed food and he was in charge of supplying it. He was the one who always went to see Mrs Rizzi and took the rabbits and fish but also now that Connie made money they could afford to pay Mrs Rizzi for her homemade pasta, for cheese since they had begun eating some dairy, for milk and eggs and salt and sugar and flour.

It wasn't a good day for gardening but by this time his grandmother could get up and dress herself. He would sit her by the kitchen stove if it was raining or dull and they would talk. Mostly it was her reminiscing about how wonderful life had been before Michael had left 'with that woman'. There was no point in his protesting that Rosa had been his mother as his grandmother sometimes got very mixed up and couldn't tell one person from another. She was failing mentally and physically and she told him the same stories over and over again. She loved telling them and she did not remember what had happened to her even weeks ago.

She did tell him about her childhood and he found it interesting though it was so far from what his and Connie's childhood had been that he found a great deal of it puzzling. He got very bored of his grandmother and then felt guilty for doing so. Before coming here he had not had much to do with old people, he had avoided them as much as possible, left his father to deal with them when they weren't well and he thought his father had understood.

It was when he was on his own like this that Mr Whitty called. Dom knew his wife and who the man was but he was surprised to greet him at the front door.

It was raining when Mr Whitty called. He introduced himself and asked if he could come in. Dom let him through the door and introduced him to Grandmother, as she didn't look as though she had any recollection of this man.

Dom was suspicious and worried. He had not forgotten that he had stolen money from Mr Adams but had tried to put it from his mind and had stopped thinking that anything would be done. Now he wanted to panic and run from the house. Mr Whitty looked all around and then asked how many people were living here. Dom told him about Sarah and Connie and the children and how his grandfather was still at the house in Wolsingham. Then Mr Whitty wanted to know how they paid for things and Dom told him about Connie at Miss Hutton's shop and the work they did. Dom was upset with Mr Whitty by then and was learning to dislike him and his questions.

'And I understand that you shoot and fish? Do you have permission for such things?'

'I don't shoot. I've never held a gun in my hands. I hunt for rabbits up on the fell with my polecat and the only fishing I do is with him and my hands in the stream at the bottom of the hill. I deal with Mrs Rizzi, we barter and then we pay for basic goods out of Connie's money that she earns. Sarah goes to see to Grandfather. They take the children with them when they go to Wolsingham and I stay here and see to Grandmother, at least at the moment.' Would Mr Whitty think him less manly for doing such work, he wondered.

'I took some books from the empty houses when we first got here and I had nothing to read but they had been discarded so I didn't think I was doing anything wrong and also I borrow some from your wife's library. In some of the houses we found old pans and crockery and such and nobody seemed to want it so we use it. Was any of this the wrong thing to do?'

'Certainly not,' Mr Whitty said, 'but people here are suspicious of newcomers and although your father's family may have lived here for hundreds of years you are very different.'

'We had nowhere to go. This village was completely abandoned.'

'What do you do for water?'

'There is a well out the back, it was a huge find because before that I had to carry it from the stream and Connie had to boil it in case there were things in it so this is much better now.'

Mr Whitty looked out at the back garden.

'You've made quite a lot of progress here,' he said.

'Do you know much about gardens?'

'No, but I can see that you've already made a difference to this place. It must have been completely overgrown when you got here.'

Mr Whitty somehow got Dom to talk about his parents and what they had done and for the first time somebody did not think they had made ghastly mistakes. It was so nice to be able to be open without worrying about giving offence or seeming strange. Mr Whitty even said that if Dom had any problems he couldn't solve or any worries he was to come to the police house and Mr Whitty would help him.

Dom hadn't known how much he missed his father until Mr Whitty left. He found that his throat ached with unshed tears. He also resented that Mr Whitty thought of him as unacceptable though it was only what other people had thought since they had come here. Why did it have to be this way, why was everything so hard and alien? He longed to run after Mr Whitty and beg to be taken in and to behave like the small child he had not been in so very long that it felt like a hundred years. Also he was scared.

He thought Mr Whitty hadn't mentioned the stolen money on purpose though why he would have done so Dom had no idea. Was he just pretending to be friendly?

Mr Whitty went home and sang Dom's praises to his wife.

'Oh, Norah what a grand young man he is. If I'd ever been able to have a son I would have wanted one like him.'

Although they wished they had had children it was not a closed subject between them. They could talk freely over the fire about Dominic Butler.

'He's very easy on the eye,' Mrs Whitty said with a twinkle in hers, 'it lightens the afternoons for all of us when he gives us the benefit of his company,' and Mr Whitty laughed and said he hadn't noticed, just that Dom was so careful and caring of his grandma though it was obvious that he would rather be out doing other things as any lad would. Caring was a thing for women to do.

After that Dom missed his father more and more. He had never felt quite as orphaned as he did now. He was having to be the only man here and it got harder and harder somehow. Leo was too young to be an accomplice in anything and the girls got on so well together that he felt left out, something he had never experienced before.

They would spend hours in the evenings sitting over the kitchen table with Grandma ensconced in an armchair and they would sew and knit and talk and arrange and rearrange patterns and then pin and cut out cloth and stick pins in again somehow and talk about colours and styles and ideas and it was another land to Dom, one which had nothing to do with him.

He ended up dealing with the children and trying to amuse them but the days would soon be shortening and he felt there was a great deal to do in the garden and it was hard to find enough time.

Finally he got to the point where he wanted to have a little bit of freedom so he announced one fine evening that he would walk down and see his grandfather and when Connie suggested he should take Leo with him Dom refused. For once she understood and didn't push her point. He left Sid with Leo so that Leo was reasonably happy at the rest of the company being female and then he set off and straight away he felt better.

He didn't know how the old man would receive him. They rarely had a conversation that wasn't cantankerous. It didn't take him long to get down the double bank to the village. The countryside was green and white and the lambs were big now, dancing around, and the grass was growing long in the little square fields. It was, Dom admitted to himself for the first time, a beautiful place. The grey stone houses were grouped around the river and when he got to the far edge of the village and to his grandfather's place the doors were open to the evening sunshine.

Dom politely knocked on the door but there was no answer. Inside all was as it should be because Sarah was keeping it so. The shadows were long and he could see the back door open as well as the front door and his grandfather was sitting like a king in his castle. This was what a well-tended garden looked like. Dom thought it was the neatest thing that he had ever seen. His grandfather was a farmer basically, Dom thought. There were rows of neat fronded carrots, tall tops of green and white leeks, potatoes and onions and cauliflowers. There was not a weed anywhere and the soil was rich and black and everything was so orderly. There was a big greenhouse further over and little huts

here and there for various reasons which Dom had no comprehension of and there his grandfather sat on a wooden bench,
smoking his pipe and surveying his kingdom.

There were also small raised enclosed beds with glass covers –
were they called cloches, Dom thought – and inside these also
stuff grew.

In another area various-coloured flowers were blooming. It
made Dom think of his mother. His father had had nothing of
the farmer about him. He couldn't have grown anything but then
perhaps he had wanted to leave that part of his life to Rosa so
that she could shine. He was a great one for letting other people
bloom. Had his grandfather been like that at one time and was
it just the years and disappointment which had turned him sour
and gruff? Perhaps everybody ended up like that.

His grandfather was in his shirtsleeves and was wearing a dis-
reputable hat, half dozing in the warm sunlight so that Dom
paused and then almost went away except that his grandfather
either saw or heard his soft footsteps and said,

'You,' in a most unwelcoming tone so that Dom did not go
any further forward. 'There's nowt for you here.'

Dom knew it was his dead son he was hitting out at. He didn't
want to care about anybody new. Why would he when his best
efforts had gone so wrong? His son was dead, his wife was being
looked after somewhere else. His broken-down house and his
few acres were all he had left.

There was a long silence. Dom walked around the garden on
his own and ventured into the greenhouse but he didn't know
what the plants were. Huge round-headed flowers. It was very
warm in there. He heard his grandfather come up behind him.
Warriors always knew when somebody was at their backs and
Dom was no exception but he didn't acknowledge it.

'Chrysanthemums,' his grandfather said.

'What?'

Then Dom did turn around. His grandfather was looking at the plant pots and gesturing with his pipe.

'You take them in in the late autumn and they grow from this time and in late summer or early autumn the next year you get a big show of them. Some of them go outside and they come in lovely colours like this, yellow and white and lilac and purple. They have great big round generous heads on them. My father used to grow them by the score and I used to put them into shows but I haven't the patience any longer.'

He went into the other greenhouse and there he showed Dom tomato plants and cucumbers.

'Your father never took any interest,' his grandfather said. 'What did he like doing?'

Dom had to think, he was so surprised at the question.

'He liked going away to different areas to help people, not just with their health but they liked to talk to him and he enjoyed telling stories. He was no use with plants. It was my mother who had the many talents. I think he should really have been a doctor had he stayed here.'

'He could never have done that. We couldn't have afforded it.'

'He did it in Tokyo in his own way. He helped a great many people.'

'Why did he not come home?'

His grandfather's pain was palpable, Dom thought, and he could not say 'Because you would not accept my mother.' He couldn't think of anything to say and in the end settled for,

'He thought he could do good there and he did.'

'So far away. A lot of people leave because they can't make a future here, they go to new lands. Some prosper, some die and sometimes they come back in defeat,' his grandfather said. 'I had family who went to Canada and some to Australia.'

'Did you never want to leave?'

'There was no money, I had a younger brother and his wife to feed and my parents were both ill and died while I was young. I had to pay for the medical attention and then their funerals. I hadn't been married long, your father was a little boy. I didn't think of leaving but also there was this land. I didn't want to leave this place I cared about so much.'

Dom wanted to say that he felt like that about Japan but he didn't think his grandfather would have understood so he stayed silent and they walked up the garden paths together. And still he felt like the older man here, was he always to be the parent? There seemed to be no comfort for him anywhere.

The old man didn't even ask after his own wife. Was he so entirely defeated, Dom wondered. Was this place all he had left? It seemed pitiful somehow that this small space should be his realm. And yet it brought him comfort. Dom had no comfort and wondered whether he would ever do so.

This place meant nothing to him, it was too tiny, too tight, too ingrained, too old. He felt that people had held this place so close to them for so long that it had begun to suffocate them. They needed to strike out as his father had done and not be tied to such a poor thing as this.

Was it that his grandfather had longed to get away and yet could not? Did he envy his son? And now Dom thought that in some ways he was tied to Japan as the old man was tied here. They were both destined to be stuck somewhere that perhaps they would not have chosen.

It was one thing among many that his father had conquered

and he had found such a love that Dom envied him. Would he ever find a woman like Rosa?

Without encouragement he sat down beside his grandfather on the bench and talked of the people his father knew and the things that he had done and although his grandfather said nothing Dom knew his ears were longing for the sound of Mickey's voice, his sweet north country lilt which Dom could not imitate and would not have done had he been able out of respect for his father's unique and beloved self.

He told of his father's wanderings in a land he knew little of to aid the people who had needed him, of those he had rescued from flood and famine. Of those he had taught to trust him and go forward. That was what a missionary should be like, good and true and humble.

He made people laugh. Dom never knew how he did that, just that he was like a sunbeam, a moonbeam, a shining star. He gave himself away each and every hour, each and every day. And yet somehow Dom had no need to be jealous of those who consumed his father's days. The more his father gave the more his family and those he cared for prospered and grew rich in his love.

He didn't know what he had said but there came upon Joshua's face a look of contentment such as Dom didn't think he had seen before, perhaps it had never been there. His grandfather said nothing but when Dom stopped his grandfather waved his pipe in front of him as though to enthuse and so Dom talked of his home and the people his parents had loved.

He did not talk much of his mother for he sensed it would sit badly here and he didn't want to disrupt the serene look on his grandfather's face and in the end it was only when the evening grew late, and dusk and then darkness came down upon them, that he went and left his grandfather still sitting on the bench, the red glow of his pipe having long since gone out amidst the beginnings of his late summer garden.

Dom was glad to have the three miles to walk. It made space between the garden and his grandfather and the night and how he was reluctant to go back to the responsibilities which life had pushed onto him.

It was very late when he got there and he thought that they had all gone to bed but Connie met him in the hall.

'Is he all right?' she said.

'Yes, I think so.'

'And you?'

'I wish I could go home.'

Where was home? Was it where you were happy? Was it where your parents chose for you or could it be some place in the future that you could look towards and hope for? Dom didn't know. He couldn't sleep. He lay awake hour after hour.

He got up in the middle of the night and left. He didn't intend to leave, he just couldn't stop walking.

Twenty-Two

Connie was concerned from the very first. It wasn't like her brother to go off without saying anything or without breakfast or without Sid but there Sid was with Leo. She waited for him to come home presuming he would be there for the midday meal but he wasn't and when he didn't return for dinner she was even more worried. She was now the one lying awake, listening for his footsteps, for the sound of the door but nothing happened.

He didn't turn up the following day or the one after that. Connie went into the garden where the weeds were already trying to take over and she cried. He was his father after all, he had run away, or like his mother who had known no home before she met his father. Surely without money or food he would come back to her.

She had checked the food and the money and was dismayed. He had taken half of what money they had and it made her think that he had gone for good. She could not accept it. He would not do such a thing, they were family, closer than most siblings. Twins were different and yet she had not suspected that this would happen, had no idea that Dom was planning to run away. Had he planned it or had he just gone and would possibly come home? It was something to cling to but she did not hold out a great deal of hope. He must have planned it to a certain extent or he would not have taken the money but then he liked carrying money on him as men did, she thought. She tried not to think that he had gone for good.

Also on a practical level it made life difficult. Somebody had to be there to see to the old lady. Between them she and Sarah had to try and share all the caring and the work. Connie was obliged to work, it was now their only form of income. No more pigeons, fish or rabbits so she had to pay for everything and one of them had to see to her grandfather three days a week and so she started taking work back to the Hilda House and there she tried to get everything right and not to wonder what on earth had happened but as she thought about it she saw that it would not do.

Dom had been attempting so many things that he didn't want to be involved in, she knew now, and there was a great space where somebody else ought to have been. The hollow where their parents were not, seemed to get bigger and bigger. Now but for Sarah she would have been here all alone with two children. And responsible for two old people who were getting more frail and less easy.

Dom's leaving had confused their grandmother and she cried and would not eat and asked for her son, for Michael, over and over again until Connie thought Dom pitiless and selfish for what he had done. At night their grandmother began to get up and wander about the house, calling his name and then falling asleep during the day as her body tried to make up for lost time.

And she wanted to go home. She wanted to go home to her mother, she wanted to go home to her son, she had to get home. She could not stay here, she was needed, Michael needed her and the fire was going out and the food was not cooked and the housework was not done. There was dust, she could see cobwebs everywhere. She would get out of bed and look for her duster and her sweeping brush.

It got worse. She began to run away so that Connie was always running after her as her grandmother tried so hard to get back home. Connie began to question how sensible she had been to bring her grandmother away from everything she knew, from her house and her husband, her belongings around her, the place she had lived for forty years. Everything was gone.

Her grandmother turned night into day and day into night. She was by now totally unpredictable and would run away into the darkness which meant that Connie got very little sleep.

Sarah therefore had far too much to do, as she was still going to look after the old man. She now collected Connie's work from Miss Hutton and took it back and together they managed the children. They tried to rescue the garden but the work was heavy and Pearl cried a lot during these times and gradually became afraid of the old lady. She could not bear to be in the same room. Leo kept close to Sid and out of everybody's way although he did not venture far. To Connie his gaze seemed always on the horizon as though his longing would make Dom return.

It took Dom three days to cover the thirty miles to Newcastle because he tried and tried to turn back. It was like he was a new person, so grief-stricken and lost that his feet carried onward even though he would have given almost anything to go back to the Hilda House and his family. His mind wouldn't listen to him. He tried telling himself that Connie could not do without him, that he was betraying her in the worst possible sense, but there was a part of him that was so angry at his circumstances that he walked on.

From time to time he stopped and asked for food and water and was not refused. He slept in barns in the countryside and when he reached Newcastle he felt much better. He liked it, the busy streets and the quiet alleyways.

He already felt better in one way. He had hated the country, he told himself. It could have been just that he missed his parents but when he remembered the role he played he felt as though it was that of a woman except the parts when he went hunting with Sid. He missed Sid. He knew it was wrong of him to miss Sid more than the others but he had been starting to resent Connie for how capable she was, as though she was the man of the family. His mother had never done that, she had always had what he considered to be the secondary role, but Connie ordered everybody about and had no respect for him.

He was glad he had left. No more fields for him. He liked Newcastle from the moment he got there as he had liked his home somehow. He did not remember much of Liverpool, just docking there and then the walk to the station. Indeed he had been glad to leave it but now he would not go back to the country and Connie lording it over him and how the Hilda House was full of women. He was tired of it.

He slept on the streets, it was much harder than any way he had slept before but he liked the way that nobody asked him to do anything, that nobody spoke to him. He carried his money carefully, he was aware there were people who would steal from him and judging by the rags many people had nothing. He did not share the food he bought though hungry children watched him eat, hoping he would drop a crumb or two or offer them a little. There were so many of them that he turned away. His money would only last so long and then he was not quite sure what he would do but one thing was certain. He would not go back.

The weather was dry so it was no great hardship to have nowhere to go and he felt gleeful that he had escaped and then he began to feel guilt that he had left Connie to cope without him. They had never been apart and he was sure that she wished him home, missed him, longed for him to come back, but he was too stubborn to return to the life that he had come to dislike so much. He missed Leo but it was quite good not to have the younger boy around, always wanting him to do things he didn't necessarily want to do, but he also wished he could have brought Leo with him. He had left him to the women and that was unfair in a lot of ways. He felt as though he had deserted Leo but then Leo was a survivor, they were all survivors. They had got this far and they could do all kinds of different things. Connie was good at most things, so capable. He thought she would worry a little but would guess that he had had enough and would not return.

Just as he was starting to enjoy his freedom his money began to run out and short of stealing and risking being caught by the law he eyed the windows of cake and pie shops eagerly and one shop in particular where they had a bakery at the back he thought wistfully about when his stomach was full. He had not considered how much food he needed just to get through the day.

Sometimes fruit fell from stalls onto the floor but the younger children were quicker than he was and grabbed an apple, even fought for it. Dom thought it was beneath his dignity to fight for a piece of fruit.

Then it began to rain, hard and cold, and now he was hungry all the time, cold all the time. Sheltering under the bridges meant joining a lot of other folk who had the same problem and the gilt began to run off his ideas of what the city was like.

He began to think almost wistfully of Connie and the Hilda House but he did not go anywhere. Also having nothing to do for the first time in his life did not suit him. He was tired of walking about and seeing the same buildings. The only really lively place was the docks and here he liked how the ships came and went. He thought of the ships he had come on and how he would have enjoyed helping on those ships. He rather envied the men who ran them and he imagined how he might be able to join a ship here and go somewhere, anywhere, it didn't really matter. He was enthused. He was young and fit and he felt sure he could use his brains and his fitness to work.

He listened to some men on the quayside talking and they were sailors. They had come off a ship that had recently docked. Dom steeled himself and asked them where they were bound next and it turned out to be America.

'Could I be taken on, do you think?'

The men stared at him and then one who was friendly grinned at him.

'Why would you want to do that, lad?'

'For food and somewhere to sleep. I've been on ships before.' He thought he knew quite a lot about how they worked and didn't tell them that he had been nothing but a passenger.

The man nodded at a big man who was standing on the deck and told Dom that he was the captain and he decided who would be taken on and who would not. They were leaving the following day. Dom turned it over and over in his mind and then, knowing that the ship would go with the tide, he went on board, quite enjoying the feel of the boards under his feet, and he approached the captain.

The man merely nodded when Dom said he had been on ships before and then he became part of the ship's company. Now he had found what he wanted, now he would have a place here and make friends and he would go to a new country where people were welcomed and taken in unlike this place that he had learned to hate. He would go to New York and make his fortune as many a man had before him.

Connie was starting to believe that her brother would not come back. A week went by during which she watched and listened for him every minute of every day. She lay awake at night and was hopeful but gradually that hope began to fade. They had never been apart before and she could not believe that he would not come home, there must have been a good reason for him to absent himself. She knew she had become impatient with him and scolded herself but she had not imagined he would take it like that. She had not understood how unhappy he had become. She had thought they would be together always.

The first week turned into a second and the second into a third and still he did not come back and she had to face up to the fact he might not be there for some while, if ever. It was the hardest thing she had had to bear since her parents had died and it sat on top of those losses and made everything worse. She also felt now that she had no protection but her own wits and the burdens were growing.

She was concerned about Sarah. She was much too young to have to bear all these things. The old man kept asking about Dom and Sarah did not tell him that the boy had left. He had always spoken of him as useless and that he didn't matter. Connie knew it was his son he wanted to hurt and since he could no longer blame him he chose the only other man and talked bitterly of Dom not going to see him. On the other hand she didn't want to have to tell him that Dom, like his father, had found the situation too difficult and had left.

Would it make the old man feel better or worse that he was apparently the only man in three generations who had stayed to take care of his responsibilities?

Slowly the early autumn weather took over the countryside and at the Hilda House the weeds grew in profusion among the vegetables and flowers until it was difficult to distinguish one from another, so very tall and green as everything was.

Leo altered after Dom left. Right from the beginning he seemed to know that Dom was not coming back and worse still that Dom had not taken him with him. He was now the one lad in the place and he resented it from the beginning.

Leo took Sid to bed with him every night and it was the only comfort he seemed to find, Connie thought. She felt so sorry for her little brother and wished very hard not just that Dom had not gone but if he couldn't have done otherwise he should have taken Leo with him. They had a bond such as she did not have with him and Leo was a very unhappy boy.

He seemed to take against Sarah too and didn't speak to her. Connie saw the rift between them and knew what had caused it and in a way she didn't blame him, he missed his brother as they had never been apart before and he was at the age where he did not like being the only boy around. He was slightly jealous that Pearl was a favourite with Sarah and she talked down to him as though he was the small child that his sister was. There was nothing Connie felt she could do about Dom's disappearance. She didn't want to upset Leo but she couldn't have Sarah offended so she had to ask him not to be so rude but he stormed off into the garden and when she looked later he was not there.

She didn't believe he would stay away long. He was not old enough to get by on his own. She was inclined to curse Dom for what he had done but she couldn't blame him. In so many ways it was all just too hard. Had he gone back to Tokyo? She had the feeling that he would. It was his home, he had loved it as Connie felt she had not. After her parents died she saw that it was her situation and not the place. Perhaps she would never feel at home anywhere.

She had felt a slight affinity for her grandfather's house but that had gone too. She felt trapped and unloved and overburdened and exhausted.

She waited all afternoon and evening for Leo to come back on the first day but he didn't and then she panicked. What if something had happened to him? What if he had thought he should go after Dom and had got lost? Dom was probably out of the country, being useful on some ship and making his way slowly home. She wanted to wish him well but she missed him so much that it was impossible.

She had the idea that Leo had gone to his grandfather's though she didn't understand how that would work out. Leo was almost formed as a person and she wasn't sure that her grandfather would want anything further to do with him. It was the only sensible explanation she could think of.

She would have liked to ask Sarah when she cleaned to find out if Leo was there but Sarah and the old man weren't getting on very well at the moment, he seemed to turn against everybody after a while, so she left Sarah to take care of Grandmother as best she might – it wasn't really much of a choice, she was aware – and she took Pearl with her walking down to the dale.

Pearl was quite eager to see the old man as she had finally warmed up to him. Connie was just relieved that somebody got on with the old man though when he asked about her grandmother she wasn't sure what she would say.

It was a fine day and therefore when she reached the house she could see her grandfather in the garden.

'Is Leo here?' was her first question as she looked around her in panic.

'What?'

He so obviously wasn't.

'The boy.'

'Never seen any boy,' her grandfather said, going back to his vegetable patch.

It was so neat. Connie was comparing it with what was becoming a wilderness at the back of the Hilda House and wished her grandfather would agree to leave here and go up with her so that they could all live together. Then she reminded herself that in a very short time both lads had run away and she was now worried so much about Leo that she felt sick.

Pearl had obviously taken to the old man and he to her though Connie had no idea why. She was as unlike this old man as any child possibly could be and of course she was no relation to him. She did speak English now but was not a talkative child except with him or with Sarah for some reason and occasionally with the women in Wolsingham who paid her special attention. Her circumstances had been so difficult that Connie had doubted she ever would be able to do more but that was one fear being put to rest and at least she stayed by his side and when Connie decided to see Mr Whitty she gave Pearl the chance to go with her but the little girl shook her head.

'Can she stay here? I will not be long,' Connie said.

'Where are you going?'

Her grandfather really hadn't taken in what she had told him. Was that his age or was it just that he was not interested?

'Where's the lad? Where's Michael?'

Connie didn't reply. She left the garden and went off to Mr Whitty's house, hoping that somebody might have seen Leo or Dom. Mr Whitty did not look pleased to see her but then she and her family were causing him trouble and she had the feeling that Mr Whitty liked an easy life. He frowned but he did ask her to sit down and when she told him the story he frowned in a different way as though he was considering what to do and then he said,

'They went off together?'

'Dom left almost three weeks ago and Leo has been gone one night but he's ten and I'm worried about him.'

Mr Whitty looked gravely at her.

'I don't think you need to worry for your twin, he seems more than capable of looking after himself and young men get rest-less, but as for the child, that's different. I'll ask all around the village and see what I can do. He probably hasn't gone far.'

'I think he is trying to get to Dom, to follow him, and I don't know what to do.'

The sympathy made Connie want to cry and she struggled and Mr Whitty saw it and promised he would do everything he could to find Leo.

Connie was somewhat comforted though she tried to tell her-self that somehow she would earn enough money to take them home to Japan when Leo came back. She regretted now that she had wrongly believed she could come here and have some kind of family who would support them. How laughable, she thought. Instead of that she now had two old people who were like sponges. They soaked up all her time and energy, money and food while she got so little back. What she could do in Japan she could not imagine. She didn't seem to fit anywhere.

Downhearted, Connie went back to her grandfather's garden.

'How is Flo?' the old man asked.

She didn't know whether to tell him how she was in case it upset him or to let him know so that he might offer to see her or stay with her.

'She forgets things.'

'Nothing new there then,' he said. He seemed happy to accept this so perhaps he needed to hear that he didn't have to do anything.

She and Pearl went back up the hills to where thankfully her grandmother had slept most of the day. Sarah was keen to know about the state of the house but Connie had to say that she had not been inside so the following day Sarah went and Pearl seemed happy to stay with Connie.

Connie heard nothing more from Mr Whitty. She hoped that he would turn up something but after a week she got used to being in a blind panic about what had happened. She didn't know what else to do.

Twenty-Three

Thomas had almost finished his morning surgery and was about to start his home visits when he saw a carriage and four grey horses pull up in front of the house. He was astonished. Nobody in the dale had such a thing. The best he had was a pony and trap but this was an ornate vehicle, very old but shining and well kept.

As he listened there was a polite knocking on the door and when Ada answered it a young man told her that Mr Reginald had come to see Mrs Neville. Was she at home to callers?

Thomas trembled that Ada had never met such a thing before and would not know what to say. Ada seemed stunned but recovered quickly.

'Yes, sir. You had better come in. If you will just give me a minute.'

She whisked herself through the hall and Thomas stepped into it and she looked flustered and shot off into the dining room where his mother was reading the morning paper as usual.

Thomas took the squire into the sitting room and bade him good morning.

He had thought the squire might call long before this but his mother had said nothing after the gift of sherry and he had taken to imagining that neither his mother nor the squire had anything to gain by knowing one another better and he had put the matter from his mind. Now he was quite excited and could barely keep the smile from his face.

As Thomas made small talk with the squire Ada trembled before the mistress of the house.

'The squire is here, Mrs Neville.'

She looked up as though accusing Ada of making a joke.

'What?'

'The doctor is with him in the sitting room,' Ada continued, red-cheeked with excitement.

Mrs Neville stared and she also went first pink in the face and then pale.

Laura got up and looked at herself in the mirror. She thought she looked presentable and she could hardly keep the man waiting so she followed Thomas into the sitting room.

Moments later Thomas left the house though he would have given a good deal to stay and hear the conversation which was about to start in the sitting room.

'Madam,' the squire said and turned from the window, 'I know that it is far too early in the day for you to receive callers but I was so nervous about coming to see you that I could barely wait for breakfast. I do hope you aren't busy?'

Laura's tongue seemed to have vanished and her mouth had gone dry. She was only grateful that it was a fine morning and that Fiona had made sure the sitting room was all done before the missus, as they called her in private, got up from her breakfast and went in there.

There was no fire because the day was fine for autumn and the big doors were open to the garden. Laura always told herself that this house was not a patch on the house by the river in Durham where she had gone as a young bride and fallen in love with it, but the truth was that her lasting memory was of finding her husband when he had killed himself in his study. She thrust away the picture but it kept coming back. The turkey rug had been thrown out because the blood would not come off it. She had not even made sure that the room was made habitable again. She knew she would never go in it and she was glad not to be there so that she did not have to think about this every day.

Oswald, who did the gardens and looked after the doctor's horses, and was gallantly repairing the stables, was a farmer's son and knew everything there was to know about animals. His uncle worked up at the big house and therefore was head gardener for the squire and saw to the hothouses and Oswald had obviously taken in everything he was told because the doctor may not have been in the house for very long but Oswald spent most of his time digging the beds and tidying the paths so that now there was a myriad of flowers. It looked glorious that day in Laura's eyes.

Also she had ordered from Mr Smithers a table and chairs for under the big tree which spread shade. There was not much sun in the garden this early but it was warm and bees buzzed into the beech hedge. She sat the squire down and wondered what on earth she would say to him. Fortunately he spoke first.

'I wondered whether it might be possible for us to be friends,' he said having mentioned how beautiful the garden was and asking after her health. 'I suppose it is very unorthodox and that you are a city dweller and perhaps don't care to be friends with crusty old men who are at least twenty years your senior but the truth of it is that I have no one to talk to.

'I have thought long and hard about this and I do hope you are not insulted that it has taken me many months to come to this decision but I'm sure you understand that my wife has not been long gone from me and friendship with another woman seemed insulting to her at first. Now it doesn't and I am hoping so very much that you and I can be friends.'

Laura couldn't believe that he wanted to be friends with her. Socially she was well below him but then he had been good friends with Harry when younger so perhaps that meant something and yet the squire was admitting to loneliness and she felt the same though she now had women friends. In some ways it made her miss her husband more but she didn't like to say so.

'I need a woman of my class to talk to.'

There again she was not a woman of his class as she well knew but then she had married a well-loved and well-respected man so for all her humble beginnings she was a lady. In fact she remembered the last thing her father said to her on her wedding day was,

'Laura, you have always been, and always will be, a lady just like your mother. It isn't how much money or status we have, it's all to do with how we treat others and you are always kind and loving.'

Still she had very little idea of how the squire lived and was not sure what either of them would gain from the friendship but she was very willing to try.

She thought of him now and that her father had always been a gentleman, caring for others and doing his best in all ways, never saying anything bad of anyone though they had lived in a pit row and had very little spare cash.

Laura realized as the squire spoke to her that he must feel very solitary up at that big house with no children or grandchildren and nobody but the servants. It was a harsh grief that afflicted him and he needed someone to stem the flow of feelings, she knew that only too well.

They talked about books, which was all she knew they had

in common, and he told her how proud he had been to be a friend of Harry's when they were young. He told her the story of how he had wooed and won his wife and she told him of her childhood in Langley Park.

Ada brought coffee and newly made ginger biscuits at eleven. The squire took his leave at twelve. By then he had kissed Laura's hand and asked if he might see her again soon and she had agreed.

After he went Laura didn't move until lunch was announced at one when Thomas had returned from his calls and was ready to eat. Laura couldn't eat, she sat in glazed shock over her beef pie, potatoes and peas.

Thomas was dying to hear what had happened but didn't like to ask. However, he learned a great deal from Ada who gave him tea when he was in his surgery making notes on various cases. He was so pleased for his mother, she might have another life now, something she deserved.

Ada told Fiona privately in the kitchen that if the missus was to marry the squire she wanted to go up to the big house and lord it over the servants there and when he proposed she would ask the missus if they could both go with her. They both forgot at that point their loyalty to the doctor, they did not give him a single thought in their excitement.

Twenty-Four

Leo hadn't intended to run away, it was just that he awoke one morning and Sid wasn't there. Everybody else was still asleep. He searched the house and then he went outside and called Sid's name everywhere but he could not be found and Leo convinced himself that Sid had left to try to find Dom but where could Dom possibly have gone to, and why?

Leo couldn't make anything out. Mickey had rescued him and his sister after their parents died and taken them back to be part of the family and Rosa had treated them just like her own children. Mickey had taken to calling him Leo, it was a nickname.

It did occur to him now he was older that Mickey had not known Leo's parents all that well and if required he would make up stories about them so that they should always live with him in his head. Mickey would tuck him into bed at night and get him to close his eyes and he would conjure up the good times that Leo had had with his parents. His first love was Japan and the people.

Leo knew now that somewhere along the line Mickey had discerned that his children would have to go back to England and so Leo should learn to speak English and although Leo hadn't liked this at the time he had trusted his new father to look out for him in every possible respect. Meanwhile he wasn't sure how much he remembered of his birth parents and how much

Mickey had embroidered the stories so that he would always have such good thoughts of the village he came from and the way he had lived before he was taken to Tokyo.

He had been devastated at first but Mickey would wrap him in his arms and talk to him and his voice was so lilting. Leo had not heard that accent until he had come back here and it reminded him of the man who had taken him home, saved his life and told him how beloved he was every single day. He missed both sets of parents and then he had had to go thousands of miles and ended up in this place where nobody wanted him, nobody was kind to him, not even the nasty old man whom he was meant to call Grandfather as though somebody so horrible would have anything to do with him.

A big fight was going on inside him so that he would not forget either his first set of parents or his second. He missed them all. His own culture had completely gone now as if it had been swallowed up by this new place and these new people.

Grandmother had been all right at first but now she had gone all weird and scary and made Pearl cry. Grandmother was always yelling and shrieking and crying and accusing them of having taken her away from her mother and from her father and from her husband, which Leo knew was nonsense because it could not all be true.

She walked the floors at night so that he felt scared in case she came anywhere near to him and worst of all she was weird and odd and Leo had taken to wishing she would die. She cried all the time and Connie was so busy taking care of the dreadful old woman that often Sarah would tell him what to do and he didn't like Sarah, she was nasty and bossy and nothing to do with him. She was not family, she had pushed her way in here and made herself important when Leo had a feeling she was nobody at all.

Sid had been all he had left. He had considered going after Dom but it was too long now, Dom was probably on a ship so that he could go back home. Leo gave up on the search for Sid after three days. Connie had said she would help but she never did and when he told Sarah she said that Sid was just an animal and could take care of himself. Probably he had gone back to his family. Sarah was stupid.

Leo waited day after day but Sid did not come back and that was when Leo decided that he would find Dom. He carefully took quite a lot of money, waited until early morning and he too left.

He knew from what was said generally that Dom would not go back to Liverpool, he was a lot more likely to go Newcastle which was the nearest big place though not big and wonderful like Tokyo had been, Leo felt sure. But it seemed logical to him that Dom would make for the nearest port. He therefore walked to the railway station and got on the first train. He didn't ask any questions, that would have been suspicious. He walked tall and tried to sound confident and there were two platforms, one going south and one going north, so it didn't take a lot of working out. He got on the first north-going train and was in Newcastle by teatime

Newcastle was a lot bigger than Leo had thought it would be. The train came into the enormous station which had a big entrance hall with huge stone pillars. When he got beyond the station he had no idea how to get to the river but it was obvious that he must head downhill so as soon as he could he turned right and kept on going and therefore it was not long before he reached the quayside and what a scary place it was.

It was well on into the day by then and dark before the evening grew late. Leo didn't know what to do. There were a great many ships on the water but it occurred to him that Dom would be long gone and so he stood by the water for a while and after that he wondered how to go on. He very much wanted to be back with Connie even though he was convinced he would never see Dom or Sid again ever but it was too late to go anywhere.

The nights were growing cold. He hid in a corner down by a building where the trains went over the top with the railway arch high above the street just away from the immediacy of the river. He hoped that nobody could see him and it was shadowed. He had never been outside or alone at night and was so down-hearted he told himself how stupid he had been, whatever had he been thinking. He folded himself up as small as he could and waited for the dawn.

Twenty-Five

It was very odd, Laura Neville thought, that the squire should choose to be friends with her. At first after he had left and the initial euphoria had worn off a little she wanted to back off. Her husband had recently died. He was younger than the squire, even though the squire talked of them as being young men together. Harry had not been so much older than she was so the squire must have been in his late thirties when he knew Harry as a lad. Perhaps he had got mixed up about it, his memories were imperfect.

She did not want to love another man, did not feel as though she could, but she was excited at having attracted such a man whatever the reason. When she explained her fears to Thomas he said,

'Being friends with him seems to make you happy.'

It was true. Perhaps twice a week the squire came to see her and then he asked them both to go to dinner at his house that autumn.

The squire's home was wonderful to Laura's eyes, shabby but lovingly cared for. She had not expected other people to be there but he took her around and introduced her as his new friend. Laura was not used to being singled out in such a way and she enjoyed it.

She drank champagne and then dry white wine with fish and a good red wine with the meat and all around her people talked and listened to her and it was very respectful.

Thomas was happy that his mother was enjoying herself but he felt no more at home here than he did in the Bay Horse. Was this how other doctors felt? Also the young women here knew that socially he was well below them and they ignored him.

His mother was shining in the candlelight and yet she was so modestly dressed. He had never seen her so beautiful and he saw now what his father had seen when he first met her and she was very lovely. She had a quality that shone from her which had nothing to do with her looks somehow, could it be her very goodness? He didn't know, just that it infected the people around her and he listened to her laughter and it was silvery and others were smiling too.

The squire had seen that immediately, he could tell. The squire kept turning towards her, his eyes caressed her, his conversation was all about 'my new friend'.

Thomas wondered what it would be like if they married and she came to live in this house. He would be so pleased for her but he would miss her even though she would be less than two miles away. It would be totally different. He could see himself moving back to London. That would be his step forward. He would get out of this place which offered him so little.

And perhaps he would be able to get rid of his regard for Connie Butler and move forward on his own and make a new life.

Twenty-Six

It was only when the ship began to leave the harbour that Dom realized he had made a terrible mistake. He didn't know what he had been thinking of. He had talked his way into being taken on and now all he could think about was that he had left Connie to deal with everything. How could he have done that? He didn't understand why he had panicked and walked out and been unable to change his mind. He watched as the land began to drift out of sight and then the moment that he was able to he jumped over the side.

He had been supposed to be helping so there was some commotion and lots of shouting and swearing and people seemed to think he had fallen but Dom had been a strong swimmer all his life, having lived on an island, and he did not hesitate in going back to the shore. There was no way in which the ship would have turned around for one man, be he swimming or drowning. Just as well he wasn't drowning, that would have been it.

The water was so cold that it caught at his breath and towards the end he began to tire. He was fully clothed and his boots dragged him down but he went on and on. He could do nothing else now. He must get home and as quickly as he could.

When he finally reached the docks and was able to drag himself out and up onto solid ground he could barely breathe. His teeth chattered. He needed to get inside somehow but when he tried he staggered and then fell, knocking himself out on something hard.

When he came round he didn't know where he was or what had happened but he could see the Seamen's Mission and managed to get to its front door.

The man on the desk stared at him. Dom couldn't think and after that he knew nothing until he woke up in a strange bed in a place he did not know and could not remember anything.

The man on the desk was Mr Forster. He and his wife ran the Seamen's Mission. He had noticed that his visitor wore a silver cross around his neck and so he called the resident chaplain, Mr Leslie, and partly because of it, they thought he was a Christian and partly out of compassion, they called a doctor.

Dom could remember nothing and was amazed when Mr Forster told him he had swum ashore from a ship, judging by the state of his clothes, and then had banged his head.

He had been soaked and bleeding and had passed out. The doctor said that the blow to his head was causing a problem and with luck he would get better. Dom was horrified. As soon as he was well enough to get out of bed he saw in the nearest mirror the thin face of an ill man and gazed at the cross around his neck and tried to think hard who he was or what he was doing here.

Dom felt sure there were any number of religions that had such a symbol. He didn't understand why he knew that when he couldn't remember anything about himself.

Mrs Forster gave him the washed and dried clothes which apparently he had arrived in and a pair of stout boots which were obviously his because they fitted him.

It was quite a big place and seamen from all over the world

went there so that they could be looked after. And since the ships had turned from sail to steam and they were able to come in to dock at quaysides, instead of having to anchor out where they would catch the wind to fill their sails, the seamen had needed somewhere cheap to stay and eat and find a bed.

Dom also discovered that there were rooms for reading and playing games, there was a huge kitchen as well as dining and sitting rooms, and the food was good and wholesome.

Mrs Forster regaled him with the story of the Flying Angel: when the Reverend John Ashley was holidaying near Bristol he had discovered that the seafarers had no chaplain, so instead of joining a parish he became a chaplain and started up such places so that the seamen could be cared for. There were now many such places, she said.

Dom discovered the chapel. It seemed familiar to him but he didn't know why. Was he religious? He found himself at home there. He felt as though he ought to move on but he didn't know where he could go and when he suggested to the Forsters that he ought not to stay when he could not keep himself they wouldn't hear of it so in the end he tried to think of how he might help them.

The first time was when some sailors who were drunk came inside and Mr Forster was trying to send them out because such behaviour was not tolerated here and they became abusive and threatened Mr Forster. Dom heard them and came into the reception area and when they started trying to knock him about he dealt with them in a way in which he had not known he could. He downed them immediately with high kicks that must have been a form of martial arts.

When they were all on the floor he gazed down at them in awe and shock. Mr Forster stood by, looking relieved and rather surprised. The men were not badly hurt but they did leave as soon as they could stand.

'Well,' Mr Forster said, 'where did you learn to do that?'

'I don't know.'

'You see, I think that English is not your first language from the way that you use it. You must be highly educated and also have been taught how to get your way out of difficulties. It could be very useful.'

Dom also found that he could read all the books in the library and several of them were written in languages he did not know he understood until he took them from the shelves. Consequently he was useful because when men came in from ports all over the world he could make himself known to them and he became a bridge between them and the people here, and afterwards the chaplain asked him to read the bible to them at the various services which were provided and he found he could do this in English, French, Spanish and two languages which came from the east, one being Japanese and the other a form of Arabic.

Also he found that he was eager to be at the services and he had ideas about religion. The men who came here were meant to be Christians but no one was turned away and so he found himself able to talk to believers of Judaism, Islam, Hinduism, Buddhism, Sikhism, Taoism and he understood Confucianism immediately. It became a great joy to him and to the Forsters and to all the seamen who came into this port to find such a person like Dom that they could all relate to in different and yet the same ways.

He learned to stop worrying about his past and live in the present and he thought that he had been taught somewhere along the line to do such a thing. Also he had slight medical skills and was able to assist the doctor, Mr Hardy, whose family were a well-known seafaring family in Newcastle and who came here to look after those who needed him. Dom was especially good at listening to the problems the men had and talking to them in their own languages about how much they missed their wives and families. Some had not been home for years, while some had drunk too much and gambled and wasted their money so that they had had to go on another ship because they were left potless.

Dom dealt with those who drank and was able to stop them to a great extent. Also they had seen shipwrecks and death and been to many places so they were interesting to him. He grew to like his new life very well.

The doctor was keen for him to take up medicine and the chaplain was keen for him to become a minister but Dom didn't want to go any further just now. He was quite at home here and Mr and Mrs Forster said he was much too valuable so that they would not give him up to any profession he did not care for.

Also Mrs Forster confided to him that they had had a little boy who had not lived. They had called him Frederick and so Dom became Frederick Forster because it pleased the kind people who had taken him in. Dom knew they were paying him a huge compliment.

They had only one child left, a daughter, Rose. She sounded familiar to the new Frederick though he could not place her but then he had no memory of anything before he woke up in the Seamen's Mission. Her mother talked a lot about Rose, she obviously missed her.

Rose had gone into service. She had not wanted to marry the man who wanted her and Mrs Forster confided that he had been a sailor and not of good character but neither did they want her to leave them. She would go into service no matter how often they told her that she could do better. They had not seen her for two years because she had only half a day every other Sunday and since she was a maid, a lady's maid she proudly said when she wrote, she was needed there but her mother thought it was probably not true. She knew plenty of young women who had gone into service and been neglected, badly paid and given no time off.

Mrs Forster acknowledged that her daughter had wanted to get away and that she had been working at a big house at a Northumberland estate and there she was doing very nicely thank you, so she said, since she was lady's maid to the mistress of the house. When they went to London and sometimes to Scotland she went with them and no doubt found it exciting, but Mrs Forster wanted her to come home because she missed her so very much, they both did.

Mr Whitty made it known in the village that the Butler boys, as they had become known, had left home. He told his wife, she told her friends and since Mrs Whitty and Mrs Rizzi and the doctor's mother got together at Mrs Whitty's library afternoons they decided that they must do something to help the two girls.

Laura went home and talked to Thomas and he wrinkled his brow just like his father used to and said that he would sort things out. It had not escaped his mother's notice that he tried not to talk about Connie Butler which gave him away. Laura thought her son was in love. She didn't think this had happened before and she was curious to see what would happen. Connie had become popular among the womenfolk, she was noted as kind and considerate, good to her family and not afraid to take on anything, but she now had too much to do.

Miss Hutton was already giving the two girls work they could take home so they did not have to come down to her shop so very often though both their faces filled with dismay when she separately told them this – since one had to stay with Grandmother.

Miss Hutton had never had any family and she now regarded the two girls as near to family as she had ever got. Connie did not need mothering but Sarah and the little girl did and Miss Hutton took to them all in big way. They brightened what had been a very lonely existence. Miss Hutton was not an outgoing person though she went to Mrs Whitty's book afternoons, she was fond of her own company, but suddenly she had people she cared for who cared for her.

She liked it especially when Pearl came to see her. Pearl loved the shop. Miss Hutton thought it was because of all the bright wool and sewing threads but also when women came to the shop they would talk to her and Pearl was learning English fast. Dearest to Miss Hutton was that she gave the little girl some big needles and thick wool and within days Pearl could knit. She tried hard with her little fingers and became adept in a short time. She could only do plain stitch but she had begun a bright blue scarf and within a couple of weeks it was almost done. Pearl was very proud of herself and showed the two girls her big achievement.

Sarah had never had anyone who cared for her in such a close way and she also was blooming like a flower under the way that people were so kind. She always looked carefully on the street in case Mr Adams came for her, but she began to realize that there was nothing he could do and she stopped scouring the streets of Wolsingham for him.

Twenty-Seven

Leo, like Dom, did not come back. The best and worst thing of all somehow was that Sid returned. Connie burst into tears which startled him and then he went around looking for Dom and Leo and she found herself talking to Sid and somehow it helped and then it didn't. If Sid had not left then perhaps Leo would not have gone, she told herself, though Sid being a weasel she could hardly blame him.

Connie had no idea what to do or how to go after them and she could not leave Sarah to face everything to do with Pearl and her grandparents, she was too young to know very much and was already having to learn so very much that was hard for her.

One sunny morning about three weeks after Leo had left, when they were trying to do everything and not doing too well, the doctor called.

Connie would have been pleased to see anybody but he greeted her like an old friend and his presence was a huge relief to her. Not only did she like him more than any man she had ever met but her eyes took him in and noted the details of his clear skin, his shiny dark hair and his tall lean body. She tried to hide her blushes and kept looking down but she glanced up again in concern when the doctor told her the reasons for his visit.

'I understand that both your brothers have left home. You

must have an awful lot to do. I hope you don't mind but I have asked Oswald who looks after my horses and garden if he could make time to come here when he isn't busy and help in the garden when the weather is favourable and do any odd jobs about the place, he has a lot of skills. He will bring you wood and coal and draw water for you and see to it that you have a warm and comfortable winter. The wind must blow shockingly up here and from what the locals say the snowstorms are legendary. You need access to the village. I went to see your grandfather. He isn't coping at all, one of the neighbours told me so. When I got there I realized that neither you nor Sarah had been so I thought something must be badly wrong. It's hard for you and six miles, while it shouldn't be a lot, somehow sometimes is. I'm sorry he cannot manage but I expected nothing less which is why I wanted to bring him here but he wouldn't come and you can't force people to do such things. Fiona and Ada do their best but I find so much for them to do that we need to engage other help. My mother has got together with her friends and will make things easier and Mr Smithers and Arnold will be able to take you back and forth when Oswald is too busy or out with me.'

Connie could have wept she was so grateful. She would have worked herself into the ground but it was not fair on Sarah and they could all do with a little relief.

Connie found herself making excuses to talk to the doctor and he seemed inclined to linger or to find new excuses so that he could come up here to see her and she was only glad that they would be around one another so much. She thought that his voice softened when he spoke to her and she was eager for every word that he said.

She asked him about London and he told her lots of things which made her want to go.

'It sounds so exciting,' she said.

'There are so many theatres and so much going on.'

'I would love to go to the theatre some time.'

'I would love to take you,' he said and then stopped and they didn't look at one another again for a little while. 'I've never met anyone like you before,' he said finally and in a little rush of words.

'Like me?' Connie said, eager to hear what he liked so much about her. She found herself gazing into his eyes and feeling so happy there.

'Different, worldly-wise and mature and you are so good with other people.'

'So are you,' she said.

'It's my job.'

She told him about her father and how she thought that he should have been a doctor and he told her about his father.

'I don't usually discuss him but he is so often on my mind,' Thomas said. 'He was a clever man, a lawyer, the best barrister in the county, that was how people spoke of him.'

'It's terrible that he died,' Connie said, and then added frankly, 'My mother killed herself.'

It had never occurred to either of them that they would find such an awful topic something they had in common and yet it was a relief for her to talk about her mother who she missed so very much and he said the same of his father.

'Do you blame her?' he asked.

Connie shook her head.

'I try not to. It was the right thing to do. None of us can live another's life.'

'Some people would call it selfish.'

'I don't think that's true. We belong to ourselves. It doesn't mean your father didn't love you and your mother very much,' Connie said and she found the doctor smiling at her and she knew she had made him feel better. How odd that he was the doctor but she was doing the healing but perhaps it was the same for both of them.

Thomas was so glad that he had cause to see Connie very often.

Another problem which Thomas had in Wolsingham was the Methodist minister, Mr Adams. Thomas tried not to listen to gossip but he heard rumours that the man drank and badly treated his wife so taking his courage in his hands Thomas called in at the manse.

He did tell himself not to interfere when nobody was ill but he was glad he had gone and he was one of the few people who could go without a valid excuse. The place was not very clean and both children were howling. Mrs Adams was visibly pregnant and Mr Adams was nowhere to be seen.

She ushered the doctor into the study and Mr Adams jumped up from a shabby armchair. He had so obviously been asleep and the doctor had the awful impression that the man was drunk. He couldn't smell it from across the room but Mr Adams was unsteady on his feet and it was the middle of the day. He had seen a great many drunks at the hospital in London and knew what it looked like. How sad it was and he wondered what was the huge need in Amos Adams' life that he tried to obliterate it. He had a wife and children and a calling and a house which could be sound if it was looked after but there was such a falling off here, such a loss, that he longed to know what it was so he could help the man.

'Have you brought Sally back here?' Mr Adams questioned him. 'We could certainly do with her. Mrs Adams is having to do everything herself.'

Thomas tried not to judge, it was not his business.

'Sarah cannot come back. She is needed where she is. Perhaps it would be better if you employed someone older.'

'I can't afford to pay anyone.'

Thomas knew he could not say Mrs Adams needed help, it was not part of his job. He could go no further. Neither could he ask his mother or any of her friends to come here because he didn't trust Mr Adams to treat them well and even though they were all capable women Mr Adams sober had been bad enough. The same man drunk was very different and Thomas dared to think that Mr Adams drunk could be violent.

'Why can't the girl come back?' Mr Adams insisted. 'She ought never to have left, ungrateful is what I call it.'

Thomas wanted to call it something else but of course he couldn't. The fact he disliked this man should not mean he judged him. He was at a loss to know what he could do to help there but he sent Mrs Adams a bottle which would help her to feel stronger in her pregnancy and when he talked to his mother she said that she would go to the manse and see Mrs Adams on a regular basis despite the awful husband. Thomas told her to be careful but his mother was so energetic these days and so involved in everything that she wouldn't necessarily take any notice.

Thomas had never seen his mother in this capacity but her early life had been poor and industrious so she started going to the manse quite often. Mr Adams would not dare to get in the way. Laura could be formidable when she chose and she was perfectly capable of organizing and cleaning and seeing to the children. Thomas knew she had wanted a big family and could not have any more children after him so perhaps she was fulfilling things other than her friendships in the village. He knew how good it made you feel to help someone; it was his whole life. Perhaps he had got some of that from his mother. He certainly had it in quantity from his father.

She came back from the manse bright-eyed and full of energy and reported that she had made sure the house was clean and the children were fed.

Thomas had never lived in a village before. It was a proper community. His mother had been brought up to be capable though having married well she had not needed to be but now she was remembering all those skills she had lost and she had made a big hit with Oswald. He was always bringing great armfuls of flowers to the back door and as autumn advanced exquisite-coloured leaves and Christmas roses and other late flowering plants.

Thomas so wanted to do more for Amos Adams and had taken to going to the manse every few days but often Amos was not there, nor did his wife know where he was. Thomas wondered how Amos got his drink and he must be paying a lot for it because Laura reported that there was little coal for the fires, the food was scarce and not good and the children and Mrs Adams were so badly dressed that it was obvious they bought nothing. Mrs Adams had second-hand clothes given to her for herself and the children and Thomas was certain that Mr Adams had extra clothes given to him but he never seemed to change his apparel, neglect was another symptom of drunkenness, he knew. He suggested that Amos and Mrs Adams should go to the surgery dining room one Sunday and bring the children to dinner but Amos shuddered and Thomas knew he was afraid someone might see that once he began to drink he couldn't stop, that he was not fit for company and was lost in a sea of self-pity.

Thomas wished he could find out the source of the drink and prevent it but he knew drunks were devious people, he had met many such sufferers in London hospitals and addiction was almost impossible to deal with. He would try to get to the root of the cause but Amos declined to talk to him and if Thomas found the man at home he was always just on the way out.

Twenty-Eight

Two or three times a year Amos Adams had a letter from the chaplain at the Seamen's Mission in Newcastle, Mr Leslie. They had studied together at Leeds to become ministers. Amos had longed to be a missionary and to go to other lands but he had been disappointed when he was not considered suitable material, he was never told why and that was when things had begun to go downhill for him.

First of all he got his wife, who was not his wife then, pregnant. That went down badly and was when his troubles started. He blamed her for letting him have her, women were meant to prevent men from such sin. He was only thankful that she lost the child and then he considered that he need never have married her and began to resent her very presence in his house and the way that he had to keep her and the children she did bring forth. Now there was another on the way.

The whole thing was appalling. The half-grown boys did nothing but shriek and scream and run rampant through the rooms. He wished he could send them away to some boarding school and pretend they did not exist but that cost money which he did not have.

Also people in the village headed by the wretched new doctor were interfering in life at the manse and he did not like it. He could not very well say so and it was not that he disliked having a clean house and good meals but the place was not his own any more. He felt as though they were interfering and that he could not escape into his study without some blessed woman coming in to check the fire. He had liked having it to himself, it was his private place, but in vain did he say that he was composing his sermons and writing letters. It did not stop the doctor's mother from barging in when he least expected it and giving him good reports of how his wife was and how the boys had enjoyed playing football in the manse garden with Oswald.

He would have to find somewhere else to do his drinking. His old home was the first place he thought of but then there were a lot of women there too now, not just the girls, but he could go there when the old man had gone to bed and take his whisky and stay the night and dream of what it would be like when the old people died and it would become his home once more.

In the meanwhile he was more than happy to receive a letter from Mr Leslie who had his own work as well as the Seamen's Mission and wrote very chatty letters without managing to make Amos feel that he was missing out on things but Amos was feeling so now.

He heard about the seamen from various countries and the people who were friends to both clergymen they had known from the past and then Mr Leslie told Amos an interesting tale about a young man who had turned up wet and suffering from amnesia and Amos frowned at the letter because he recognized from the description that this boy was Dominic Butler. It could not be, his sensible self said. It was just a coincidence.

He shook off the worrying feelings. He was glad to be going to Newcastle and having a little time to himself. He would enjoy meeting his old friend and having some new company.

But then Mr Leslie had said how grateful Mr and Mrs Forster were to have found someone so gifted, useful and full of knowledge and learning, and it made Amos feel blackhearted that Dominic Butler or any of his family should be having a good time of it.

Amos had been pleased to see the back of Dominic Butler and it was even more lucky when the younger boy left. He hoped the boys would never come back and that they would never meet again.

Twenty-Nine

It was not exactly a surprise to Laura when the squire proposed to her. She had been thinking about it, going backwards and forwards in her mind, worrying and considering. He was a lot older than she was, did she want to marry an old man who might need nursing, but then did she want to go through the next twenty or thirty years by herself, bored and listless and even perhaps, oh horrors, doing more good works because she had nothing else left?

He taught her to ride. Laura felt silly trying because she had never been on a horse before and wanted to refuse but the squire told her she would love riding once she got the hang of it and she did. She had not realized that horses were such large creatures but the horse he loaned to her was so biddable, so easy, that she came to love these mornings, for they went out early almost before the village was awake. Laura was aware by now that the whole place was talking about her friendship with the squire but she didn't care for that.

He would send his groom, Beverley, to pick her up in the pony and trap in the early mornings and she loved these times best of all.

Weardale itself was beautiful but she preferred it up here on the felltops with nothing but rabbits and sheep and acres and acres of land with the odd farmhouse or barn so be it clear skies or rain she was equally happy.

They would retire to his house for breakfast and then spend most of the day together, sitting in the library if it was cold, walking in the gardens and going to see and help various people in cottages around them. The cottages were owned by the squire and well kept by him but Laura could see herself here too. He introduced her to all the wives of the men who were out on the farm and doing various jobs on the estate. She loved seeing the children and how the squire would give each of them a shiny penny. He was well loved.

So, although Laura was dithering inside when he did ask her tentatively whether she would deign to become his wife, it was as if a firework went off in her head. She was elated, thankful, and in a way she was grateful that the little lass from the pit village could go so far and yet her dad would have known it could happen and her mam would have bragged about it.

Her old age need not be lonely. She and John could have a lot of fun together and she would learn to love his house and to help look after his tenants and she would give big parties for them at harvest time and at Christmas and on as many other occasions as she could find an excuse, Bonfire Night, New Year, she would make something of Valentine's Day.

'I'm a lot older than you, Laura, I know, but it would give me so much pleasure if you would have me for your husband. I think we could have a great many good times together. What do you think, my dear?'

And there was no way she could refuse.

It was difficult to tell Thomas. He had loved his father very much and Laura was worried in case he might think she was being stupid. Also that she had put her first marriage behind her and was ready so quickly for another relationship when she ought to have been content with what she had done in her life and sit in an armchair and knit for the next few years, however many she had left.

She had heard of other people's children being upset when their remaining parent found someone new. Usually of course it was the husband because so many women died in childbirth and men did marry again and within months sometimes so she was unsure of how her son would react when she told him that the squire had proposed.

She was so nervous that she didn't know how to approach it. She waited until the evening after the last surgery and then she thought that perhaps he was tired, he had a hard job and worked awful hours and there had been a lot of night work lately so she wanted to put it off to the following morning but she knew she would go through the same thing again and she must tell him some time.

She told him as shortly as possible about the proposal of marriage and heard the silence which followed it but just as she was about to go on and explain further he said,

'And have you accepted?'

'Not yet.'

'Aren't you sure about the idea?'

'It's not that, it's just that, well, I wasn't sure what you would think.'

'I think if it's what you want you should do it. That's what I would do.'

'Would you?' she looked anxiously at him.

'Everyone is entitled to love another person,' Thomas said.

He thought about it afterwards and although he wanted to tell his mother how he felt about Connie he didn't think it was quite fair or appropriate at that moment. If his mother had another chance of happiness she should take it with both hands. She hesitated and then she went on,

'I don't love him. Not as I loved your father.'

She half wished Thomas was going off to the Bay Horse to play dominoes though she had not approved of his friends there when she had first reached Wolsingham. Now she could not wait for him to go out and then he said,

'There are all kinds of love,' and she began to breathe more easily.

He was smiling. Perhaps he had half expected it.

'And an old man's love?' she prompted.

'Why not if the relationship shows promise? He is a very grand old man and I feel sure that you have sufficient regard for him so that you will both be happy.'

'I have a feeling that a lot of it is pride on my part that he would ask me to be his wife.'

'Why wouldn't he? My father was as much of a gentleman as the squire and he adored you.'

'I was young.'

'To the squire you are still young.'

Laura felt happy now, warm and excited. She had not felt happy in a long time so it was a welcome feeling. She could not wait for what was to follow.

She did not think of herself as vain but just for once she wanted to brag, to see her day with the people who had shunned her because she had no married status.

So she ordered thick cream invitations to her wedding, which was to be at Christmas, and added a personal note to each saying that there was a lot of room at the house and she and the squire would be so glad if they could come and stay overnight before the wedding and enjoy the celebrations. She and the squire would be delighted to have their company.

The squire also invited his own friends and what an august company they were, with many titles among them and all were well off. They were coming from Cumbria, Yorkshire and deep into Northumberland and beyond the border for the wedding.

There were to be Northumbrian pipes playing after the ceremony and later there would be dancing. The ballroom had not been used since his wife had died and it would be glorious with winter foliage if the head gardener, Evans, had his way.

Miss Hutton and Miss Butler had fashioned her a lovely dress, dark blue and demure such as became a bride who had been a bride before, and Laura loved how it folded around her body so neatly and yet there was a swish to the skirts.

Laura remembered what happiness was like and grasped it with both hands.

Thomas was not as pleased to have his mother marry again as he had told her. He knew he was being ridiculous but there was a part of him that could never and possibly would never accept that his father had died.

His parents had had a very good marriage and he had missed a lot of it. He knew they had missed him too but had thought it better for him that he should go to good schools where he could have the best education but his plan after he became a doctor was to come back to the north-east and spend time with them as never before.

Yes, he would be away from the city. In Durham he would

have his father's reputation to live up to, not professionally but people thought his father a great man and Thomas did not want to have to compete.

He wanted to leave the immediate past behind him and go back to what he had hoped to have here, a profession in which he could do well and have his parents close enough so that he could go home and they could come to see him and that his father would watch him succeed and be proud of him.

Thomas knew how mean it was of him to want his mother to stay as she was. She had been so lonely, she did not take well to being widowed, he doubted any woman would. Now she had a chance of a different kind of happiness and in a way to also set him free from the responsibility of having his mother living with him.

He could go ahead and make plans to ask Connie Butler to marry him. He was not sure what his mother would make of this, but having recently decided to marry again herself she could hardly complain that Connie was so different than they were but in fact there was little to object to. Connie was a lady, she had fine instincts. Also if his mother settled happily here with the squire he might change his mind about staying here in the dale. He had dreams of carrying Connie off to London and of them being prosperous there and having children and he could go forward with his ideas that he might specialize though he had not yet worked out in what field this might be.

He knew it was a pipe dream, Connie would not leave Pearl and he knew she was waiting and hoping that the two boys would come back and they needed her. Sarah needed her too. Also he doubted she was even aware of his existence except for his kindness and his professional zeal to her grandparents. Maybe she would never think of him like that.

He tried to put the problem to the back of his mind and told himself that once his mother was settled he could go ahead with his plans and that would be wonderful. He must accept that his father was dead and that he and his mother would go on to be happy. He felt certain that they both deserved it.

Thirty

Connie went back to Wolsingham to speak to Mr Whitty. He told her that he couldn't think of anywhere else Leo could have gone. He had looked high and low for the lad. She didn't quite believe him though what she thought of high and low and what he did left a great deal of room between them. Mr Whitty was good-hearted but he was not very energetic and although she knew he had asked everybody he could think of and put up notices in all the local villages nothing more had happened and Mr Whitty had run out of ideas.

She, however, had not and was convinced that Leo had gone to Newcastle because Dom would have gone to the closest port. Mr Whitty looked baffled. He had never been beyond Wolsingham and did not therefore understand how anybody would want to leave this very place where he and Mrs Whitty were so cosily situated so none of this had occurred to him.

Connie tried to impress upon him how hard it had been to leave Japan and come here but to Mr Whitty everybody who didn't come from the dale was a foreigner and to think of a country thousands of miles away was so obviously beyond his comprehension that Connie despaired.

'I think I have done everything I could. I contacted the police in Durham City and in Newcastle but there are so many children who are alone, have been left or gone astray which makes it difficult, Miss Butler,' he said.

Mr Whitty hesitated. Connie wished that he was more energetic, more involved, more curious. He was the last person on earth who should've become a policeman, she thought uncharitably.

Connie was inclined to go to Newcastle herself. Leo had taken quite a lot of money but then he could hardly have walked all that way by himself and the money might keep him safe, at least she told herself that for comfort. It was by now too late that anybody would remember seeing him and anyway he would have been on at least three trains. She thought hard and wondered whether there was any other place he could go.

Liverpool was too far and would cost too much and anyway she thought that Dom would have gone to Newcastle. It was the sensible thing to do considering what a stupid idea it was in the first place but she knew now that Dom must have been almost out of his head with homesickness. Indeed she felt like that too, though she had duties here and women were more susceptible to duty as far as she could tell. There was no way that she would ever have run.

She missed her home and her parents very much indeed but she could not have left, knowing what a mess there would be behind her. She could not have left without the children or when her grandparents still needed her. Really, being female was a wretched nuisance in some ways.

Thomas made Connie's grandmother's failing health an excuse to come up to the Hilda House almost every day.

Her grandmother was easier to deal with now that she had more visitors. It took her attention away from being confused and running outside. So it was not that the doctor was strictly needed there but Connie by now knew that he wanted to see her and she wanted to see him. They talked about his mother's future.

Connie knew he told her things he would never have dreamed of telling anyone else and she was proud that he confided in her. They had talked a lot about his father and his parents' marriage.

'Now she is ready to move on,' he said, 'and I'm so grateful for it.'

Connie had heard the gossip from Wolsingham and there was a lot of discord among those who envied Mrs Butler not only her position as a barrister's wife but how that not being enough for her she had come into Wolsingham shortly after her husband's death and almost immediately taken up with the squire.

'I only hope she doesn't hear such things,' he said to Connie and she reassured him that none of his mother's friends would talk like that but his mother would not care what other people thought when they did not like her.

'Women ought to be able to lead the lives they choose,' Connie said, comfortingly, but he looked so warmly at her that she almost wished she hadn't said it.

'Once she is married and settled everything will change,' he said.

Thirty-One

Connie made several attempts over the next days to get into her grandfather's house now that the weather was cold. He was being his usual difficult self and rejected those who would have made his life easier. He refused to let anyone over the doorstep and when the women of the village had tried to insist he had taken to living outside. Connie was so very worried.

He had made a kind of camp in his tiny garden shed and from what she could tell he was living there, eating vegetables and not going into the house for anything. She decided there was nothing she could do but occasionally bring him bread and butter and cheese and meat and leave them in the hut when he was busy in the garden. So she left a basket of food for him whenever she was in Wolsingham. It was all she thought she could do until the weather would drive him indoors and just now she had sufficient to worry about with both boys seemingly lost to her.

It did not occur to Thomas Neville that his mother thought he was doing anything wrong until a couple of weeks later when his mother waited until after evening surgery and then collared him in the sitting room.

'I was just going to the Bay Horse.'

'I know.'

He felt guilty already and hadn't got out of the door yet. He was getting bored at the pub. He wasn't any good at games so everybody beat him and they talked about the families and their farms and he could contribute nothing to the conversation. He could tell nobody about his work and sometimes he wished he had stayed at home with only his mother for company. He knew now how much he would miss her after her marriage.

'Has it never occurred to you what people will think about you and Connie Butler?' his mother said.

Talk about frank. Thomas stared at her.

'Obviously not,' his mother said dryly.

Thomas felt helpless, he felt found out, he felt yet another form of guilt.

'I'm just trying to help her.'

'I know but people are talking.'

'They have to talk about somebody.'

'Not you. You are the doctor. You can't afford to give them fuel to turn small flames into bonfires.'

Thomas said nothing.

'You like her?' his mother pursued.

'No. No.' He paused there and sat heavily on the nearest chair. 'I'm in love with Connie Butler. I can't stop thinking about her.'

'Oh no.' His mother sat down heavily too by the fireplace.

'I didn't mean to.'

'She's totally unsuitable,' his mother said. 'I understand she's very beautiful but she can't be more than eighteen and she has so many problems in her life. It would make her nothing but a burden.'

'My father married you,' was all the answer Thomas could manage.

'He wasn't a doctor and I wasn't a foreigner. We were from different classes of course but the law is very different and your father would never have let such a thing happen.'

'I know and I know that it doesn't make an argument but I haven't been in love before.' He smiled in apology. 'All those women I met in London. There was one I preferred but she was as unlike Connie Butler as anyone could be. And looking at her now it was not love.'

'And does she care for you?'

'I don't know. I think she likes me.' He hesitated.

His mother was silent for a few minutes and then she said,

'Why don't I go with you more often and in my capacity as your mother and not just to help and perhaps I might be able to tell whether she has feelings for you? I know it sounds fussy and pointless but it would give the whole thing respectability. And if Miss Butler ever has thought that you mean anything by her it would clear that up, at least from her viewpoint.'

Thomas didn't want his mother there. He wanted to spend time with Connie on his own but then he reflected that he rarely got a chance. She had so much to do and so many people to help. There was also the possibility that if she became aware of his feelings she would panic, close up against him, and it would be a huge loss.

'Miss Butler is well liked in the village but that isn't the same thing as you wanting to marry her,' his mother said. 'You need to marry someone local, preferably someone from Wolsingham if you can find a girl like that. I haven't seen one so far but it's important that you marry the right woman. Everybody looks up to you. Personally I like Miss Butler very much but I don't think that you ought to marry her.'

Thirty-Two

Leo lived on the streets. Snow fell at the beginning of October and he was never warm. He felt strange that he didn't know anybody. He had never been anywhere by himself before and had he had sufficient money he would have gone back to Connie, he longed for her so much. He spent what money he had on food and wondered how long he would survive in such a big city where people hurried past him, where everybody but him seemed to be going somewhere. It was very odd having nowhere to go to.

There were a lot of people living on the streets and many of them were children. There was nobody to look after them. He wandered about a lot, sleeping under bridges and staying there when it rained and also when the winter sun was warm and the Tyne dazzled him.

It was bustling down by the quayside and there was a market on Sundays where people came to buy clothes and eat and drink. There were food stalls, and he managed to run off with the odd cake. It was so busy that nobody noticed, it was always thronged with people who came to buy and sell and just for a look round. He had never felt as lonely in his life.

He thought more and more about Connie and how eager he had been to get away. What must she think of him and of Dom that they would go and leave her with too much to do as if she didn't matter? He felt ashamed. And all his comforts were gone. He thought longingly of his best times at the Hilda House and of how much Connie had done for him and would have continued to do had he been more of the man he had hoped to become and less of an idiot. He tried to comfort himself that he was not very old but that wouldn't wash. He had behaved badly, stolen money from the house. Now he had nothing to eat and nowhere to go and the odd tear of self-pity ran down his face only to be scraped away with a grubby hand. He felt so lost and so stupid and he missed Sid and Pearl and even Sarah sometimes. He had been really stupid when Connie had held them together and done so very much. He wished and wished that he could go back.

One day in November he thought he saw his brother and it was the only good thing that had happened to him since he had left home. He shouted and ran then lost sight of him, there were so many people about. He tried to follow in what he thought was the right direction but it was no good, he couldn't see Dom. It was frustrating to know that he was somewhere in Newcastle but not where. After that he spent all his time looking for him but he didn't catch sight of him again and some days it was all he could do not to sit down and cry.

However, he was down by the quayside hanging about because he was convinced that Dom was going there or had come from there and after seven days he saw his brother again and this time Leo ran after him, shouting his name. Eventually he came to a halt and saw Dom go in at the door of the Seamen's Mission. He couldn't work that out and didn't care, following Dom inside and shouting the more and when he found Dom in the reception area he tugged at Dom's coat until his brother turned around. Dom stared at him.

'Didn't you hear me?'

Dom went on staring until Leo wanted to cry with relief and frustration.

'I came here to find you. I've been here for ages. I didn't want to be there without you and Sid ran away and I felt as if I had nothing left,' he said.

The man behind the desk came out and asked what he thought he was playing at.

'This is my brother.'

'Oh yes?' the man said. 'Do you think I'm stupid? Anybody can see that you come from China.'

'I do not!' Leo yelled. 'I'm Japanese and so is Dom.'

'I don't think so.'

'Tell him, Dom, tell him you know me.'

Dom looked blankly at him.

'I don't remember having seen you before.'

Leo had no idea what was going on here. He stared and despite how old he thought he was he started to cry. Somehow to him it was the last straw.

The man seemed to take more kindly to the tears and was sympathetic and told him not to mind, that they would get to the bottom of this, and he offered Leo a chair and told him not to cry and Leo sat down thankful for somebody's kind voice after the struggle he had had for what felt like so long.

'Where did we meet?' Dom was asking him now.

Leo couldn't believe this. Was Dom pretending but why would he? The blank look on his face was not reassuring.

'Yes,' the man said to Dom, 'but you don't remember anything before you came here,' and he spoke gently. 'Frederick came to us after banging his head in an accident.'

Leo was aghast at the idea but the man was softly spoken and he said,

'Why don't you tell us about you and about Frederick's life if you really do know it?'

So they sat down and Mr Forster and his wife sat with them and Leo told them about the life they had led in Japan and about his parents, how Mickey had been ordained a minister in England and how he had worked in Japan in a different way. He told them about what Japan was like and about the ships that had brought them there and how they had got to the Hilda House and then he eased his mind by saying that he had run off and left Connie and Pearl and he didn't understand how Dom hadn't gone back and Sid was missing.

'I wish I could remember it,' Dom said, 'it's all just a complete blank.'

Leo was so relieved that Dom was being truthful and he was, it was just that Leo had never heard of anyone losing his memory like that, but the way Dom spoke was sincere and Leo was able to accept that.

'And so you too ran away,' Mrs Forster said, shaking her head at such behaviour.

'Sid went and I set out to look for him. Sid is my polecat. And then I decided it wasn't worth going back without you, Dom, and I'm glad I've found you even if you don't know who I am.'

'You'd better stay with us then,' Mrs Forster said, 'and I will write to your sister and let her know that you are safe. She must be frantic with worry. In the meanwhile you look like you could do with a wash and something to eat, young Leo,' and she tutted over the state of Leo's clothes and took him into the back and gave him hot water, soap and a towel and when he had washed she sat him down at a big table and there he was able to shovel a huge bowl of lamb broth into his mouth.

He watched Dom who sat down at the table with him. They

stared at one another. Dom encouraged him to say more about the Hilda House and the life they had led and Leo was happy to do so if it would jog his brother's memory.

'If you would just come back with me I think everything would be all right,' Leo said. 'You would remember Pearl and Connie. It would all come to you.'

Dom was upset, Leo could see just by his confused look. It seemed to Leo that his brother had gone through things he had no idea of and hopefully never would but nothing had prepared him for a Dom who didn't remember his twin sister or the circumstances that had brought them there and although he didn't dispute any of it he could not take a dark leap forward in case something should go wrong again.

The other awful thing was that Leo didn't want to go back now that he had been taken in and comforted, and fed. He felt even more guilty after that. The Hilda House was in the middle of nowhere and he had been left there with four females. It was not a happy thought and then he felt worse because he knew how upset Connie would be and even Pearl would be missing him by now. So he was torn in half here but he had decided that he would not go back by himself and if Dom would not go there was little he could do.

'I don't remember any of this,' Dom kept saying sadly as they talked and then they heard the outside door and Mr Forster went to open it, thinking it would be men wanting bed and food, but shortly afterwards they heard a cry and it was an exclamation of delight. Then the woman got up and followed, leaving the door open, and she too laughed.

When both of the older people let go of the girl who had come in and was now smiling Leo took an instant dislike to her. She reminded him so much of Sarah though he didn't know where he got this idea from. It was just that he was upset and angry because Dom did not even remember his name, never mind the past. Leo thought that if he would just try to remember a little bit it would help.

Mr and Mrs Forster made a great fuss of their only child, Rose, who Leo disliked even more when she smiled at his brother. Thankfully Dom didn't smile at her in the same way, Leo thought he must be thinking too much of all his family and the past that he didn't remember.

Leo had no idea what to do next, he stayed with them but he wished that Mrs Forster had not said she would get in touch with Connie. Connie would be there like a shot, urging them back to that house in the middle of the fells where nothing interesting ever happened, and he certainly would go nowhere without his brother.

Luckily Mrs Forster sent Leo to the post box with her letter to Connie so he tore it up and watched the little pieces of paper fall into the Tyne. He immediately wished that he hadn't. What kind of selfish boy had he turned into that he would do such a thing? But it was done now and he could never confess what he had done. Connie did not deserve such treatment. He was wretched.

It went on being hard that Dom did not recognize him. He had known that his brother had loved him, that he was important in Dom's life. Now he wasn't. It felt as though they were not brothers. There was no special place for him here. Was he not to feel good ever again?

He avoided Rose but there was always a lot for the women to do in the kitchen making meals for all the seamen, washing their clothes and changing their beds and cleaning the big house. No wonder Mrs Forster had been glad that her daughter had come home. 'Home to stay,' she said contentedly.

Leo felt like he had no home now and no brother. He did like Newcastle though and he did start to enjoy being here. Mrs Forster mothered him and was very keen on keeping his stomach full and making sure he was warmly tucked in at night. It was an exciting place to be especially where the Seamen's Mission stood right on the river. He got to listen to the tales the seamen told and go down and watch the ships, loading and unloading their cargo. There was an activity about the place which Leo had not seen before.

Nevertheless he worried about Sid and to a certain extent his sisters as well though he knew Connie would get on with things, just as she always did.

Rose seemed strange to Dom, almost as though they had met before. He wondered whether his sister looked like her and perhaps that meant that he could be remembering the rest of his family and that would be good. He wanted his memory back but he was confused and conflicted by his feelings. He felt happy here, so very happy, and it began to involve Rose. They started spending a lot of time together. He also had time for his little brother but he found that he wanted to be on his own with Rose and so they would go for walks along the quayside and into the town.

He caught her mother eyeing him with suspicion and went into the kitchen and said,

'Do you not want me to be friends with Rose? Is it because I don't know who I am?'

Mrs Forster looked down at her washing-up for a few moments before she gazed at him and said,

'You are both very young and I don't want you doing her a mischief.'

'I don't understand.'

She hesitated for another second and then she said,

'We don't want any babies.'

Dom was horrified.

'I would never do such a thing,' he said. 'After you have all been so very kind to me and to – my little brother.'

'She is beginning to like you an awful lot,' her mother protested.

'I like her very much too,' Dom said.

'I just don't want my daughter's heart broken by a good-looking lad who doesn't care for her.'

'I do care for her very much and I will make sure that I don't hurt her,' Dom said and after that Mrs Forster made no more objections.

Dom needed to think. He had not realized that Rose was falling in love with him but he knew he was falling in love with her and he was amazed and pleased he had found so much that mattered in this new life.

She loved reading as much as he did so they always had lots to talk about and he made sure that they did often spend time alone so that her parents would get used to him being there and perhaps in time he would be accepted as the man who would eventually marry her.

The Forsters had a very good friend, James Leslie, who was a local Methodist minister. Dom liked Mr Leslie very much and Mr Leslie encouraged him to go to chapel and Dom got very excited when he saw the chapel. It was as though it had been waiting there for him all that time. He liked to discuss the bible and the rise of the Methodist church, the education and the trade unions, and he began to admire John Wesley and think that he would very much like to be a part of this church.

He also asked Rose whether she would like to go with him to the chapel and Mr and Mrs Forster said they would let their daughter go with him if she wanted to.

Dom was surprised that the Forsters were friendly with such a man. They did not go to any church but the Seamen's Mission was the main goal for all three of them. It seemed to Dom that the pieces of his life were beginning to slot into place and he had the feeling that it was for the first time.

Mr and Mrs Forster said he was to bring Mr Leslie back with him from chapel the next Sunday and so Mr Leslie went to the Seamen's Mission not just to work and to look after the men's welfare but because he was at home there, Dom knew, and it was there that Dom said rather breathily because it worried him,

'I don't even know whether I am a Christian. '

Mr Leslie looked across the dinner table at him.

'You could always become one if you aren't sure about that.'

'I have come to the conclusion that I would like to become a minister, that if it was possible I would like to go to a seminary and learn.'

Mr Leslie positively glowed past his beef and Yorkshire pudding and said he thought it was wonderful.

'I always hope young men will have a calling and you are so bright and educated. We are about to open up a seminary here and I will put your name forward so that you can go.'

Dom was so excited that he could barely sleep and when he was next alone with Rose he said to her,

'Do you think the ministry would be a good idea?'

'I think it's a wonderful idea,' she said.

'Then I would be able to make a living and—'

He stopped there, embarrassed and scared.

'Yes?' she encouraged him.

'If we could become betrothed then when I am ordained we could think of getting married. I know it's early days yet and we aren't very old but this would be my aim. What do you think of that?'

And that was when she gave a little squeal and threw herself into his arms. It was their first kiss and Dom was not disappointed. It made him think of Connie and Pearl and how he would be able to introduce the girl he loved to the family he had loved so much and felt certain that he would again if he could just meet them. Perhaps when he did so his memory would come back.

Leo had already told him much of what their life together had been like and Dom was entranced by the thought that he had family, that he had people he had belonged to before he came here. He got Leo to describe them and Dom could tell that Leo also loved them very much because of the way his eyes warmed when he talked about them.

'We came from Tokyo where our parents had died,' Leo said, not far from tears but also keen to talk about what the past had been like.

There was so much to tell and yet now that Leo had escaped there was a large part of him which wanted only to go forward, to forget about the past as if it had never happened. He had already tried to blot it out with his destruction of the letter that was to tell Connie her brothers were safe. Leo could not forgive himself for what he had done to the letter which had been destined to reach Connie and yet he was too ashamed to admit it. Each day he told himself that he would tell Mr and Mrs Forster what he had done, each day he waited for a way out of his predicament, but he knew that as an honest child he should not have needed a way out. First of all he shouldn't have done it and secondly he had added insult to injury, as Rosa would have said, by compounding the bad deed.

His guilt made him angry and resentful with himself and yet he did not feel as if he could do anything about it. He wanted to live in this world of half-truths where he had his brother and had got away and also daily he conjured pictures of all the times when Sarah had been sharp with him, treating him like a little boy which was obviously what she thought him. He wanted so much to be grown-up and so far he was making a complete mess of it.

Dom said, 'Shall I stop asking you about the past, it seems to upset you so much? We can go back and see our sisters and the place which took us in and perhaps some day we will even go back to Tokyo and then I might remember our parents and the life we had there.' Dom hugged his little brother to him and Leo closed his eyes over how things were and how he had wanted to them to be and how he had failed this far and yet he was so pleased to be there with the brother he had always loved so much.

Leo wasn't sure what to think of Rose and he saw that he was jealous of her. He had had to share his brother always and he found it hard. He didn't know whether to be glad or displeased when the girl looked into Dom's eyes in a completely soppy way as though nobody else on earth existed. Leo was now losing his brother for the second time and he wasn't sure he could stand it but he knew that if he was going to do any good at all in any of his family relationships he must learn to share all the people in his life with all the other people.

He liked how the men talked and laughed and sat about after they had been fed and housed and looked after, and then they went outside and sat about, smoking and telling stories. They didn't seem to mind when he went and sat with them, they just smiled.

He understood several languages as all his family did so he didn't miss out but best he liked the story of the mermaid who had been on some island in the Pacific, who had sat there, sunning herself on a rock and combing her hair. The man who told the story had a golden comb to prove that he had seen her. Leo was mesmerized and more entertained than he had been in many months.

Different seamen turned up every few days and Leo could see that they paid for their board and lodging or if they had nothing they would be taken in anyway and a lot of them became better men and if they could not pay straight away they would go away for however long the voyage was and come back and pay what they owed. Mr Leslie would keep them out of the pubs and clubs and out of the way of the prostitutes on the quayside and those who would cheat and rob them, take them down dark alleyways and beat them for their belongings, but Mr Leslie took Dom with him when he set forth upon these adventures. Leo begged to go too but they said it was too dangerous.

'I don't want to stay here with the women,' Leo protested. This was turning out to be not much better than the Hilda House in that way. Seemingly he was besieged by women and he was starting to resent it but he didn't regret having found his brother or the other good things in his new life.

Thirty-Three

The next time that Thomas went to the orphanage he took his mother with him. He wasn't very happy about it but he understood what a sensible thing it was to do. He did not, however, think that his mother liked Connie because he loved her or liked the situation she was in but he kept these ideas to himself.

Connie too was such an innocent. She never thought of people as having more than one motive. She greeted his mother with warmth just as she always did and took her straight through to see the old lady and she said to her grandmother,

'Look who has come to see you. Mrs Neville has called especially and she has brought lots of good food as she always does and some chocolate especially for you,' and her grandmother seemed equally grateful as Laura was obliged to sit down on the bed and make the kind of small talk which she deplored but then the woman was old and failing and unwell and so she did her best. Women such as this had meant nothing to her, they had poor humdrum lives like the women she had lived among in Langley Park.

Connie Butler frightened Laura, that was the truth of it. She had not seen this girl as a potential wife for her son before and now that she had met her and seen her with new eyes she was very afraid for him. She knew Connie was a great many things a woman would want for her daughter-in-law and yet she had never met anybody so young who was so self-possessed, so capable, so caring and yet so devastatingly attractive. Connie had the sort of beauty every woman envied. She was tall and slender with brown skin and graceful limbs. Her thick lustrous hair was neatly twisted and pinned at the back of her neck as plainly as it could be and her clothes were not there to be paid attention to, she wore them easily though Laura could see how soft and flattering was the material.

She was educated, clever and yet so humble with her grandmother, thanking Laura for having come to visit them as though she deemed the favour very special and she was always like that, so generous when anybody did anything for her and yet she gave so much away to other people.

Sarah was there too and Laura liked how straightforward and hard-working Sarah was. As for Pearl, the little girl made her long for a grandchild, she was so taking and yet so foreign with huge dark eyes and a ready smile which showed Laura that Connie had made the child feel secure even though they had had such a hard time.

Also Laura could imagine how beautiful a child her son and Connie could have and she could not help hoping that despite how young Connie was a grandchild would be the very best thing that could happen for her.

So when they reached home and her son looked quizzically at her Laura took him into her arms and told him that although she worried for how young Connie was and for all the responsibilities she had, as long as he honoured those responsibilities and made sure he did not upset the balance of Connie's life, nor ask too much of her, he should ask her to marry him.

'Do you think she will have me?' he said, hesitating.

Laura smiled.

'She ought to be glad to have you but whether she thinks of you like that I'm not sure.'

'I cannot be happy without her,' he said and Laura kissed him and let him go.

Thomas wanted to ask Connie to marry him so much that waiting any longer was agony to him and yet he was terrified that she would turn him down because of Pearl and Sarah, because Connie longed for her brothers to come home to her, because she was in that sense a mother to her family and she could put no one in front of that.

He knew Laura might have had had other ideas for him and he had argued with himself so often about the concept of asking Connie to marry him when all along he had been aware that she was vital to him. So without telling anybody he went up to the Hilda House and he had not even the excuse that her grandmother was ill. She was always ill and he went there often. This would be different.

He tried not to go, he told himself he was being stupid and that Connie would never accept him, but he must do it so he took his courage and his horse and went.

It was a crisp bright cold morning and he felt sick, anxious, worried, everything negative except that she must marry him. He could see no way forward but for that. When Connie opened the door he wanted to run away but he thought she looked so beautiful and she smiled at him and ushered him in as though he was her best friend and of course in a lot of ways he was.

She took him in to see Pearl and Sarah and her grandmother and then she went into the kitchen to put the kettle on and he quietly went with her and closed the doors and then he said, 'Connie, I have come here to ask you something particular.'

Connie put the kettle on and then turned in surprise.

He shifted his feet like what his mother would have called 'a spare part', he was so nervous.

'My mother is keen for me to take up a post in Durham or somewhere else rather than staying here after she marries. I want to give her some space to be the squire's wife rather than the doctor's mother.'

Connie's face fell, he could see it.

'But you can't,' she said immediately. 'You are needed so much here,' and then she stopped and she said,

'I shouldn't have said that. You must do what is right for you but you would be so badly missed if you left, you have been so good for all of us.'

He nodded and smiled and then he said,

'I don't want to do that, I don't want to go anywhere without you. I want to be wherever you are.'

There, it was said but his breath was all over the place and his arms were moving like windmills. He had never felt quite so stupid.

'I love you, Connie. I've never been in love before and I didn't know that it was quite so wonderful and if you will marry me I will take care of you for the rest of our lives.'

Connie stared.

He had been too sudden with her, he knew, too forward, she looked aghast, she looked mystified and perhaps she didn't look happy. No, she definitely didn't look happy. He wished he could go into the pantry and close the door and hide.

'What?'

'I'm sorry, I didn't say it well. I've rehearsed it over and over and tried to be sensible and take everything into account. I know that you have a lot of responsibilities but we can share those. I will look after all of you. You could come and live in the surgery house, I've got lots of room and . . .' Here he stopped. He couldn't think of anything to say.

Connie sat down suddenly on one of the kitchen chairs and then glanced at the closed door in case Pearl or Sarah should come back in and as though she would have welcomed an interruption and then she looked back at him and she said,

'I couldn't do that.'

'You don't love me?'

'No, I – no. You are the best friend I have ever had,' she said, 'even more so than Dom.'

It was a huge admission, Thomas knew, and he was glad of it and yet he wanted so much more. He wanted a commitment from her.

'I could be so much better than you think if you would let me,' he said.

She shook her head, she looked perplexed.

'I think you have got carried away,' she said, 'blinded by your feelings.'

His heart sank, it really did, he could feel it, it clonked onto the floor and skittered down the hall and out of the house.

'You couldn't possibly take on a whole family. You aren't very old yet and you are young as a man to settle down. What if you changed your mind? Then where would we be? There are four of us, all women, and also I am hoping that my brothers will come home so that we can be a family again. You couldn't take on six people, all of them difficult and different. You couldn't do it. And I wouldn't let you do it, it would be wrong, very wrong. I think you would tire of us in time and wish you had done otherwise. And your mother would be appalled.'

How was it that Connie was the sensible one and he was the impulsive one, that she seemed like the adult and he felt like a young boy, and stupid?

'Just let me try,' he pleaded.

'No, I can't. It would be a huge mistake and everybody in Wolsingham would laugh and as the doctor you are respected for your abilities and expertise and you couldn't do with that. They would look down on you that you had been no more sensible than to take on a huge burden. I couldn't let that happen.'

'It wouldn't be a burden.'

'I think in time it would be and the local people would say that I had set my cap at the young doctor who was so very eligible and that I am strange and from another country and they would resent me and in time so would you and perhaps you would even learn to hate me.'

'I could never do that,' he said. 'Never. Never,' but she wasn't having it, he could see. She made him go from her and he knew now that it was not because she didn't love him but that she would not let him shoulder her burdens in case his shoulders did not prove wide enough and she led him into making a terrible mistake.

Thomas never knew how he got away. He hoped he didn't run, he hoped he managed to maintain some dignity, but afterwards he could never remember what he had said or what he had done, just that he had to go back to Wolsingham and pretend that nothing had happened and he had no idea how to do that.

He rode back very slowly, hating every step, hating how beautiful the dale looked in front of him, the neat square fields, the stone houses. None of it meant anything to him any more now that he couldn't have the girl he loved so much.

He tried to school his face before he got back and then he had work to do and he was glad that he did not have time to think about what had just happened. There were patients waiting for him. He must get on with it.

Worst of all he had the feeling that Connie was right, that it wouldn't work, that no matter how much he loved her it was not going to happen and worst of all she had not said that she loved him. Now perhaps he would never know. He tried to recall how upset she had been and that that had been love but he couldn't be sure of it and the more he went over it the less sure he became until he felt tortured.

Connie's eyes ached because she wouldn't cry. Luckily Sarah came into the kitchen and Pearl with her and Connie had to get on with her sewing and her cooking and her baking and being generally kind to everybody because she had to be. Thomas would never know how she felt about him, she could not have said it, it would have hurt him too much. She would have given almost anything to have married him but her practical self knew it would be a disaster and so even when her whole face ached with suppressed emotion all that day she did not give in.

Thirty-Four

Amos Adams had been to the Seamen's Mission before. The chaplain, his friend, James Leslie, sounded delighted when he wrote to say that he would like to visit and stay overnight if it was all right with James. Amos tried to put from his mind that he had learned to dislike the man who had been his best friend when they were at the Methodist college together in Leeds. The trouble was that he knew James was a better man than he had ever been.

It caused him feelings of resentment. He didn't want to be the way that he was but he was too weak to be any different. He hated himself but he did not know how else to go on, he did not know how to change, he hated other people because they did not struggle and suffer and know defeat. They did not hate the awful people that they had become, they did not have to be him.

And now in attempting to make things better he was making things worse. He was drinking. It was against his church, his better ideas, his very ethics, against everything that he was. Each day when he woke up he wished he was dead. He had thought the whisky would alleviate his feelings whereas in fact it was making everything harder.

He was skinny and shaking. He could not leave his house to visit the people from his church, he had no energy for such things, it was all used up with the whisky and his hopes and dreams which had never left him. He had wanted so much to go to the east and claim souls against the devil.

He liked the idea of teaching strange people to embrace the correct faith so that they should be saved. There were no souls to convert in Wolsingham and it was a fruitless task. How much more could you impart to those who had already embraced Christ, though a great many of them were Catholic and Church of England and had ruled there and pushed down the workers for too long, but people here were faithful to their chapel and he had nothing much to say to them any longer.

Yet something made him go to Newcastle to see his old friend. He wished he could talk to Mr Leslie about the mess he was making of his life. James would have understood but he knew himself too well and that he would not be advised. He could not change, he could not even try to.

It was good to get away. He felt better. He was tired of being poor, of his moaning wife, his screaming children, how he knew he was drinking money that would have kept them warm and well fed. His wife was almost in rags. He was learning to hate how small-minded and boring she was, she never had an interesting thought.

He could not imagine that he had been foolish enough to marry her. She was skinny, plain and of no credit to him. He wished that he could get away. He was starting to breathe more easily as his train journey went forward. This was helping. He was beginning to remember what joy felt like, somewhere in the recesses of his mind he found a glimmer of hope.

He enjoyed the journey. He liked the feeling of being away from everything. He wished there was some way in which he could just keep going. He understood now why people ran away from their impossible lives.

He wanted to go on and on. He was sleeping badly and because he drank he was tired and irritable. He nodded off and was sorry when the train pulled into Newcastle Central Station. He longed for the end of the world where he was certain he would find redemption waiting for him.

James was at the station to meet him and to take his small amount of luggage and then they went to his house. James lived alone. Amos was amazed that men lived like this and began to envy it. The house was small in a dark terraced street not far from the quayside. It was humble and modest and yet it worked much better than his own traditional lifestyle. There was a house-keeper to manage everything and a woman who came in to do the washing and hard work.

Amos was given a comfortable bed, good food and his friend gave him rather too much whisky as though it was a special occasion and no doubt it was for him. For Amos it was an everyday thing and even then he could have drunk a lot more. He slept well because he was not at home, no screaming children or whining wife, no need for him to do anything.

He felt better when he got up. He had been in good company, had eaten and drunk well but not too much. After a breakfast of bacon, eggs, local black pudding and pork sausages washed down with lots of coffee they set off for the Seamen's Mission.

Amos felt a strange excitement. He was almost certain that he would find Dominic Butler and that morning it was the only thing on his mind. He was obsessed with the boy and sincerely hoped that he was having a bad time of it and that he would be seen to be at a loss, not just his mind but his whole self.

As they drew nearer his breath shortened and he stopped listening to what his friend was saying.

The waterside was an alien place to him, he suppressed the

memories of being a boy there, they had hurt and damaged him too much. He knew nothing of shipping or of seamen. He was kindly greeted by Mr Forster and tried not to keep looking around for his first sight of the boy he had learned to despise and envy. He could not bear that Dominic Butler should inherit the house that was meant to be his, that a ghastly foreign upstart should take his place there. It could not be, it was never meant to be.

Mr Forster showed him the comforts of clean beds and good food and he and James sat down and ate with them and James obviously got so much out of it but Amos became impatient when the young man did not appear and he wanted to leave, to turn and run back to his mousehole, that was how he thought of it now. He needed his study, his whisky, his oblivion and he needed to go to the house which was morally his, he ached to be there.

He had got through the morning without a drink but he knew he wouldn't last much longer. He made excuses. James so obviously didn't understand and frowned when he said abruptly that he must go, he would miss his train.

He was at the door when it opened and Dominic Butler stood in front of him. Amos panicked. Would this boy remember him? But the boy looked vaguely at him and smiled. He was differently dressed than he had been, in more usual clothes, but there was in his face somehow the same arrogance Amos had learned to hate. Why had he thought this boy would change? He'd wondered if losing his existence would mean he would suffer but there was no sign of that suffering in his face. Amos was disappointed and he could not help but stare. Why should this foreign boy who stole and had run away have such a good life and why did he not?

As Amos froze in shock there was a noise behind Dom and

then the younger boy came into view and it was as though he could not believe that he was seeing the minister and he gawped and then he said loudly,

'Mr Adams, what are you doing here?'

Amos tried to pretend that he did not know the boy.

'Who are you?' he managed.

'You know very well who I am,' Leo protested and Amos couldn't think what to say. 'I'm Leo Butler.'

Mr Leslie coughed.

'He knows your name and you have spoken to me of his family.'

It took Amos several seconds to recover and then he wished Leo into hell and he wished his brother even further if there was further to go. He said,

'Yes, of course. I remember you now, you lived in the Hilda House. And I remember you especially,' he nodded at Dom, 'you stole money from me, a goodly amount, and you stole food and drink. Goodness knows what else you took from other people.'

It seemed so unfair that having invaded his life once Dominic Butler should do it a second time, though as long as he didn't remember who he was he was no threat to Amos.

They had done him great wrong by coming back here and invading his life and taking everything that he had worked so hard for and needed so much.

'We did not!' Leo, like anybody his age, would not be put right when he thought he was already there. 'You charged us for spending the night in one cold room and all we had to eat was a slice of bread and butter each. And this is my brother, Dom. Surely you know it's him.'

Dom in turn stared at Amos.

'I don't remember you.'

'Yes, but there is a good deal you don't remember,' Mr Forster said gently.

Mr Leslie, his good friend, was staring at him as though they hadn't met before either and as Amos stared back he saw that James thought he was lying and that he could not bear. He couldn't be there any longer.

He turned and ran away. He mumbled something, he didn't remember what, and then he quickly left the place, stumbled into the nearest pub and downed two huge glasses of whisky before his hands stopped shaking. It felt so good, the tears of relief welled up in his eyes.

It had not occurred to him that he would find the younger boy there. He had wanted to find Dominic Butler unhappy. He had wanted to gloat, to see the boy lost here as he deserved to be. Things were working so very badly. On the way back he fell asleep to the rhythm of the train and when he got home he fell into his bed and after he had slept for a long time he went downstairs into his study and there he found the bottle of Scotch which was hidden in the deepest drawer in his desk. He had an arrangement with the man who brought it in to him by the back, leaving it in various places, and the money was put there and the whisky picked up. It took almost everything which Amos earned. Whisky felt like all he had left.

Thirty-Five

'I was thinking that after you get married I might find a post in a London hospital,' Thomas said to his mother. 'I need to get away from here.'

His mother looked sympathetically at him.

'You must not be defeated so easily,' she said.

'She has told me that she could never marry me and I cannot stay here and live without her. I feel as if I must leave and do my work in other places.'

He felt brave about this but he knew it was the thing to do. He could not stay here with Connie so close and once his mother married he would feel the responsibility of her slide away. And then he felt precarious like he had felt balancing on a sheer drop from a wall when he was a child. He wanted to go and yet there was a boy in him that didn't want to leave his mother. He tried to scoff at the feeling but that didn't work.

His mother would need him so much less after she married, he knew, and in a way he wished she wouldn't because they were becoming very close but she would be happy and that was his paramount wish for her.

He could see that she too was conflicted in her thoughts because she lowered her gaze to the breakfast table and didn't look up for some time and when she did her beautiful eyes were full of tears.

That was when he got up and she got up and they embraced and she called him my son, my son, so that he feared a fog around him when he would cry and he broke away and went off into the surgery to recover himself.

Thirty-Six

Amos could not stop the way that Holy Well Hall drew him in. It was as if it whispered to his mind that there was a place for him, that it could be his if only the old man would agree to go up to the orphanage with his old woman and stay there. The way would then be open for Amos to take over. As it was the old man went to bed early, so as soon as the light had gone – and up here on the tops in December the light came in no sooner than nine in the morning and it was dark by half past three in the afternoons – he went and it gave him plenty of time in which to own and enjoy the place he coveted so much.

Amos was deft and quiet and he would push open the window which provided entrance and sit there in the kitchen because the other room was the shop. There was nothing in the shop now and it offended him to see it with empty shelves and vast windows. He wished that somehow he could make the house be as he remembered from childhood and it would be his once again.

Sometimes Amos would take food from the manse if one of the girls had been there or other people from the village who interfered in his life and got in his way. Women, he thought, always bossing other folk about. He knew when they had been to the old man's and when they had not. The clean and tidy house deteriorated over the days they were not there and since the old man ate very little there was always something to eat. The old man had no idea of tidying up anything and so the sink was full of pots and the table and chairs were laden with shoes and cardigans and various half-eaten dishes which he did not like or had forgotten about.

Amos thought the old man was losing his mind. He took no care of himself and the odd time when Amos made a noise he listened in case the old man should wake up but Joshua was deaf these days, Amos assumed. It made him gleeful that he could go there and stay all night if he chose and nobody would know the difference.

His wife seemed not to notice whether he was in their bed or not and so he came and went and it made him happier than he had been in as long as he could remember. He was learning to hate how she whined at him and he wished to God he had never married her. She had lost another child recently and was so pale and sickly that he wished she had died with it. At least he could get away from her.

He would steal out through the empty streets with a whisky bottle in his pocket and when he was feeling very bold he would light the fire at the house or stir up the embers and sit there most of the night with his memories which he was making real now as never before. He almost expected his mother to appear and that the place would be full of light and life and he would be a child again with all his sorrows somehow far in front of him. The past had become the present and all he had to do was stay there.

Sometimes it was daylight when he went home but his wife said nothing, she just assumed he had been called out early to visit a parishioner, something he rarely did but she couldn't know that so it became earlier and earlier when he left the manse in the afternoons and later and later in the mornings when he returned.

He went on feeling so good and then the night came when he fell asleep in the chair by the fire and the first thing he knew was that the old man was shouting at him to get out and threatening him with the poker just as the day was getting light.

Joshua had become frail since his wife had been taken away from him and he was not the man to wield any weapon with authority. Amos was shocked but recovered himself in seconds and jumped up and said that there was no need for concern, he had just called to see how the old man was.

'How did you get into my house?' Joshua yelled though his voice was thin and reedy.

Amos stared. He did not know what to say. It had not occurred to him that the old man would wake up and find him there.

'The window was open,' he said, not sure what to do or say now.

'You broke into my house and you a Methodist minister.'

Joshua looked around the other man and then stared at him.

'This isn't the first time, is it?' he said. 'I thought I could hear somebody but I told myself it was the wind coming through the cracks in the walls and all this time you've been breaking into my house and swilling drink. I can smell it from here.'

'No, you can't,' Amos said. 'And anyway I have a right to be here.'

'What right would that be then?'

'I belong here. I was born here.' Amos felt better for just saying it. He had never said such a thing aloud and it made him feel lighter, more in charge.

'What do you mean, you have a right?'

'I'm your nephew, I'm your brother's child. I spent the first years of my life here and I've missed it ever since.' A sob was on Amos's lips. He managed to stall it but the recollections gave him long summer days when he'd played in the garden, his father plodging in the ponds with him.

'I haven't got a nephew.'

'I am he! My father was your brother.'

'Aye,' Joshua said, 'I did have a brother and he brought his wife and a bairn with him but it wasn't his bairn. She had it before they met. He picked her up in Gateshead from the streets. He was always a soft bugger. Anyroad, you are nowt to do with this place. They went off and I never saw him any more.'

Amos stared.

'That can't be right,' he said. 'It can't be. I was his son and I'm your family, I'm a lot nearer to you than those – those foreign people, that boy who stole all my money. They have no place here. Their father ran off and took that whore with him and there is no nobody to say who they are.'

'What rubbish,' old Joshua said and Amos could see by the look in his eyes that he thought he was right.

It couldn't be. And he was an old man now. He was failing, Amos thought with glee, he would not last five minutes and after that the house would become his own and he would leave the manse for good and move in here.

Old Joshua's ire made him lunge at his enemy, however, and Amos was obliged to defend himself. He looked around for something to help and seeing nothing he ran, not knowing which direction to go and he fled upstairs and tried to lock himself into the bedrooms first one and then the other. The old man struggled, wheezing after him. Amos tried to close the bedroom doors but neither had locks, he discovered, neither shut properly and he was obliged to hop over the bed and make once more for the stairs as the old man screamed and swore at him as he made his way inside the second bedroom where Amos felt like a beast at bay. In the darkness, in the deep shadows, he stilled and in the silence then he pulled the door ajar and slid into the upstairs hall. Confused, the old man tottered onto the landing and headed for the stairs. There he tripped in the baldness of the stair carpet such as it was, frayed, worn and coming to pieces. He might have righted himself but that Amos followed him to the edge of the stairs, gave him a solid shove and he fell and when he hit the bottom he lay still.

Connie and Sarah spent a lot of time sewing, mending, making new clothes and knitting. Christmas was only a short time away and the commissions had doubled. They also had long discussions over Miss Hutton's kitchen table deciding what they would make and for whom, the orders that had come in for various garments. Also on half day closing which was Wednesday and on Sunday afternoons Oswald would convey Miss Hutton up to the Hilda House. It made a change for her, she enjoyed it very much and the girls liked having her there.

They were also doing work from several miles beyond Wolsingham. Women had heard of Connie's skills and word had spread. She bought materials from the market and sometimes the local men who cleared the houses of those unfortunates who had died bartered with her over cloth and garments but also Connie found now that people would sell her clothes that their children had grown out of. It had always been that you handed down clothes in the family for the next child but this was an alternative and local people were enthusiastic that they could make up their minds as what to do when there were no more children to clothe and it made money.

On this particular day, however, they had a lot of sewing to do so Connie would have go to Holy Well Hall alone and leave Sarah to take care of Pearl. She would have taken Pearl but Pearl was happy to stay there and this was a relief because she would not often walk back and was now too heavy to be carried. Mr Smithers or Oswald could not pick them up every time a lift was needed so on a decent day they walked and felt less guilty about the whole thing.

It was a crisp fine day so Connie enjoyed her freedom and stepped out and made good time. She hadn't seen her grandfather in three days and each time she saw him she felt worse. Having retreated to his house and locked the doors he would not let her in and if she found him in the garden which he so often lived in if the weather was good, he had lately shouted at her and thrown bricks such as he had sometimes done with other people.

Connie knew he was coming to the end of a long life but nothing was easy. So today she was surprised when she found the outside door unlocked and when she ventured inside to find him stiff and cold at the bottom of the stairs she stood completely still for a moment unable to believe it.

She had wanted so much to aid her grandparents, she had tried so hard to set up a reconnection so that they would be a family such as she had so often dreamed of. It was as though she tried to turn her grandparents into her parents, she missed them so much, but it was not to be. The old man lay there inert and Connie, after the first few moments, understood that he was no more.

She looked around her. The place was in disarray. What had happened here? The outside door had been unlocked but surely her grandfather locked it when he went to bed?

The fire was out but still warm and there was food on the floor. Although he was a messy person he was not usually as bad as this. Also while she watched she saw the poker which he must have held in his hand. Now it was lying not far from the bottom of the stairs.

Had there been an intruder? Had somebody killed her grandfather? What had happened here? She was at once afraid that somebody might still be there and was so scared that she ran all the way to the doctor's house.

She wasn't sure whether to run to Mr Whitty first but she changed her mind, he had not been of much help to her so far but then perhaps she had been wrong and her grandfather was still alive and she was just too stupid to understand. She must find him some help before she did anything else. She was frightened now of somebody being in the house and perhaps was there still and of how she felt that she did not want to leave her grandfather to anyone else's mercy but could think of nothing else to do. She ran to the marketplace and in by the surgery door.

The pharmacy was deserted, morning surgery having been over for a good half hour, and she worried about facing that awful lad who usually handed out various bottles and pills but could barely say a polite word. Also the doctor might have gone on his rounds and if he had she didn't know what she would do.

The door opened. Connie felt the relief surge through her. Thomas was there, had not gone yet but he had his bag in his hand. When he saw her he forgot himself and called her by her first name. Not pausing to correct himself he asked what the matter was.

Connie wanted to burst into tears but she contained her breathing and got beyond the ignominy of such behaviour and within moments he was following her through the market square.

When they reached the house he moved gently because he thought it might cause her less distress and then he kneeled down to the dead man. Having seen a lot of dead people before he could not make her feel better and even though both of them knew there was nothing more to be done he gave them a few moments before shaking his head.

Connie thought she might stand there forever as though she could hold back the time which would make it official, if she could only delay the moment before she had found him it would be so much easier but she could not. She let go of her breath and tried to act naturally even though she was shaking

'Do you think that somebody has killed him?' Connie said, trying to hold on to her sanity now that somebody else was there.

Thomas didn't answer her. Very carefully he picked up the old man's body and laid him down on the couch and then he looked around him and went upstairs. Connie wanted to follow but for some stupid reason she didn't want to leave her grandfather even though he was no longer breathing. It seemed disrespectful somehow. Worst of all her grandmother must be told and after that she didn't think the old lady would last much longer.

Thomas came back downstairs but slowly.

'I think that possibly somebody was here and there was some kind of fight. Your grandfather tripped over the carpet,' he took her back upstairs and showed her where the big hole was where her grandfather's foot had gone and he had lost his balance. 'It looks as though he was fighting off an intruder and fell.'

'But who would come here?'

'There are always people looking for shelter and something to eat,' Thomas said. 'Why don't you come to my house with me and I will go and find Mr Whitty?'

'I don't want to leave my grandfather.'

'Connie,' it was the second time that the doctor had used her first name that day and he said it so gently that it made the tears stand at the front of her eyes so that she could barely see him, 'your grandfather will not know whether you are here or not now and I don't want to leave you here in case somebody comes back. You do understand? I will take care of your grandfather.'

She nodded dumbly and abandoned her grandfather's body and followed him to the house. There Ada and Fiona gave her tea which she didn't drink and Thomas went off to see Mr Whitty and they went back together to Holy Well Hall so that Mr Whitty could see what had happened and so that they could look after the body of the old man.

Connie felt defeated and abandoned. First of all her parents had gone, then Dom and Leo had turned away. Soon she would have no family left. She would have nobody. She felt bitter that it should have come to this. When the doctor came back, and she thought he was away a very long time, he took her into the sitting room where his mother was and there they talked about what had happened and what was the best thing to do now. Mrs Neville was kind to her though Connie could barely think. It was as if the picture in her mind of her dead grandfather was all there was room for. She could barely move. And then Thomas took her home.

It was three days before the vicar went up to the Hilda House to see her.

Connie found that she liked the vicar. They had met vaguely several times but she had not known how comforting it was to have somebody to take care of all the difficult things a death entailed and he made it easy for her.

He invited her to the vicarage to see his wife and it was at least something to do so the following afternoon she made her way down the hills to the little town which now reminded her over and over that her grandfather was dead and there was nothing more to be done except practical things. She was coming to be grateful for practical things.

The vicarage in Wolsingham was in a lovely situation amidst fields and not far from the river. The church had once been a beautiful building but had been somewhat altered by somebody's enthusiasm a few years back so that the additions looked odd and clumsy. To Connie, because the vicar and his wife were kind and welcomed her, it was the most wonderful church in the world. But she had also heard bad things of the Church of England, how greedy it was, how it had taken away all the silver and lead in the area and how the clergy had grown rich on the backs of the people.

It was not a new or uncommon story but from the moment she went into the vicarage and Mrs Wilson sat her by the fire and talked sympathetically to her Connie was converted. She felt almost as though the vicar and his wife were her family though they were less than twenty years her senior.

Mrs Wilson took her hands and said how sorry she was for all the woes her family had had to face. Connie wanted to cry. She wanted to be taken in and given good meals and a soft bed and some gentle companionship. Gentility and kindness had not been constant in her life.

She felt awkward when Mrs Wilson took her into the vicar's study. He got up and greeted her warmly and told her how sorry he was that her grandfather had died. He also asked after her grandmother and then about what hymns she would like, what kind of service. Connie blushed and then she said,

'I don't think I can afford a service.'

The vicar coughed and didn't meet her eyes for a few moments and then he looked her steadily in the face and he said,

'Miss Butler, I understand that your family has lived in this valley for almost a thousand years. I would be failing in my duty as the vicar if I didn't give your grandfather a decent burial.'

He didn't say so to Connie but he had had the doctor there to see him earlier that day and the doctor had sworn him to secrecy but everything would be paid for. Mrs Neville had also called and offered help independently of her son. Mrs Rizzi had come and Mrs Whitty.

Mr Wilson was so pleased that this girl was not without friends at this time. He didn't quite know how to tell her that she had nothing to pay for and it would have been less than tactful so he named a small sum so she would not feel humiliated but that evening when he and his wife were in bed he said,

'I think the doctor is in love.'

'You are not the only one to think so. She is very lovely.'

'Isn't she? But not just that, clever and charming and educated.'

'It sounds to me as though you are a little in love too,' and they smiled at one another before they kissed goodnight.

Mr Whitty was not a happy man about what he thought had happened at old Joshua's house. It seemed obvious to him that there had been a struggle. The upstairs of the house was where things had been pushed to the floor. Several items were broken including a china figure so the struggle had not just been downstairs.

The old man had died because he had fallen but somebody had broken in and upset him and maybe even helped him down the stairs to his death. The windows were unsound and he could have climbed in at any of them but as far as Mr Whitty could see there was no other evidence of who had been the intruder.

Nobody local would go there. There was nothing to steal, there was little comfort to be had in such a house. There were much better places to go for somebody who wanted shelter, warmth and something to eat. The old man had no enemies, nobody that could gain from this. It seemed to him that somebody had taken shelter for the night and then, surprised when the old man heard him, woke up to find old Joshua trying to defend his house against a tramp. Joshua had then fallen down the stairs and broken his neck.

It didn't make Mr Whitty happy to think anything other than that had been real. He didn't want unsavoury characters in his area. The very idea would come between himself and his sleep so he put it from his mind and thought no more about it. Nobody had broken in anywhere else. The story was what he thought of as a nine day wonder. The villagers were shocked at what had happened, such things were rare in such a peaceful place. There was little crime here, folk looked after one another so it was an isolated case, he decided, and it was just unfortunate that the old man had woken up and done battle for his home.

Connie argued with herself as to whether she ought to tell her grandmother that her grandfather had died. They had been married for forty years and more but her grandmother was becoming less and less coherent. Would she understand what had happened? Connie decided not to tell her and when her grandmother did ask – if she ever did or lived that long – she would say that it had just happened and try to go from there. If not then there was nothing lost.

On the day of her grandfather's funeral Connie was driven in Mr Smithers' pony and trap, courtesy of Arnold, Mr Smithers' son since Oswald was taking his mother to the funeral and other older women in the village who could not walk so far. Usually Arnold was chatty but today he had little to say and Connie had heard gossip that he was wanting to court the blacksmith's daughter, who was a big bonny black-haired lass, but his father apparently did not think much of it. Connie couldn't see why not. Mr Smithers and Arnold had a good living, she was a very respectable girl and the boy was distracted, obviously in love.

Sarah and Miss Hutton had insisted on Connie being got up properly as they called it and though Connie hated show of any kind in such circumstances she appeared at church in black and with style, her dress and hat had been made by Miss Hutton who would not have any less, so she said. It also occurred to Miss Hutton, though of course she didn't say so, that the stylish though respectful garments would be seen by a great many other women that day who might in time make further orders and not just in black.

Connie was amazed when she got there and followed her grandfather's coffin into the church that half the village had turned out. Rosa, for all of her lack of spiritual guidance, had always regarded hymns as part of her strange life and so the congregation was treated to her mother's favourite psalm, 'I will lift up mine eyes unto the hills'. Rosa had told Connie that it always reminded her of her times in the dale and how occasionally she went to church. Then there was 'Lord of All Hopefulness' which she had thought so cheery. Connie had wanted to include 'Abide with Me' but it always made her cry and things were bad enough so she went with 'How Great Thou Art'.

The congregation seemed to approve Rosa's favourites and roared out the ones Connie had chosen. It also seemed strange and had a good flavour to it that although her grandfather had disliked her mother, Rosa was there in spirit at the old man's funeral.

Mr Wilson also spoke of her grandfather in such glowing terms and proved that though he was a fairly young man he understood youth and age. Afterwards everybody was invited to the vicarage and Connie stood beside the window in the loveliest afternoon they had had for weeks, cold and bright, and she saw how good her friends had been to her and how many she had.

They came and told her about her family and how revered her grandfather had been. She had seen him only as old and worn out but a lot of older people remembered his youth and her grandmother when she was young and they sent their best wishes to the old lady.

By the time her grandfather was laid to rest in the churchyard Connie was feeling a whole lot better about a great many things. She had had Mr Whitty there reassuring her. All she wanted now was not to have to go back to the house where her grandfather had died and somebody must be to blame but nobody was to be found.

She tried not to think about it too much but it got in the way of her life every minute of every day and she wished with all her heart that Leo and Dom were there. She felt unsafe. She knew it was ridiculous to think that somebody would break into the Hilda House but she could not quiet her mind. She tried to tell herself that she could deal with whoever might be there but she found that she was afraid now for Pearl and Sarah and her grandmother.

Flo woke up and knew that something was different. At first she understood where she was, comfortable in her bed at the Hilda House where her lovely granddaughter was looking after her.

She went back to sleep but she dreamed of her husband and when she woke again all she knew was that he was not there and she must get back to him.

She managed to push aside the covers and started across the floor. To her dismay she could not see Connie when she reached the hall. Sarah and Pearl were in the kitchen. She asked Sarah where her husband was and when Sarah tried to persuade her back to bed she remembered that it was Joshua she wanted to see most of all.

She wanted to go home to Joshua and to her mother and father. She began to cry and to fight to get out of the house and away down the hills to where her family was waiting for her but she could not open the door no matter how hard she tried. She began to weep from frustration and to say his name. All she wanted was to go home.

Exhausted soon she let herself be put back into bed by Sarah and the two girls sat with her, Pearl showing her big pictures in a book Sarah had given her. It always soothed her and eventually she fell out of consciousness with a blissful sigh.

When Connie came back from her grandfather's funeral she wondered yet again whether to tell her grandmother that her grandfather was dead. Was her grandmother capable of remembering? She decided to do nothing for now and when her grandmother awoke she did not remember the distress and the longing and the tears, she was only glad that Connie was there.

After that somehow her grandmother became confused and thought that Connie was her mother. It calmed her so Connie told stories about her childhood, it was easy enough. Her grandmother's main topic was her wonderful childhood and it worked every time. Connie was only glad that something was going right. She no longer felt safe up there now that her grandfather had

had somebody in the house and had died and even though Mr Whitty tried to assure her that he thought it was not somebody local Connie was not convinced, she thought he was just trying to reassure her. She didn't blame him for that but she knew very well that anyone who would chase her grandfather and cause him to fall downstairs and break his neck was not somebody she could be easy about and there was no saying whether he was still around.

That week she had a letter from the local solicitor, Samuel East, telling her that he wondered whether he might come and see her since he had her grandfather's will. This had not occurred to Connie. Her grandfather and legal documents were worlds apart to her but she waited for Mr East, who was a middle-aged man, to come to the Hilda House. He was tubby and grubby and smoked so that the ash gathered on his waistcoat. His horse seemed happy to wander outside. She was a little bit worried about this but he told her the horse knew the area and since the horse was fifteen years old he had no curiosity left but if she could spare a couple of apples that would be nice.

Pearl and Sarah therefore spent a lot of time feeding Hercules apples and carrots that afternoon and Hercules had such a good time that he would have liked to be adopted except that he was loyal to his master, especially since when the solicitor had a particularly knotty problem he always took it to the stables to discuss the matter with Hercules.

It transpired, however – as the solicitor told Connie – that her grandfather had left her everything he owned.

Connie had had to excuse to Mr East that she could not take him into the living room, since her grandmother was there so the kitchen would have to do. Her grandmother did not always understand what was being said but sometimes she was fully coherent and Connie had not yet braved the idea of telling her grandmother about her grandfather, or rather she had judged that it would not help until things were different and to cause her grandmother any distress at this point would be silly.

Mr East said genially that he was at home in kitchens though Connie dismissed this as kindness. He looked to her as though he had never seen a kitchen before and stared at the big stove and the cupboards before being seated on a very hard chair. He put his papers down on the table and set his chair sideways and then looked seriously at her.

'Your grandmother of course must be looked after but since we know you already do such a thing that will be no problem. He wanted you to give her a home and as she has one—'

Here, Connie could not help but interrupt.

'When was this will updated? It must have been not long since for the circumstances changed.'

'It was but a few weeks ago.'

Connie's heart hurt for the fact that her grandfather had acknowledged her, had done such a thing when he was alone and his wife was ill and the future was uncertain. Maybe that cleared the mind.

'Why would he leave it to me? Why not to my brother?'

The solicitor hesitated. She thought he was almost embarrassed.

'Forgive me for saying this but he trusted you and I think it had something to do with your father leaving.'

'Oh no,' Connie said, having to breathe hard when her whole world had turned to salty tears. It was true. Joshua was the only man in the family who had stayed. Somehow her grandfather had known that Dom was lost to them. She could not believe it.

'What would you like me to do with it?'

Connie stared.

'You mean sell it?'

'When the legalities are settled. I can do that if you choose. I don't think it's worth a great deal of money as it is but it could be made into something wonderful if somebody spent a lot of money on it.' He looked more wisely at her than Connie had given him credit for and she said,

'I don't think I want to sell it, not just at present.' It would be an easy way out, she thought, she would not have to worry about the place any more. She could not bring herself to go there now that her grandfather was dead and somebody had been startled by him or had deliberately gone to him but she knew it was not good to make a decision when you were having a bad time so she took comfort in not having to.

Mr East smiled and nodded and she was glad.

After the old man died everything changed for Sarah. She didn't know why. She had thought she liked the way she lived now but she found herself ungrateful somehow. She didn't really like the quietness of the Hilda House and the way they had to go to Wolsingham for any kind of life and when she was there she found that she preferred it. It was so lonely up on the tops.

She loved the old woman and the little girl but it seemed one-way traffic. Nobody had time to care for her and both she and Connie had so much to do that she was always tired. She couldn't complain because Connie gave her only the tasks she could not manage herself but they were many so although Sarah didn't have to see to the old man now when she had time she was less appreciative of the good things in her life.

The best part of her time was spent with Miss Hutton. It was not just the shop and the sewing and the pretty materials. Miss

Hutton was very kind and though a maiden lady she showed Sarah love just as though Sarah was a relation until Sarah began to long to spend more time with her.

Miss Hutton made cosy meals, informal where they sat over the fire and toasted teacakes or Sarah was able to help with the baking. Miss Hutton had good fires in both downstairs rooms and when the shop was closed she always had lots of things to say and she began to make clothes for Sarah in colours which she said suited the girl.

Also Sarah wanted to go to school. Connie tried to teach her to read and write but it had taken a back seat lately as the little girl and the old woman took up so much time and work and the house and the garden took the rest.

Connie sensed the restlessness in the younger girl and that she was not as happy as she might be but there was little she could do about it. She did notice that if she stayed at the Hilda House Sarah perked up as she was able to go into Wolsingham and Connie watched Mr Smithers or Arnold take Sarah off to the village and she saw the girl smile at him and start to chat.

It wasn't easy never having a change and having to do everything there and then face the sewing too but Connie didn't see what she could do to change it. She was also thinking of Pearl and how Pearl would benefit from living in Wolsingham and seeing and playing with other children her own age. She could go to school and see another side of life. They had all become lonely, Connie knew.

Connie was surprised when a clergyman she didn't know turned up on her doorstep. This man, while about the same age as Mr Adams, was quite different so she calmed her fears. He was as unlike Mr Adams as he could be. Rather stout, middle-aged, balding, and yet his sweet grey eyes reassured her.

She urged him inside and sat him down by the kitchen fire for the day was wet. The others were in Grandmother's room but she suspected this might be something private and therefore kept the doors shut. Sarah would understand not to intrude.

He told her that he was James Leslie from Newcastle, and then he gave her the best news she had heard in months.

'I have seen your brothers. They are safe and well and staying with some friends of mine. The people they are staying with, Mr and Mrs Forster, they did write to tell you but since you didn't reply or come to Newcastle to see them we thought that the letter must have gone astray and so here I am.'

Connie was so pleased and surprised that it was just as well she was sitting down.

'You have? Oh, I'm so grateful. I've been worried sick about them.'

He explained that Dom and Leo were living in the Seamen's Mission but when he said the next things Connie became as upset as she had been elated. Dom had had an accident and hit his head. He didn't remember his real name or anything about his past life and Leo would not go back to the country, he wanted to stay with his brother. Dom had been taken in by the people who ran the mission and was to marry their daughter but it was not for a long time because he had to qualify as a minister first.

Connie's emotions were rampaging. First she was relieved they were all right, second sad that Dom did not know who he was and worst of all that they were not coming home.

Thirty-Seven

The squire sent Laura a note saying that he didn't want to go riding, he was coming to see her. It would be something to do with the wedding, she knew. It was less than two weeks away now and she could not remember having been so excited. Every day she went to the estate and rode around what would become hers.

Also she had been told that she could alter anything she wanted but since it had all been chosen to be as it was when the squire married the lady then to become his first wife, she did not want to intervene too soon. She thought of it as Phoebe's house and it had been her house for a very long time.

The squire, she knew, was sorry that his marriage had not produced the heir it might have done but he spoke vaguely of his cousin who lived in Cumberland so she merely bided her time to see how she would fit in and if there were things she wanted to change. It was all tasteful and it was not as if she was a young girl, going to spend a long life there, but she thought she was happy enough to grow old along with the squire, enjoying his acres and the rooms and views, sitting by the fire with him on long winter evenings and in the garden with him in the summer.

That would keep her occupied and if they did choose to entertain from time to time it might be fun. In the meanwhile she had been kept busy at the surgery house where the squire's servants came to work out who had replied that they would be coming to the wedding and the wedding feast, who would stay overnight, how many beds were needed. The squire had left her to do all that wedding stuff, as he said, and she was enjoying that he had given her this freedom. Miss Hutton and Connie came to the house several times about her dress and about who should wear what and the squire's housekeeper, Mrs Mills, came down to talk about food and the butler to advise her about wine. She told him she knew little of such things and would be happy to let him do what he might because he was the expert. He had, however, taken to coming to see her about champagne and claret and they had little tipples in the middle of the day which she very much enjoyed.

In the meanwhile she rode every day and had forgotten how much she had loved her life in Durham until Harry had died. Now life was making up for these things and she had the chance to start again.

She thought the squire didn't look very well the morning when he came to see her at eleven. She would of course have coffee served and his favourite biscuits. When Ada came in with the tray the squire merely waved at her so that Laura nodded towards the door and Ada went back out with the tray.

'Summat's up,' Ada told Fiona. 'The squire looks awful. I wonder whether he's poorly.'

'Or come off his horse,' Fiona said. 'Any signs of that?'

The squire had always been a very bad rider and had fallen off his horse several times over the years though thankfully had never been badly hurt. However, the people around him knew how old he was and shook their heads and said that his next fall might be his last and then there would be some dreadful foreigner coming to take over the acres.

'He wouldn't have been here then, would he?' Ada said. 'But he's awfully pale.'

'If it was catching he wouldn't come, so if it hasn't been a fall and it isn't something nasty it can't be that bad,' Fiona said and they were both comforted.

'John, are you ailing?' Laura said, coming over and putting her hand on his arm. He shook his head and then sat down heavily and not in the chair he particularly favoured. She let him and then she sat down across the fireplace from him.

'Is there something wrong?'

'My dear—' he stopped there, hesitating, looked briefly at her and then got up and wandered around the room. 'I – I don't know how to put it well so I will just come out with it. I can't marry you. I wish that it had been different but I can't.'

He wasn't looking at her, he had turned away as though what he was saying was no part of him.

Laura thought she must have misheard though her hearing had always been perfect. Then she heard the sentences repeated in her mind and she knew the squire had been told he had a terminal illness and could not marry her. She couldn't think of any other reason but was that a reason? Did men usually think more about another person than they did about themselves? Did he love her that much?

'Oh, John why? Whatever is the matter?'

'Something happened.'

Laura waited for him to go on and when he didn't she wished

he would look at her so that she could see the reason somehow in his face.

'Whatever it is you can tell me, surely. The wedding is so soon, all the arrangements are made. I have even had a lovely blue dress made especially.' She smiled encouragingly at him and finally he looked at her, frowning as though he had not understood.

'I know and I'm so sorry.'

He fidgeted, made his way around the room a couple more times and then stood in the centre of it for such a long time and yet she waited.

Did he think he was too old to enjoy marriage, to have such a close relationship, that she would regret marrying a man twenty years older than herself? But he didn't need to think about it, she had taken all that into account and was eager to marry him.

He didn't say anything and then, looking past his well-polished boots to the living room carpet, he said in a low and ragged voice,

'I cannot marry you, Laura, because I have to marry someone else.'

Laura had always scorned women who passed out, whether it was their corsets or just that they were silly and didn't eat enough she did not know, but she was glad that she was sitting down because she felt peculiar.

He said nothing more and she thought once again that she was in bed dreaming and that in a minute or two she would come round and smile at her fears. Everyone had notions like that. They meant nothing. You woke up and the sun shone and Ada was bringing you your first cup of tea in the morning. How wonderful.

But she did not wake up. He was still standing there.

'You cannot marry me?' Surely he hadn't said such a thing.

'No.' He spoke as though the worst had been said, he was regaining his composure. There was even a little colour coming back into his face. She could see it as he looked at her. 'I can't. I'm very sorry but it has to be done. I hope that you will forgive me.'

'Is there someone else?' Laura managed.

'No. At least yes, there will have to be. I need to marry somebody young, a girl who can give me an heir.'

Laura stared and as the silence lengthened she said into it,

'But your cousin—'

'I have found out that Aloysius has died and the only family I have left is some dreadful person who lives in the New World and always hated my home. My acres are all I have, you see, so I need an heir.'

She stared. Was he mad? Laura was going back into the horrible way that she had felt after Harry died. It was as if she was caught in a nightmare and she had thought she was coming out of it now but apparently it wasn't so. It would go on and on until she died. She felt sick, she felt strange, she could not believe that it was happening. It was like the same day all over again.

'We are less than two weeks away from the ceremony,' she said.

He didn't answer her. He didn't look at her. Laura became angry and then she heard what he had said and the blood rushed into her cheeks. She stared at him.

'You would give me up for a tumbling-down old house, a few acres and half a dozen shoddy little farms?' she said.

The squire hesitated. She knew he hated having his home described so disparagingly and inaccurately but for once she didn't care. She was hurt and trying to hurt him in the only way she knew how.

'No, Laura, not that.' He wasn't looking at her as though ashamed.

'Then what?'

'The idea of men being able to hand down what they have worked for all their lives to a son.'

'But your cousin had no children. Didn't it occur to you sooner?'

'I thought it would be his problem in twenty years and not mine.'

'If he hadn't married and produced an heir he would have had the same problem.'

'I wouldn't have been here. I wouldn't have had to take the responsibility for it but now I do. I have to think that someone belonging to me would carry this place forward and so would his son and so on for hundreds of years. That's what it's all about.'

'Is it? Is that really what marriage is all about? I thought the whole point was to spend time with someone you cared for?'

He didn't answer. He hesitated and then he said slowly,

'My family has lived up there for at least six hundred years. I cannot give it up for the sake of my own happiness.'

'Or mine?' Laura said. She was on her feet and would not acknowledge to herself that she was swaying. She tried to control it and then the ground came up to meet her and everything was black.

The squire left in a great hurry, observed by Ada and Fiona who watched him from the kitchen window as he went out into the stableyard and with an oath urged Oswald out of his way once the lad had helped him to mount his horse.

They looked at one another and then Ada went straight back

into the sitting room and there she found her mistress in a faint. She shouted to Fiona who went and got smelling salts. By the time Thomas came in for his lunch Laura was conscious again but very pale and Ada ran out into the stableyard and told him that his mother had lost consciousness and wasn't well.

'She fainted, sir.'

'My mother did?' He stared. She had never fainted before, not even when she found her husband dead by his own hand. Dr Crawcrook had spared Thomas none of the awful details. Thomas ran in.

'The squire was here, sir, and he left in a big rush and I just knew summat was up so I came in and found her there. She won't go to bed, sir, she won't.' Ada's voice was trembling.

Thomas found his mother sitting on the edge of the sofa like a visitor. She was so pale that he was frightened. His mother was never ill. They joked sometimes that she never needed a doctor. She needed one now.

'Ada, fetch some brandy,' he said and the girl scuttled off to do his bidding.

'I don't need brandy,' his mother said. 'I don't like it.'

'I never saw anyone who needed it more.'

Ada came in not with one of the big balloon glasses but a large sherry glass which she had filled to the brim so that unsteady hands would spill it. Thomas took the glass and tried to put it to his mother's lips.

'Drink it,' he urged her.

'I'd rather have tea,' she said, smiling just a little at her maidservant.

'Very sensible, Mrs Neville,' Ada ventured and went off again in search of the preferred beverage.

The doctor, having then tried to hand the glass to her and

failed, was rather glad of that. She was in shock but his mother was unlike anyone else. She always rallied. A woman who could go on like that after her husband had killed himself could handle anything.

'Don't fuss and don't crowd me,' she said, getting up, standing there rather unsteadily for a few moments and then she was still and her face had stopped being putty-coloured though her eyes were bleak.

'John has decided that he cannot marry me. His cousin has died who was much younger than he is and now he needs to produce an heir.'

Thomas was about to laugh in disbelief. He put down the glass in case he should be tempted to drink it himself. It was some kind of joke. The idea of a man of seventy being able to produce an heir was – well, it wasn't ridiculous, it could be done and the squire was hearty for his age but really, the whole idea was – yes, it was stupid. He would not live to see his child grow up. And in any case, though Thomas would not have said so, it could be that the squire could not produce a child. Men always thought the woman was to blame.

Thomas sat down and his mother walked about the room like a patient who had not wanted to be seen by the doctor and wished she could go home.

'But surely he doesn't need an heir,' Thomas said. 'Such a house is not entailed. If it was one of those big Northumbrian estates with thousands of acres it might be different but all he has is a very small estate with a few farms attached. Whoever inherits, and there must be someone, could just sell it.'

'He doesn't want it to be sold.'

Thomas was not often silenced but he was now. He couldn't think of a single thing to say and was glad when Ada came back with the tea though he thought he would have mightily enjoyed the brandy at that stage except that he had patients to see and another surgery to do at teatime.

Ada did not ask, she just poured out the tea and then she went to Laura and said,

'Sit down, madam, do sit down,' and Laura obeyed her and even thanked her for the cup and saucer which Ada gave carefully to her, making sure that Laura's hands were not shaking before she let go.

She gave another cup and saucer to Thomas and then she left the room, closing the door softly behind her. The tears came into Laura's eyes without her summoning them. They drifted down her cheeks, unwanted and unacknowledged.

Thomas tried to contain his anger. He could not go to the squire and call him a bastard and a blackguard, much as he wanted to. The man was old and quite obviously pitiably stupid. Nobody in his right mind would do such a thing. It was preposterous.

'He must be losing it,' was all Thomas could think.

'That's a very good, rude explanation even though I doubt it's true,' his mother said, sipping her hot tea. They sat there for a long while. Nobody mentioned lunch and Ada did not announce the meal as she usually did.

Thomas went off to see his patients as he must that afternoon and though his stomach rumbled he did not take any notice of it. He was relieved to get away. What to think or say or do he could not imagine. He would work off his temper.

When he had gone Ada brought Laura a huge glass of sherry and when she had drunk it Laura went to bed. She had never been this tired except after Harry died and it took every ounce of her energy. Now she felt the same, it was as though the squire had died and to her it meant the same thing, that she would be alone and lonely once more. She had dared to grasp at happiness and it had eluded her. She fell into bed and instantly into sleep. She had not been so grateful to sleep during the day like that for a very long time.

Thirty-Eight

Amos was shocked when he discovered that Joshua Butler had fallen down the stairs and died. It had not been because of him, had it? When he had left the old man was still alive and fit, he told himself. It was quite a usual way to go, that or falling on the fire or burning the house down from a single candle, old folk did such things every day, but he was aghast that the place would be left empty and perhaps even sold. He could not bear that it should be sold, that it may be given to some well-to-do family and done up and inhabited so that he would not be able to go there any more.

He wanted to be there. It was his by rights. He found himself thinking so much about Holy Well Hall that he started going there every day and being there all day. He was no longer at the manse. His wife nagged about his not being there and how he never did anything and how she had no money. He went to see the solicitor and told him that he believed he had a claim on the place, that his father had been the old man's brother.

'Joshua was the elder brother, so I understand,' Mr East said. 'The property was left specifically to him, the will is here and I can show it to you. Mr Butler was of course able to leave it to anyone he chose. There is no entailment. He left the place to his granddaughter.'

'Morally my father had a right to it and so do I,' Amos said. 'I have nothing but my work and my family. I am poor. It's not right that I shouldn't be entitled to half of it. As for that girl – she's foreign and ought not to have rights here. A foreign woman cannot have my inheritance.'

'I'm afraid, Mr Adams, that legally you haven't a leg to stand on,' Mr East said. 'Connie Butler inherits the house directly from her grandfather and it is now hers to do with as she will.'

Amos went to the Hall. It was so dark and dismal but it was the only place he felt safe and at home. He couldn't sleep at the manse. It was too quiet, like he was lost, he knew now that he had felt lost all his life. He knew he was entitled to go back and start again and he could only do that here. Now that old man Butler was dead and apparently that awful boy had deserted the place it was his. He would take it and live out the rest of his life there in the place he belonged. That foreign girl did not deserve and would not have it. He would live there and make it his.

His wife had taken to asking him not to go out.

'You go away from us for days,' she said, 'and I have no money to feed the children. What is going on with you, Amos? We would starve if people here did not look after us.'

He told her roughly to come out of the way and while he remembered he took the two bottles of whisky which had been left for him and put one into each pocket before he went. He could hear her calling after him but all he knew was that he needed to go to the Hall and listen to the sounds there.

They were sounds of long ago when he had been a small child and had parents. He remembered pigeons cooing in the nearby wood, and there were fish in the ponds which were sleek and orange. Or had he just been told that they were there and men had fished for them hundreds of years ago? He had so much in common with these people. Their voices made sense to him. He was always a small child when he was there and it was where he was meant to be, always when his heart was light and his mother sang to him.

Had she sung to him? Somebody had and there had been music from violins and laughter as of many people talking together. Parties. Always in his mind there were parties. He could remember the food, beef and good white bread and butter and pale cream cheese.

There was game, pheasant and partridge and woodcock when the men had been away in Scotland. They would stay at various castles or big houses and shoot woodcock. Woodcock was the best bird for eating, they would say, whereas grouse was disgusting. There was a joke about how you wrapped bacon around the grouse and roasted it and when it was done you threw away the grouse and had the bacon between two slices of bread with Worcester sauce.

Partridge would be roasted over a slow fire so that it was not tough. The cook chopped up the liver and put it inside the bird with various herbs and juniper berries and when it was done it was a feast.

He knew all these things though he was not sure he could even remember the taste of such delicacies. All his life he had eaten tough meat and woody vegetables and had nothing for himself, nothing to please him.

He would have this to please him now. The whisky would take him back to way beyond his childhood and into the history of this blessed place which held people so close to it like a mother.

He would lie down and could be back in any time, when he

was small or even before he was born when he had been just part of a day or a night or even a minute in the time beyond where his ancestors lived who had been a part of this place. He would be a part of this place now. He would lie down and cover himself in blankets and if he had the energy he would make a fire and pull up a chair and watch it until it died or until he slept. He was happy then. He had found his home.

Thirty-Nine

Flo woke up one morning not long before Christmas and she knew everything had changed. She looked back on how she had been, how she had lost the sense of who she was and where she was. Now it was all coming back. She was safe here at the Hilda House with Connie but there was something very much the matter. She didn't know what it was, she couldn't think, just that she felt fit and well. She climbed out of bed and went into the kitchen and there Connie looked surprised and pleased to see her.

'I feel better than I've felt in months,' Flo said.

She tried to put from her mind whatever it was that bothered her. What did she have to worry about? She couldn't think but things had altered. The boys had not come back of course and Connie worried.

Sarah was spending more and more time in Wolsingham with Miss Hutton and when she left the house in the mornings Flo could see that Pearl longed to go with her. Children needed other children, Flo thought.

She sometimes wondered if that had been Michael's downfall, that he had hated being an only child and taking all the responsibility for carrying on the family which his father had expected him to do.

He had lived up to none of that expectation. Looking back now Flo thought how very hard everything had seemed and it came to her when she had had her nap that afternoon that Joshua was no more.

She didn't know how she knew it, only that she did. That was what was wrong, that was why Connie looked even more sad than usual and that the quietness of the Hilda House was not just that the boys had left but that things had altered. Sarah no longer wanted to be there and Pearl should move into Wolsingham and go to school and lead a different kind of a life yet how could they?

She put it to Connie that Joshua had died when Connie brought in the tea things and scones which Mrs Rizzi had baked and Mr Smithers had brought up with the rest of the groceries earlier that day.

Connie's face fell and Flo could see guilt and horror pass across it.

'I was going to tell you but you've been so poorly I thought that you wouldn't remember,' she said.

'I knew it. We hadn't been married for forty years without my knowing such things. Tell me what happened.'

Connie therefore told her that Joshua had died in his sleep and that when the weather was better she would take Flo down to see his grave. The weather was turning hard this December so it would not be any day soon.

That changed everything for Flo. She resented though she understood why Connie had said nothing but also she resented that life had treated her so badly. First Michael and now Joshua and even Connie did not make up for it.

She thought of how Joshua had died alone in that bitterly cold house and of how she wished she had been a stronger and better wife to him. It grieved her and it was a different grief than she would have felt had she been there. She felt like a bad wife, she felt stupid and weak. How had she gone into this old age illness, how had she left him there to suffer on his own? She could not put from her mind that she had not done her duty as a wife. She was a bad person. She had had only one child who had left her, she had neglected her old husband and he died without her and worst of all somehow she had deserted her home, the place where she had lived for so very long with a man who loved her. She sat and cried and the tears were not tears of relief, they were hard cold tears that did not ease the ache inside her.

She was so distressed that she did not sleep or eat and when Connie pressed her to try and eat she threw up the food and that also was a disgrace. Was she so covered in self-pity that she had turned into this dreadful old woman? When she looked into the mirror, as she rarely did, all she saw was weakness.

Connie tried to help, telling her that she had done the best she could, but it would not do and she could not forgive how she had left him. She turned her face to the wall and lay there in a guilt-induced stupor until finally she slept. It seemed the only thing to do, to lose herself in sleep. She even wished that she would die while she was unconscious so she did not have to face this awful person every day.

Mr Smithers had taken to complaining about things to Connie. Was there something about her face which encouraged people to unload all their troubles, she wondered. She had sufficient troubles of her own but Mr Smithers was not a happy man.

Arnold had taken up with a girl in the village, the blacksmith's daughter.

Connie could not understand why that was a bad idea. The blacksmith's daughter was one of the bonniest girls in the dale. She had thick black hair and equally bright blue eyes and a shapely womanly figure and she was what they called her 'brazent fond', which was cheeky and thinking well of herself, but then there was no reason why the girl shouldn't think well of herself, Connie thought. She did not roam the streets of the village at night looking for young men, she did not cause problems, she looked after her father well, but people said she was sly and stuck out her chin and would be told nothing.

Connie felt an affinity with this girl but she said nothing. Mr Smithers was afraid of things going forward and why wouldn't he be? His wife had died a few weeks ago and Arnold was his only child. Arnold was well thought of. He worked hard and had no vices but now he had upset his father and Mr Smithers was bitter against his son because he had fallen in love. It occurred to Connie that it would not have mattered who Arnold loved, his father would have felt the same, but she could say nothing because he did not understand that he could be jealous at being pushed out of first place in Arnold's life. He had always come first, now he didn't, and he thought Arnold had chosen wrongly and that the girl was nothing but a hussy. Connie thought he should have left well alone. The blacksmith had been furious at the idea that the girl was not good enough for Arnold and had given Mr Smithers a piece of his mind.

Mr Smithers was unhappy and Connie caught the brunt of it.

She did attempt to talk to Mr Smithers about it in a positive way but he was never going to understand even though by rights Arnold should marry and have children as his father and forefathers had done.

'Why can't he be happy at home?' Mr Smithers said. 'He's just a boy. He's not old enough to take on responsibilities.'

In vain did Connie talk about very young people falling in love – she knew a lot about that, she was in the same predicament herself.

She also felt like saying that Mr Smithers was making things worse by objecting and that everyone had the right to marry whosoever they had chosen.

'He would leave me,' Mr Smithers said as though Arnold should have no life of his own.

From what she heard in the village his father's objections had turned Arnold from a nice young man into a person who had secrets and told lies and went behind his father's back, and according to gossip Arnold was spending a lot of time with the blacksmith's daughter and why shouldn't he, but she held her peace since she was getting nowhere.

Mr Smithers was a stubborn selfish man and he had been a much nicer person when he was not lonely. He did not know how to set about finding his own life when Arnold married and it would happen, Connie felt sure.

She tried to put such concerns out of her mind. There was nothing she could do about the boys, it was their choice to stay in Newcastle. Here she must go on providing a home for Sarah and Pearl and most of all for her grandmother. Mr Smithers was there daily picking up her or Sarah with the pony and trap, he would carry her back and forth so she could spend time with Miss Hutton and make plans and discuss new ideas. Luckily the weather was cold and windy without sleet, snow or ice, so Mr Smithers said, and the pony had no problems with the hills though Mr Smithers would advise Miss Butler to move into

Wolsingham for the winters in the future. What use would it be to be stuck up there on the felltop?

Mr Smithers made Connie feel uncomfortable because it seemed to her that he spelled out her most anxious thoughts. She was aware of how lucky they were at the moment but she knew the winters were long here and a decent snowstorm would mean she could go nowhere.

She tried to prepare for this, she bought in coal and logs and stored sugar and flour, and Mr Smithers brought her supplies from Mrs Rizzi. The arrangement with Mrs Rizzi was a good one so they had milk and tea and coffee and Mrs Rizzi sometimes sent ready-made meals. The women in the dale were good cooks but for people like Connie and her little family it was nice to have somebody else to take a little of the load.

That winter also Connie sometimes walked to see the old house. She made herself go. She was still worried there had been an intruder who had killed her grandfather or unwittingly caused his death but she knew the less she went the less she would be able to go and it was hers. She had to make it more hers and she would.

When she could afford to she would make the house safe and secure and she would hire somebody to do the vegetable garden and in time perhaps she would let the place to a tenant so that the house might earn its keep.

It made her sad thinking of how her grandparents had lived there all their lives and that probably she would not live there now and Dom and Leo would not come back but also she liked how her grandfather had not wanted to leave the dale.

She admired his spirit in that he was determined to die there and she couldn't see what was wrong with it except that having spent most of her life without him she had wanted to keep him safe. Nobody lived forever.

She walked in the garden and thought of her grandfather sitting on the wall smoking his pipe and she went into the house and tidied and cleaned. It was in such bad repair that she couldn't understand why she was making work for herself and then one day, when it was particularly dark and starting to snow and she should have got Mr Smithers to take her back up to the Hilda House, she realized that somebody was actually living here.

The whole idea made her skin crawl. The intruder had come back and perhaps he would try to kill her. She got out of the house very quickly and saw Mr Smithers and he took her home and told her that he would try to keep an eye on the place though he was very busy but she was not to go there without him any more.

She knew this was common sense and so she agreed and there was a slight feeling of relief at not going. The time to be there was not right but she could not stop thinking about it.

There had been a fire in the kitchen grate and one of the chairs had been moved close to it. The bed had been slept in. All the items she had folded so carefully and put into cupboards were out and had been used. She did not know whether to take them away and therefore make the house even less uninhabitable because part of her was glad that somebody was using the place and she felt envy because she could not live here and take what was rightfully hers. She began to resent the Hilda House and all that it represented, when she already felt lonely at the thought of the Hall being used by someone else.

She tried to think about what it would be like in spring. How she would be able to come here and begin growing things. She liked the idea that the ground was always fruitful and that even after all these years this place still belonged to the Butler family.

She loved the Hilda House as a project but this place was ingrained in her bones and sometimes when she lay in her comfortable bed at night she thought she could feel the Hall missing her and wishing her there so that she could carry on her life in a new way.

It would take an awful lot of putting right, this house, she thought as she made her way between the four rooms, trying to think of her father being here and the family before her grandparents and how it would always be special to her.

Perhaps when she could afford to do up that house and make it safe and sound she and her grandmother and Sarah and Pearl would be able to move in but she was so short of money that she could only sigh over the idea.

Connie told Sarah that she was afraid somebody had spent time at the Hall but Sarah said she had no inclination to go now that the old man was dead and yet sometimes Sarah thought about the place and wondered what it must be like to have a house of your own. She had nothing but happy memories of that house. How strange that she should have become fond of old Joshua yet there had been something about the countryman she had liked.

It occurred to her that if Dom had been like his grandfather, and she a little older than she was they might have got married and she would have lived there and made it so much better. She would have helped him in the garden and made wonderful dinners for him – even though she knew her cooking was dreadful her daydreams transformed it.

They would have handsome children and take them all to church, no chapel-going for them, and in the winter when it was cold they would sit by the kitchen fire and she would knit and sew and she would read the newspaper to him while he smoked his pipe. It was such a beautiful dream that despite what Connie had said she longed to see it one more time and imagine the future as it was in her head.

It was the talk of the village when Amos Adams went missing. The weather was foul and he had taken nothing with him as far as Mrs Adams could see. She, as a lot of people now did, went to the doctor rather than to Mr Whitty for help. She did not know what else to do. He had been gone a week by then. She didn't feel able to tell the doctor that he had been gone that long but he often went away for two or three days. This time she had waited for him to come back and it had not happened.

Thomas had known that Amos Adams was in a bad way. Mr East, while not being able to talk about such things, let slip a few details when they met at the Black Lion because he liked that the doctor must keep everything confidential.

Thomas had started going there because of Mr East and a few others who were on his social level and though they did nothing but sit about and talk he liked how different it was from the Bay Horse so when he was alone with Mr East for a few minutes they talked about Amos Adams.

He was badly liked, that Thomas had already known. He drank and neglected his family and you could not do such things in a village of that size without people resenting you. Also he had a position to keep up, clergymen were well respected and relied on for morals and to give people guidance, but Amos Adams had not managed this. Thomas had the feeling the man was getting worse.

When he went missing, however, it made matters harder. All it took was one snowstorm and people got lost up on the fells or froze to death in the fields.

Laura was no longer going there to help, she was sitting at home brooding about what might have been, but when Mrs Adams came to the house Thomas got the village to help and in a lot of ways it was easier now that her husband had deserted them. She had a brother who lived in Scarborough. They had been estranged for years because he did not like her husband but Thomas said that if she liked he would write to her brother and see if something could be done for her and her two boys.

The doctor was coming very little now but even so Connie couldn't have asked any more of him. She knew it was partly her fault, that after he had proposed marriage and been turned down he was less eager to be there, but also she thought he knew that her grandmother was getting worse and in fact it was nothing more than old age and all the complications which went with it. Flo had altered. Connie knew she missed her husband so very much that she grieved and could not put from her the idea that she was much to blame. Physically Flo was dying but it was her mental state which brought her down so far, Connie knew, and neither she nor the doctor could do much about that. And she could not ask him to come when what she really wanted was sight of him, to be a part of his life, to hear him laugh and to make conversation, to take part in his days and not be just somebody on the edge of them, turned out and turned down. If the doctor was angry with her Connie did not blame him though she little knew how she could change anything.

Sarah was the one who went down into the dale with Mr Smithers that morning the week before Christmas. She had been longing to go out but had tried to be content staying with Pearl. Connie sensed it and asked her why she didn't go to see Miss Hutton by herself that day and Sarah was so pleased that she went with him and after she had spent a couple of hours with Miss Hutton and talked about cloth and designs and had a lot of sketches and material to take back to Connie she decided that it was too soon to go back. It was a bright cold sunny day and she thought she would go for a walk.

She walked to the place where Connie's granddad had died. She hadn't been there since before he had died but she had happy memories of it and since the day was fine and it was not far she went. Connie had said she thought that somebody had been living there but she had seen nobody, just a dead fire and things taken from cupboards so that somebody could find shelter there. It did not bother her that when she got there the door was unlocked, but when she opened it there were signs that somebody had been there recently.

She hesitated but could hear nothing. She called out but nobody replied. She stepped into the room where the grand-parents had lived and then she stopped short. Somebody was huddled in the chair near the fire. She was half inclined to run back to the village and get Mr Smithers to take her home but she didn't.

She ventured nearer. There was the sound of somebody breathing. It was the breath of sleep, she could hear it, regular and yet there was some kind of disturbance in it, like a rattle, as though the sleeper had breathing problems. She tiptoed into the room and stopped well before she reached him. She recognized the sleeve, frayed and dirty, and the thin grubby hand and wrist that protruded. She knew to whom it belonged. She stopped again but when he did not awaken or move she went on until she was in front of him and the dead fire.

It was Mr Adams. She almost ran out, she had been so afraid of him, but he did not come round and so her fear abated and the more she stood the more her worries retreated and she realized that he was very ill. She had seen old people like that before they died but he was not that old.

She remembered how he had treated her, she thought of all the hurtful things he had done to her but these were now interlaced with how Connie had taken her in and looked after her so they were nowhere near as bitter as they had been. She felt like going and leaving him there like that to die and then she remembered how much Connie felt for this place and she couldn't do it.

She went back to the doctor's house. He wasn't there but Ada and Fiona welcomed her into the kitchen, they had known her well. When the doctor came home Ada went to get him. Sarah would have gone with him to the house but he said,

'Don't worry, I will take care of this. Why don't I get Mr Smithers to drive you home?'

'But sir, what if he dies?'

'It will not be your fault,' the doctor said and he smiled at her.

Forty

It was not long after the squire had jilted Mrs Neville that she told Thomas over breakfast that she wanted to go back to Durham. He was not surprised but had been dreading it. Gossip said that the squire was about to marry the local blacksmith's daughter, Emma Lee, who was all of eighteen years old, the girl whom everybody knew that Arnold loved.

It had been the cause of a lot of talk in the village, that the blacksmith was pleased with the idea his daughter would marry so well and that Arnold's nose had been put out of joint because he was not able to marry the girl he cared for. Connie felt sorry for Arnold but perhaps Emma Lee would refuse. That seemed unlikely. What girl would not have her head turned when she was able to marry the most eligible old man in the whole area?

The squire had gone to see the blacksmith, Jonty Lee. They had met before of course on mart days in St John's Chapel and at the various shows in the autumn and Jonty Lee looked after the squire's horses and was therefore familiar with his outdoor servants but Jonty Lee was quite concerned when the squire turned up at his front door. Friends went around the back so he was worried as to why the squire should call.

Emma had directed him into the parlour and called her father inside.

She kept his house so clean and neat, Jonty thought, she was a fine lass. It had hurt him very much when Mr Smithers had not thought her good enough for his son. It struck him forcibly at the time that she was too good for anybody in the village.

Now Emma, being a girl of sensible mind, brought them a decanter of single malt, a jug of water and two thick square glasses. She had gone out and had closed the door to the kitchen so she would not overhear their conversation.

'What are you thinking of to do with your daughter?' was the squire's first attempt at his subject after the small talk they managed.

Jonty didn't know what to say and waited for the squire to go on.

'I would like to marry her.'

This took the blacksmith aback. He knew – everybody knew – that the squire had jilted the doctor's ma so what was going on?

'I need to marry a young woman. I need an heir, you see,' and the squire explained his problem.

At first Jonty was aghast at the idea of an old man marrying his child but he remembered how Mr Smithers had said she was not good enough for his lad. That would show them. He thought about his daughter and how good and beautiful she was. She had not said that she was disappointed when her brief walks and talks with the lad had been curtailed because Arnold's father did not like her. She took things well but he had no idea whether she would ever consent to marry a man old enough to be her grandfather, no matter how much her father wished it.

After the squire left he called her into the parlour. Her eyes gave nothing away as he explained and he said carefully,

'The squire has asked me for your hand in marriage. You are my sole child and I would have you do nothing you don't want to do and I know, though you have said nothing, that if Arnold Smithers had been a better man's son you could have married him. I know how fond you were of one another. Will you think about it? If you did marry such a man it would be very good in so many ways but I would not have you leave me if you didn't want to.'

In answer to this she came to him and threw her arms around his neck and began to sob. Jonty had not expected this and didn't know whether to be glad or sorry but she told him in a whisper that she would be pleased and grateful to marry the old man and go to live in the richest house in the area. He was a lovely old man and she would do her best to take good care of him as she had always done for her father.

'I think we would need a builder in before you could go home,' Thomas said when his mother voiced her desires.

'I don't care. I just want to get out of here. I hardly dare leave the house for people watching and pitying me.'

'I doubt they mean any harm.'

'That is not the point. This is not and never will be my home. I would like you to come with me but if you make it difficult for me I shall go anyway.'

'Of course I'll go with you.'

His mother said,

'I'm sorry, Thomas, it's just that—' She didn't finish the sentence. He went and stood behind her chair and then he leaned in and kissed her cheek. She patted his hand and then he went to his surgery.

He didn't think he behaved much like a doctor that day. The last thing he wanted was to leave Weardale even for a day or two but then his mother felt that she could not stay and who was he to say anything when she had already been through so much.

The squire's new wedding day was to be in March but Thomas knew very well that his mother would be pleased to be long gone as soon as could be arranged. Christmas was always a bad time for coughs and colds and flu and pneumonia but there was little else to be done. He could hardly let her go alone.

Laura Neville could not believe the state of her house when she got back to Durham. Her memories fed her better times, easier days when she had been married and was happy.

She was appalled. Thomas had got builders in to sort out the leaks that happened after Harry had died and although the place was drying out it was a mess. She must have been in shock or she would never have left it to such a fate.

Her beautiful garden had suffered neglect and there must have been a great storm which she did not recall from Weardale. Trees had fallen over and been left where they lay. The grass was knee-high and the flower and vegetable beds were choked with weeds. No horses filled the stables and there were no dogs to run out and give her a good homecoming.

Worse still somebody had broken into the house, smashing the windows, and no doubt finding nothing of value there had smashed the furniture, put out most of the windows with bricks and thrown on the floors everything from the cupboards that they could find. The kitchen was sticky with a mess of disintegrating sugar and flour. As she stepped in there various mice scurried into dark corners.

Upstairs the roof had not been repaired as she had hoped and she could see daylight through the bedrooms. Everything up there smelled of damp and decay.

'Mother, you cannot stay here,' Thomas said.

'I have no intention of doing so. I will go to the County.' She meant the County Hotel, the best in the city.

She could see by his face that he didn't approve.

'That is not a good idea,' he said. 'How would you feel going down to dinner by yourself?'

He was right. People would start talking about her again and she had had enough of that.

'You must come back to Wolsingham with me.'

'And face that man and the little trollop he's wedding?'

'We will both stay at the County for tonight,' was Thomas's compromise.

In the end she agreed. This was hard work and she had had enough for one day.

But that too was a mistake. The minute she got through the doors of the County Hotel her mind gave her the dinner dances she had attended here. She thought of how handsome Harry had been in evening dress. She had been so proud to walk in anywhere with him. He was well known, well loved.

It was almost Christmas and dinner dances and celebrations for various groups happened every night of the week except Sunday. It was bad enough the squire getting married and she having nothing, dreading going forward in any way, but this just made things worse.

She had owned so many lovely dresses, silver and white and green, claret-coloured velvet which swept the floor and he had bought her diamonds for her neck and her wrists, her ears and even in one case a tiara for her lovely golden hair. Every dream had been fulfilled by her marriage to him.

He had been such a good dancer too. Round and round the floor they waltzed and she was in his arms and the world had nothing more to offer.

After dinner they would split up and go around talking to various people at the tables – friends and people about to be friends who they would ask to their next party at Christmas or New Year or Easter or during the summer because their house was on the river and lent itself to those lazy evenings.

They'd watch the rowers go by and wave, and see younger couples walking hand in hand. Dogs would be barking over a ball which had got into the river and then the Labrador would swim out to it with sure strokes and bring it back. Laura could remember the yellow gleam of the Labrador's coat and the shine of her dark eyes that she had retrieved this most precious subject for the people upon whom she had bestowed her life.

Most of their close friends had ignored Laura when they understood that Harry had killed himself, because after all it must have been her fault, something she didn't do, something which hadn't pleased him, and so he hadn't wanted to be with this woman any longer. She was a pariah to them. It was one of the reasons she had left her house and retreated to Wolsingham and the comfort of her son's love and his house and even his servants who had been so kind to her.

Now as she walked into the County Hotel with her son by her side she saw a couple who had ignored her since Harry had died. They came coolly across to her while she could hear strains of the music for it was a Saturday night and there was a dinner dance. She had not remembered it until she got here.

Through the big doors she could see people dancing and beside it the dining room where the tables glittered with silver and shone with glasses amidst candles white and flickering.

'Why Laura,' the other woman greeted her and Laura could not remember her name for which she was thankful. 'How lovely to see you.' Her husband was shorter than her, a fact Laura was thankful for which showed how low she was, Harry had been six inches above her and she had so liked that.

Laura merely smiled and did not reply.

'Congratulations. We hear that you are to be married again and to such an august man as John Reginald. We thought you did very well the first time to marry as you did but to triumph again after Harry died and in such a way we never thought to hear from you again. You and the squire must come and stay with us. I will write to you.'

Laura stood like she had been turned to stone.

'Who on earth was that cow?' her usually correct son muttered in a low voice when the couple had gone away.

Laura turned around and walked out the main front door of the hotel.

'I cannot stay here,' she said as her son went after her.

'Why don't we find the little writing room at the back?' was his compromise. 'There'll be nobody in it now and I could bring you a glass of sherry.'

Laura wanted to be petty and childish and say that she didn't want any bloody sherry but it wasn't true and it wasn't fair after all he had done since his father had died.

So Thomas guided her away from the busy part of the hotel into a little back room with a roaring fire, small tables and large armchairs. It was empty of other people, as he had said. It was all she could stand. There were Christmas decorations everywhere, streamers across the ceilings from corner to corner, even a Christmas tree. She could hear far off in the backstreet somebody singing 'Away in a Manger'. She had always disliked that tune but she thought of the many happy Christmases she and Harry had had and while she wanted to be grateful for these she missed him so much.

'I'll go and sort out rooms for us. Sit down,' Thomas said with swift urgency.

She did. The sherry arrived shortly afterwards, in a glass decanter. It reflected the firelight in its pale cream clear glow. The waiter poured out a large glass for her and then retreated.

Faintly now she could hear music from the ballroom. She felt that Thomas was away for a long time. She felt sorry for him having to deal with all this. If he had had half a dozen siblings it would have been so different and she would have been occupied with grandchildren and being widowed would not have been nearly as difficult as it was. At least she thought so.

'I've ordered room service,' he said.

Oh, how wonderful, Laura thought.

Less than an hour later they were eating dinner and looking out over the river from her sitting room.

'Tomorrow I'll find a builder who can put the house to rights,' she said. 'Your father was friends with Fatimus Brown so I shall ask him if he will help me. I think I can stay here by myself now. Go back to Wolsingham and your patients and your cook and bottle-washers.' She smiled at him and put a hand on his arm.

'I can't leave you here by yourself,' he said.

'I'll be fine. Putting the house to rights will give me something to do. I just want you to go back to Wolsingham now where you are needed.' Also, though she didn't say it, she couldn't bear to be in Wolsingham for the lead up from Christmas to the New Year. She shuddered. She knew she couldn't stay at her house but even in the hotel there would be so much merriment, so many people rejoicing. She remembered how she and Harry had gone to the cathedral. There weren't many times of year she could get him to go to church after they married but he did like carol singing and how they would walk home by the river in the dark nights, with stars and a decent moon and the fires on in the house and silly drinks like punch and eggnog over the fire. She had been happy then.

Thomas knew exactly what she meant. After the squire was married life would be easier though Thomas had the feeling that his mother would never leave Durham again.

Thomas felt abandoned and although he wasn't the kind of man to feel sorry for himself he did now. He was going back to work and but for the servants to an empty house. Connie had refused to marry him and his mother had left. He did not want to be in Durham yet when he got back to Wolsingham he didn't want to be there either and despaired of how stupid he felt. It was a good thing there was work to do though the weather became bad in the dale and he had problems reaching outlying farms and even walked to some of them so afraid was he that his horse might slip and break a leg. Having to have one of his beloved horses put down might finish him off and make him want to run away.

'If it was up to me I'd pull it down,' Fatty Brown said. Even his name somehow made Laura feel better. He was tall and slender and therefore his name was beautifully inappropriate. He was a man Harry had liked and trusted but Laura was horrified when he spoke so plainly to her.

'Surely it's not as bad as that,' she ventured.

'It's dropping to pieces, Mrs Neville. It's been there for hundreds of years and to be honest it was never a good house.'

The scales fell from Laura's eyes. She had loved it because she had loved Harry and he would never have moved. He had liked being by the river and on fine nights would sit out there with his claret and his dogs and she would go and sit with him on the bank below the house and they would watch the lovely Wear flowing away to Sunderland and the North Sea and perhaps even beyond.

'If you put your business head on,' Mr Brown said, 'you would pull it down and build smaller houses here. There are lots of good honest Durham folk looking for a place to rent or buy. A terrace of well-built houses would be a godsend to them and it couldn't be in a better place. If they were affordable it would mean good business in Durham and good business for growing families, tradesmen and their like. Otherwise you end up with an exodus and they have to live outside the town and it makes life difficult for them. It's a prime spot,' he said.

Laura was amazed to be able to talk about this house she had thought she dearly loved in such a businesslike way and she found that it was simpler than she had thought and that she no longer wanted to live there. She was happy at the hotel for now and she could think about the future later.

When he had gone she lingered, trying to look forward instead of back, not to bring up once more the old memories of how happy she had been then. She could be happy again perhaps doing something useful, constructive. She retreated to the hotel and sat over the fire with her sherry.

The waiters were used to her now as she spent her evenings in the little back room which she had made her own. She had learned to know them all by name and they seemed to like her. She had kept her big rooms upstairs and sometimes had dinner there and that night she stayed upstairs and watched the river she loved so much and thought that Harry would approve of having terraced houses built in the location he had loved so much. It would be like a tribute to him and when she enabled other people to buy a reasonably priced house Harry would be smiling down from heaven.

She decided in the end that she would get Mr Brown to do her bidding. They could design the houses between them and he could do the building and she might even get some satisfaction from watching the old place come down. Time to move on, Laura, she urged herself.

Mr Brown came and had a drink with her in the little writing room, nothing more serious than a single pint of dark beer, which she found disappointing but liked him for it in a way. There was a table and several chairs and they began to plan and sketch. They could have big back gardens on the street side, there was plenty of room and people could grow vegetables and flowers and keep hens if they chose or even a pig.

The houses would be sideways to the river with a big common piece of land between them at the front. There would be room here for three lots of terraced houses. The green was where children could play safely and at the bottom beside the river there would be a fence across so nobody could fall in.

She even invited Mr Brown to dinner and not in the back room but in the main dining room. She didn't care whether people talked about her now, she was past that, and she was very excited about what they were about to achieve.

Mr Brown was a hearty eater. She had forgotten that men ate so much. Poor Thomas was always trying to make time for meals and never managing it. She smiled to herself that her son had become Poor Thomas. In a secret way she was rather proud of herself for managing her independence.

She wore a plain dress but for the first time in months she enjoyed wearing jewellery and diamonds glittered around her neck. Mr Brown was all done up too and they had champagne to toast their new venture. He caught on to what she was saying – as much light as possible, space and lots of fresh air and the houses built well from local materials and sold as cheaply as they could manage, but that Mr Brown could still make a fair living and she would have a profit in case she wanted to build another house for herself.

Strangely, she didn't want to. The responsibility didn't feel right just now. Maybe it was too soon to think of such things. She had got the hang of living at the County and rather taken to having other people do everything for her. No worries, no washing, no cooking or thinking about servants or making sure that everything was right and done. She was starting to enjoy herself.

Laura had the feeling that they would manage other projects. She was rich. Harry had been born rich and had made money. She had never wanted for anything, she thought with affection. Her pledge to Harry now was that their legacy should be something for the people of Durham.

She could still hear the music at night but by then she and Mr Brown were at the site every day and he had begun demolishing the old house so she no longer cared about dinner dances and bad friends.

Laura was surprised but rather pleased with herself when she invited Fatty to dinner on February 14th. She told herself that it was a coincidence but it wasn't. She had been managed by circumstances so very often and now she was taking charge. She hesitated for a few moments, unsure what she would do if he turned her down when it was such an obvious thing to do but much to her glee he didn't.

He came suitably clad in a gorgeous suit and did not seem disconcerted when the waiter left them by themselves when the dinner had been served. Laura, after two glasses of red wine, ventured,

'Why did you never marry?'

He looked at her across the table, but the look told her nothing.

'You never met anyone?' she prompted. 'You aren't romantic? You're the one man in the world who didn't want sons?'

Fatty looked disconcerted.

'I have sons,' he said. 'I thought you would know.'

'I never heard anything about it,' Laura said, wishing she had been more tactful. 'But you never married her?'

'I was an idiot. I was seventeen. Her father took her away to Canada when I wouldn't have her. I've never seen my sons.'

'And it put you off?'

'Well, if I'd been her father I would have beaten me to a pulp but he wasn't like that and my father thought it was funny that I'd got away with not marrying her. I couldn't forgive myself when I got older. She got married and then had three daughters. I did write several times but she didn't reply after telling me her present circumstances and then I lost touch and now my sons will be adults and have their own children and I missed it all.'

'So she got over you?'

'I do hope so. She was braver, she got on with her life, whereas I seem to have got bogged down in mine.' Fatty shrugged in disgust at himself. 'After that I worked.'

There was a long silence. The waiter came back with coffee and Laura silently blamed herself for making things so very difficult. Perhaps she would never see Fatty again except as a builder and suddenly she didn't want that to happen. She wanted him there in her life. She liked how tall and well tailored he looked tonight with his shiny hair and blue eyes. She had lost two men. Was she going to lose a third? She was terrified of the loneliness if this should happen. She had been lucky and then bereft so she could barely look at him and he didn't look at her for quite a while.

They sat and watched the river. The fire sparked and the room was cosy but Laura thought she had spoiled the mood.

And then Fatty said, all of a sudden, abruptly, like it was something he didn't intend to say, or didn't want to,

'I brought you a present.'

It was the very last thing Laura expected.

'Why?' she queried. 'Christmas is over, New Year has gone and my birthday is in August.'

Harry had given her jewellery but she was not the less impressed by the sapphire earrings which Fatty gave her. They were balm to her damaged ego.

'Oh Fatty,' she said, 'they are exquisite. They must have cost an awful lot of money.' She knew this was tactless but she couldn't think of what else to say.

'They did,' Fatty admitted, but there was a twinkle in his eyes. 'Happy Valentine's Day, Laura. There's music playing downstairs. Will you come and dance with me?'

So she did.

The squire married his new lady amidst much talk but of course he did not hear it and Emma Lee's father was very proud that she had decided to marry the old man.

It was Dr Alexander Blair from further up the dale who attended Mrs Reginald during the birth and it was a comparatively easy one. The girl did not seem to be worried about the whole thing. Dr Blair would have thought it a full-term child, yet it was apparently only seven months since the squire had married her. Dr Blair was just glad he had the heir he had wanted.

Mrs Reginald was young and fit and very cheerful. She came through the ordeal so quickly and so easily that she was soon back to full fitness and Dr Blair could see that she would be a doting mother to her lovely little boy.

She breastfed easily right from the start and like many other country women she carried the baby around with her all day in a sort of sling fashioned from a large shawl. The child was very contented.

The squire did not live to see his child grow. He died within days of the baby being born but at least he knew it was a boy and that made him happy.

Six months later Mrs Reginald married Arnold Smithers, whose father had not thought the girl was good enough for him. Mr Smithers was happy about it then.

The squire had had dark hair and eyes whereas Arnold had bright red hair and blue eyes and so did the squire's young son.

The dale agreed that Arnold was a good lad and had done well to find the squire's widow eager to marry him. He therefore went to live up there at the big house with his new wife. Dr Blair was glad that they prospered up on the tops.

Forty-One

Thomas hadn't realized what a relief it would be to get back to Wolsingham and leave his mother with some kind of a future to think about, but now that he had sorted things out he found that he was not satisfied here. Maybe his mother changing her life like that was the right thing for him to do as well. He was beginning to believe it, especially when he got a letter from his mother to tell him of her huge new project. He could hear her voice through her writing and she sounded better.

Amos Adams moved into the bedroom, which Thomas's mother had previously occupied. Thomas couldn't think what else to do. He didn't want the man to die but neither did he want him there. The man started to recover and acted as though he had always been there, issuing orders to the two maidservants and demanding whisky which they did not bring him.

When they would not feed his habit he threw things across the room and muttered terrible oaths. Fiona burst into tears more than once. Ada, being made of sterner stuff, told the doctor that they would stand no more of it, yet Thomas couldn't think what else to do. He could hardly turn the wretched man out into the winter weather.

Sometimes he was less than coherent and talked incessantly about Holy Well Hall until Thomas understood how cruel things had been for him and how much love he had squandered because of something which he could never have.

That house had meant something different to everyone who knew it. To Joshua it had held him back and yet held him up, to Mickey it had been a curse, to Amos it had been an unfulfilled dream. Thomas felt that Connie was finding her responsibilities very hard to bear and yet she would not let him take her away from it and that the Hall was just another burden pressed to her. He also wondered whether, considering its immediate unhappy past, he could persuade her to let him put money into the project of doing up the Hall. He did worry about her up there with very little protection so he thought also about the Hall and whether it could be changed and made useful. Also he did not know that she would care to have him involved in any such project.

Thomas decided that he would let Oswald deal with Amos. Oswald was taciturn. He would take no notice of cursings so after that Amos's meals were delivered to him without whisky and his bedroom door was locked so he could not roam the house. The walls were thick and nobody could hear him ranting.

More than two months after Amos had been rescued by the doctor, Oswald came up to give the wretched man his breakfast to find the window open and snow blowing onto the carpet. He ran downstairs and although few of the men had any affection for Amos Adams, they remembered that he had a family and that he was their minister, bad as he seemed to them, and so they organized a search party.

The storm got worse until they had to give up searching for him. The days in March barely got light and the snow deepened. It was typical weather. Just after the lambs were born there were what here were called lambing storms and March and April could be even worse than January.

They went out when they could if there was any light but in the end Thomas saw a glow in the Hall and he guessed that the man had somehow got back to what he thought of as his home. Thomas had been there every day thinking that Amos would attempt to get back there but this was the first time he had held any hope.

He plodged through the snow, worried about what he would find or what he might not, and sure enough the doors were open, the windows were open and a tiny fire was burning in the grate. Amos Adams had lain down by that fire and there he had died in the place which had possibly, Thomas thought, been the only place that he had ever loved.

Amos Adams' funeral was well attended, partly from curiosity and partly because he had lived among them and the villagers were too generous to let his memory be besmirched by his many shortcomings. There should be nothing bad said about someone who was part of the community and especially since he had been so unhappy. Most of them had enough experience to remember 'He who is without sin among you let him cast the first stone' and so they wanted to give him and themselves respect, pity and even love.

A nearby minister from Crook came to take the funeral service and Thomas, who had written to Mrs Adams' brother some short while ago, decided to go and see what he could do for the poor woman.

The door was opened by a well-dressed man who resembled her very much and he ushered Thomas into the house. Mrs Adams looked shocked and yet relieved and why wouldn't she? Her marriage had been so hard for her.

'Thank you for getting in touch and telling me how matters stood. I didn't like him,' the brother confided in Thomas as he walked the doctor from the house. 'He parted us and set her against me a long time ago. Now I will do what I can to help her and take her away from this wretched place and give her the kind of decent life she deserves.'

The man shuddered. Thomas wanted to be offended for Weardale but he could see what he meant. He lived in Scarborough where he ran a number of grocery stores and could well afford to take in his sister and his nephews, he said.

Forty-Two

Having realized that his mother was happier than she had been since his father died Thomas became more restless. It was not that he didn't feel at home here but his love for Connie Butler got worse and worse if it could be described in that way. It certainly wasn't a comfortable feeling. He knew Connie was right in that she would not let him take on her responsibilities and he admired her for it but he hated that there were obstacles between them.

The only way to get past this was to leave, he had finally persuaded himself. To stay there and eventually to find that Connie married somebody else or he settled for another woman was unthinkable so he did what in his heart he knew he wanted to do, he applied to the London hospital where he had trained. He thought that he could do so much good there and he might specialize in some way.

He still had friends there and some of them were in a position to help him towards his goal and he had liked being there. He had enjoyed the bustle of the capital and the places of leisure and the pace of life. Here everything seemed slow and measured. He did feel rather guilty that he was leaving folk here after such a short time but he knew he was right to move on. His mother had her independence and she was not very old. He might as well do the things he wanted and live somewhere he felt was right.

Connie's grandmother would not last long and after she died he had the feeling Connie would not stay either. Why would she when she had no family here?

Connie was not very surprised to find her grandmother had died in her sleep. It must have been an easy way to go and she knew very well that Flo longed for her husband and why would she not after they had been together for most of their lives?

Everything seemed to change at that point. She had been debating with herself whether to go to Newcastle and see her brothers. Mr Leslie had said they were well and happy and although she wanted them to be happy she wanted them to be happy with her.

Also she did not want to leave her grandmother just as the old lady was failing. It was not fair to any of them and so she sat by the window while snow fell and she sewed and she let the days go on while her grandmother slept easily and peacefully and when she awoke Connie would feed her and tell her good things and she would smile. Connie knew it would not be long now and she wanted to cherish her grandmother's last days on earth.

It was all so quiet and still and while she knew her grandmother would have preferred to die in her own home with her husband by her side this was the next best thing.

Connie sat by her side for her last few hours and spoke softly to her and saw that her grandmother was in no pain and had no bad dreams that she was crying out from and so her grandmother passed into what Connie hoped were better hands than hers and if there was any justice she was with her husband for eternity and it was a kinder place than this had been to her.

After they had buried her grandmother Connie began to feel

as though she had no future here. She took no joy in anything. There seemed to be so little left. Her family was ebbing away from her like an outgoing tide.

This house was not right for them and yet how could they leave? They had nowhere to go and would only be a problem to whoever might take them in. She had not forgotten that the doctor had offered to take the whole family. She could not do that to him even now.

It was therefore late April when the weather turned wet and she could go to Newcastle. Sarah had said she would stay with Miss Hutton where she liked being best and that she would take Sid to Mrs Rizzi. Mrs Rizzi would take care of Sid and he in turn she hoped would kill the rabbits which plagued her garden so that she could make pies and pâté and stews.

Pearl was eager to see her brothers.

Connie had written but after she sent the letter she set off for Newcastle almost immediately. She had been so worried about them but in her heart she knew that had her brothers wanted to come back to her they would have done so before now.

She was almost relieved to go from the Hilda House to somewhere new and not feel as though she was neglecting some duty she believed was hers. She felt some guilt still as though she was turning her back on something important, as though there was something left in the old broken-down village she had tried so hard to make her home.

She was also nervous and worried about Dom. Mr Leslie had said that Dom did not remember who he was or who anybody else was. She hoped that when he saw her he would remember. She also had the feeling that she would not be liked by Dom and Leo's apparently new family. It was not like her to be jealous but she was now.

The journey did not seem to her to be long enough. It went over at such speed that she felt breathless. She wished she could turn back the clock and put it off, put it back for days and possibly for weeks.

When she had written she had told Dom and Leo that their grandmother and grandfather had died. She did not want to surprise or hurt anybody any further.

Mr Leslie had told her where the Seamen's Mission was and she found it easily but she felt sick and tearful by then and was so afraid of what would happen now. It seemed to her that Pearl understood and she was also afraid. She clasped Connie's hand tightly.

From the moment the door opened and she saw Mrs Forster all those feelings disappeared. The woman took Connie and then Pearl into her arms and welcomed them. It was the best welcome Connie had ever had. She ushered them into a huge sitting room and gathered the family around them. First her husband and then her daughter and finally the two boys.

Dom had changed. Connie could see that he did not remember them but she could see that also he was sorry he could not. Tears stood in his eyes and he embraced his sisters and told them that he was so glad they had come.

Leo said very little. Connie could see how ashamed he was that he had run away and yet he was not sorry he had done so because he was happy. She merely said how glad she was to see him again and to meet them all.

She talked to Dom about his future and to Rose about the wedding which would not be for a long time yet and how Dom would make such a good minister when he got that far but in her heart she grieved for she could see that her brothers were lost to her and why would they not be? This was the best place they could have gone to.

She and Pearl stayed there. She did not know what else to do. Leo was eager to show her what a wonderful city Newcastle was and introduced her to various seamen and talked of how he would become a sailor.

Dom walked with her so that they were by themselves.

'I'm so sorry for what I did,' he ventured.

'You mustn't be. Especially when you don't even remember it. It was hard.'

'Yes but it must have been hard for you and yet you didn't run away.'

'Oh, Dom—' she would never get used to calling him Frederick and didn't care to. 'I wanted to so very often so very much but for Grandmother. Sarah was there for me, we helped each other.'

'That doesn't excuse me.'

'You must forgive yourself,' she said, 'nobody blames you and you have your whole life in front of you. In so many ways it was exactly the right thing to do and look how it is working out.'

Dom said nothing for a long while and then as they stood by the river, watching the daylight fade to mid evening he turned to her and said earnestly,

'I have talked to Mr and Mrs Forster and to Rose and we want you to come and live here with us. We would be a real family again. People from all over the world come to live here because it is a port and welcomes everyone. There are good schools, I have persuaded Leo to go to the nearest one, they have said they are happy to have him and they will want Pearl too. The children will have a bustling community, a safe place to live and people who truly love them even if they aren't closely related.' He paused here but Connie was too moved and too overwhelmed to speak.

'They will take Sarah too if she cares to come.'

Connie turned away and added a few tears to the Tyne, she was so close to the river. Wasn't this what they had always wanted? Dom had achieved this, while she had struggled so hard to get it right and had not. She couldn't understand how people could be so generous as to take in strangers and yet that was what Mr and Mrs Forster did, alongside Mr Leslie.

They welcomed those who needed them whether it was just for a few days or a lot longer and she knew by the softness of his sweet voice that they were in earnest and that they had either chosen or learned to love her difficult brother so very much.

If only their grandparents had behaved like Mr and Mrs Forster but then too much had happened and they had been hurt too badly to start again and they were old, they could not do it.

Dom put his arms around her and held her for a few moments and then they walked very slowly back to the mission.

Connie and Pearl had a view from their bedroom which looked out over the river. Connie thought that the mission was one of the biggest buildings she had ever seen and it served so many purposes. It was big enough that there was peace, and yet nobody got in anybody's way. The beds were comfortable, the meals were good. There was so much joy here. Dom took to introducing her to seamen who had been to Japan and could tell her tales of the home she had loved so much and she told them of how her parents had died. She was unburdening herself as never before and her heart lightened of the very load it had carried for so long.

She liked Rose. She had been almost determined not to like her since she blamed Rose for stealing her brother's heart but now she saw how much this girl loved him and could blame her no more. People were meant to fall in love and marry and have a future. Connie was sure of it now like never before.

She was even allowed to help in the house and with the sewing and it seemed to her for the first few days that she would be content here but it wasn't so and the more she looked at the river at night in the darkness the more she knew that she had to go back to the Hilda House, she owed it her presence somehow.

She didn't understand why. Part of her really wanted to stay here, why not, she could have everything. She even wanted to write to Sarah and tell her that there was a place for her here whereas in her heart she knew Sarah would not leave Wolsingham or Miss Hutton. Sarah's future was to be so very different from hers.

The more she resisted the more she wanted to get away as though some invisible ties were tugging at her. She didn't understand it. She told herself over and over that she had nothing left in the little broken-down village that she had thought she loved so much. Everything she held dear was with her in Newcastle and yet after two weeks had gone by she explained tearfully that she could not stay.

Pearl began to howl and raced from the room. Connie ran after her and caught her into her arms in the big wide hall and the child sobbed.

'I don't want to go back. I don't want to leave Dom and Leo. I don't want to go anywhere. Haven't we gone enough places? Haven't we really, Connie? I want to stay here for always and for always and I want you to stay with me.'

And here was the child who had not been fluent in English, Connie thought, holding her sister to her.

And yet she left. Was it impossible for her to be happy? She had been offered so much and had yet rejected it. All she had thought she wanted she discarded now as if it was waste paper. She saw herself in a new light and did not like it. She had worked so hard for this and now it had happened and still she could not rest there with the people whom she had claimed mattered most of all to her. There was a part of her that was appalled at what she was doing and yet she had sacrificed herself for others for so long and now a new selfish voice had come from somewhere inside her and demanded to be heard.

Connie did not recognize the young woman she had so suddenly become. She wanted to get away from her, to go back to being the Connie who was there for everybody, who had looked after her brothers and sister, tried not to begrudge her mother's death, seen to the grandparents who only wanted her out of despair, and somehow she was done with it all. She did not want to care, she did not want to be relied on, she just wanted to get out, and if Dom had felt like this then no wonder he had left.

She wanted to cry all the way back on the train. Her teeth ached because she would not give in to it. She felt as though she was giving in to her worst self and that nobody would ever like her again. Would she care? She wasn't sure she would.

She thought that at least she might feel better when she reached the Hilda House but she remembered now that she had wanted to leave so badly, that there was a part of her that did not want to come back, but neither could she be happy in Newcastle with the lovely family who had offered her everything any decent young woman could possibly want.

The Hilda House was dark and silent and cold since there had been no fires on in more than two weeks. There was nothing and nobody to welcome her home and yet the place seemed to echo with the people who had lived there. It was as though her youth had died, that it was over, and she didn't know where she was going or what she could possibly do next.

She tried activity. She lit the kitchen fire but remembered her grandmother and what a huge loss the old woman was to her. She wished the years back that she could have seen her grandmother and been there with her. But for that she would have to blame her parents for leaving and that was one thing she could never do.

Her mind gave her Dom and Pearl and Leo there and yet there was nothing here for them now. It was all past and done and there must be something new.

She sat over the kitchen fire, she made soup, she even baked some bread. It was so cold upstairs that she went to sleep on the kitchen settle and kept waking up not remembering where she was.

Already despairing of her own company and even though the wind and rain were driving hard across the tops she decided the following morning that she would go down into Wolsingham and see Sarah and Miss Hutton and she could even go and see Sid and Mrs Rizzi. Having a plan made her much happier and as she got further down into the valley the wind and rain had almost ceased and the raindrops clung like a million diamonds on the little square fields.

When she stepped into the shop Sarah threw down the scissors she was holding while Miss Hutton tut-tutted over how dangerous this was and she ran to the doorway to greet Connie with such enthusiasm that Connie felt a lot better. She laughed and said she was so pleased to see them and Sarah said excitedly,

'I thought you weren't coming back.'

They sat her down, Miss Hutton insisted on closing the shop even though it was not yet dinner time and they sat in the back room over the fire and Connie told them all about the life in Newcastle and how settled the boys were and how Pearl had not wanted to leave.

Sarah looked disappointed and Connie knew how much Sarah had loved the little girl.

'You can go and see her,' Connie said. She was tactful enough not to say that there was a place for Sarah in Newcastle too because she knew instinctively that Sarah would not go. She was the happiest now that Connie had ever seen her. And the old lady had a new life in her, bright-eyed and nimble-fingered.

She had some food with them but did not want to stay. The house was small and it seemed to her that she did not sense there was any place for her here. Wherever was she to go and whatever was she to do?

Sarah solved the problem.

'The doctor was so sorry to go without saying goodbye to you and Pearl.'

'Go?'

Miss Hutton chimed in.

'He's been offered a place in London. He will be a huge miss here in the dale but he wanted to be away and why wouldn't he now that his mother is in Durham? He says she is content and that there is nothing to hold him here. It was what he wanted to do all the time, so he says, though I never heard any talk of it before. Dr Blair will come down and cover for him until the new doctor arrives. He wanted to be away all sudden like and it has upset a lot of folk. He was an incomer in the first place and by the time he was accepted he decided that he didn't want to be here any more as though we got doctors so easily. Goodness only knows how long it will be before we have anybody new.'

Miss Hutton sighed over her mince and dumplings and shook her head at such goings-on.

'He is very young,' Connie said. 'I think young people just get restless.'

Was she restless? Was that her problem? That she could find nothing here and she heard herself ask when he had left.

'He's just gone, I think,' Sarah said and that was when Connie knew what her problem was. The blood rushed her cheeks so that she turned away and then her eyes filled with tears. She called herself stupid. She tried to finish her dinner but couldn't get another mouthful past her lips. She made an excuse, much to their joint surprise, and left the house.

She walked up the street to the surgery, thinking of all the times Thomas Neville had been so kind to her, and not just to her but to her whole family. She brought to mind his declaration of love and faltered. He had gone to London and the chances were that she would never see him again.

As she made her way to the surgery she saw a small knot of people gathered outside. It was the two maids, Ada and Fiona, Fiona with a hanky up to her eyes and also Oswald and Jimmy and one or two more folk. They were saying goodbye.

Connie hung back. She was too late in deciding what she wanted.

Would he forget her? Did he still feel the same or had it just been a passing phase? She had said herself that he was very young. Young men often changed their minds about such things. Perhaps he had already changed his.

The maids stood back with Jimmy and the doctor and Oswald got into the trap which was filled with the doctor's luggage. Connie was silenced and wished to be invisible but as Oswald clicked his tongue at the horse to set off the doctor saw her and told him to stop and even got down to her.

'Why, Connie,' he said, smiling. 'I thought you had gone for good. Everybody seemed to think you would go to where your brothers are so well established and where is Pearl? Are you here just to say goodbye to everyone? You almost missed me.'

'Pearl is in Newcastle with the boys. She thinks she will be happy there.'

Connie couldn't think of another thing on earth to say.

'We can give you a lift back to the Hilda House if you like. It would save you the walk,' the doctor suggested.

He helped her up into the trap. Connie wanted to run from him.

'I don't think I want to,' was all she managed. 'I don't think I will after all.'

Connie got down from the trap and then couldn't seem to move a step away no matter how hard she tried.

They did not set off again as she had hoped. She wasn't looking at either of them. She willed her feet to move but they wouldn't.

The doctor got down too and he said in a conversational tone, 'You know that I am off to London.'

'Yes, I – yes, Sarah said, Miss Hutton said. I do hope that things work out for you there and I – and I—'

And then Connie disgraced herself entirely. She burst into such floods of tears that she wished herself anywhere but where she was. The doctor stared. Oswald stared. The whole street stared, she knew even though she didn't see them, couldn't see anything. She wished only to disappear. She had the feeling that even the horse stared. This was the worst day of her life, that she should behave in such a way in Wolsingham main street. She would never live it down. She would have to go and stay in Newcastle now.

And then the doctor took her by the arm and walked her back to the surgery and escorted her inside and he said, as he sat on the front of his desk in his surgery and held her arm,

'Connie whatever is it? Talk to me. Has something awful happened? Has somebody done something?'

She shook her head, thinking deplorably of the way that he sat on the desk and so close to her such as she was convinced he had never done before.

'Are you all right? Are you ill?'

Connie sobbed and shook her head and then she cleared her throat and scraped the tears from her eyes and face with her fingers and then she said, trying to make a joke of it,

'I'm turning into what they used to call a watering pot.'

'I don't think I would have described you quite in that way. You are the bravest person I ever met.'

'I'm not going back to Newcastle. They are lovely people but I just don't want to be there.'

He frowned.

'But if Pearl and your brothers stay there and Sarah goes on living with Miss Hutton as everybody thinks she will what will you do up at the Hilda House?'

Connie tried to be positive about living there at the Hilda House, that she would be able to help any children who came by, as though people appeared from nowhere up on the tops and yet she and Dom and Leo and Pearl had done exactly that. She wanted her parents to look down on her and see all the good things she was doing just as they had done but the words wouldn't make themselves in her mind or on her lips no matter how hard she tried.

She wanted to tell him that she would be all right, that he must go to London, she was so certain it was the right place for him, and she couldn't utter a single word while further traitorous tears ran down her face like melted ice in the howling gale which was now coming down from the tops and sweeping its way across the street, as though reminding her how much she was needed, all the work she could be doing in this place where her ancestors had lived probably for a thousand years, but her throat stopped her, her voice gave up and she swallowed hard and then in the shakiest voice ever she said,

'I don't want to be there either.'

Thomas went on looking at her but Connie couldn't meet his eyes. She was just relieved that she had now managed to stop crying. There was a silence that seemed to go on and on but when she finally did meet his gaze he was leaning forward and drawing her ever so gently into his arms. Connie closed her eyes. The kiss was only the merest touch of lips but it was more right to her than anything that had happened before in her life and then he moved back slightly and so did she and he was looking at her as though she was a star that had fallen from the sky and was shining especially for him.

'Will you come to London with me then, darling Connie? Will you come with me and be my wife?'

All she did was nod and let go of her breath.

'Yes, yes please, yes I will. I want to go with you, anywhere that you want to be except here.'

'There's no chance of that now. I think you will like London. After all, you have lived in a city most of your life. I don't suppose it's much like Tokyo but all cities have similarities. I will buy you a beautiful house and look after you all my life. My best and dearest girl.'

It was strange, Connie thought later, that she had not realized what was happening to her but her instincts had got her to there. Now she had a future and although it was not the future she had envisaged she knew immediately that it was the right one.

She thought back to her brothers and sister. She could leave them knowing that they would be happy and she must tell Thomas – it was the first time she had thought of his first name like that and it brought the colour flooding into her cheeks but she was so glad of what was happening to her now that she could not help laughing amidst her tears as her mother had always said was the Irish bit in her. Connie knew nothing of the Irish bit – no doubt another story of her mother's family life and Connie did not doubt that many of those family stories were yet to be told.

Thomas promised her right then and there that he could not possibly leave his mother for too long, as goodness knew what scrapes she would get herself into in Durham, and he wanted to invite his mother and Fatty to London once he and Connie were married and established there.

Connie said also that there was a part of her left in Newcastle with her family but she had high hopes for the future which might bring some happiness for all of them and she must come back here often and they must go and visit her in her new life.

'It's going to be a very busy life,' Thomas promised her, 'but we will also have to return here. There will be ghosts of happiness in the Hilda House because of your time there and the strength and courage you give to everyone you meet and everywhere you go. And there is the old Hall. It is still yours and there is a big place here for you as there was for all your family always.'

Some day she vowed when she was an old woman she would come back and rebuild her family's old house and make it into something splendid so that future generations could enjoy it. There was something in it of all of them, even, she managed to admit, Amos Adams had been happy there at one time. The old house would wait there for her until she was ready to come home. Her grandparents were buried in the churchyard but maybe they could see her going forward into her new life and perhaps even they were glad of it. Her parents were pleased about it all, she felt sure.

Acknowledgements

I would like to thank everybody at Quercus for their hard work and support. It's a lovely feeling that you have special people at your back. In particular, my editors, Emma Capron, Ajebowale Roberts, Celine Kelly, Rhian McKay and Nicola Howell-Hawley. Also, thanks go as ever to my agent Judith Murdoch who has been there for me for over twenty-five years.

Special mentions to Katy, my lovely daughter and her husband Allan who have brought me through the isolation of Covid and cheered me on. Most especially I would like to thank our wonderful golden Labrador, Izzie, who insists on beach walks seven days a week. I get my ideas from throwing tennis balls on the sand and watching her duck under the waves.

The Foundling School *for* Girls

She may be an orphan, but she has hope for the future . . .

After Ruth Dixon's mother deserts her on Christmas Eve, her father comes home drunk and commits an unthinkable act. Without money or friends, she has nowhere to go, but when he hurts her a second time, she knows what she must do.

Ruth is rescued by Jay, a businessman, who takes her to the convent where she meets Sister Madeline. Along with the rest of the nuns, Maddy provides food, shelter and education for orphans.

Ruth comes to see her new friends as family and things are finally looking up. But then a pit accident changes everything, and they all stand to lose something – or someone – they love. . .

Available now in paperback and eBook

QUERCUS

The
Runaway
Children

All they ever wanted was a place to belong . . .

When little Ella's grandmother dies, she is turned out of her home and forced into a life of cruel labour. Even her own mother wont help, too busy with her new husband.

Seeking refuge at the Foundling School for Girls, Ella meets Julia, who has been torn apart from her twin, Ned. They must take matters into their own hands if they're to stay together despite their parents' wishes.

In a world of hardship and betrayal, three children begin a search for belonging. But years of strife have left their mark on Ella, Ned and Julia . . . Is it too late, or can they find the new start they need?

Available now in paperback and eBook

QUERCUS

The
Miller's
Daughter

A poignant story of love and betrayal,
and of hope in the face of adversity . . .

When the miller learns of his previous wife's death,
he tracks his daughter Mary down at the Foundling School
and brings her and her siblings to his new home. But the
miller remains desperate for a son, so when Mary's
newest sibling turns out to be another girl, he begins
to court a lonely young woman called Isabel.

After Isabel gives birth to a boy, the miller believes that
the son he has been waiting for is finally here. But when
rumours abound that the miller may not be the father
of Isabel's child, he begins to lose control.

Will Isabel escape with her child, or will the miller's wrath
destroy everyone in his life, including his own daughter . . . ?

Available now in paperback and eBook

QUERCUS

A Miner's Daughter

A heartbreaking story of love and loss in the big city.

Determined to escape a troubled history in her hometown, Rosalind West flees to London for a new start working at the Doxbridge Motor Company.

As she is swept up in the excitement of city living, Rosalind meets the handsome and aristocratic Freddie Harlington, the son of a once-wealthy Northumberland landowner. Against her better judgement, the pair begin a relationship, but Freddie's family have plans for him . . . Plans that do not include him marrying a miner's daughter from Durham.

When Rosalind turns to a close companion for consolation, she suddenly finds herself torn between two men, both of strong passions and fierce ambition. Can she choose between them, or will she lose them both . . . ?

Available now in paperback and eBook

QUERCUS

The *Lost Child*

Durham, 1877. After a traumatic and harrowing incident at the hands of a stranger, a woman gives birth to a child. However, she is persuaded by her husband to give him up to a local couple.

On the same dark and stormy night, a local pit owner turns his wife out onto the bleak moors, telling her son she is evil. The woman is never seen again.

Twenty years later, these seemingly unrelated events have shaped the characters of two unloved boys, who have now grown to be men. As the past reaches out and casts a shadow over the present, will mistakes be repeated as two innocent lives hang in the balance, or is there hope yet for change?

Available now in paperback and eBook

QUERCUS